The Quarant

The
Quarant

GRAHAM BULLEN

Matador
9 Priory Business Park,
Wistow Road, Kibworth Beauchamp,
Leicestershire. LE8 0RX
Tel: 0116 279 2299
Email: books@troubador.co.uk
Web: www.troubador.co.uk/matador
Twitter: @matadorbooks

ISBN 978 180046 021 8

British Library Cataloguing in Publication Data.
A catalogue record for this book is available from the British Library.

Printed and bound in Great Britain by 4edge Limited
Typeset in 10.5pt Baskerville by Troubador Publishing Ltd, Leicester, UK

Matador is an imprint of Troubador Publishing Ltd

Visit the author's website at www.grahambullenauthor.com

To Joanne

MAP OF VENICE

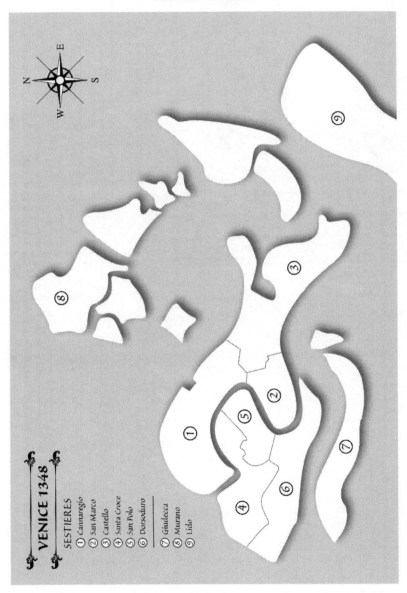

VENICE 1348

SESTIERES
① Cannaregio
② San Marco
③ Castello
④ Santa Croce
⑤ San Polo
⑥ Dorsoduro

⑦ Giudecca
⑧ Murano
⑨ Lido

VENETIAN GOVERNMENT

Arengo
The electorate (male citizens only)

Maggior Consiglio
Featuring up to 2000 members, its sessions
are largely taken up by electoral duties

Pregadi
A 120 member senate in
charge of day to day legislation

Council of Ten
A 10 member council focussed on
intelligence gathering, diplomacy
and investigation of treason

Minor Consiglio/Signoria
Authority advising and supervising the actions of the Doge

Collegio
The Cabinet

Doge
Head of State and head of all
government institutions

Chapter 1

Saturday 26th January 1348

Day 0 of the Quarant

The white veil clung to the curves of the woman's head and shoulders, spilling onto the gentle swell of the Lagoon. Her sightless eyes faced down into the muddy, quiet waters.

A beam of wood floated beside her, its lines appearing and disappearing beneath the veil's thin silk weave.

The yellow of her dress had caught Malin's eye, just yards to starboard of the *Seynte Marie*. He stood motionless against the bulwark, unable to tear his eyes away. When the ship's forward progress took the body from sight, he turned and ascended to the sterncastle deck.

The ship, a 130-ton cog from Dieppe, continued her journey north along the Lido shoreline.

He looked further out across the bay.

Beyond the city, framing the grey winter air, the snow-clad peaks of the mainland stood their usual guard. But something about the rise and fall of the Venice skyline, the dark blocked mass and splintered light of its roofs and towers, scraped at the edge of his mind.

What was it?

Thin plumes of smoke, perhaps half a dozen, rose from separate points on the main island. A thin stain of haze hung above and between them.

There was little movement on the water. Few if any of the small, two-masted fishing boats. No patrol boats searching for smuggling or import infringements. Seabirds, normally seeking food or temporary roosts, were nowhere to be seen.

All sound, bar the gentle motion of the Lagoon waters on the hull of the ship, had been sucked from the world.

He looked to port. Wharf pontoons appeared wrenched and twisted, some just shapeless tangles of timber and rope. A line of detritus extended many feet above the waterline.

He turned again. A *galere grosse* lay broken on its side a hundred yards out from the wharf, its midship shelter smashed and misshapen, the top of its main mast gone. Its curved rudder rose from the water, broken and stranded.

The *Seynte Marie* continued on, between the wrecked ship and the quay.

Had there been an attack?

A mile from their expected berth, the crew came above deck.

Yet still no sign of the pilot boat.

A group of small figures stood on the quayside, perhaps half a mile ahead. They signalled for them to moor up by the Lido warehouses, rather than continue to the anchorages of the Grand Canal.

Something was definitely wrong.

Malin's thoughts turned to Lucia and the rest of her family. And to Symon, expecting him back home. Were they safe?

The ship moved in to berth. Splintered planks and concave bowls of earth pitted the raised moorings. The men on the dock stepped through large mounds of debris.

Malin stepped off the ship and approached a stevedore.

And then he learned.

An earthquake had caused all this. Yesterday. A movement of the seas emptied the Canal and lowered the Lagoon, only to return as a single, enormous wave.

Buildings continued to fall. Fires still burned.

The number of dead and injured was high, and still rising.

The *cattaveri* completed their cargo checks. The captain's papers, issued in Southampton, tallied with the searcher's findings.

Provisional calculations of taxes were completed. The *ripalico* for wharfage, and the *teleneo* to insure their goods before deed transfer to their buyers.

Malin returned the signed papers to his shoulder bag, and watched as the men prepared to unload his cargoes of wheat and linen. They would be stored under protection of the authorities until cleared for distribution.

The date, the twenty-sixth day of January, was written under each signature on all the papers required. The obligatory forty days' storage, the Quarant, would expire on the sixth of March, a week into the Venetian New Year.

Until then, nothing could be moved. The *Seynte Marie* would remain in port as surety. The *Extraodinarri*, the commercial magistrates for whom the *cattaveri* worked, demanded it. Their regulations provided security and protection for all involved, at the cost, accepted by all, of considerable taxes.

For almost twenty years Malin and his partners had bent to the city's requirements. The protections offered were worth it.

And now? Now, these constraints offered Malin the cover he needed.

Forty days until the ship's trade would be officially cleared.

And forty days to finalise actions that would shake the Republic to its core.

He pulled out a small green phial from his jacket, removed the stopper, and took a long swig, sighing as he felt the burning in his chest ease.

No longer expecting Symon's arrival at the dock, Malin secured a ferry to cross the Lagoon, to see if the people he most cared for, those he most depended on to leave this place alive, were in any fit state to greet him.

★

Lucia sat with Malin in the first-floor reception room of the Da Segna home. Malin's beard, rough from his voyage and streaked with new grey, had provided an easy way into their conversation.

Her teasing complete, she fell quiet. Malin sensed an unusual air of vulnerability in her as she told of the previous day's events.

"It was yesterday morning, just before Terce. Maybe eight of the clock? We'd broken our fast, and Father had left to attend his office in the Rialto. I sat with Mother and Collette downstairs. A trembling filled the house, then died away, but then the whole house began to move and shriek. It felt as if the air was pushing down on our ears. Deafening. Everything was falling over. Moving. The tapestries swung from side to side and then several windows shattered. Even when the noise abated, I could still feel it. Like a deep, pulsing echo."

The last of the afternoon light framed her features. Long, raven hair, pulled back from her forehead, with a few silver threads of its own.

Strong, straight nose. Dense lashes over bronze eyes that sought affirmation of the experience.

"Collette, of course, was beside herself. Three more times the shaking returned. Each less powerful than the last, but her screams became louder and longer. Mother did her best to calm her down.

"Father returned at midday. Even he looked unnerved. The damage, he said, was widespread. He would not promise that the quakes were over. But the most shocking thing, he said, was the water. The banks of the Canal were completely exposed. The water had gone. Reclaimed by the Lagoon. He said the constables were just standing around, drained of sense just as the city had been drained of water.

"In truth, Malin, I didn't entirely believe him. I wondered if he'd perhaps been injured, or that shock had clouded his mind.

"Father said a number of buildings in the Rialto had fallen in on themselves. Pavements had risen and cracked, and people had been trapped inside their houses. The same damage had been wrought along his route home.

"He said we should leave the house. Find somewhere we could be free of the danger of falling buildings. So we dressed up warm, and walked with Penina and Tusco to Campo San Giacomo.

"The damage was everywhere. Rubble filled the streets, making them even narrower. At one point, Tusco had to lead us by the hand through an almost complete blockage. I kept thinking something else would fall on us."

Lucia fought back tears. Malin leaned forward, and placed his hand gently on hers.

"It's all right. You are past this now. Everyone is safe."

"I know. It's just been so…"

They allowed the silence to find its own natural end.

"When we got there, the square was thronged. We moved into the centre, as far from the broken buildings and fallen masonry as possible. Lots of people had blood on them. A row of bodies were laid out under the porch of the church, covered by blankets. I could see their shape against the wool. I don't know who they were, or who put them there.

"There must have been others. Lying in their houses injured, or dead. It could just as easily have been any of us."

She paused to clear her throat. "We stood there without really thinking about how long we should remain there. Every so often, we felt small vibrations in the ground. Nothing like those earlier. Father was right. Talk was of empty canals and waterways. Boats sitting in the mud, or hanging from their mooring ropes like toys on strings.

"By mid-afternoon, an odd hush filled the square. It was really strange. Hundreds of people drawn together, saying nothing. No one seemed to want to leave.

"But then the water…" Her eyes widened. The agitation in her voice returned.

"It was the noise. I couldn't tell where it was coming from. As it got louder, it felt like it was all around us. Someone ran into the *campo*, shouting. Saying that water was gushing back to the canals. Father pulled us all together, but still didn't seem to know what to do. The noise got louder. Like a wave that never stops crashing into the shore. Everyone began talking, adding to the noise.

"I couldn't just stand there. I took Collette's and Mother's hands, and pulled them towards the steps of San Giovanni. Father and the servants just followed. I didn't care about the bodies laid there. I just wanted us to get higher, and the steps seemed the right place to head.

"Some other families saw what we were doing, and followed us. We entered the front of the church, stood in the nave. Other people rushed in behind us.

"Malin, I froze." She trembled, reliving the moment. "I didn't know what to do next. The noise of the water had dropped when we got inside, but sounded more sinister. Otherworldly. The sound was deeper, echoing around the chapel, in and out of the side-altars. It felt like it was trying to trap us.

"Then there were more screams, near the door. Water was rushing into the *campo*. And it wasn't just water, Malin. It moved heavy bits of wood around like blades of grass.

"Father told us all to move further into the church, and make for the chancel. It felt strange walking up the altar steps. Do you think we will be punished for the sacrilege? Looking back again, I knew it was the right thing to do. Everyone pushed forward to join us.

"Some men closed the main doors, but the water started to come in under them. People started screaming again. You could hear them over the rush of the water. It started to feel as though we were going to be crushed. Some people even stood on the altar. By then, the water covered the whole of the nave. Those that couldn't join us at the altar just stood in it, up to their waists. Held onto each other. I thought we were all going to die, Malin. That God would just stand by and allow it."

Lucia caught her breath, her resolve broken. Her tears came, and neither of them tried to stop them.

When she finally regained her composure, the two of them sat once more at a discrete distance, except now they held each other's outstretched hand.

"The cold water rose up the altar steps about knee height, and then stopped. Night had fallen, and our only light came from the high windows around the nave and transepts. Collette was shivering. Mother and I took turns in comforting her. The servants must have been even colder, without our layers.

"It was well into the evening before someone pushed open the church doors from the outside." She shut her eyes again. "Ripples flowed up the nave and splashed against the top step where we stood. Then slowly, the water level dropped.

"We followed the others to the doors, and looked out across the *campo*. It was as though the Lagoon had reclaimed the city. I remember the floods in 'forty-one, but they were nothing compared to this. There must have still been at least two feet of water. The square was just gone.

"It was Father that made the decision that we should return home. He thought we would be better off back here.

"So that's what we did. It took us an hour to travel four streets, with so much of the damage hidden below the water. And the smell? Well, you can still smell it now, can't you?"

Lucia looked around her, as though the slightly rotted smell could be traced to just one physical place.

"When we got back, there was almost a foot of water downstairs. The house was freezing. Tusco lit the upstairs fires, and we all collapsed."

Another pause.

"I'm so glad you're here, Malin. We knew that you were due back soon, but had no idea if you'd been caught up in the flood. My God, what would it have been like, caught aboard ship in that?" She squeezed his hand, looked up into his eyes. "I'm sure Father would have been beside himself if any harm had befallen you. How could he cope without your company, and your daily conferences?"

Malin reflected back Lucia's smile.

"You know I couldn't possibly let your father down. Where else would I be able to enjoy all the hospitality of Venice, and the gentle caress of a sharp tongue."

They both looked down, to find they were still holding hands.

Lucia reached out her other hand, and they sat for a few more silent moments. Content in each other's safety, and happy to leave all else unspoken.

It was hours later when she speculated what might have happened to the bodies laid out on the church steps. Her tears, when they returned, brought little solace.

Chapter 2

Sunday 27th January 1348

Day 1 of the Quarant

The ground floor of the Da Segna home, bereft of all furniture, remained covered in a spoiled stew of seawater and mud when Malin prepared to leave the following morning. Damp climbed up from its surface, tracing the timbers beneath the thin plaster of the walls.

A sour, rank smell rose from each rippled step he took towards Donata. He chose for her sake to ignore it, not wishing to upset her further.

Her voice was surprisingly confident. "Please Malin, take care as you head back." She, too, was putting on a brave face.

He cast his eyes around. "All will be well, I have no doubt."

The woman was a living marvel, managing this household and its strong personalities. Uberto, the quite brilliant trader. Lucia, their headstrong eldest daughter. And Collette, her constantly taxing sister. Donata's composure never seemed to waver. Even during Uberto's fall from grace at the Palace.

Malin stepped forward into the terrace doorway, and embraced her. As her own grip tightened, he could feel her tremble. She was shaken more than she would ever admit.

Donata leaned back to look into Malin's newly shaven face. She spoke quietly, as if to be sure that only he could hear. "When will this all end? When will things return to their rightful state?"

He stepped back, studied her face. *Was she referring to the floods, or something else?*

"I'm sure repairs will be completed in good haste, Signora Donata. The city is resilient. As are you."

He waved farewell as he turned onto Calle Donzella. His river ferry, arranged by Uberto overnight, would be waiting at the Canal.

Heading north to the jetty by Campo Pescaria, he passed several groups of workmen, gathered around the largest piles of street debris.

Above and around them, few buildings seemed to have escaped damage.

Those most spared still displayed new cracks in their plaster, or missing or damaged lower steps where detritus had swept past on the oncoming flood.

Others had fared less well. Fallen masonry on the corner of Ruga dei Spezieri completely blocked the passage. An upper balcony and all supporting brickwork had collapsed, and the remaining frontage appeared to be suspended on just a few bared oak beams. If the owners did not support full demolition, their neighbours, not to mention the *Capo Sestiere*, would probably insist.

His journey up the Canal from the Lido the day before required his boatman to weave through an almost total covering of floating debris, washed there from who knows where. Much more, undoubtedly, lay beneath them. Heavier objects, picked up by the onrushing Lagoon waters and driven into the silt. The larger of these would have to be lifted quickly, to preserve the hulls of larger vessels.

This morning, as Malin was carried along the broad waterway, the damage to the city was abundantly, shockingly clear. Protective masonry in many sections of the canal wall had been ripped out or reshaped, exposing the basic brickwork beneath. Approaching the Riva del Carbon, close to the Rialto Bridge, many edge slabs from the top of the canal had penetrated the normally solid, unbroken pathway above.

For the first time, Malin saw the true nature of the Canal. A man-made construction that dared Nature, every day, to do its worst. And Nature had responded.

He had no doubt that Venice would recover. Not just because Venetian life depended on its maze of waterways, but also because of the character of the people that lived here. They would see this as yet another problem to be solved, a challenge for the Republic to overcome in its endless quest for power.

Despite the raw winter cold, the pungent marsh odours reminded him of high summer. Something had awoken from its rotting slumber. Each movement of the breeze carried the scent away, only for it to settle once more just above the water's surface.

The largest shock arrived as they approached the Piazza.

As the Canal widened into the waters of the Giudecca, Malin's attention drifted to the scene to his left. To the milling crowds on the broad promenade, and beyond, onto the Piazza itself.

His eye was caught by the large number of men dressed in the distinctive robes and tall, pointed hoods of the Confraternities. Dressed in the striking reds, whites and browns of their particular brotherhood uniforms, seen only in feast day processions or when administering Christian charity to the poor or deceased.

Or performing funerary rights.

An orderly line of bundled black cloth stretched the entire length of the square.

Ranks of dark-shrouded bodies appeared indifferent to the shadows cast on them from the new porticos of the Ducal Palace, plunging the muddy brown surface of the square to a glistening black.

There must be hundreds of them.

He wanted to look away, but couldn't. Instinctively, he tried to make sense of the sight before him. Of the countless human stories behind the regimented, lifeless mounds.

He forced his eyes to shut. But his mind stepped forward with sights from an earlier time. Scenes of carnage and spoil on a high Scottish heath, over fifteen years earlier.

Of his continuing need for forgiveness.

He lifted fingers to trace then rest on the scar that ran from his temple to a point just below his left eye.

Punctuated cries of grief from the shore brought him back. One source of anguish to save him from another.

Unaware of Malin's turmoil, his gondolier broke his silence. "All those people. They say it will be days before the number of dead is confirmed. But adding to the dead here for days more? Is that the right thing to do?"

Malin turned to face him. "I'm not sure. But I expect they need families to identify the bodies before arranging for burial. The Brotherhoods will be busy, no doubt."

The man's tone was brittle. "And that assumes they can find any dry ground to bury them in."

Malin said nothing, but took another swig of gentian and replaced the green phial in his tunic.

They moved on, the cloying scent of decay lessening as the waters widened.

The damage around the inner reaches of the bay seemed far greater than when he had travelled to San Polo the day before. His mind then had been consumed with thoughts of reaching Lucia.

Malin asked the gondolier to pause at the mouth of each diverging canal as they passed. The buildings on the west bank of each of these tributaries appeared to have taken the brunt of the water's assault.

By Chiesa Santa Maria della Pietà, the mouth of the waterway itself was completely lost under a collapsed house. Looking beyond it, regular gaps were visible in the normally unbroken rows of houses.

He wanted to get home. To see if his house on Calle San Domenico was still standing.

They arrived at the small inlet at the end of his street. Malin sent the gondolier back to San Polo with a few extra pennies and alighted onto the small pontoon.

Houses here were mainly still timber, although they lined the street in much the same way as the more affluent *sestieres*. In keeping with a growing number of house owners further west, Malin had rebuilt his house in stone, as had a number of his wealthier neighbours. Unfortunately, today, that simply resulted in the same mixture of timber and stone debris littering the seventy yards or so of street that lay between the quay and his front door.

Standing with his back against the house opposite his own, he looked up to assess the damage. One or two new cracks underneath the higher of his two street-facing balconies, and it looked like they had a new door. But little else of concern?

His house had been a wise purchase, enabled only through Uberto's patronage in the days when his reputation could call on any number of favours or bequests. The small house Malin had originally rented, a few streets back towards the Arsenale, had served him and Symon well enough during his travelling years, but as his time abroad dwindled, Malin made no secret of his desire to settle permanently.

14

City laws regarding the living arrangements for foreigners, and foreign merchants in particular, were clear. German merchants were required to reside in the Fondaco dei Tedeschi, an increasingly large complex on the Canal by the bridge that also served as warehouse and market. The growing population of merchants from the East had little choice but to stay in the Fondaco dei Turchi, just a few hundred yards further west.

Yet three years after Uberto was invited to join the Great Council, and nine years after his first tentative visit to the city, Malin joined the ranks of Venetian landowners. His association with Uberto, initially built on their covert agreement with the Hanse in Antwerp, offered a legitimacy that others could only wish for. Da Viscia had been most helpful in buying out the lease under which Accardi held the property, and registering it in Malin's name. Since then, the building had doubled as both home and place of business.

He wondered, quake or no quake, how long this would be the case.

*

Moments after closing the door behind him, Symon's voice came from the back of the house, shortly followed by the man himself. Their embrace, never routine, seemed to Malin to be just that little longer. That little tighter.

"My God, Malin, you're here after all! Your chest arrived yesterday afternoon, but I've had no idea where you've been. I've not been able to get any sense out of anyone at the Rialto since the disaster. Did you even bring the ship in? Were you caught up in it all?" The questions came fast, his Scottish accent thickening, as it always did, when emotions ran high.

Malin smiled for the first time in days.

Answering as many questions as he could remember, he slowly backed his friend into the office at the end of the corridor, noting the same stale smells and discoloured walls as those he had left in San Polo.

Symon went across to the large office table, and began to gather the papers strewn across it. "Just give me a few moments. These need to be moved to a drier shelf, in case the water returns. I've lit fires in all the rooms. We need to dry out."

He soon joined Malin in the front drawing room, the place they spent most evenings.

"So Malin. Tell me of your adventures. Did you complete the deal in Southampton?"

Malin outlined events at the English port, hoping his voice betrayed none of his growing indifference to trade.

He moved the conversation back to Symon. "And here? Tell me how you managed to survive the onslaught of the last two days? Were you in the house when everything happened?"

"Without you here to help and protect me, you mean?" Symon's mischievous look brought another smile to Malin's face. "I'm not sure how much you've heard. The quake, well, I've never felt or heard anything like it. Everything in the house shook, and everything that shook made a clamour. I thought the walls were coming in. And the ceiling. I was in the office, and the shelves emptied themselves almost completely. At least I piled the papers up on the table when the shaking stopped. Although I had no idea at the time that getting them off the floor would be so important." His eyes narrowed. "I wonder how many contracts are now sitting in sodden piles all over the city, all their ink washed from them. The markets could really struggle to cope.

"Anyway, yes. The shaking finally stopped, save for a few smaller tremors, so I left the house. Took a look at the outside of the place, to see if anything important had fallen off. Everyone else was outside by that point. Probably doing the same.

16

"By midday, constables were on the street, sent out by the Castello councillor." He laughed. "It's probably the most popular the constables have ever felt. Everyone wanted the latest from them. Did you know that two church towers completely collapsed? Including that new one. The Santa Vidal? The bloody thing hadn't even been finished.

"Then rumours started about the water. That it was draining out of the Lagoon. I walked down to the shore. There were hundreds of people there, doing the same. It was true. The struts of all the jetties along the side of the island were exposed. Well, that was just strange. The place fell really quiet."

Symon moved his hand to his forehead, pushing his deep auburn hair back.

"I expect you've heard what happened next. There was a faint white line just visible at the north end of the Lido, between the Lido and Sant'Andrea. Anyway, it got bigger and higher. A giant wave. None of us knew what it really was, but we knew enough to understand that it looked bad. No one stood around watching.

"I'd definitely seen enough. I ran back to the jetty. But waiting for something to happen when I couldn't actually see it was really hard. It was so different to anything we've seen at sea, even in the worst storms. When I finally saw it come around the headland? I just ran again. Ran back here, just in time to see the water breach the dock at the end of the street. Then I shut the door and waited for what would happen next. It's a good job I was standing in here, rather than the corridor, or the door would have taken my head off when it fell in."

He looked across to Malin. "How can such a thing happen? First the shaking, and then that?"

They both shook their heads.

"Anyway, how did you manage to get docked? I heard that much of the Canal frontage was wrecked. That every crane had

17

been damaged or collapsed. And that the Lido had been hit at least as hard."

Malin described how the *Seynte Marie* had been told to dock at the Lido.

"They had either repaired the least damaged berths within just one day, or the damage over the Lagoon was not quite as bad as you heard. The main thing is that we registered the cargo, and it's entered the usual protocol." Malin reached down to his battered satchel, a gift from his Uncle Haylan back in Lynn, and a constant companion since his first trade. "When you're next in the office, add this paperwork to the files." It was Malin's turn to have fun at his friend's expense. "I expect you know what to do with it, but let me know if you need any help."

They had worked together since the young Scot joined him in Venice thirteen years ago. Symon's methods were faultless, and from Malin's experience, without peer.

Malin turned to warm his hands at the fire, grateful for one last chance to rehearse the words he had planned since leaving England.

He cleared his throat.

"So, now we know we both survived, we need to make sure all our deals remain robust. Check our goods are safe, and that our friends can still guarantee the cargoes we're contracted to handle. Have we put much in the warehouses since I left?"

"A fair amount. But no more than usual. I can start a stocktake. Yes, I should do that in any case. See if we're exposed."

"That's good." Malin saw his chance. Worked hard to sound natural. "And I wonder. The impacts of this may run deep. Perhaps we should take the opportunity to examine just what we have now, across the whole business. We haven't done it for the best part of five years. I would like to know where our wealth lies."

This was where Malin felt most vulnerable. They knew each other so well, and he had no intention of lying. He would tell Symon only what he needed to know. Guard those truths that might do his friend harm. Threaten his safety.

Freshly back from England, he would keep his plans from the man who owed him his life, but to whom he owed his own.

The rest of the afternoon was spent in the office. Symon, never one to delay in the execution of any task, pulled out dozens of scrolls, making notes as he went. He also found time to send a note to arrange for the house to be surveyed for any serious damage. "I don't think the place is in too bad a shape, considering, but it won't hurt to know for sure. I expect many others will be thinking the same."

Malin, for his part, spent most of the afternoon rehearsing his next conversation, one no less delicate than the first.

Twice, with Symon buried head-deep in his parchments, he withdrew the small apothecary's phial, and took a mouthful of his physic.

★

In the chilly dusk of early evening, Malin took the short trip across the waters to Dorsoduro. Despite the failing light, men were still hard at work clearing debris on the margins of the Canal.

The gondolier, swarthier and more talkative than the boatman that morning, was full of tales of destruction. He confirmed the collapse of the Chiesa del Santa Vidal. At least ten dead there so far.

Five years under construction. Was this a sign of God's displeasure?

Approaching the imposing wooden structure of the Custom House, Malin reflected on his many days spent in such places.

Satisfying the regulatory requirements of each city, securing his profits made in the exchange of goods between sellers and buyers who rarely met, and often never would. He had made it his life's work to identify and facilitate these exchanges. To step in and act as the buyer and transporter of goods from areas of surplus to areas of need, taking his reward once contracts were stamped and duties paid.

This had become his world. And he lived for it.

Or had done, until recently.

He paid the gondolier, and stepped onto the quay, glancing across at the walls of the San Giorgio monastery opposite. What would it be like to turn your back on the world? Excuse yourself from the daily ebb and flow of needs and wants? To simply withdraw?

Malin thought of his old friend and mentor back in Wormegay Rectory. Of Jerold, a goblet of wine in hand, reading his latest manuscript by the firelight. What would his counsel be? How would he explain the necessary conflict between increased wealth and wellbeing of communities, and the drive towards conflict when enough was no longer enough?

Stop.

My path is set.

He entered the Custom House, to learn that Uberto had already arrived. One of the clerks guided him to the booth reserved by his friend the day before on learning of his return to the city.

Uberto rose immediately to embrace him. When parting that morning, they had barely said a word, beyond confirming their meeting venue later that day. They had agreed, many months ago, to discuss nothing of their latest dealings in the family home, even though they had grown to overshadow business and friendship.

Were it not for that friendship, Malin felt sure the weight of their work could have crushed them both.

Their first meeting had been fourteen years earlier. Introduced by Accardi, his Pisan friend, in the Hanse warehouse in Lynn, on the banks of the estuary where the Great Ouse flowed into the German Sea. It had brought Malin back to the world that his own father had threatened to steal from him.

Their burgeoning partnership had benefitted them both.

For Uberto, it became the basis of his final push for wealth and recognition. Led to his anointment as a noble, with a place on the Great Council and the respect of his peers. For Malin, it marked the end of a deeply troubling period of physical trauma and self-questioning. And a chance to escape, for a second time, the mortal threat of England and resume his trading business based in Antwerp.

Malin stepped back, taking the chance to see how his friend had fared during his absence.

They had agreed Uberto would nurture and protect the vitality and secrecy of their contacts in Malin's absence. It would be challenging, so Malin expected to find him drawn, fatigued from the pressure since his departure the previous November.

If anything, though, Uberto appeared to possess a vitality of his own not seen since his days at the heart of Venetian politics. He stood unbowed, his shoulders back and his head high. He had removed his beard, an increasingly ageing feature of his appearance since his demise from the Council.

"What is it, Malin? Did you expect to see me worn down by the uncertainties of winter? I have missed you dearly, my friend, yet I am able to hand back the reins to you with all in what you would call 'hale form'." He stopped himself. "You, on the other hand, look as though you have brought with you the cares of the world."

"I am fine, my friend. Relieved to see that you have fared

well while I've been away. I don't think I've seen you look this good since you sat with all those sanctimonious councillors when old Francesco Dandolo died! The years seem to have dropped from you."

Uberto laughed, recalling that week clearly. The election of the new Doge, and his first real sense that he had been accepted into the noble ranks of the Republic.

"Ah, how time makes fools of us all. And yet, I confess to a feeling that, at long last, I have a part to play that will bring those days back."

As they talked, Malin stepped back to the booth door, looked up and down the corridor, and closed it again. His voice dropped slightly, suggesting a more intimate exchange would now be wise. "I too believe those days will return. We have much to talk about. But we must ensure, from this moment onwards, that we are even more careful in what we say, and how we say it."

Despite the plea for discretion, Uberto could contain himself no longer. "So, Malin, is all still set?"

Malin raised his finger to his lips. Something in Uberto's enthusiasm was a little unsettling.

"In short, yes, it is."

Over the next hour, until Vespers rang out from the nearby monastery, the two men compared the main details of the plot as they stood last November, before Malin's recall to England, and how things stood now.

Malin tried his best to spell everything out as simply as he could. "The fundamentals have not changed. The mobilisation of Veit Libusch's mercenaries from Silesia is confirmed. It's likely they've already started their march south from Bolzano, and will contact us in about three weeks. They've split their forces into five parts, each travelling by different routes. It's hard to imagine anyone being able to put the whole picture together before it's too late to stop them. We have agents in position in most of the ports around the Adriatic.

"The money to be paid after we take over is also secure. Once the Council, magistracy and civic leaders are ours, and the new Doge and Small Council is appointed, the funds will arrive over land. I wanted to bring some of it with me in advance, but the Household would not permit it. They believe that the funds already disbursed will be sufficient to ensure the right actions will take place. It's not what we preferred, I know, but we can manage. Have you any sense that people are backing away from their agreements here?"

"No. If anything, they are frustrated at how long this is taking. None of these men take this plot lightly. Many want it to happen quicker."

"I'm sure you reminded them of the fate of those before them that acted without all contingencies in place?"

Uberto sighed. "Yes. Of course. Truthfully, none of them needed the reminder. They simply feel that their small part of the entire endeavour is ready, and assume this is true of all of us." He paused, as if wondering if he should continue. "I think they fear a note, one of the dreaded *denontie segrete*, posted into one of the Lions' Mouths at the Palace, informing The Ten that someone is up to no good. I can't really say I blame them. I know of at least ten families who have benefitted from such denunciations in the past. Three of them we now count as friends! The number of people involved in this now is extraordinary, and you know as well as I that this city runs on its secrets."

Malin nodded. "It is a danger. Each day could be the day we are discovered. Yet we have known this for nearly two years, and still nothing. I believe we are almost unstoppable now. With your networks, and the Royal Household still showing complete support for the way ahead, we can make this happen."

He tried to sound more enthusiastic than he felt.

He had sought no part in this. News of cancellation, or a change of heart, would have seen him on his knees with relief. But after his visit to Westminster, he was as clear about his responsibilities as he was of the consequences of failure. He needed no reminder of the latter. Treason, citizen or not, brought harsh penalties. An early death was serious business, no matter if the blow was delivered here, or back in a disappointed England.

Malin wondered what was going through his friend's mind. Uberto had all the reason in the world to want to see this through. He worshipped his wife and children, and would do nothing to put them in danger. Yet the man's ambition burned in him. It was this, his overwhelming need for reinstatement, that made him open to Malin's approach as broker of the coup.

They sat there, two friends, each flawed, but now dependent on each other's guile to protect their loved ones.

"So what happens tomorrow, Uberto?"

The older man reached into his jacket, and pulled out a thick folded parchment. He ran his finger down the tightly written text.

"I need to visit Sclavo at the Arsenale. I've heard nothing of the damage caused there, and need to understand if his contacts remain able to do their own part when the time comes. Who knows what new pressures they will be under."

Malin nodded. "For my part, I'm seeing Bourchier. I expect him to bring the final ten thousand. Come and visit us at the house once you're finished."

Emerging into the dark of the late winter's evening, Malin watched his friend take the first of the two gondolas pulled up against the quay. Rather than do the same, Malin hung back and walked a little further along the waterside.

Directly opposite, on the north side of the Canal, Piazza

San Marco lay framed by the Basilica and the two colonnaded walkways. Palace lighting sketched the outline of the ongoing building works, a permanent feature of the structure since the vote to expand and improve it eight years earlier. From this distance, Malin could not tell if the scaffolding had been extended to address any damage from the earthquake. As his eyes strained, a dark shape still lined the eastern side of the square. It appeared to have grown.

This place. A seat of power for much of the Mediterranean and Adriatic. The lust for wealth and influence built into every new brick of its defiant architecture. The whole edifice, built on secrets and ambition.

But what difference would it make, over the next forty days?

The Quarant.

Forty days and nights until all hell would break loose.

He turned back to the jetty.

As he sat back in the gondola, making his way home, he couldn't wait for it all to end.

Chapter 3

Monday 28th January 1348

Day 2 of the Quarant

Malin's night was filled with dreams of battlefields and cracked walls. Of the bestial clamour of blood-crazed infantry, and the dark, ominous silence of mounded corpses.

He rose an hour before dawn. Starting the day early might just banish the thoughts weighing on him.

He continued to see bodies lined up in the Piazza. The air of disbelief in the men and women gathered for their identification. Perhaps some had simply walked to the square to witness the human toll of the assault from land and sea. Taken solace in their own survival, the random hand of God passing them by this time. No amount of *aqua alta*, the high tides that visited every two years or so, could have prepared them for this.

Alone in the office, sitting between two large tallow candles, he sat quietly and allowed the past to return.

Memories of his hospital bed on Dam Gate Road in Lynn. Tended by the brothers of St John. Of Symon, his body so much more damaged than his own, drifting in and out of consciousness for days at a time in the bed next to him. The boy's savage fevers, his daily battles with demons and death. His stubborn fight to survive. Of Symon's face the day Malin was discharged, returning to Haylan's family home a mile south of the hospital grounds. Of looking down at his friend from the side of his bed on his daily visits.

He shook the images from his mind.

Three years before the battle at Dupplin, and then again after his eventual return two years later, Malin worked in Venice as an agent for the port city of Antwerp, and its powerful Hanse Kontor.

Anxiety for him, after Dupplin, had been limited to that arising from breaking new ground in foreign ports, or evading discovery of his Hanse links by authorities that took a very strong view on competition from rivals.

His trading business had become as routine as it was profitable. Deals struck. Ships chartered. Cargoes loaded and unloaded. Expansion east had brought comfortable wealth, with or without the Hanse. Their contracts secured, the Hanse allowed him to slowly melt into the background, happy to send him their annual commission from the Low Countries.

Yet now?

Here he sat. A forty-year-old man, grown soft and content, drawn into a turbulence for which he felt totally ill-prepared.

He was still deep in thought when Symon appeared.

"I'm not sure if I can get all the information you need this week, Malin, but I'll get a sense this afternoon of just how difficult it might be. If I can talk to the five or six key parties, understand if they will have time to deal with me. Lanzuoli, Polani. Maybe Arimondo, across in Cannaregio. After that, it's just a case of the Registries. That part might take a while, with all the upheaval going on."

"That's fine, Symon. I'll see Da Segna this evening. He's spending the day at the Arsenale, so we can discuss any likely impact on the charters for the summer. It'll depend on the amount of damage there's been."

Symon left for the jetty, confirming he would be back for their evening meal.

An hour later, a knock at the door removed any uncertainty Malin might have had about how to use the day.

The message delivered was a simple one.

"The Tinsmith. Calle dei Stagneri. Terce."

He was lucky. His westerly route to the tavern, one of several in the densely populated *sestiere* of San Marco, was blocked just once. A damaged bridge, by the Fondamenta di Santa Giustina, cost him time and bearings, swinging back to cross instead by the Calle de Lorenzo. When he finally arrived at the narrow, curving street a short walk from the Rialto, he was surprised to find much of his nervousness gone.

Route-finding in Venice. A great way to divert the mind.

Stepping in from the damp street, he found the tavern almost empty. A Monday, so most citizens were about their business.

He noted three women sitting at a table, disturbed by his arrival. This wasn't a tavern. It was a brothel, at its quietest time of day.

"Le Cordier. Over here."

He walked over to his right to meet the man rising from his seat to greet him. Ricaud Bourchier, a small, dark-haired man with a smile as wide as his face, reached up and placed a hand on each of Malin's shoulders. It was hard not to return the man's cheer.

"Nice place, Bourchier. One of your regular haunts?"

"Ah, Malin." His smile continued to dominate his face as they sat down. "It is fair to say that I did not have to travel far to be here this morning. Just a walk to the Rialto and back to find a messenger." They sat down, and Malin loosened his overcoat.

Bourchier picked up a goblet from the board in front of him, and took a large draught.

"But this place serves our purpose well, does it not? Please, make yourself comfortable." He signalled towards the landlord at the back of the room to bring another cup. "How do you find us now you're back? What of this flux?"

"I'm not sure if that's the right word, Ricaud. The city's been hit really hard. It defies belief that such a thing can strike from nowhere. So many people have been affected."

"True. True. But think. The Council will be focussed on dealing with the consequences of this for months. What better time for us to be here?"

Malin thought about this for a moment. "But what of our friends? They will be distracted too. Expected to help repair the city." The women seated just at the edge of his vision appeared to be inspecting the sleeve of one of their dresses. There was no one else within hearing distance. "Anyway, it's certainly made things more complicated."

The air was thick with the smell of stale beer and wine, and damp floors. Malin wondered if the surge of water from the Lagoon had swept sewage back into the city, or, in the case of this place, washed some of it clean.

Bourchier brought his attention back to the present. "We have much to talk about, either way. You have been given your final instructions by Westminster?"

"Inasmuch as they are able to offer any detail, yes. They wish us to proceed. To put the final arrangements into place. Their resolve remains strong."

"You seem surprised."

It was Malin's turn to pause.

"Not surprised exactly. It's simply that in the last two years, it's often felt as though the whole thing might just fall through. That Edward, or whoever is making the decisions, would have second thoughts. Or that agreement between Household, Chancery and Exchequer would collapse."

Bourchier nodded. "True. There have been days when I have thought the same. But don't underestimate how desperate the king is for funds. Nothing's really changed since he cancelled his debt to those Florentine bastards. Any gains secured have been more than eroded by the conflict with France. And there's never been a king that hasn't wanted to spend more than he's got."

Malin shrugged his shoulders. "I suppose it no longer matters how likely or unlikely it was that his plan would remain constant. All that matters now is how we make all that work count."

Bourchier shifted in his seat.

Malin sensed something wrong. "What is it?"

The man was still something of a mystery to him. Rumours concerning his past, of his reputation as the most senior English intelligence agent, were never far away. Time spent in France, and Scotland. Applying pressure on de Beaumont, the leader of the Dispossessed, to force him to abide by Edward's hold on the Crown. The insights he shared with Malin, into where the next conversation needed to be held, or which member of the Venetian nobility should be enrolled, had always proved invaluable. He, not Malin, was driving the plot. Malin was here only because he and his city friends could be used. And Bourchier was here to make that happen.

For the first time, Bourchier seemed to shrink from looking him in the eye. "So. I'm guessing that when you were back in England, there was no mention of any concerns about the integrity of our... little scheme?"

Malin thought back. "Well, none that I can recall. If

anything, everyone I met seemed very optimistic. Soldiery has been secured. Mainard would have told me if there were any problems of note."

The diminutive man scanned the room, and when he spoke, his voice was more hushed.

"I think you need to know. It was too late to get the message back to court before you set sail. It makes no difference to the command to proceed, but I've informed the Exchequer that The Ten have recently stepped up their activities. I think they've got wind of something. I don't know what, or from whom. But everywhere I look, I see signs that their vigilance has increased."

A dozen questions crowded Malin's mind, but he waited for Bourchier to continue.

"Soranzo. Our key to the Small Council. He came to see me in early December. You'd been gone for just over a month." Although his voice had dropped, his hands were now off his lap, emphasising the importance of what he had to say.

"He had been approached on behalf of the *Capi dei Dieci*, to test the waters on monies for extra ears and eyes. He didn't say what it was that concerned them. They wanted to ensure that when they sought additional funds at the next Small Council meeting, they would get them."

"But what is it that they think they know?" Malin glanced over his shoulder, concerned that the women might react to his raised voice. "What are The Ten looking at?"

"Bluntly, I don't know. It may be something completely unconnected to our activities. You know what this place is like. When they drained the marshes, they did little to drain the appetite for intrigue. I challenge you to name one family, any of the eight hundred in their precious Golden Book, that have not at some time schemed against the state. It would be extraordinary if some of them weren't involved in something right now. Completely outside of our own work."

31

Bourchier was right. It was naive to think that the existence of their own plot precluded the existence of all others, no matter how big or small they might be. For many, the state represented their only income. Not from their unpaid appointments, but from the influence that their appointments gave them, their ability to position themselves to do service to others and receive favours in return. With this strong interdependence sustaining their families and lifestyles, not to mention reputations, it was little wonder when interests collided. And the more serious of those cases would come to The Ten's attention.

"But Ricaud, if it was us they suspected, we can't stop now anyway, can we? Events have already started to take on a life of their own. A small army is already on the move. And our friends across the city?" He could feel the return of the pain in his chest.

Bourchier reached forward across the dining board, taking a firm hold of Malin's arm. "Steady yourself, my friend. This is nothing. Really. Just compose yourself for a moment.

"I know this is not your natural place in life. But you must understand that nothing in the world I inhabit, and that you have been asked to step into, is straightforward. Or blessed with certainty."

But he hadn't stepped in. He'd been *dragged* in. Not that he would ever admit it to a man needing assurance that he was safe to work with.

He could feel the weight of his tincture in his jacket pocket, but swore to himself to leave it untouched. "So what adjustments do you think we should make?"

"I've been thinking of little else for weeks. And I confess it's had me looking over my shoulder more times than I can say. But if there *were* a problem, we would have seen them act by now. I also believe the chaos of this week gives us an additional source of concealment. Men and money are needed elsewhere right now. We should, of course, be diligent. Take no chances." Bourchier's smile returned. "In that sense, nothing's changed."

The *Pregadi*, the permanent Senate, had spent centuries clarifying and refining the Republic's laws. Planning a coup was deemed just as treasonous as executing it.

And The Ten had the power to arrest, interrogate, try, and sentence anyone in the interest of state justice. Men had been executed and hung by one leg in the square, in full view of the citizenry, within one day of the verdict. No one, not even the Small Council or the Doge himself, ever felt it wise to appeal against them. They could be the next to attract their gaze, and hang ignominiously.

Their conspirators had been selected with care. Hand-picked by Malin, Uberto and Bourchier. It had taken them almost a year to confirm if their perceptions of each individual and their motivations were valid. It had been tense work. Vetting raised questions of its own. *Why do you wish to know? Why the sudden interest in my happiness with my lot?*

A single misstep, and suspicions could have been leaked to the authorities.

The last year had been spent developing and aligning this disparate group of citizens, each no doubt having their own prize in mind. A promotion here. A contract there. A place for a family at an important dining table. Everyone different, yet everyone in one fundamental, vital sense the same. They wanted change, and they would play their part to bring it.

His confidence returning, Malin now saw this latest information as merely a signal that they were closing in on the final stage of their work. Why shouldn't they be worried? It was naive to think that they would be able to maintain total secrecy. In this of all cities? Their friends numbered almost a hundred, not counting those they represented, and their regular discussions, at least to the point where he had left for London, suggested all remained steady and committed. They had chosen as wisely as they could, and exercised a thoroughness and patience that would serve them well in the weeks ahead. That remained important. It had to.

He glanced again at the whores at the opposite side of the room. Spies? Hardly. Their concerns would be of a kind that would continue whichever faction controlled the city.

"So, Ricaud, what has Soranzo told you since the turn of the year?"

"That's the thing. Nothing's been voiced at meetings since. Nothing formal, anyway. No more petitions to the Doge and his ministers. They've had two changes amongst the three *Capi dei Dieci* since Christmas, which can often mean a change in policy or tactics. Who knows. Perhaps they've got their money, and their work, whatever it is, is proceeding as they wished."

"So we just carry on, assume they will just do their job as they normally do, and we do everything *we* can to give them nothing to bite on. Is that what you're saying?"

Bourchier raised his eyebrows and placed his hands on the board, palms facing up. "With everything set outside the city, it's down to us to make the most of the time remaining. Nothing now should be left to chance."

Their conversation touched on tactics for the next few days, and a commitment to arrange another meeting.

As Malin moved through the brothel door back onto the street, he sensed Bourchier taking a few steps behind him in the direction of the women on the other side of the room.

He smiled wryly, wondering if his colleague was aiming to conclude earlier business, or negotiate a new intimacy.

At least the two men would not be seen leaving together.

★

He wasn't sure what made him turn left into the street rather than return the way he had come, but Malin found himself walking south, over the half-dozen small bridges before crossing the *piazetta* in front of St Mark's Basilica.

The Lagoon chill rolled in from the Canal as he turned into the main square. He felt its tightening grip on his heart. Or perhaps his rising sense of dread came from the realisation that he had come this way to see again what death on a monstrous scale looked like.

What, beneath the cries of the returning seabirds and the dampened footsteps of the bereaved, the finality of death sounded like.

The rows of the dead had grown further, although gaps in their ranks suggested that some had been removed. To his left, a carriage and its attendants stood midway along the east portico. Another body was being prepared for departure.

Unable to continue looking, yet equally unable to leave, Malin moved to the Basilica steps, and lowered himself slowly to the damp stone.

For the second time that day, his thoughts were no longer his to control.

Memories rushed in with the same power of the wave that had wrought so much damage on the city and its people.

Memories of sitting for hours on the heather-covered rise of a Perthshire moor, bodies of the recently butchered lying just below him. Some had met their fate at his own hand, consumed as he was by a rage that had driven away his fear and resentment. That had pushed it deep into the same peat that was at that moment both battlefield and open grave. His rage was long spent, but he felt now that same sense of powerlessness at the hands of forces far greater than himself.

Like his one and only time as a soldier, the role of conspirator was unsought, but unavoidable.

He forced himself to look again at the rows of bodies awaiting identification or disposal. How many of those he knew would be leaving life in the next month, swept away by forces every bit as impersonal and savage as the trembling earth and the vengeful sea.

He would see this through, if only to protect those he most cared about, and to put distance forever between himself and those who had given him this choice that was no choice.

Between himself and his father.

*

Uberto was already waiting for him when he returned home, enjoying a glass of wine with Symon.

"So, I don't know what the two of you have heard, but I don't think I've ever seen so much chaos at the Arsenale. I've not spoken to Sclavo since the disaster, but I doubt even he could have prepared me for what I saw."

Malin marvelled at the man's continuing high spirits.

"The damage was greatest in the north and south yards. The whole flow of construction has taken a battering. Many of the most completed ships, at the south end, were driven repeatedly to the edges of the dock. At least a dozen will have to go back for hull repairs."

His voice dropped a little. "Fifty workmen are dead. Most of them from the framing quadrant. God knows what it must have been like to be hit with that force of water. That's assuming they weren't crushed by falling materials in the initial quake. About sixty others are still missing, presumably washed out into the Lagoon. Three men were burnt alive when one of the caulking pots tipped over on them. Terrible."

He took a large swig of wine, the look in his eyes suggesting he was revisiting the morning. The things he'd seen and the anguish of those who related the news.

"Each part of the yard seems to be working, albeit on reduced output, but there's a distinct air of disbelief around the place. You know yourself just how much noise there is normally. It was quiet enough today to hear the seabirds out beyond the Lagoon wall."

Symon reached across to the half-empty flagon on the table, refilled his goblet and offered more to his friends. "The story's the same all over, I think. The surge caused damage as far west as Cannaregio, which is completely unheard of. Everyone is talking of retribution, a kind of divine punishment for the city's defiance of the Pope. Or for our sins." He laughed. "If that's indeed the case, I'm amazed it has taken this long for it to be delivered."

Malin laughed too, as much at the idea of a lack of divine punctuality as at his friend's customary irreverence.

Uberto fell quiet.

"What is it, Uberto? You of all people know the amount of scheming and dissembling that goes on. Do you think God has truly decided to back Venice's enemies, and teach us all a lesson?"

Uberto's frown deepened for a moment, then broke.

The banter and wine continued, before Symon offered to cook their dinner.

Malin took the opportunity once again to rib their friend. "When are you going to admit that you lose too much drinking time with us in that kitchen? Get some servants who know what they're doing in there."

Uberto could resist no better. "And when are you going to stop angering all our friends in the meat business, and cut down on the amount of fish you push on us?"

The jokes were old, but borne from a very real admiration of their Scottish friend.

Two months after moving into the house, Symon insisted

that Malin should let the servants go, and allow him to run the house himself. From that point on, he astonished Malin and any visitors with his skills in obtaining and cooking the best seafood in the city. It was as if he had memorised and then mastered every meal they had ever eaten during their travels around the Adriatic and the Black Sea, and found ways to apply every ingredient from the spice markets.

When Uberto eventually rose to travel home, he thanked Symon for the spiced *barbone*, the red mullet dish that was known to be one of his favourites, and for the Dalmatian wine that accompanied it.

Malin walked him to the door, where they exchanged a few final words out of Symon's hearing.

"So, Malin. I am guessing your day went well. Although you seemed very quiet tonight."

"Yes. Oh, yes, everything is going as it should. I met with Bourchier, and he remains confident too. He seems to think that all this chaos will aid us in our attempts to hide our activities." He paused to look into Uberto's eyes, seeking any sign of affirmation.

Uberto looked at Malin for several more moments before answering. "I've lived in this place, for good or ill, for over thirty years, Malin. I'm too old, seen too many examples of where Venice, at its darkest hour, pulls itself up and surprises the world. You've been steady in your assertion that secrecy is paramount, and that we should do nothing to threaten that. Bourchier is right. Nothing has changed, my friend. I won't allow talk of divine intervention, or any increased attention of the authorities, to affect any of that. We are so close."

Malin paused, reflecting on his conversation in the brothel that morning. On how the king's spy had wandered back to the whores at the end of their meeting, as though normal life would simply continue, wrathful God or not.

He decided once more to say nothing of The Ten to his friend.

"Safe journey home, Uberto. Give my love to Donata and the girls. They have nothing to fear. And you and I will see this thing through."

"I'll do that. And I'll tell Lucia that you send your regards."

Unsure what to say in response, Malin rolled his eyes and said nothing. Smile intact, Uberto turned to head back to the Canal, and his ride home.

Malin closed the door.

He wondered if they were all as safe as he hoped.

Chapter 4

Tuesday 29th January 1348

Day 3 of the Quarant

Malin stood in the office, barely believing what he'd just heard.

"So just let me get this straight. In less than two days, with God knows what happening in the city, you're ready to show me the state of our business spread across almost twenty years and as many countries?"

Symon, seated at the table with him, remained calm. "What's so hard tae understand? Anyone would think you were disappointed." As usual, with just his friend present, his voice betrayed more of the natural inflections of his country of birth.

Malin lent back from the table. He'd hoped to keep Symon busy for many days, creating the space for himself to meet those most critical to the coup.

"No. No, that's not it. It's just incredible that you've been able to bring matters together so rapidly." Malin's face lightened.

"I know you tell me regularly just how good you are, but I never thought for one moment that you were right."

Symon bit his tongue. "Bastard! You prance around the city, talking your talk, doing your deals, calculating margins, predicting the weather, guessing the need for copper in Alexandria, salt in Naples, or hemp in some God-forsaken corner of the Black Sea, and you think I sit here all day, every day, contemplating the dirt under my nails?"

They were both laughing now. Sixteen years of friendship and interdependence left little room for surprise. Yet Malin remained amazed at his friend's abilities. And the man's place in his heart.

The six months recovering together, day after painful day back in Lynn, explained much but not all of their bond. As did Malin pulling the dying young boy from a pile of corpses on the Dupplin *bealach*.

It was as much about how he, Malin, had felt, the moment before he heard Symon's cries. Lost. Sick with self-disgust. And how helping Symon had put that feeling behind him.

He had spent much of his time on the *Seynte Marie*, sailing back from Southampton, reflecting on those moments.

Malin pulled out a seat. The table was covered in scrolls and bound pages. "I suppose you will tell me next that you want to do this now?"

"Well, I thought that you were keen to know everything. I still have a few questions anyway, so talking now would give me a chance to act on the answers. It's probably going to be another two or three days before the city grinds to a halt with all the funerals."

Malin ran his eyes across the piles of paperwork. These records defined much of his life. Of *their* lives. "So where do you want to start, my friend?"

Symon took two deep breaths and waved his hand over the table.

"These are all our contracts and letters of current concern. All the open agreements in force with the Commune, and their associated merchants and shipowners. Over here are the *commendas* related to your business holdings in Antwerp, both contractual and in stock." He twisted in his seat. "This third pile covers the deals that might mature over the next few months.

"And these represent the best information I have on the value of our six contracted ships, and their locations as of today."

Symon pushed back his chair and walked to the shelving running along the back wall of the office. He took out another small pile of parchment, and returned to the table.

"I updated this yesterday, partly based on the conversations I had over in San Bartolomeo. I'm pretty sure these numbers are accurate, but as I'm not sure what you want to use them for, it might be wise for us to sit down and go through them together. I kept the coinage values in ducats."

He passed the papers across.

Malin looked down at three sheets of tightly written columns.

These dense black marks summarised his entire life's achievement. Deposits of money in banks in cities as far north as Bergen, and as far east as Trebizond. He pictured himself as a twelve-year-old, his first deal done without his uncle's help. What that boy would think of such wealth.

The numbers took his breath away. At what point did his wealth begin to approach this size? He knew he had built solid foundations, first in Lynn, then from Antwerp, and finally here, yet the figures suggested a growth in recent years that was astounding.

In his youth, he had carried every document governing his business in a leather satchel given to him by his Uncle Haylan. Flicking through them each day, despite Radley's mockery, had given him a real sense of satisfaction. It was also the basis of his growing reputation at the Lynn Guildhall, as the young man who could quote the details of every transaction, every cargo and its value. Perhaps it was this skill that had helped Haylan recruit Elyas to smuggle him out on a Hanse ship to Antwerp, away from his father.

It had been years since he could fit all his business in the satchel. Although still a permanent part of his dress, it served a different purpose now. In any case, he had Symon.

"Malin. Is everything all right?"

The question brought his attention back into the room. He cleared his throat.

"Yes, of course. Everything here is in order. I commend you, Symon. Really. How have you kept on top of this so well over the years?"

"It kept me busy, that's for sure. All that time with Elyas when I first came to Antwerp. You teach well, Malin, but you were always away on your travels. Without him to help me understand how to keep all these figures, well…"

"And if he hadn't smuggled me out of Lynn, I might not have made it past fifteen. And then we certainly wouldn't have met."

A short silence followed, each thinking back to earlier times.

Malin slapped Symon on the back.

"Anyway, let's go through these remaining items, and see where it gets us."

★

The morning flew by.

Malin's initial frustration at being distracted from other more pressing matters soon disappeared. He had stepped back into the world in which he felt most comfortable.

43

Their conversation was relaxed, yet remained focussed. Symon made notes throughout. It was clear that his knowledge of Venetian regulation, or the latest likely rates of exchange when visiting ports of the *Oltremare*, had now outstripped Malin's.

By late afternoon, with just a small pile of scrolls demanding further conversations with traders, they were finished.

"So, Le Cordier. We have finished, have we not? I think some wine is due."

"Almost. There's just one more thing." Malin leaned forward, and laid out each page of the summary document Symon had produced that morning.

"I'd like you to visit each of the banks shown here, that have their holdings in the city, and arrange for the funds to be transferred to Antwerp. I am happy to pay any fees that may apply."

Symon looked puzzled.

Malin continued before his friend could say anything.

"I think we've seen enough the last few days to encourage us to be cautious with the money we have tied up here. Until I'm sure that the city can rebound from the damage caused, and get its mind back on trade, I think we should put a temporary hold on business. Take our money back to Antwerp, where we know we can find good, safe uses for it."

"But without these deposits, we could miss out on the summer trade here. Doing what you suggest could put a whole year's business in jeopardy."

"As would continuing as we are, Symon. I have thought this through, and you've given me every confidence today that we have more than enough reserves to see us through a light summer, if that's what is needed."

"Are you sure?" Symon rarely challenged Malin's decisions.

"Yes. What I ask is that you make this happen as discretely

as possible, and do so by the end of the week." Malin looked directly at Symon once more. "Am I clear?"

Something in Malin's tone suggested that Symon should say no more.

An uneasy silence settled on them both.

Symon finally excused himself, returned to his desk and removed some blank sheets of paper.

★

Malin went upstairs and brought down his satchel.

Sifting through the sheaf of thin, unbound parchment, he found the most recent, half-filled page. The writing was so small, it was barely legible.

All his notes to himself. A diary, not of things that he had done, but of things he had learned or felt. He'd begun it as part of daily life in Lynn, at the insistence of an uncle determined that the young boy made the most of every new day.

He could still hear him. Still see Haylan returning from the Guildhall.

"Find time to think about the most important thing the day has taught you, Malin. And write it down. Your life will soon be too long to remember it all, and you will be the poorer for it."

He wrote something most days. And carried the growing record in his satchel, folded into a pocket away from his business papers. At his loneliest point in Antwerp, far from home and cut off from all those he knew, he began to consolidate his thoughts. Elyas had found him a quill that offered the tightest, smallest script, and he transcribed his entire life's reflections onto a small number of pages. He had been doing so ever since.

Arranging the soft, scuffed leather of the bag on his knees, he took out quill and ink, leaned forward and began to write.

Misleading, or withholding the truth from his friend, was

45

an entirely new and sickening departure from their customary openness. Little matter that his motivation was to protect him from worry and danger. From any knowledge of his true goals on his return to Venice, or accusation of involvement.

To most, it might appear that the Scot owed Malin everything. Rescue from the carrion crows on Dupplin Moor, soon to grow fat on the further slaughter wrought by the forces of the Dispossessed. Malin's almost impossibly strenuous walk back to the barber-surgeons with the young boy draped over his own damaged shoulders. Passing off the unconscious young boy as an English man-at-arms. Their shared journey south to Norfolk, pausing only when it looked as though further movement might kill him. Then, eventually, recovery back at Lynn.

Yet in truth, Malin's debt to his friend was one of at least equal measure. It was shame and self-loathing that moved Malin to wander back up to the *bealach* of the Perthshire hill. Looking down from the western slope above the col, upon the thousands of bodies funnelled into the narrow pass of the engagement disgusted him. Worse still, the memory of his mania of the previous day, when the two forces met.

Already traumatised by the prospect of fighting from horseback, his fear had multiplied when, in a change to centuries of battle wisdom, all men-at-arms were ordered to leave their horses at the bottom of the hill. It would be the longbowmen, attacking from the second rank, who would lead the way against their enemy.

Perhaps it was the immediacy, the churning, brutal intimacy of the fighting that saw Malin's swift descent into something bestial. He had hacked and swung and hewn like a man possessed, losing all sense of himself. At many times during the battle, he neither understood nor cared who was friend or foe. Bodies piled up around him, and all he wanted to do was to add to them. To fight back, not against a bloodthirsty aggressor, but against the man who had sent him there. Against his father Jefferey, the seventh Earl of Wormegay, and the man's lifelong resentment of his matricidal son.

Or perhaps, more disturbingly yet, against a newly surfaced part of himself. A willingness to indiscriminately kill and maim, whether in the name of his own survival or not.

The Dispossessed, a large group of English nobles that lost their lands and wealth north of the border in the negotiated peace ten years earlier, had been granted permission by Edward to conduct an undeclared invasion to wrest back their lands from the young King David and his regent. Henry de Beaumont, a man renowned for both his spleen and his willingness to act on it, led a force of nearly three thousand men north.

Pressed by royal summons into joining their forces, Malin's exposure to all that he detested and feared of the military life was as traumatic as it was unsought.

He had already escaped his father once, when he was fourteen, his uncle fearing for his safety at the hands of Jefferey. News had come that Malin's brother Brenner, moulded and shaped to be his father's worthy successor, had been declared first missing then dead in the skirmishes at Burton-on-Trent, fighting to weaken the position of the problematic Earl of Lancaster. Jefferey had by all accounts descended into a melancholic rage, from which he was said to harbour murderous intent towards his sole remaining son.

Ten years later, with Malin firmly established as one of the leading independent traders in the city of Antwerp, his father had used his power at court to instigate a royal command for his estranged son to return and lead the Wormegay retainers.

Malin had no doubt that his conscription, as a young man totally without military experience, was contrived purely in the spirit of resentful, festering vengeance.

Symon's enrolment into the opposing army arose from his village's lack of choice. As an orphan, adopted as much by the whole village as by any one family, he was the only adolescent with no blood ties. Unlike Malin's, *his* betrayal, while no less momentous, was at least performed with a heavy heart. He seemed to have let go of any resentment years ago. Malin, sixteen years later, could still not say the same.

Thoughts of his escape to Antwerp returned. Had Elyas done for Malin what he himself had done for Symon? There was some truth in that idea. Symon of course had had little say in Malin's decision to remove him from the battlefield. To leave him there would have meant certain death. But was the threat over Malin's life from his father's anger any less serious? Haylan must have genuinely feared for his nephew's safety. He certainly held no illusions regarding the callous and unpredictable nature of his sister's bitter widower.

Malin had passed the Hanse warehouse hundreds of times over the years on the Staithe, often wondering what happened behind the veil of secrecy that seemed to enclose it. Their business was a matter only for themselves. Even the men of the guild seemed to know little of how they operated. Yet Haylan had seemingly earned the respect of their senior representative, an Antwerp man named Elyas Scepene.

When news of Malin's father's growing resentment of his only surviving son reached Lynn, Haylan acted swiftly. Malin would travel on the next Hanse vessel with Elyas to Antwerp, from where he would work under his protection. Haylan bought every one of Malin's portfolio of contracts from him, funding Malin's journey across the German Sea to safety.

His first sight of Antwerp remained imprinted on his mind even now. Losing count of the cranes on the shore of the narrowing Scheldt estuary. Following Elyas through the increasingly dense streets to his house on Wolstraat, nestled between the churches of Our Lady and St Carolus. His introduction to the three other apprentices already living there.

So here he was.

In Venice, ensnared in a web less easy to escape.

Deceiving his best friend into safeguarding his own wealth against the possible failure of a plot of which Symon had no knowledge.

Malin reached, not for the first time that evening, for his phial of gentian. Since Dupplin, he had suffered from a burning in his chest, particularly at times of worry or uncertainty. It was Luchas, his Pisan friend, that had first witnessed his pain, and suggested the herbal remedy he now relied on. He had secured a large box of the deep green miniatures in Southampton before departing England.

He took another swig and replaced the cork.

Returning the documents to his satchel, he rose from his chair, and walked through to the office, determined to ensure that Symon bore him no ill will for his earlier bluntness.

The room was empty. A plate of cheese and bread sat on the table.

Damn the man. Already out visiting one or two of the bankers featured in the accounts. Where did he get his energy?

Malin picked up the food and walked upstairs, taking his unreconciled wishes for his friend with him.

Chapter 5

Wednesday 30th January 1348

Day 4 of the Quarant

Malin left early to travel the short distance to the Arsenale.

An hour later, he found himself prostrate at Sclavo's feet, the air above him still churning from the violence of the younger man's closed fist.

The blow had come from nowhere. He had simply followed Uberto's son into the privacy of his office, turned to watch Sclavo close the door behind him, and then the blur as the punch landed.

He fell to the floor as if struck by a cannonball falling from an empty sky, with no galley in sight.

His arm out, reaching for the table well beyond his grasp, Malin rose shakily to one knee. His head continued to spin, and he dropped back to sit on the floor.

"What? What was that? What have I…?"

Sclavo stood above him, and put an arm out, offering his

hand. While his anger was not yet sated, he seemed almost as surprised as Malin at what he had done.

"Here. Get up."

Malin reached up and took his hand. The blood pumped in his ears, and his vision was still muddled. He ran his free hand along his jaw.

"Just sit down here, and we'll start again." His friend's words were harsh and gruff.

He dropped into the chair, straightening the satchel on his shoulder.

Sclavo, looming over Malin from his full height, mumbled through the falling mane of hair now masking part of his face. "I'm not sorry. Be in no doubt that it was deserved, but know also that I will not do it again."

He then moved to sit down at the top of the table, just a few feet from the stunned Englishman.

"What have I done, Sclavo?"

The sounds of office business, murmured fragments of noise that marked any large gathering of men, could be heard through the door. From outside, the intermittent smacks of heavy loads on decks. The movement of timber or sailcloth on carts around the numerous construction or repair berths.

Sclavo took a deep breath and cleared his throat.

"So, you finally came back. I was convinced you wouldn't. That you'd leave Father to cope on his own. Do you know how much I've cursed you since you left? Watching him carry all this weight?"

Still rubbing his jaw, Malin sat silently.

"Why did I think this was all such a good idea?" Sclavo had calmed a little, at least, his words more considered. "A year ago, you helped convince me of the *justness* of all this. The possibility that anything even vaguely *real* could even come of it, yes, was beguiling. That you could help reinstate my father. Help him regain his belief that good men that do good things should be rewarded. They crushed him, Malin. You know that.

"You tempted us, Malin, and we? Well, we were weak enough to go along. And here you are. Back again to see if Father has held up his part of the deal. On his own. How could you?"

Malin looked down at his hands. "That's not fair. I had to go back to England. To finalise things. And Uberto seems in good health."

"Really? He told me yesterday that you'd met him twice since your return. Do you really think he is coping with all this?"

Malin looked across at Sclavo. "Look. I'm sorry I didn't come to see you sooner. I assumed you were busy assessing the damage, and—"

"Do you think I care about how long it's taken you to come *here*?" Sclavo's tone tightened to a forced whisper. "That my anger comes from some kind of *jealousy*?" Sclavo jumped up, his jaw tightening.

"I don't care about those kind of things now, do you understand? I care only about the way you have plunged our family into this thing. How you've made my father a mere instrument in the ambitions of others. God, you've seen him. It's as though he is *bewitched* by it all. You've stolen his soul, Malin, and he simply doesn't see it. He will not see it. All he sees is his best friend leading him to redemption, when in fact you are leading him to hell.

"And what of others who, despite your words of comfort and encouragement, have no thought whatsoever for anyone in this city? Of your bloody king, who cares only for the prize, and to hell with the damage wreaked on his way to grasping it?"

He paused, as if unsure if his next words should be spoken.

"I thought you cared for us, Malin. For the years that we have worked together, the discomfort we have shared on any number of godforsaken ships across the three seas. For the years you've been happy to be received by Mother."

He glanced toward the door. His deputy sat only a few feet from it.

"And what of Lucia? She knows nothing of this still, Malin. Are you using her too?"

Sclavo was shaking. Malin reached a hand across the table. Sclavo looked down, but made no move to take it.

"I understand your anxiety, Sclavo. Truly I do. It is a tense time, for all of us. You have a lot of responsibility here. To secure the supplies and men to return this place to normality."

Anger flashed in Sclavo's eyes. "Do you think I give one damn about this place right now? Have you listened to nothing I have said?"

"As you wish. I'm sorry. I'm simply trying to show that I understand the pressure you are under. Our scheme, as you call it, is not sullied by its backers. Your father remains a justly aggrieved man. He deserves wrongs to be put right. Venice will never thrive without its best and finest able to shape its destiny."

The edge in Sclavo's voice was new. "Is that how they got you to do this for them, Malin? Are you one of *their* best and finest?"

"Sclavo. It's clear that we need to talk this through. But I tell you now, that I have never had anything but the best for your family in mind. I have always striven to ensure that our work together, and our friendship, adds to our success in equal measure."

"Only if you could come out of it smelling of roses."

"But that's the world we live in, Sclavo, your father and myself. That doesn't mean that we don't look out for each other, or share the pleasure of success when it comes. Surely you must have seen that over the years."

He paused.

"Do you no longer trust me to look out for your interests? Do you believe I mean your father harm?"

Malin watched as a scarlet flush rose up from the man's neck.

Sclavo stood and walked to the side of the room. He looked out at the teeming landscape beyond the window, and spoke without turning.

"If I thought you meant us ill, I would kill you where you stand, and to hell with the consequences. But I can't just sit by and watch you drag them deeper into this insanity."

"You misunderstand, Sclavo. I'm sorry. The decision is neither yours or mine to make now."

Sclavo turned, his colour remaining, but now his eyes were moist. "What do you mean?"

Malin joined him at the window.

"I don't mean to suggest that we have no control over our actions, or that we are somehow powerless pawns in the games of others. We could choose to call off the entire plot right now, and stand down every one of our friends. Ensure they do the same for those they have in turn recruited. We could even recompense those that have spent large sums in patronage and gifts in the right, necessary places. Or hired men for when the time comes.

"But the real issue is that our crimes already exist. We may choose not to call it treason, but others will have no trouble calling it that."

Malin turned to directly face his friend.

"Be under no illusion, Sclavo, I would dearly love to bring this to a safe halt. I have no liking for any of this deception and secrecy. But that option ceased to be available to us many months ago. You have to understand. The only path to safety for all of us, for you, your family, is to complete what we have planned. Make this a success, and remove power from the hands of those that would see us imprisoned or executed."

Malin stepped forward and put his arm around Sclavo's shoulder, guiding his friend away from the window and back to the table.

"Let's just take a little time to reflect on just how well we have done to date, and on how well set we are in comparison with those before us who have tried and failed."

They resumed their seats.

Sclavo, showing little sign of his earlier aggression, told Malin of their progress since his departure for London.

Three of the five senior Arsenale foremen, the *protomaestri*, had each pledged their support for the planned coup. The form of that support was still to be shaped, but Sclavo was confident that when the time came, these men could either neutralise their workforce, or possibly gain their support to take an active role. For Malin, and his co-conspirators back in London, this was key. Many of the craftsmen, whether shipwrights, caulkers, mast- or oar-makers, were also members of the respected *Arsenalotti*, the part-time militia spread around the city.

Sclavo had courted each of the foremen, slowly strengthening their commitment. Unlike the three members of the *Patroni*, appointed by the Small Council for a mere thirty-two months at a time, these men would lose little in the event of a change in their political masters. They rarely had anything good to say about any of the three *patrons*, feeling that their masters' contributions were at best symbolic. Any sign of the crimson-clad nobles usually saw the foremen running for cover.

The *protomaestris'* trust in Sclavo was built in no small part on his extraordinary efficiency. And on how he helped them solve urgent problems within the workforce or at the stores.

It also helped that, without their knowledge, he been drawing off money over the last year or more to build the foundations of his 'action fund'. His occasional gifts to them were well received.

Malin left just before lunch, leaving Sclavo the rest of the afternoon to complete his assessment of the damage to the shipyard from the previous week.

★

The day could not have begun more badly, but Malin's confidence in his assailant was, if anything, higher now than when he left Calle San Domenico that morning.

The Arsenale carried a huge amount of weight in the minds of the *populari*, the ordinary men and women of the city. Much of the city's safety was due to how well its ships were constructed and kept afloat. As the largest employer in Venice, it also offered an escape from poverty for many families.

An Arsenale sympathetic to the imminent coup would be an enormous factor in the outcome of their actions. Malin could think of no one better than Sclavo to coax this giant in the right direction. As long as he kept his temper under control.

Another brisk walk.

He headed further east, facing into the stiffening north-east breeze crossing the Lagoon. To his left, the buildings gradually lost their industrial look. Cutting inland through the park, gaining shelter from the raw breeze, he passed the respectable houses of well-to-do families.

He turned from the path onto the broad wooden bridge spanning the Gardini canal. It appeared intact, although Lagoon flotsam hung from its latticed sides. Further still, the older bridge across to the isle of St Elena had fared less well. Swarms of workmen surrounded the entrance ramp. He picked his way through, holding his breath in anticipation of falling through into the cold water beneath.

He wondered briefly at the possibility that these men could be called as future witnesses to his journey.

The church of St Elena finally came into sight. The most easterly tall building on the Castello mainland, the roof of its high central nave stood stark against the winter sky. He wondered what it must have felt like to stand at its door, witnessing Thursday's wave crash across the low plaza, on its way to the centre of the city.

There was no sign of anyone at the front of the building, so he continued around the south end of the church, back into the full strength of the breeze. A figure sat on a large pile of ruined masonry. As he approached, Malin inspected the imposing structure of the church above him.

"It appears that even the house of God is subject to His earthly might."

Bourchier turned as Malin drew close.

"Ah, there you are, my friend. I was beginning to wonder if my note had reached you this morning."

"Have no fear on that score, Ricaud. My only challenge is to ensure that I reach the front door before my friend."

They embraced as though long apart.

Malin rubbed his chin. "I've just come from the Arsenale. Things appear in good shape. We can discuss their readiness."

"That is good news. And for my own part, I wish to recount the fruits of my efforts since we last met." He winked. "At least those relevant to our endeavour."

The man's ebullience could not be resisted.

They walked further around the church, to the northernmost tip of the island, and took a seat at the very edge of the protective wall. Isola La Cetosa stood just across the narrow waters, and the small inlet leading to Murano.

He imagined he could smell Murano's glass furnaces, burning all year round since the glassmakers were banished from the main city. Their enforced departure had been unpopular, but the number of fires in the largely timber-built city had dropped dramatically as a result. For the artisans themselves, the island had become a glorified prison, for fear their secrets would be passed to rival cities. Resentment amongst the glass-blowers guild was being usefully exploited.

Bourchier seemed to be entirely relaxed, sitting on the last open ground of the city before it gave way to the Lagoon and then open sea. He had a remarkable mind, yet at the same time, an almost insatiable appetite for life, in all its tawdry glory. Perhaps his time spent in the taverns and brothels was simply a reflection of the precariousness of his position. Knowing such a man remained at the helm offered hope for what lay ahead.

He gave Malin a long, hard look.

"I have to say, you're looking a little drawn, my friend. Sitting here, pondering the great imponderables. I sense you are not enjoying your first few days back."

He threw his hands wide, and took a dramatic and noisy deep breath in, as if trying to embrace the whole of the city.

"So, what is it about this ridiculous, wonderful place that fails to get your heart beating out of your chest? It's magnificent, yes? There is no other place on earth like it. I used to think that the wiles of Westminster were enough to keep an observant man intrigued and busy for a lifetime. But Venice? It is like walking through a labyrinth, where the pulsing sides of the maze are never in the same place from one day to the next."

The man's eyes shone. He always seemed able to seize upon any news, good or bad, and derive energy from its consumption. Ingesting threats and opportunities alike, without being cowed or unnerved, was something Malin could only hope for in himself.

"So tell me, Ricaud, just what has changed since we sat on the Calle di Stagneri?"

Bourchier placed his hands palm-down on his thighs, and rolled up his bottom lip.

"Well, I've been taking the temperature of our friends in the Council and the *Pregadi*. It remains to be seen, of course, if they speak truly, but I feel that resolve remains in good supply. Their commitment remains unchanged, although I detect impatience. A desire to simply get going and make this happen.

"I've not had a chance to visit every *sestiere*, so I'm unable to confirm if the support is truly holding steady across the whole city, but I have to say, things are looking good. I've told them that we'll confirm the date for action soon, but that they should know it for certain by Holy Week."

Malin thought this through. "And for that to be true, we need news of the progress and disposition of Libusch and his men. I hope to God that their arrival goes unnoticed until it's too late to stop them."

The small man glanced up into his face again. "Relax, my friend. All is good. As I said last time, we should allow events beyond the Veneto to find their own way. No one has heard anything to suggest we have a problem." He cleared his throat. "Anyway. I would rather hear of the latest from the Arsenale. How is your young friend Da Segna?"

Did he know of their confrontation that morning? Malin knew almost nothing of Bourchier's methods, but he knew enough to wonder.

He dismissed the possibility. "Arrangements are maturing just as we would want. Sclavo is meeting those remaining *protomaestri* yet to offer their support this afternoon. If the *Arsenalotti* do what they are told, as they normally do, we should see militia positioned around the Palace, the six halls of the *sestieres*, and the Treasury. The Arsenale bells remain the signal for them to act. Within the walls of the Arsenale itself, the foremen will keep the men's minds on their work and away from interference. If I get word tomorrow, I think it is time for you to transfer some funds to these leaders, through Sclavo, to strengthen their powers of persuasion."

"Of course."

Malin changed the subject. "And have you heard any more on the subject of The Ten?"

"Nothing, my friend. In fact, I have spent the last two days doing all I can to put them from my mind. An effort worthy of you too, if I may say. The trick is to not alter our behaviour. Quite the opposite. If they are starting to show an interest in us, the last thing we should do is make any obvious adjustments."

Again, Bourchier's tone struck Malin oddly. "Adjustments?"

"Yes. Anything sudden or different." Bourchier turned to face Malin directly once more, their knees almost touching as they sat on the sea wall. "For example, the despatching of a colleague to close out a large number of contracts. Arranging to withdraw all monies from local banks. That sort of unusual activity."

Malin's face coloured then dropped. "I don't... How the hell did you...?"

Bourchier said nothing, but something new, something colder and more prying lay behind his eyes.

"Listen to me carefully, my friend. Never underestimate the skill and persistence of those whose business is the business of others. You are lucky that it is only I that sits here and offers this advice. How would it feel if it was someone, let us say, less in harmony with our goals, that was pondering the significance of your actions?"

He waited for his question to sink in, then continued.

"So let us imagine that my words will reassure you that there is little I fail to see or hear in this place. Feel glad that I am on your side, and that *our* side will be victorious. Yet please also consider how much more careful you should be when deciding what to do, and how to do it. We are in this together my friend, and will be until it is over. As are your friends. I need you to be positive but vigilant. Always."

★

On his walk home, Malin felt the bite of the rising north-easterly through his tunic and leggings. He had done his best to mask his shock at Bourchier's thinly veiled warning, but it shook him badly. Had Bourchier instructed a man to follow Symon as he went about his business? Did he have informers at each of the trading houses and banks that Symon visited? Or had he simply heard rumours from others not necessarily directly allied with their goals, and procured the information from sources keen to profit?

In the end, it didn't matter. The point had been made, and yes, Bourchier was right.

But what should he do?

He sat at the centre of the plot with Uberto, regardless of questions of how much control they had. Their safety was entirely dependent on the health of that plot.

Discovery or failure would be fatal.

Malin shuddered, and pulled out a half-empty phial of gentian. Without a replacement tomorrow, he would be doubled over by noon.

He hugged his satchel close to his side. The strap, relieved of its weight, caught in the breeze and slapped gently on the side of his neck.

He turned back, losing his view of the remaining winter light over the west of the city. It would soon be dark. Unwelcome eyes might find it harder to observe him. Could they know him simply from his fading silhouette?

His eyes watered, disrupting his view across the Lagoon to the Lido. He blinked, and the sharp contours of the Church of San Nicolò resolved themselves, punctuating the low skyline just a mile or two away.

Uberto had once told him of his arrival back from one of his most successful trading voyages. Of entering San Nicolò to offer thanks for his safety, while others headed home across the Lagoon. That moment had marked the date from which his friend's wealth was assured. When he first truly believed that his family could look forward to an affluent and safe future in his adopted city.

He turned to walk back home, the full moon above the horizon, pricked by the long thin line of buildings rising from the bay.

He needed warmth, and a chance to regather his confidence.

To consider ways to silence all the signals he was sending to friend and foe alike.

Chapter 6

Thursday 31st January 1348

Day 5 of the Quarant

An unforgiving full moon bathed his every dream step in bright, unequivocal guilt. Enemies laughed at his feeble attempts at disguise and misdirection. Bourchier stood in the meagre shadows that remained, a silent rebuke on his lips.

It was past dawn before Malin gained any peace. Before heading downstairs, he re-read last night's journal note.

Change must be masked if it is to go unnoticed.

Symon looked up from a plate of cold meats and cheese, sitting quietly in the grey early light.

Malin's mood rose immediately. "I see you're happy to fill your stomach without waiting for your so-called friend."

Symon pointed to a second plate. "There's plenty, Malin. Although by the look of you, I'm not sure if you'll do it justice."

Malin pulled out a chair, ignoring the obvious question lurking just beneath Symon's jibe.

"Thank you for caring so much. I'm sure I'll survive long enough to give you your next instructions."

Two mouthfuls passed before laughter filled the room.

"So Malin, what will it be today?"

Here it is. Take back control.

"So. I feel we need to make a statement. Establish ourselves once more in the convoys. Demonstrate our commitment to the Republic." He paused, his mouth so dry he could barely swallow.

Symon turned to face him. "We need to do what?"

"Well. The chaos of the last week will have shaken up the listed participants. Some more than others. The *Savii ai Ordini* might well be reconsidering the makeup of the spring *mudae*. Things may have changed for many people. The corn stores have suffered considerable damage. Perhaps room for other business will open up. Perhaps the admirals will decide to stock the fleet differently. We should make enquiries."

"But Malin, only two days ago, you asked me to put all our affairs in order. I thought—"

"It doesn't matter what you thought. Things are moving rapidly. We have never allowed a genuine opportunity to pass us by, and I don't intend to start now." He heard the insistence in his voice, and softened his tone. "It's possible that there is nothing to be gained. But let us at least understand if there is anything we might do."

Symon said nothing.

"We'll go across and see if we can catch any of them before they meet to discuss their plans for the year. We can at least plant the idea in their mind."

They finished their meal in silence. Symon gathered his papers, while Malin, dressed once more for the cold, walked to the front of the house and examined the street.

"Come, Symon. No one ever made money by spending the whole morning filling a bag."

Symon stood by his side, his preparations complete. "Aye,

but many's the time that folk lost money, or worse, without doing it."

★

An hour later they took their place with a dozen other petitioners in the high-panelled waiting room of the *Savii* for Land and Sea.

The mood was sombre. What little conversation could be heard behind the desks was terse and abrupt. The announced move of staff into their new chambers in the Palace had been put on hold until damage inspections in the new wing could be completed.

They watched as the reception clerk, a short, middle-aged man with an unruly shock of grey hair, met every approach with a deep scowl. Each new arrival was greeted with mounting irritability. Malin and Symon worked harder, with each approach, to suppress their grins at each confrontation.

A young man came towards them. "Please, gentlemen, if you could follow me."

Both sides of the passageway were lined top to bottom with shelves full of documents. Above their heads, a large crack ran the length of the ceiling, then divided to spread across the top of the door to their left.

The official noticed their gaze. "Yes. It's hard to imagine that things could be any worse in our new home. Yet we must remain patient, and hope that our records can be kept safe."

They took a seat in a cramped room at the end of the corridor. As their escort turned to leave, the seated man behind the desk looked up.

"Good morning. I trust you had only a brief wait. Although as you have no doubt seen, we are in some state of transition. Half our material is no longer here. We are, how shall I say it, *unaccustomed* to this level of disarray."

The man, not long in his twenties, smiled and tugged down his uniform. "My name is Pietro Selvo. I understand that you are interested in the spring fleets?"

Malin introduced himself, confirming his previous participation in the state convoys. "I'm sorry to hear that you're experiencing some challenges. It must be difficult to focus on matters, even those dear to the Republic's heart, when so many people have lost their lives, or suffered the loss of their homes or businesses."

"It's harder for some than others. No doubt some of the builders in the city will be rubbing their hands, looking forward to all their new work."

He reached forward to straighten the quill and paper on his desk. "My own family is still trying to make sense of what has happened, so as a city, it could be months before we truly understand how we have been affected." He removed the purple cap from his head, and ran his hand slowly back through his thick dark hair before replacing it. The strain in his voice became more pronounced.

"I'm not sure if I can help you today, Signor Le Cordier. I have just agreed with my colleagues that we will not meet until next Wednesday to examine our position regarding the fleets. We only commenced our enquiries with our bond holders three days ago."

Malin commiserated. "It is so unfortunate. I myself have asked my colleague here to assess our own position regarding our stocks, and those of our partners. We had not originally sought to participate in this year's convoys, but in light of recent events, I would dearly love to be considered. If you identify any difficulties, that is."

The young noble lent back in his chair.

"Well. I could point out the potential lack of respect that you show to those struck by tragedy. Yet it remains possible that changes may be needed. We will need every ducat from the convoys to pay back the loans being negotiated for the rebuilding. The *massari* will not want to produce more coins to fund the work when there could be shortages of men or resources. So I will overlook your presumption. What might you be able to offer?"

Symon glanced at Malin. "If I may, Signor Selvo. I have with me a record of our current dispositions. I could sit with one of your clerks? Take them through what we have."

"That may be helpful. But I am curious. Why is it that a week ago, you had no part in this year's fleets?"

Malin cleared his throat. "Allow me to be honest, Signor. We have lacked the opportunity for some years now to participate directly. Doge Dandolo's insistence that only state ships may participate in the fleets has left me unable to offer my own vessels. I have chosen instead to work with those best placed to hire ships from the Commune. You will find I have contributed fully in taxes, but have not sought to engage in any primary contracts of my own."

He paused, scanning Selvo's face for any further sign of distaste.

"So I come to you now, aware that my actions may be seen as opportunistic, yet wondering if at this time the interests of the Republic and myself are sufficiently aligned to allow me to re-enter the fleets as a primary charterer."

Selvo brought his hands together on the surface of the desk.

"I commend your openness, Le Cordier. One of the more intriguing propositions I've heard since this whole sorry business started.

"In return for your honesty, I will share with you that I am not unaware of your reputation in the city for profitable and honourable trade. And, sadly, that the plans passed by the Small Council in December are currently deemed to be in shreds. By the end of next week, we must explain our revised plans to them. At present, we do not know which galleys will be seaworthy or available. The complexity of the contractual arrangements alone could see us tying up the *savii* and the wider magistracy for years, if our worst fears are realised.

"I have two more years in this role, and I do not wish to spend the majority of that time in court, wading through claim after claim, or the rest of my life afterwards distancing myself from any damage to my reputation."

Selvo looked across at Symon. "So, young sir. If you could wait here until this afternoon, I will arrange for one of my assistants to make a note of the commodities and sources you are proposing to use."

★

It was past noon when Malin and Symon reached the Rialto market. Nothing better illustrated the Venetian character under duress than their determination to observe their noon break.

A number of empty pitches were cordoned off, isolating the worst damage to paving slabs laid no more than two years earlier, yet stallholders and their customers had already gathered around the food boards.

Leaning up against one of the sidewalls of the extended market, large cuts of wild boar in hand, the two of them relaxed back into their preferred relation. Two friends, sharing a meal.

"I'll head back there this afternoon and take them through the details of the five most likely shipments." Symon put his head back to take in a brief ray of sun as it crossed the busy square. He wiped his mouth with his sleeve, animal fat darkening the fabric. "I won't know for certain how secure each of our own suppliers are, but by the time the *savii* have pulled together their new plan, I'll be able to let them know of any final changes." He belched. "But I still don't know what it is that made you change your mind. I thought we were pulling out. What we discussed this morning will take us right back into the centre of things. Are you sure that's what you want?"

"I'm sorry to have behaved in such an unpredictable way this week, my friend. I'm not quite sure why. Perhaps I had too much time to think on the journey back. Perhaps it's just the chaos of the last few days. Everything feels somehow different. I just need to understand exactly where we stand here. The options we have. You've really helped, Symon."

They left the market and its ripe, thick smells of raw and cooked meat, and made their way along the Canal.

The Rialto bridge appeared largely unscathed, its wooden slats still tight and smooth. The decorative side walls showed none of the twisting and warping of some of the smaller bridges further east.

Once on the north bank, they sought out the offices of the *Extraordinarri*. The clamour and din of the city dropped as they passed under the imposing figure of a lion, complete with protective shield, and closed the door behind them.

Across the room Giradino Da Viscia, the Da Segna family representative, looked up and acknowledged their arrival.

The man, his moustaches almost escaping the sides of his ruddy shining cheeks, explained that the papers exchanged and signed on Malin's arrival at the Lido were all in order, and that he was close to reaching agreement on the preliminary freight charges due to the city. He had already taken receipt of the Bills of Lading, confirming the warehousing of all cargoes. Five days into the Quarant, and everything was going to plan.

Malin looked up to his left. A solid-looking constable, on permanent assignment to the office, betrayed no sense of suspicion at what was, to all appearances, just another routine mercantile transaction.

Their business done, the three men returned to the street. As agreed, Symon took his leave to return on foot to the magistrates' offices.

Malin and Da Viscia turned right at the canalside, and made their way slowly back to the bridge, and then on to San Polo and the Da Segna house.

★

Their arrival took the house by surprise. Malin was not due to meet Sclavo until nightfall, but he hoped that Lucia might be available to receive him.

Da Viscia disappeared into one of the rooms at the back of the house while Tusco ushered Malin into the spacious and ornately decorated reception room just off the main entrance hall. Alone with his thoughts for the first time since leaving his own front door, he reflected again on how much the occupants of this house meant to him. A life spent without a real family, apart from Haylan and Radley back in Lynn, had been redeemed in a very real way by the warmth and generosity of the people here.

He looked around at the tapestries hung on three of the four papered walls. The hand of the wall-mounted timepiece, one of few in the city, pointed down and to the right. Gifted to Uberto while he was still ascendant.

All visitors had this same chance to reflect on the family's wealth and sophistication. Only those whose friendship went back through the years understood the gentle irony that the clock represented. Of the world that Uberto had once but no longer occupied.

He closed his eyes. His mind emptied as his breathing harmonised with each small regular click of the clock's mechanism.

Footsteps and rustled clothing could be heard beyond the door, then Donata walked in to greet him.

"Such a nice surprise, Malin."

Her embrace caught Malin off guard. She stepped back, and looked directly into his eyes. Her face betrayed immediate concern. "My dear. What is it? You look so tired."

"Really? And there I was, thinking I was looking my best." He smiled. "Of course, if you feel I would be better resting, I could always leave."

Donata returned his smile. "I'll hear no such thing. Are you here for the evening?"

"I'm afraid not, much as that would please me. I'm hoping to attend a meeting with Sclavo later, but thought to arrive early to enjoy the inestimable fruits of your company."

Her eyes sparkled at the light-hearted flattery. "Come now, let's get that cloak off, and see if I can find us somewhere comfortable where we can await our young master of the Arsenale."

As they walked upstairs to the family sitting rooms, he asked, "Is Lucia in the house?"

Donata chuckled. "I'm afraid not. She went across to San Marco to see if there was anything she could do to help the bereaved. But don't worry. I'm sure she'll be back soon." She paused. "In the meantime, I'm sure Collette will keep you entertained."

*

Lucia was only a few steps behind her brother when they walked into the house. Despite the weakening daylight, Sclavo had recognised her familiar stride easily from his own boat as it pulled into the ferry stop. They travelled the last few hundred yards together, comparing their experiences of the city in the aftermath of the earthquake.

Their conversation continued up and into the house, until Lucia's eyes fell on their visitor. Malin took pleasure in her momentary hesitation.

"Sire, so kind of you to call. I trust you are getting your fill of local gossip?"

She glanced across at Collette, who seemed oblivious to the gentle slight. "We've covered the full range of subjects, sister. I've learnt much about the damage to the east of the city, and Malin shares my views about the indignities of the latest dress laws."

Lucia laughed. "I'm very pleased to hear it, Collette. Perhaps he could spare me a few moments later to judge whether I fall within their boundaries. I would hate to think that my appearance might cause any man to fear my accidental criminality."

She crossed the room and embraced her mother, whispering something into her ear. Donata smiled, and gently patted her daughter's shoulder.

"Now then, you two. Now you're here, let's get settled, at least for a while, and catch up on all the latest news together. Sclavo, it's so good to see you. How are you coping at the Arsenale?"

Her son, almost two hands taller than his mother, brought his arm up to his forehead in mock fatigue. "Oh, I suppose I'll manage, Mother. I'm taking regular naps, and eating all my food up before leaving the table."

The next hour flew by, shaped by the relaxed atmosphere that Malin had witnessed and become part of for so many years. The five of them sat in the richly upholstered chairs, exchanging questions and stories, and the occasional mild rebuke. When it became clear that Malin would have no chance to spend time alone with Lucia, he eased instead into the ebb and flow of the conversation.

Penina entered to tell them that dinner would be ready shortly.

Sclavo looked across at his mother. "When do you expect Father home?"

Donata sighed deeply. "Ah, who knows. He told me not to wait for him this evening. I dare say he has yet more meetings to further his quest."

"Quest, Mother?" His voice lacked its normal confidence.

"Well. Let's just say that he dreams of the day when he can show those men on the Great Council that he is able to grow his business without their patronage. Or friendship, for that matter. He'll be sitting somewhere, negotiating a cargo, or a ship's crew, or some other thing that brings in the next sum of money into that ungrateful Treasury."

Malin jumped in. "I'm sure he'll be able to share news of his latest venture when he returns. In the meantime, I'm looking forward to seeing what is on the table next door. Lucia, will you join me?"

As they rose to walk to the dining room, Malin glanced briefly across at Sclavo. The man's thoughts remained known only to himself.

★

They left the house as soon as the meal was over.

Sclavo led the way to the *scuole*. His white uniform, befitting his role as Grand Guardian of the brotherhood, took Malin's eye each time they passed under a lit *cesendeli*.

The air was still but raw. Malin wore his cloak fastened up to the neck, but Sclavo simply carried his over his arm. His impatience led to several small trips over raised or damaged paving stones. "We should make haste. The brothers do not look kindly on lateness. I cannot set the wrong example, or what will become of the Republic?" His idea of a joke.

73

Once across the St Agostin bridge, the street narrowed. Residue from the flood still stained the walls on both sides. The entrance to one unlit building was blocked by a large pile of surge debris. Workmen still had much to do before reaching this far from the Canal.

Ahead of them, several streetlights converged around a large entrance, its three stone steps leading to a deeply recessed oak door.

The old lunatic asylum.

A place seen by some as the mark of Venice's growing civic conscience. By others as the place where the disturbed and strange could be hidden away, no longer able to unsettle or threaten more genteel members of society.

Doge Soranzo had originally closed the place when scandalised by the treatment of his own father-in-law. The dilapidation that followed had proceeded without hindrance for almost thirty years. No one wanted to buy a property with such unpleasant associations.

At the turn of the century, the *banca*, or supervisory council of the Scuola di San Giovanni Evangelista voted to move out of premises granted them by the nearby church, and rent the broken-down shell of the old *ospizio*.

There were no objections to the move. The rent was low, and the local *consigliere ducale* was delighted at the possibility of the notorious eyesore being restored.

What the magistrate failed to account for, however, was the *scuole*'s frugal nature, and its desire to spend money only on the most basic of repairs. The main facade of the building, facing directly onto the Calle de ca' Donà, remained crumbling and unpointed. External walls remained a dirty grey blight on the otherwise well-kept street.

Inside, the brothers directed their main funds, raised by donations from the membership, to restoring the top floor of the property, and establishing a clean and effective hospice for the *sestiere*'s old and infirm.

As they approached the doorway, Malin noted the guard posted by the local representative of the *Signori di Notte*. In response to a recent crimewave, the Lords of the Night had increased the visibility of law enforcement, particularly in the evenings, and where there was any increased chance of pickpocketing or more violent street crime. *Scuole* meetings across the city were deemed to be such occasions.

At least Malin hoped that explained the constable's presence. The two men walked directly under his gaze, trying hard to maintain a look of disinterested innocence.

The buzz of unregulated conversation grew louder as they entered the main hall.

A few moments later, Sclavo called the meeting to order, a task he'd conducted every month since his election as chief officer six years earlier. Malin stood at the back behind the fifty or so seated members of the *scuole*, each of them displaying the white armband of their confraternity. It was Malin's first visit, and he was struck by the sense of discipline and order on display.

Sclavo took the group through first one agenda item then the next, with an authority that merely strengthened Malin's admiration for the younger man.

Predictably, most talk centred around their response to the natural disaster. The need for additional donations to assist in the rehousing of displaced families. One member, a salt merchant, volunteered to coordinate the burial of those unfortunates from San Polo who had been killed by falling masonry or swept off their feet by the onrushing waters. Debate was lively, but at all times Sclavo retained control of who spoke, and for how long.

The longest discussion concerned the status of the *scuole*'s long-term goal of securing a fragment of the true cross, which would require spending a potentially enormous sum at a time of domestic misfortune.

Their funds had grown slowly and steadily, helped in no small part by the recruitment of three successful spice traders and the endowment received on the death of Signor Ziani, a long-serving member whose family had made their fortunes in transporting Chioggia salt to the annual German fairs.

Some argued that it was at precisely such a time that they should bring such a holy object into the city as balm for the people's ailments. Others sought to delay a decision until they knew more about the immediate needs of the *sestiere*, and how well they could meet them.

The discussion ended without resolution. The *banca* committed to revisit the subject later in the year, when the situation in the city would be much clearer.

As the majority of attendees filed back out into the night, three of the *banca* remained with Sclavo at the front of the room. Malin joined them, as agreed, and together, they took the staircase to the upper floor.

They crossed the main ward, through the four long rows of beds. Isolated conversations hung in the sour, still air. Few occupants appeared young, and all looked frail. Three beds held supine, unmoving figures.

They entered a small, windowless room at the far end of the floor. Malin shuddered to think how it might have been used in the past.

Sclavo spoke first. "So, gentlemen. This is my colleague and friend Malin Le Cordier. Malin, these are friends of mine. Between us, we hold positions of chief, deputy, treasurer and director of processions. We speak for the body of the *scuole*, and guide the membership in all matters."

He shook hands with each in turn, before Sclavo continued.

"Malin and myself would like to brief you on where we

76

are to date, and the expectations we have of each of you in the coming weeks. Malin?"

By the time they left the building, the steps outside were empty, and the night constable was nowhere to be seen.

Chapter 7

Friday 1st February 1348

Day 6 of the Quarant

A rriving home late the previous evening, he had retired to his bed immediately, pausing only to look at the most recently amended page of his journal. The day had been so busy, he had not had time to reflect on any of it. He returned the pages to his satchel unchanged, and slept deeply.

Refreshed, he rose to find the house empty. Setting the fire in the front room, he sat with a simple breakfast of bread and cheese, and a customary tankard of weak ale.

The occasional flutter of flames from the hearth was the only thing that broke the silence.

At rest, his mind went back to his first meetings in Westminster. His anger and confusion at his summons. How nothing in the discussions between the Household and Exchequer suggested they had any interest in what their scheme might mean for him. He recalled the first moment that he consciously felt his fascination turn to frustration and a gnawing sense of dread.

These men would decide as they would, and he would be

expected to fall in behind them. Any debate on that matter had started and ended prior to his arrival.

No one had appeared interested in his absence from noble life. The question simply never came up. It was his years in the Republic, and his knowledge of how things worked that had drawn him there. That was all that mattered, apparently.

Though showing enough faith in him to demand his presence, they refused to consult him on anything but relatively trivial concerns. The mix of trades present in the wharfside warehouses. Variations in the price of salt. Gossip in the drinking houses and brothels. Levels of civil obedience. All while sitting in any number of rooms within the buildings of the Chancery and the Exchequer, around a seemingly never-ending array of heavy oak tables.

In the middle of his second week, conversations shifted to larger matters. To alliances sought or required, to enable the sharing of intelligence or funds. Favours pulled in or promised, in return for cooperation or a willingness to cast a conveniently blind eye on their actions. Monies obtained, or chances to be taken or ignored.

As the details mounted, the implied form and content of their plan began to take shape, without ever being stated clearly.

The English Crown had run down its coffers to the point where war with France had become unaffordable. All recent steps to address this were exhausted.

Edward had defaulted on all debt with their traditional lenders, the Peruzzi and Bardi families of Florence, writing off staggering sums amassed since the beginning of his father's reign. The move was bold, yet still not enough. To make matters worse, options for raising more funds were limited. Edward's recent levies could not be repeated for fear of noble dissent. Wool taxes were already at their highest rate since the collapse of trade in the 'tens and 'twenties.

Challenged with finding ways to solve the problem, senior members of the Household had gained the king's approval to pursue a plot to destabilise Venice, the powerful trading state at the northern reaches of the Adriatic. To install men in their governing councils who would offer the English greater access to the growing wealth of the Adriatic and Black Sea trade routes, in return for the use of English ships and men in the event of any future hostilities with Genoa, their primary rival.

Edward had instructed the Lord High Steward, Henry of Grosmont, to establish a small but powerful group of men, drawn from the great offices of state, to establish how such a scheme could succeed.

That had been a year before Malin's arrival. By then, it was no longer a matter of whether they would proceed, but of making it happen.

At first, on each return to his room, Malin tried to reckon the impact of the latest decisions on his own safety. That lasted a week. Once it became obvious that failure could mean death, it seemed pointless. There was nothing to be done, except reach for the gentian.

He decided to concentrate his mind on those issues that carried the greatest threat to his survival. From that day to this, sitting by the fire in Calle San Domenico, he ignored any detail that had no bearing on his ability to stay alive. Or on the survival of his dearest friends. All other details emerging from the Household, Exchequer or Chancery held only secondary interest. His new colleagues barely seemed to notice his long periods of silence.

Malin's father had appeared only once.

He had never considered that their paths might cross.

The day it happened, Malin sat with a small number of men that included Mainard Glyn, a senior official in the King's Exchequer. In matters of state, the man's experience was unrivalled. Posts in the Royal Household, the Treasury and then the Exchequer made him the obvious choice as one of the few at the heart of the Venetian plot.

Malin had felt an immediate rapport with him. His manner was courteous, even friendly. He seemed to instinctively understand the nature of Malin's own genius and experience, and had never patronised or confused him with the intricacies of Crown power and practice. In return, Malin had happily described his experiences in the Adriatic. An early mutual respect had developed, with a promise of potential friendship.

When the old man walked into the room, Malin's breath left him.

The years had taken their toll, yet Jefferey's glare had lost little of its power to pierce his son's skin.

The reason for Malin's presence was no longer a matter of conjecture. His father had used events, and the authority of his position, to put him once more in harm's way.

Used the state to act as both hunter and master.

He will never let me go.

The moment of mutual recognition passed. Glyn, knowing everything of importance across Westminster, would be fully aware of the significance of the event.

Jefferey took a seat at the table.

He broke his silence in response to the first mention of Malin's need to liaise with Bourchier.

"You will need to follow this all the way to the end, boy."

His father's tone fell just short of hostile.

Glyn saw Malin's hesitation. "I'm sure your son understands the importance of his role, sire. He has been fully briefed, and by the time he returns to Venice, there will be a network ready to benefit from his presence."

Jefferey grunted, as though clearing something lodged in his throat.

"You need to push him. Do not allow him to set his own pace."

Malin did his best to remain impassive. Turning to face his father, his voice was calm and controlled.

"You forget sire, that I am no longer the child you knew."

"Oh, I remember all too well, boy. You don't have that bastard Haylan to watch your back now, and if you fail in this task, the consequences will be grave." Jefferey looked across at Glyn. "For us all."

"Your son is uniquely positioned for this work, as you know. No one is better placed to pull all the disparate parts of this together, and do so through his reputation as a leading trader in the city."

Jefferey grunted again. "And God knows how that came to be. Must have stumbled into it. Let's hope he doesn't stumble in this."

After the meeting ended, Glyn asked him to stay back. "Has anything changed for you, Malin? Will you still help us?"

It was the first time he had been asked directly. He searched the man's face for any sign that he was being tested. What he saw surprised him. Confusion, perhaps, but also compassion.

He stumbled over his words, thrown by Glyn's unexpected openness. "I assumed my involvement had already been decided."

"By us, undoubtedly. But I wonder. Le Cordier has been urging us to recruit you for months, yet how he just spoke to you? Something worries me. Are you willing to do this? For reasons we can accept?

"Let me say this differently. There will be times ahead when your commitment to what is needed will be vital. Are you prepared for this, or merely going along with what is expected of you?"

"I don't know, Mainard." He was mumbling. "Really, I don't. My father—"

Glyn interrupted. "Forget your father."

Malin looked up, and cleared his throat. "I have friends in Venice that need protection. And I know how the place works. I am the only sensible choice, and will not let you down."

The rest of the visit was unremarkable although, sitting by the hearth, he could still shiver at his father's thinly cloaked malevolence.

Since his first return from Westminster, Malin had lived two very different lives. On the one hand, he spent short, intense periods back in England, under the guise of chasing new trade opportunities in England and the Low Countries. When back in Venice, while maintaining a semblance of normality in his business dealings and social life, he worked with Bourchier to tighten the weave of their increasingly intricate plot.

He leaned forward to place two new logs on the fire. A new column of sparks rose from the disturbed embers.

He recalled the day when he sought to bring Uberto into the circle. Not the details of their conversation, but the guilty churn in his chest as he took the irreversible step of declaring his role in the coming plot.

He was back there. Back in the reception room in San Polo. Treading up to and then over the boundary between innocent friendship and something that could end them both.

This was the father he had never had. The man, unaware even as he did it, who had filled the void at the centre of Malin's life.

Others had played their part, of course.

Jerold, the old priest back at Wormegay, who removed him from the spiteful attacks of Brenner, and the suffocating world of his father. Haylan, also willing to defy his father, who treated him like a third son. Elyas, the instrument of his escape to Antwerp and his mentor on adulthood and commerce.

Yet it was in Uberto that Malin had first experienced what it meant to have a father. As a grown man, Malin had been unconditionally shaped by Uberto's wisdom and experience, and drawn comfort from a relationship based on mutual care and respect.

In that moment a year ago, Malin had ransomed years of familial love and trust to the needs of a foreign power. He exploited Uberto's frustration and disgust at his ejection from the Council. Fuelled his basest desires for revenge on Grimani, the magistrate leading the move to cast him from the nobility and back, after a mere six years, into the ranks of *cittidani ordinari*.

He could no longer remember his words that night. The words no longer mattered. Uberto had needed little persuasion. What *did* matter was that he knowingly steered their relationship into waters that neither of them could ever sail back from. That night remained the lowest point of his mission.

"Tell me what I need to do, my friend."

With those words, Malin had felt the final plunge.

He had steeled himself since that day. Taken every step to put it from his mind. To do otherwise would tear him apart. Recruiting Uberto's worst self. Hiding his biggest secrets from Symon. Staring into Lucia's eyes, knowing how he had irredeemably compromised her father, and in doing so, betrayed his love for her and her family in the worst way possible.

Piece by piece, contact by contact, he and Bourchier had been the beating heart of the plan to tear the fabric of the city apart, and change the course of an empire.

★

The knock at the door brought him back from his thoughts. How long had he been drifting? The fire's heat was still intense enough for him to feel its absence on his shins as he moved through the house to answer it.

The package was addressed to him in a broad, ornate hand. The care with which the package was secured, with wax and a complex weave of thick blue hemp, betrayed its origin.

Whitby.

He paid and thanked the messenger. Closing the door, he leaned back into the corridor wall, his knees trembling and his breath shallow. His fear of arrest was more intense than he realised.

He took the package through to his office, and applied one of Symon's stationery knives. Once opened, he took a step back and cast his eyes over the wide leather cover. The book was almost two feet wide. The flourishes of ink were similar to many of his earlier purchases. He read the title.

Duns Scotus. Lectures on Lombard's Sentences.

The four spine cords protested when he swung the manuscript fully open. The spread of colour on the very first page was astonishing. The red ink of the headings glowed as if meeting light for the first time. The sharpness of the marks suggested the finest parchment. It was a long way from the cheap paper copy of the *Book of Days* Malin had commissioned from the Abbey on one of his first voyages north from Lynn, nearly thirty years ago.

He closed the book. Its imminent receipt had been pushed completely from his mind. It felt strange that an object of such beauty could co-exist with the tawdry concerns enveloping him.

His mood lightened nonetheless. He had something to look forward to later that day.

Two hours later, he stood on the shore of the Lido, looking west across the paving stones of the Riviera San Nicolò and into the Lagoon. A small fleet of crabbing boats moved out of and then back into view with the gentle rolling of the water.

The skies were crisp and clear, throwing off the overcast pall of the last few days. He took several deep breaths of salted air, and felt a welcome sense of peace. He was early for his meeting with Uberto, and the relative solitude of this stretch of the island quietened his mind.

In his younger days, it was sailing back to Lynn with his return cargo, confident of a sale and its profits, that brought a sense of tranquillity. No one to answer to, the tension of his last transactions behind him, and the fresh breezes of the German Sea clearing his head.

No. The Lido wasn't the Staithe. But equally, it wasn't some dingy brothel, selected to avoid prying eyes and enable treasonous conversations.

He continued to walk along the margins of the Lagoon, the water dappled by the thin, bright sun.

The narrow straight leading to San Pietro and the massive complex of the Arsenale drew his attention. Then, first lowering and then closing his eyes, he cast off one unresolved problem after another.

Make the most of the afternoon. It can do you no harm. You might even enjoy it.

His gaze was drawn next to the Campanile San Marco, the highest point of Venice to breach the heavens. The city continued to beguile and amaze. Nearly twenty years since his initial trading visits, these views were still intoxicating.

He opened his satchel, and pulled out the letter. He had read it many months ago, yet he found it and put it in his bag before leaving the house.

Opening it, he searched for a phrase that had stayed with him since he had received it from Wormegay Rectory.

He re-read it, the breeze gently wafting the edge of the paper.

"Remember that you have become who you are through your actions."

The words struck once more, like the fumes from a poorly stored cargo of salammoniac destined for Murano.

Jerold had no doubt wished them as encouragement. For days like this? He had transposed them word for word into his journal, but there was something about reading them in Jerold's own hand that he needed.

A further half mile along the Riviera, he arrived at his destination.

He had attended services at Chiesa San Nicolò many times, during the period when he personally accompanied each of his major trading voyages to Africa and the East.

The tradition, whereby a ship's charterers, investors and crew attended a Mass for divine protection and good fortune prior to departure, had always given him great comfort. St Nicolas had long been adopted as the patron saint of seamen, and a failure to attend the ceremony was deemed both ill-advised and presumptuous.

Looking through the decorative porch, he saw three figures silhouetted against the candlelit transept. Clergy, going about their duties. He waited there, doing nothing to alert them to his presence.

Uberto's footsteps, when they came, lifted him out of his reverie. "So here you are, my friend. I see you've been paying your respects."

"Perhaps. I just thought I'd spend a few moments gathering myself." They embraced, Uberto still breathing hard from his walk from the jetty.

They entered the church, and set about sharing their activities and observations gained since the beginning of the week. Between them, they had crossed the city many times.

A small warning voice sounded in Malin's mind. "Are you confident that no one is following you?"

The older man sat back in his chair, and looked at Malin.

"I don't think anyone really cares much about what I do these days. Perhaps, a few years ago, when I was still raw and bruised, well, from my misfortune, there may have been some who might have looked for signs of behaviour consistent with a vengeful man. But now?"

He raised the back of his hand to his mouth. Tapped his lips thoughtfully with his fingers. "Now, my friend, I fear I am considered by most to be an irrelevance. Someone to be left alone to make money and pay taxes. In answer to your question? I have noticed no one, and think it unlikely that I shall."

Malin shook his head slowly. "My friend. That was then. And I will say nothing to contradict you. Yet surely you know how much your reputation for honesty and endeavour still plays in the work we are doing. And do not forget for one moment, that there may be those in the city who have long memories."

He reached over to hold the top of Uberto's arm. "You have to take great care now. It is not just your own safety at stake."

Uberto pulled back sharply. "What do you mean? It has never been about my own safety. You know that. I would never put my family in harm's way. Any more than I would do anything to jeopardise you." Malin gestured for him to lower his voice. "If I thought for one moment that you were completely safe from Grimani and his friends, I would never have thrown in with you."

Malin struggled to find the words. "Please. I did not mean to sound harsh or critical. I just want you to truly recognise the danger awaiting us in these last days. That is all."

"I know you mean well, Malin. But I also know how this city works. God knows I've had to learn the hard way. But I honestly think we will succeed. We have been meticulous. *I* have been meticulous. Each one of us knows to keep their words as close to them as their thoughts. Come, walk with me. I need to show you something."

He rose and walked forward into the transept. To their left, the gold leaf of the altar glimmered in the wavering candlelight. On it rested a beautiful triptych, depicting Moses, Abraham and Solomon, each caught in their own unique moment of obedience and triumph.

He beckoned to the three priests at the front of the church. The eldest of them approached.

"Good afternoon, sir. Is all well?" The man's voice betrayed slight annoyance at being disturbed.

"Yes. I'm sorry to pull you away. I was having a conversation with my friend here, and I could not remember. Perhaps you could help. I recall this wonderful altarpiece being purchased for the church a few years ago. Could you remind me who was so generous to bequeath it?"

The priest looked across to the paintings.

"I'm afraid I cannot help you, sir. The inscription of the man's name has been removed. I believe he was one of the more generous members of the Council, though."

Uberto thanked the man for his time. They both watched as he re-joined his fellow priests.

"The church was so grateful to see this commissioned, Malin. At the time, I could do no wrong. Their good words undoubtedly had a part to play in my ascension to the Council. Just nine years ago. And look at me. My money is no good. My views even less welcome. None of my former friends on the Council even acknowledge my existence. I'm a ghost to them. And to everyone else from that time. Unless, of course, they remember me only to visit further humiliations upon me. Upon my family.

"It's important you understand. These changes we seek together. They are the one thing that will allow me to hold my head up once more. I cannot bear another year to go by like this. My son works day and night to create a reputation that will convince them that he is nothing like his father. My wife has to dress once more as an ordinary citizen. My beautiful daughters are banished from the best houses..."

Malin reached a second time to grasp Uberto's arm. He could feel the man's struggle to control his emotions.

This time, he did not pull away.

"I will not let you down, my young friend. Trust me when I tell you I have invested every part of my being into this, and I will make this work. For both of us."

They walked back into the remaining afternoon light of the quay, and then to the ferry station, agreeing to meet up the following morning at Calle Donzella. From there they would travel together to the Candlemas celebrations.

Halfway across the Lagoon, Malin recalled the flotilla of crabbing boats. Searching across the gently undulating waters, he finally saw them, further north now, in the narrow channel between La Certosa and Sant'Andrea.

He hoped they would spend the evening congratulating themselves on a good catch.

Chapter 8

Saturday 2nd February 1348

Day 7 of the Quarant

Candlemas offered nobles and commoners alike the chance to put recent tragedies behind them. Services across the city celebrated Mary's presentation of her baby son at the temple, marking the end of Christmas and a chance to seek blessings for the year ahead.

Malin stood between Symon and Uberto in the nave of San Giovanni, with the Da Segnas and his assistant Giradino Da Viscia further to his right.

Most, though not all, of the smells of the Canal had been purged from the building over the last week. On the day of the flood, many of the people around them had taken refuge at the front of the church. Today the altar, laden only with the church's finest gold and silver statuary, was attended solely by the priests.

In the years of Uberto's membership of the Great Council, under the brief dogeship of Bartolomeo Gradenigo and the first two years of the current Doge, his family had worshipped in the Basilica of San Marco. But it was to here they returned, their parish church since first moving to Calle Donzella, in the weeks after his fall.

Recalling the bitterness with which Uberto spoke to him yesterday, Malin wondered at the thoughts now running through his friend's mind.

Symon, he hoped, would be oblivious to the potential discomfort playing out under his nose. Malin had surprised him with the invitation extended to him the previous evening.

Neither of them played much part in the ceremonial life of the city, content simply to do what was necessary to fit in. When it came time for each family to take their candles to the front of the church to be blessed, neither of them moved, hoping no one would take offence at their lack of participation.

Malin took his mind off the growing ache in his back with thoughts of his arrival on the *Seynte Marie*.

His anxiety had grown as they travelled along the Mediterranean coast and down past Sicily, worsened further by their passage through the narrow Strait of Medina. Past the mythical Scylla and Charybdis, apt symbols of the challenges that lay ahead. The need to navigate the tightening space between the six-headed monster of discovery, and the unsavoury and unpredictable whirlpool of Venetian intelligence.

Danger unquestionably remained.

Yet now, at the end of the first full week of the *Seynte Marie*'s Quarant, the strength of all the threads of their web had been tested. Bourchier and Uberto had worked wonders to keep it all together.

When Malin arrived back home from the Lido the previous afternoon, he had sent a message to Bourchier, arranging to meet him at The Tinsmith the following Monday.

Clear of any further duties, he'd spent the evening drinking with Symon, slipping easily into the comfortable and familiar exchange of small, sometimes trivial anecdotes of their day, or reminiscences drawn from their long history together.

When he ran out of credible explanations of how he spent his afternoon, Malin opened the new manuscript.

Symon could not believe how fast time was passing. "Is that a year since the last one?"

Another year, another gift for Jerold. Malin was fairly sure that the priest knew the origin of each year's newly transcribed text. Yet he had never ventured to raise the subject with him.

Perhaps the old man wanted to honour Malin's apparent need for anonymity. Perhaps it embarrassed him.

On Malin's first visit to the rectory after the arrival of his gift, the illustrated *Book Of Days*, it was clear that he had chosen his form of thanks well.

Isolated from the intellectual stimulation of the monasteries, Jerold had little to entertain him beyond his normal parish and estate duties. The small number of books he did possess, many of them probably stolen during his time at the monastery in Lincoln, had long since been committed to memory. Sitting together by the rectory fire, Jerold thumbed through the freshly written pages and speculated several times as to where the book had come from.

Six years since the priest had enabled Malin's escape to Lynn, Jerold had no idea of just how far Malin's apprenticeship had taken him. It would not have crossed his mind for one moment that the boy could have conjured such a gift.

Malin's joy at the man's reaction was immense.

From that point on, the pattern was set. Malin's agreement with the prior of Whitby and the head of the scriptorium meant the arrival each year of another newly commissioned, often controversial new gift at the door of his old friend.

Malin's arrangement with the Abbey had one more important benefit. In return for an increasingly attractive sum, the text chosen would be at the forefront of emerging thought, and was to be sent to him first, before passing to its final destination. Since then, Malin had taken the opportunity to study some of the most respected and progressive thinkers in Europe.

The service finally over, the congregation filed out of the church and into the still winter air. The sombre but immaculately tailored clothes of the worshippers contrasted with the vibrant blue and red facades of the newer houses on the *campo*.

A newly optimistic mood informed many of the conversations taking place.

The New Year could safely begin.

Malin held back from the lighthearted discussions around him. His attention instead fell on the Da Segna family group.

Collette stood next to Symon, intent as usual on having him to herself. Symon's stance suggested that she had her work cut out to hold his interest for much longer. Donata was saying something to Sclavo, attired in his Arsenale uniform. Their heads were down, and he couldn't tell what they were discussing.

Uberto descended the broad steps of the church, approaching first one party then another, eager as always to cast himself and his family as important and natural members of local society.

Malin wondered how much energy it must be costing him.

Finally, his eyes fell on Lucia. She quickly moved to join him.

"So, Signor Le Cordier. I trust the bags under your eyes have been gained from virtuous pursuits only?"

He laughed. "From late nights, trying to think up witty responses to your attacks on my character. Does that ease your mind?"

Her eyes danced. "Well, the truthfulness of your statements would need to be judged on their individual merits, before I could decide. In general terms, however, time spent on worthless tasks is barely distinguishable from indolence." She stopped to judge the impact of her words. "Why, sir, you blush."

Lucia's victory was as complete as it was predictable, but Malin was not done. "Certainly not, Lucia. It is merely the reaction of a man readying himself for further battle. That is what you want, isn't it?"

Her smile disappeared. Malin swallowed hard, unsure if he had gone too far. "What I mean is, of course, that I have to be in full command of my faculties if I am to offer anything even mildly interesting in response to your wit and knowledge, Lucia."

"Hmmm." She took his arm, and they wandered away from the family group.

She guided him to the perimeter of the square, and then pulled gently on his arm.

"Malin. I no longer jest. You look tired. Are you sure you are well?"

"I have been finding it a little hard to sleep. Perhaps the sight of the bodies in Saint Mark's has put me a little off balance. But I am in good health." His eyes tightened. "Why, do you have qualms about duelling with an ill man?"

"Malin. I'm serious. Since you've been back, you seem distracted. Difficult to find, almost. I can't explain it, but I worry about you."

The last thing Malin needed was to cause concern within the family. Concern led to questions, and questions to answers. Answers that could easily prompt a further, more difficult round.

He reached forward, and touched Lucia's face gently with the back of his gloved fingers. "I am fine. Let's get back to the house, and prepare for the feast. I will prove to you that I have the appetite of three well men."

★

Two hours later, Malin, Symon and the family emerged from the Da Segna house, and walked to their gondola.

Feast days in Venice were something to behold. As they travelled east, shouted greetings reached them from a number of the many boats using the waterway to move across the city.

The high spirits continued as they joined the queue of other passengers waiting to alight onto the waterside steps of the recently renovated mansion. Its three floors of newly pointed brickwork dominated that stretch of the Canal.

When their turn came to enter under the ornate portico, they were greeted by their host. Antonio Stornello was one of the leading cloth merchants in the city, and had used some of his wealth and influence to make his home in the centre of the prestigious Dorsoduro waterfront. His wealth was greater than at least half of the nobility of the Golden Book yet, like Uberto, he was excluded from high office.

Unlike Uberto, he seemed not to care. His name had never come up in Malin's discussions with Uberto or Bourchier.

Relieved of their coats on entry, they emerged from the broad, ornamented corridor into an enormous reception room, and the large throng of fellow partygoers.

The citizens of Venice seemed determined to put their recent troubles behind them.

Many of the women flaunted the most complex plaits, draped alluringly in several cases down over their open-fronted dresses. Many of the new fabrics arriving from the East competed for attention. Even the men had sought to keep up appearances, many of them sporting the latest fashions in hose, shirts and tunics. Malin felt considerably underdressed.

Music emerged from the dining room beyond. The collective murmur of voices, punctuated by occasional and high-spirited exclamations, possessed a sense of the secular absent from the *campo* that morning.

Thoughts about his upcoming business with Uberto and Sclavo could wait a little longer. He might even enjoy himself.

Conversations during dinner, spread over a full seven courses, saw the noise level increase further. Despite his need to stay relatively sober, Malin was pulled along by the general air of goodwill. Symon, for his part, was showing no such restraint.

Between each course, Uberto introduced him to many of his fellow guildsmen and other gentlemen of the city, in some cases reminding them of business they had already done with "his dearest colleague and friend". With no nobility present, every man considered himself among equals.

By early evening, the servants began to light the hundreds of candles throughout the mansion. Guests moved into the other ground floor rooms to await the dancing.

Symon's good-natured enjoyment seemed to infect the others at the table. Malin noted with a smile that several of the young ladies seated at other tables had made their way to join him. Collette was at first delighted in being next to the centre of attention, but as other women slowly grew in number around them, her demeanour began to sour. Symon, if he noticed this at all, chose to ignore it, and continued to share his good spirits generously with anyone who sought them.

Malin left his side and drifted from room to room. Several faces were familiar, from chance meetings in government offices, or through more targeted dealings that led to mutual benefit. Conversation was polite and easy.

The San Banaba bells had just rung Vespers when a tall, slim man approached him, goblet in hand. His flushed face suggested an afternoon in the company of good wine.

"Dear sire, I find I have no knowledge of your name. Allow me to introduce myself. I am Pietro del Chiaro. I am newly arrived, but have a good eye for those who enjoy equally good standing." His words were slightly slurred. "I have noticed you enjoying the company of many of our fellow guests, but remain at the disadvantage of not meeting you myself."

Malin could not quite place the man's accent. He offered his name and shook the man's hand. "Although originally from England, I have been fortunate to conduct business here for a number of years."

"Ah yes, the mercantile empire. It must take a special sort of skill to make your name in such a place as this." He moved his eyes dramatically around the room. "In a place where you are never more than a few steps away from a man who makes money as easily as he sneezes."

Malin laughed. "Well, I'm not sure it is quite that simple. But yes, it does seem at times that the city encourages a certain determination to find ways to better oneself."

"And yet." The man hesitated. "And yet. There seems to be limits on what can be achieved. No one here this evening seems to possess any real power. The hegemony of trade, certainly, but is that *real* power?"

The implied intimacy of his comment felt a little out of place.

"I'm sure you have a point. None of these men, myself included, have the honour of serving in civic positions. But we make our contributions in other ways. The Republic has much to be grateful for, I'm sure. As do we."

Malin saw Uberto approaching, and beckoned for his friend to join him. "Ah, now here is a man that can tell a tale or two about the rewards of a long life in business. Uberto, please met Signor del Chiaro."

"A pleasure, sir."

Malin stepped in when it seemed that neither man would break the awkward silence.

"Signor del Chiaro has arrived recently in the city, and is keen to get to know people."

"The *right* people, that is true." Despite the drink, it seemed that the man was still choosing his words carefully. "I have made it my life's work to identify and then invest in those men of honour and standing who have earned their wealth through persistence and acumen. Through an unwavering belief that wealth is there to be made, and that the trade routes of the world exist for their use."

Uberto responded immediately. "You make it sound like exploitation. As if we take something owned by everyone, and make it our own."

"And what's wrong with that if it's true?"

"But it is not. Routes are merely the most efficient path to take. It's the connections we make at each end, and our steady accumulation of suppliers, customers and trust that *we* possess. Everything else is merely sea and squalls, and all are welcome to take credit for those."

The tall man nodded slowly, considering Uberto's response.

"I apologise. I had not meant to diminish your achievement. Quite the opposite."

Malin stepped in. "No offence taken, I'm sure."

News that the speeches were due to start reached them through the open door, and the three men walked back to the main dining room, now completely cleared of tables and chairs.

After Stornello had fulfilled his obligations as host, Malin looked around the room to see if he could locate the curious man with the forthright tongue. He spotted Symon, a young woman on his arm as he moved with real passion towards the dance floor, but the man was nowhere to be seen.

★

An hour later, Uberto and Sclavo negotiated their absence from dancing duties and joined Malin in a small reception room at the back of the mansion. It was accepted that gatherings such as these might be the only opportunity for business partners to meet together.

Almost a dozen other men were already present when they arrived.

Uberto was last to enter the room, and closed the door behind them.

They turned to face him, and he began.

Malin had not heard Uberto address a room of people for some time. He stood in awe at how his friend repeated their arguments with such clarity and conviction. With the self-assurance of a man at one with his cause and confident that others would follow.

The guilds represented in the room that night were a critical element within the Republic. They took almost no part in events outside the boundaries of the city, yet within it, they spoke for almost all of the working men on the islands. Forty years earlier, when Tiepolo failed in his attempt to overturn the changes of the previous decade, it was the painters, unimpressed by the man, who marched from their guild building in Santa Sofia and helped disperse an armed band of rebels in the Campo San Lucca.

Guild leaders remained engaged as Uberto moved from justification to instruction. The date of the coup had not yet been set, but it was clear that their members would play an important role.

Romaso Grisani, a master joiner and head of the carpenters' and builders' guild at the Arsenale, led the questions that followed.

"We stand with Sclavo in your desire for change, Signor. Our masters at the Arsenale barely know one end of a ship from the other. But how will we coordinate our actions?"

Uberto looked across to Malin, who then gestured for Sclavo to step forward.

"It is not yet decided how we will direct events across the whole city, but for the men of the Arsenale, we will use the normal work bells. At worst, the population will believe we are calling out the fire wardens to attend an emergency."

A few more questions, and then Uberto brought the meeting to an end. "The important thing to remember is that we must remain discreet. Just meeting here, under the noses of those that have no part in this, or who might even decide that their best interests lie with maintaining our current system, could expose us to discovery. The authorities are more than adept at picking up signals, big or small. We do not need to see the informer boxes at the Palace overflowing with accusations or alarms."

The meeting closed, and the men filed out in groups of two or three, re-joining the festivities next door.

Malin made a note to compliment Uberto the next time they were alone. He had no desire to offer Sclavo an excuse to feel that his position as sole dutiful son was under threat by any public words of praise.

Returning to the dance, Malin found Lucia standing with her mother and sister. Symon was nowhere to be seen.

"Lucia. I wonder if you will join me. I imagine many in the room are eager to observe your elegance."

Each time he held her, this beautiful intelligent woman, he did not want to let go.

Chapter 9

Sunday 3rd February 1348

Day 8 of the Quarant

The world seemed determined to end him.

This morning, it was the excruciating pain in his head that would kill him. The nausea rising from deep in his gut into his chest. The refusal of the room, eyes open or shut, to remain still. To offer a sense of attachment to anything solid.

His memories of the night before threaded their way through his torment.

Dancing with Lucia had been punctuated by regular and increasingly rapacious journeys through the wine from Stornello's cellar. He had no idea why he did it; the meeting with the guilds had gone better than expected.

Before his sobriety withered, he had seen something in Lucia's eyes. Something beautiful, yet sad. There, in the space between their stolen glances as they moved around the room. He couldn't recall seeing or feeling that before. Something had shifted, in a way that he had neither sought nor hoped.

He could not remember their parting words, or even the manner of their leaving. Had they left together, with the rest of the family? Had he made his own way home?

He swallowed hard. Another excruciating flash of pain linked his temples.

He had never been a drinker. The effects of ale and cheap wine had been apparent from his days as an adolescent travelling to and from the Staithe in Lynn. Market days meant solving a maze, weaving through drunks spilling from the local taverns or lying prostrate at the foot of unappreciative stall holders. And the bloodshot eyes of seamen, pleading without success to sign on to the next departing ship.

In some of his lonelier moments in Antwerp, he had seen the lubricating effect of wine on business and had, for a while, joined in. But he deplored the loss of sharpness. How he could drift unwittingly into a clause here or a clause there that could undermine the profits Elyas expected of him.

He envied Symon, and his ability to soak up enormous amounts of liquor, and emerge the following morning as if nothing had happened. The man was a walking miracle. In their darkest hours together, sore and weak and broken from the carnage of Dupplin, he had resisted what might have been an understandable retreat into his cups. Symon found all the distraction he needed in new learning. In skills that would benefit Malin's father's estate and then, later, Malin's expanding Antwerp trading business.

No.

Symon drank to be entertained, not as an escape.

Sounds from downstairs reached him. The Scot was home, and from the sound of it, already finding his own way to exploit the day.

Sundays were always different. Commerce ceased, ensuring proper religious observance and, as importantly, full attendance

103

of the nobility at the weekly Major and Minor Councils. As foreigners, Symon and Malin enjoyed an unusual degree of freedom from religious obligation. As long as they did nothing to offend the sensibilities of those they traded with, did nothing to embarrass Uberto's family, or to build a reputation that could prejudice their chances of state contracts, they were left to determine their own level of visible Christian piety.

Malin groaned.

This would not do.

He gave himself an hour to steel his nerves.

To try and fill in some of the blanks of the night before. Understand what it was that was different in his relations with Lucia.

And join the annoyingly active Symon downstairs.

*

Symon was no help in piecing together Malin's movements at the end of the previous evening. While imbibing his own share of wine, his attentions had been on matters of the heart. Or another part of his anatomy.

He had last seen Malin re-entering the dining room looking for Lucia, but was preoccupied with the two Valeresso sisters. By his own admission, he had found new and gifted ways to offend first one sister then the other. He had left to pass the night in one of the brothels in the narrow alleys of Cannaregio, and had only just returned.

Malin envied him for his minor fatigue and carefree debauchery. Symon travelled through the world with a smile that could cause the most unforgiving of men to smile back.

Conversation turned back to Malin. "So what was it that led you to partake of so much wine?"

"Is it so unusual?"

"Well, now that I think of it, yes. When was the last time you drank that much? Really. I'm interested."

"I often spend an evening with the best French and Italian wines."

"Yes, but you're usually able to taste it as you drink. I doubt if you could appreciate anything you drank last night, from what little I saw. It was as though you were determined to drown in the stuff. God knows what Lucia must have thought."

Malin looked up with a start. "What do you mean?"

"Well, from what I could see, she had to pretty much keep you on your feet. Each time your dance finished, it was as though you were trying to get away from her in a hurry. She returned to her family, and you returned to where you'd put down your last cup."

"Nonsense. That's simply not true."

"Are you sure about that, Malin?"

Yes. Absolutely."

"Because from what I've seen of you this last week, it seems as though many of the things you've always valued..." Symon hesitated, as if chasing down a thought that had only just formed. "Things that have always seemed to matter so much are somehow less important to you now."

"What does that mean?"

"Exactly that. Since you got back from England, it's as though you want to turn your back on all you've built up here. You seem to have backed away from anything reckless on the finances, but still. First you ask me to complete a reckoning of the whole business, then you behave in a way that will lower your reputation with people you've spent a decade befriending."

"It's my choice to do what I wish with the business, Symon. Don't forget that."

"Yes. Yes. I know. But whether you like it or not, we're in this together. I won't step back and watch you unravel everything. It just doesn't feel right."

Symon's voice trailed off, and he glanced away.

"At what point do you feel you've earned the right to talk to me like this?"

The response came quickly. "Do you really need to ask?"

Neither man chose to breach the silence that followed.

Symon calmed down first.

"Do you remember the last two or three months we were together at Wormegay? How ill-tempered you became. Almost indifferent to the challenges we still faced there?"

Malin's head was throbbing. "I needed to get away. You know that. I could not be away from Antwerp or Venice any longer. You saw for yourself, once you got here, just what I'd built up. And how important it was to protect it."

"So help me understand." Symon gestured at the wall of shelves. "You're prepared to walk away from all of this, considering a withdrawal from the city that has been our life for so many years. And yet there's nothing elsewhere that I can see that offers a better prospect for you, or your ambitions. Just what is going on, Malin? Help me understand, because right now, I have no idea what to think. You owe me that, at least."

The assertion hung in the room.

"I don't know what to say to you. The carnage of the last week is almost too much to bear. It could so easily have led to the death of those I love. You included."

"Yet it didn't. And you are stronger than this, Malin. Much stronger. What is it you're not telling me?"

"Not telling you about what?"

"About what happened in England?"

"Nothing. Nothing at all." His composure was almost gone. "I don't know how many times I have to say it. Deals were hard to come by, but I found them."

Symon rolled his eyes. "Deals. As if they could cause this. What is it that distracts you so? Your thoughts are always in some other place. And our business needs your mind on it more than ever at this moment. The city could make choices that could set us back years. If they pull back from trade while they rebuild, we could be left out in the cold."

"I know this, Symon. Truly I do. And I am working to secure our future. Why do you not trust me?"

"I trust you, Malin. But I am not blind, and I know you well enough to know that something else troubles you." He looked straight into Malin's eyes. "And it concerns me that you cannot, or will not, share it with me."

"Symon. This is the last time I will say it. All is well, and the precautions I've sought to take over the last week will prove to be both wise and necessary. Now if you'll excuse me, I have to go and lie down again. If you're right about one thing, it's that the wine has bettered me."

Malin climbed the stairs back to his room, nausea threatening to overwhelm him.

This deceit was intolerable. But he could think of no other way to protect his friend. The less he knew, the better it would be for him.

Symon was right about one thing, though. He was finding it almost impossible to spread his attention across business and the plot. In attempting to keep both in check, he could fail in each. With consequences he would rather not think about.

Bracing himself, he knelt and built the fire, laid down on the bed and closed his eyes. As the throbbing in his head slowly quietened, the conversation downstairs repeated itself.

Symon had alluded to their time back in Wormegay, when they were both recuperating from their experiences on the battlefield.

After the trauma of the fighting, Malin felt ill-prepared for a return to the business he ran in Antwerp. Haylan, always keen to see his nephew, had offered to provide a home for him, and subsequently Symon, while they completed their recovery.

Rumour in the town was that the estate on Wormegay was struggling. Michaelmas contributions to the Exchequer had fallen, according to Haylan, in each of the previous ten years. A sure sign of trouble.

Malin's curiosity, and a desire to visit his old mentor Jerold, finally got the better of him, and shortly after Symon's release the two men took the half-day journey on horseback to the estate.

Jerold greeted them fondly, and offered to host them in the rectory for as long as it took to tour the estate. Over those mild spring days of 'thirty-three, they became a common sight on the land's poorly maintained tracks.

It took less than two weeks for Symon to make his first suggestions on how things could be improved.

On enquiring how Symon knew so much about running an estate, Malin came to learn of his friend's history.

★

Symon was an orphan from the age of three.

When his parents died of a winter pleurisy, the elders of their small Perthshire village decided that each remaining family would take an equal part in the infant's upbringing. His placement would be discussed every Easter.

For his first two years, he lived with the family of a young cottar and his wife, as they had no children of their own. He could remember little of that time, except that he missed his mother and father.

At the age of four, the cottar put him to work in the fields around the village, tending the small herds of cattle and pigs that, apart from the few geese or chickens owned by each family, represented the extent of the communal livestock.

The two elder boys he shared his tasks with, the sons of another family at the east end of the village, were initially rough and unforgiving, but they were disciplined enough to understand that the boy's growing usefulness was their responsibility.

After a desperate winter and the late spring that followed, he could be trusted with each of the main tasks alone.

That Easter he moved into the home of Wylyam, a weaver who had lost his wife many years earlier. His days were then dominated by the collection of water and the beating of harsh linens, his hands often chapped to the point where blood would seep from his palms. He rarely escaped the confines of Wylyam's workshop, a small extension to his dwelling house. Although his strength grew, the work was hard and unrelenting. When Symon joined the gatherings of worship of the Virgin, making offerings for her bounty in the clear waters of the River Lyon, few adults would meet his eyes.

Although Wylyam's sourness rarely moved to violence, Symon yearned for his next move.

By the age of twelve, he had laboured for almost half the families in the village. His skills and trustworthy disposition had made him an essential part of the village economy.

In the months following the winter solstice that year he helped fertilise and plant the small arable areas of land on the outskirts of the village. Throughout the summer, he was regularly pulled away from his duties with the crops by the blacksmith and, for a week of almost unbroken drunkenness, the local brewer.

His popularity was such that in the month leading up to the following Easter, a hushed bartering between households began, keen to have him for the following year.

Walking in and out of each family's life, providing the

necessary muscle or time in return for a roof over his head, he started to truly understand how the place functioned. He witnessed first-hand the consequences of argument and disagreement, and the impact this had on the delicate balance of village life.

In his thirteenth summer, Symon went on his first cattle drive. Entrusted with three mature cows and the best village bull, he left the narrow glen for the first time, joining other peasants and landowners at Aberfeldy for the drive beneath and around the broad, rolling mountains. The sound and movement of so many men and animals was overwhelming.

He arrived in Braemar, three weeks later, with a changed view of his place in the world. His village seemed so much smaller.

When his new friends left to begin the walk back, he chose to stay a while, offering his labour to a local landowner in return for basic lodgings.

When he finally returned home through the rough Cairngorm passes, he was greeted warmly by the villagers, and shown to a newly constructed dwelling of his own.

From that point on, he was free to make his own choices on the work he did, judging which households were most in need of his help. His decisions were always respected.

On occasion, he reflected on what he was still doing there. At such times, adults and children alike gave him space. At the end of each two- or three-day period, when he wandered in the high hills between Loch Tay and Loch Rannoch, he would always return refreshed, quickly catching up with his outstanding tasks.

One morning, deep into Whitsuntime, men on horseback arrived from the Menzie stronghold at Weem. The English could no longer tolerate the Scots' recently won independence, and were sending an army north. The local laird was charged with gathering and delivering fifty foot-soldiers for the upcoming battle, in addition to an allotted quota of men-at-arms.

Each father in the village argued to keep their sons at home. Reluctantly, they offered Symon.

*

Any bond that Malin had had with Wormegay had been broken at the age of six, so when Symon began to suggest how to reverse the estate's decline, he stood back and let his friend discuss his thoughts with Haylan.

Within days, his uncle had written to Jefferey, strongly recommending he appoint the Scot to the vacant position of Franklin.

Working initially through Malin, Symon spent the next eighteen months addressing each weakness in the estate's performance. Changes in crop rotation, and the related workloads that would come with shifting use of pastures. Revised tenant responsibilities to complement changes made in the spring plantings. Improvements made in the arrangements for crop storage, distribution and sale, and the allocation of supplies for consumption and cattle feed. He sought further advice on the impacts from the following year's expected rise in livestock, and adjustments needed to keep the feed-stock in balance with the likely outcomes.

Within six months, Malin was not needed. Yet secretly dreading his return to Antwerp, he became increasingly poor company. Evenings spent at Lynn with Haylan and Radley became sullen, turgid affairs. Radley in particular found these times hard to take, finding reasons to stay out in the town during the long dark nights, often not coming back home at all.

It was Symon who finally confronted Malin's assertions that he was still keen to help. For two weeks they'd bickered, until

Symon simply told him to stay away. That it would be best if he left for Antwerp as soon as possible. For each of their sakes.

What he didn't know was that Malin's unrest had been amplified by the surprise appearance in Lynn of Uberto Da Segna, the man at the heart of their Venice operations. Having overseen an increasing number of trades through his man Da Viscia, his lucrative business out of Antwerp had slowly reduced to a trickle. Finally learning the truth of Malin's extended absence from the Pisan, Uberto had insisted that he meet the young Englishman in person. The only way to do that, in stark contrast to his normal direction of travel, was to head west and then north, through the Mediterranean and up into the German Sea. Accompanied by Accardi for the final leg from Antwerp, the meeting between the three of them, held secretly in a dimly-lit room at the back of the Hanse workshop on the Staithe, had been eating away at him for weeks. His discontent at the looming decision he had to make, and his desire to shield his friend from the subterfuge of the arrangements between the Hanse and Uberto, was becoming almost impossible to contain.

Uberto was right, of course, about the need to resume business. And also, he reflected, right to comment on how Malin would feel re-engaging with a past that had given him so much pleasure. Within days of Symon's suggestion, Malin was on a ship that would take him back to what he hoped would offer a comforting distraction from his experiences north of the border.

Were Symon's comments downstairs borne of what his friend saw as the same behaviour now?

If so, he was probably right. Over the last week, he had become a little less convivial, a little less tolerant, every day.

He picked up the fire-iron, and poked the embers. Did his friend feel, as he did back in those days in Norfolk, that Malin no longer cared about how he treated him? They had mended their friendship back then, with Symon finally heeding his repeated calls to follow him out of Wormegay, tempted in part, Malin felt sure, by the lure of learning yet more new skills.

He resolved to do what was needed to prevent this argument getting out of hand. Short, of course, of sharing *everything*.

Dusk arrived without him realising it. The day was lost. Malin sat back, still deep in thought.

Later, he went downstairs to get some water. He was relieved that Symon had gone back out.

His journal entry took little time to compose.

No more drink until it's over.

Head clear in the morning, ready to do what he could to ease his friend's fears, he would head out to meet Bourchier.

Chapter 10.

Monday 4th February 1348

Day 9 of the Quarant

The morning brought bright skies. Stepping out onto the street, Malin could almost smell the oncoming spring. Salt tang with a hint of warmth. The gulls wheeled above the dock at the end of the street, perhaps sensing the same.

He stepped with renewed vigour towards the widening vista of the Lagoon. The ferries were busy this morning. Waiting his turn, he stood at the water's edge and scanned the horizon.

He was headed east, to the warehouses and docks that pulsed with the lifeblood of the city's trade. The markets and shops of the Venetian mainland were the public symbol of city commerce, but it was the rows of large buildings along the Lido that enabled the Republic to thrive.

Symon was wrong. He could never grow tired of the sound of waters, calmed by harbour walls and jetties, the gentle lapping against staithes and piers. Of watching stevedores at work, enabling goods to move from city to city, country to country. Of the endlessly fascinating rituals of regulation and trade, and their earnest application through officials sharing the same goals in every coastal city.

And yet it was his immersion in this world, as much as Jefferey's manipulation, that had brought him to this point.

He shook his head free of the thought but, the damage done, reached into his tunic for another dose of the gentian tea.

Feeling the fluid work its way down to his stomach, he turned slowly to observe the traffic heading west against the onshore breeze and into the city. The manmade estuary, slowly narrowing to the head of the Canal, was dotted with boats of all sizes, appearing and then reappearing in the choppy waters. While he waited, three low-keeled boats passed close by, heading to the dedicated salt warehouses clustered in the northwest *sestiere* of Cannaregio.

The fabric of the city remained badly damaged, but trade was back on its feet.

He felt good.

Today would be the day he grasped Fate tightly around the neck, and told it how things would be.

Moving to the front of the dock queue, Malin passed the gondolier the customary silver coin, and pointed to the far side of the Lagoon. The boatman gestured to the quay foreman, informing him of the likely duration of his return trip, and pushed off into the bay.

An hour later, having reassured Symon that he would handle the Quarant procedures personally, he walked into the local customs office, half a mile north of the Stolado warehouses.

Malin had to shield his eyes from the sun flooding through a skylight to better see the approaching figure of Signor Polani.

"Ah, Signor Cordier. I thought it was you. So good to see you again." Immaculately dressed, the jovial, red-faced man reached out to shake Malin's hand. "Please, please, take a seat. Da Viscia has already been and gone, so the Da Segna witnessing is already complete."

Although they had conducted business together for many years, Malin and Uberto debated long and hard about the wisdom of jointly underwriting the contracts for the cargo. In the wrong circumstances, it could be just another piece of evidence of their collusion. They had finally agreed that to not do so would be more likely to arouse rather than reduce suspicion.

Malin would thank Giradino for his promptness when he next saw him. "And was everything in order?"

Polani leaned forward, pushing the neat pile of documents on the desk towards him. "Yes. As you will see, he has signed without amendment."

"That's most encouraging, Signor." Malin reached into his satchel, and withdrew a similar number of documents. "So let's see if I share his confidence."

Polani walked around to Malin's side of the table, pulling his chair noisily across the wooden floor to sit next to him.

Malin lost track of time as they worked through the quantities of goods listed, and the commercial terms applicable to each, pausing every so often to countersign each other's papers once parity and completeness in each had been confirmed.

Polani put down his quill, the final signature drying on the last of Malin's papers. Both men sat back, satisfied by the faultless execution of their business. "Come, Signor. Let us step outside and get some fresh air. I believe we are in a position to witness the final stages of the inwards inspection."

Malin allowed the man to guide him along the wharf. The official paused regularly to demonstrate his grasp on the many cargoes currently in his care. Polani's bright demeanour was infectious, and he found his own mood lightening further. Without agreeing to do so, both men chose to ignore the obvious and widespread damage along the entire quayside. They lowered their heads as they passed one particularly sad sight, a warehouse that appeared to contain only the shattered timbers of its own collapsed roof.

They approached the warehouse containing the *Seynte Marie* cargo. A gang of stevedores crossed their path, pulling several high-packed wagons of untreated cloth to the large warehouse entrance.

Polani paused to let them past. "Your cargoes are all safely accounted for here. Stolado has fared better than many. The warehouses under his charge appear to have suffered little damage, despite being three of the oldest buildings on the quay. In fact, I'm eager to talk to him to see if he has any explanation for his good fortune. Perhaps we will learn something we can put into effect with the reconstruction."

The entrance finally clear, they walked into the dim echoing space of the warehouse. The inside of the building appeared as undamaged as its outer shell. There was no sign of any water ingress or flood damage, and the long runs of shelving, raised above the bare soil floor, showed little sign of disruption.

Malin turned to his companion. "You could do far worse than learn from this Stolado. I have rarely seen anything so well organised. When I next see Da Viscia, I will make sure to discuss the merits of these facilities. Most impressive."

Calling over the warehouse supervisor, Polani established the precise location of Malin's cargo, and the two men were consumed again by the checks and assurances demanded of all arriving goods.

It was only when halfway across the Lagoon on his return journey, that Malin reflected on the absence of the piercing heartburn overshadowing his earlier passage.

★

Choosing to alight at home and travel into the city on foot, he retraced his steps to the brothel on Calle dei Stagneri.

He continued to feel a surprising yet welcome sense of fortitude.

The fear of failure remained real. Any one of their arrangements could unravel, or be disrupted by forces seeking to thwart them. Just one unreliable participant, one loss of courage or conviction, one loose communication, could cost him and those around him everything.

But for today at least, he would accept that the many possible roots of any failure might be so deeply planted that worry was futile.

As he walked the increasingly familiar route, avoiding the still damaged Santa Giustina bridge, he reflected on the times in his life when he had confronted plans almost collapsing under the weight of uncertainty. He had worked through that dread, pushed himself beyond his known capabilities.

He recalled his first trade voyage to Trebizond, back in 'thirty-five. It was not so much the sense of navigating the streets alone that pulled his thoughts back there. He had covered almost every yard of the city's flagstones over the years. It was, instead, something about the way he had *felt* that day in the east Black Sea port. His temporary loss of nerve, negotiating with three Persian merchants he had never met before, in a port he had never visited.

His objectives had been ambitious yet vague. His Hanseatic partners, no doubt believing that his natural sense for profit would serve them all well, had simply asked that he strike the best deal available. At stake was a twenty-season agreement to secure and import fine silks, and a range of highly prized spices from China. Saffron. Cinnamon. Pepper.

The deal involved receipt of four caravans per year, with the option to warehouse goods that arrived at the port during the winter season break. Profit from the side deals, Uberto's ships travelling east with leading cargoes of pig-iron, grain and salted meats, would easily finance the costs of the goods on their arrival from the Caspian, leaving all signatories a generous surplus.

The freedom to improvise thrilled him as usual, but it also scared him. To make things worse, the Persian distaste for the failing Byzantine basilikon had cost him a further two days in currency negotiation on his purse of Venetian ducats.

A month later he was in Constantinople, still unsure if he had met his investors' wishes. He would not be able to objectively assess his performance until meeting with Accardi and the Hanse on his return west.

To pass the two weeks before Uberto and Sclavo were scheduled to arrive to collect him, he spent many hours each day exploring the city, returning to his lodgings each evening through the large ornamental entrance of the Roman hippodrome.

Each evening he would sit, staring at the line of obelisks and plinthed statues that ran along the centre of the amphitheatre, reflecting on the steps and choices he had made to bring him to that point in his life.

When Uberto and Sclavo finally sailed into the Golden Horn, a week late, his anxiety vanished within moments of Sclavo declaring the reason for their delay. Uberto, against all convention, had been invited onto the Great Council, in recognition of his remarkable services to the growing wealth of the Republic. On their return, the Da Segnas would be added to the Golden Book, and their celebrations would live long in the memory.

Here, walking along the Calle de Lorenzo, the echo of those days, a life full of anxiety and reward, felt recent, and all too real.

Expecting the tavern to be as quiet and empty as the previous week, he was greeted instead with a wave of heat and sound. Every table was occupied, and the atmosphere felt as though it had been building for hours.

His initial survey yielded no sign of Bourchier. It was possible, of course, that his fellow conspirator was upstairs, enjoying female company. He moved in from the door and wove his way through the boisterous ranks of men and women.

Reaching the bar, he turned and reassessed the room. No sign of the man.

He felt a tap on his shoulder and turned, unsure what to expect. He was greeted by the sweaty, swollen-faced smile of the landlord. "Greetings, Signor. Is it wine, or something more *companionable* that you are seeking?" The man's smile drifted into an unmistakable leer.

Malin felt his colour rise, and fought to retain a dignified expression.

One small drink would do no harm. "I would take a flagon of your wine, Signor, if you would kindly find me a table at which I may be seated." He turned to scan the room. "Perhaps you could clear one of those?"

He stood and watched as the landlord shuffled out from behind the bar, and walked across to confront a group of four men and women. He couldn't hear what was said over the general noise of the room, but the men, one with an arm over a woman's shoulder, another around the other's waist, were prepared to make room. First one couple then the other rose to their feet, and with unsteady steps ascended the stairs opposite.

Taking his seat, with a view of the entire room, Malin placed his satchel on the table in front of him, and waited for the landlord to bring his order. His face burned from the sudden rise in temperature.

The wine was not the best, but it would do. Bourchier

would be here soon, and watching the often bawdy interactions between customers and courtesans distracted him for a while.

The arrival of a second, unrequested flagon, carried by a heavily perfumed redhead, suggested that more time had passed than he realised. Rejecting her proposal of company, but telling her to leave the wine, he watched her move instead to another table. He was soon forgotten.

Drink refreshed, he wondered once more how long Bourchier would remain absent.

*

It was dark when he left.

Any sense of resilience he had enjoyed earlier in the day was left in the stifling tavern air.

What should he do now?

He had learnt nothing of Bourchier's activities of the last few days, and been unable to pass on an account of his own progress. He had his own plans, of course, but they now felt untethered, without any assurance that they remained in line with events beyond his sight.

Bourchier, for all his apparent flamboyance and nonchalance, was an accomplished and reliable partner. In the two years they had known each other, he had never failed to honour an appointment.

What could have caused him to stay away?

Malin reflected back on their last meeting in Castello. Bourchier had been in fine form, and given no suggestion of any concerns he might have for meeting again.

And yet.

Pulling his collar around his neck, Malin started to walk south to the Canal. He would pick up a river boat and return home.

He passed several lamplighters as he moved down the Calle Bosello, their tapers glowing in the early evening breeze.

Turning a corner, a man stepped out from the shadows, and made to intercept him. Malin halted, but the man continued to approach.

Before he could begin to take defensive action, the man was upon him. His face was covered by the hood of a dark cloak.

The man stretched out an arm. "Take this."

Malin instinctively raised his own arm, fearing a blade.

A flash of white caught his eye.

The scroll of paper was knocked from the man's hand as Malin's arm swung through between them. The man turned and walked back into the darkened alley to his right.

Malin was unable to move.

His heart raced, and his breath came in short, tortured bursts.

He looked down at his feet, and saw the rolled paper. Bending down, he retrieved it and turned back to the nearest streetlight.

His eyes ran down the flickering page.

He felt his heart thump, and then fall silent.

Bourchier is in custody. We must meet tomorrow. Soranzo.

Chapter 11

Tuesday 5th February 1348

Day 10 of the Quarant

Malin crossed the Campo San Salvatore just before midday, and stood at the side entrance to the church. Scents from the spice stalls, temporarily relocated from their badly damaged site south across the Ponte del Lovo, hung in the air.

He and Nicolo Soranzo had never met. His family had been part of the Venetian nobility for generations. Providing funds to the Fourth Crusade, their reputation and wealth increased when the crusade, rather than liberating Jerusalem, conquered Constantinople. With Byzantine power reduced, the Soranzos acquired significant land and trading privileges, and from that point regularly filled positions at the centre of the Great Council. Nicolo himself was currently serving for a third time on the Small Council, as the elected *consigliere ducale* for the prestigious San Marco *sestiere*.

To Malin's knowledge, Soranzo was the most senior member of the conspiracy. He breathed the same air, stood in the same rooms as Dandolo. The Doge was not even permitted to open his own correspondence without Soranzo or another member of the Small Council being present.

The church bells rang Sext. Stallholders pulled down their awnings and drifted from the square, heading for one of the local taverns. Malin tightened his arms across his chest, the burn rising from his guts.

Moments later, two figures approached him from the south.

One of the men walked with his head slightly lowered. He was dressed in the same dark clothing worn by Malin's assailant from the previous evening. The older man to his right bore the distinctive violet colours of the city's highest rank, and walked as though he owned all around him. As he approached, his white beard and moustache bristled with impatience. Soranzo was clearly in no mood for small talk. His eyes flashed.

"Le Cordier?"

"Yes. I'm here as requested." He would not be intimidated by this man. "Is it wise to meet in such a public place, Signor? Your dress does little to assist in concealment."

Soranzo took a small step back. His eyes ran slowly down and then up Malin's body.

"Given *your* position, I suggest you do nothing to antagonise me. My standing in this part of the city is based in large part on my visibility. I am well known for it, and chose to do nothing to raise suspicion."

He looked again into Malin's eyes. The challenge was obvious. "To change my daily habit would be to invite questions neither of us would welcome." He paused. "Come, we will find somewhere a little more private to talk."

He set off at a brisk pace around the south side of the church.

They crossed the Ponte dei Bareteri, moving undisturbed past haberdashery shops and local clothiers. A few streets later,

Soranzo stepped through a door into a damp, high-walled courtyard. Sounds from the street died out immediately. They crossed the courtyard and entered the house.

Plaster had fallen from the wall of every room they passed through. Malin gagged at the blended stink of salt damp and vermin. At the top of a staircase with several damaged or missing treads, Soranzo entered a room off the landing. He beckoned Malin to follow, and closed the door behind them. The man in the dark clothing remained outside.

Soranzo gestured to the two simple chairs at the centre of the room.

"Please. Sit."

The councillor loosened his jacket and stood between Malin and a small, filthy window embedded in the back wall. A thick layer of dirt on the glass blocked out much of the light from outside.

Malin's breath was still laboured from the exertion of their walk. "So, Signor Soranzo. Please tell me what you know of Bourchier."

"I would rather not. At least not yet. Instead, can you perhaps tell me how you have managed to get this whole *adventure* of ours so badly wrong?"

"I'm sorry. What?"

"Actually, no. Before you explain yourself, I want you to know that the man outside that door is more than content to follow any instruction I give him. Any."

Malin began to say something, then closed his mouth. He needed to listen.

Soranzo continued. "I have spent the last eighteen months seeking to fulfil my part of this... *endeavour*, with the utmost discretion and diligence. The closest members of my family know nothing of my actions. You of all people should know what it is to hazard the reputation of your family. Of those

125

before you who have achieved their rightful place in the world."

Family? What did this man know about him? Malin glanced at the dusty floor. At the holes in the bottom of the wall. And then back up into the face of the man looming over him.

"We all have our reasons for doing this, do we not, Le Cordier? For gambling all to emerge in a better position. But I have more to lose than all of you, do I not?"

Malin could no longer wait for the man to get to the point.

"I understand that you are angry. And that you want answers. Yet I too find myself ignorant of what has happened. Please. Tell me what you know of Bourchier."

Soranzo took a further step forward. Malin became aware of the man's shallow breathing. Was he frightened?

"We are discovered."

Soranzo dropped down onto the empty chair.

Malin waited for him to continue.

"I attended the Great and Small Councils as usual on Sunday. The assembled masses had their usual trivia to discuss. Spiced up considerably by the latest information on the damage. We sat for hours, listening to an unending series of reports from well-meaning but tedious men outlining the smallest details of what we had all already seen with our own eyes." He sighed. "How we ever thought the city would benefit from having so many unremarkable men sitting in such cramped conditions, listening to the flapping of their own jaws and breathing in the worst of their own humours…"

He caught himself. "The Great Council was long and uneventful, and I had no reason to believe the Small Council would be any different."

He went on to recount the events at his second meeting.

Soranzo had joined the other five Ducal councillors in the more intimate chambers to the east of the Doge's Palace. In customary fashion, they had each spent time telling their peers of progress on previous *Consiglio Minori* matters, and agreed those topics to be raised with the Doge.

When Dandolo entered, he was flanked by three men. The *Capi dei Dieci*, the triple head of the Council of Ten. The councillors' shock pinned them motionless and silent in their seats. By convention, the three elected heads were forbidden to leave the Council of Ten quarters during their month in charge, for fear of corruption by bribery, or knowledge of any baseless rumour. Yet here they all stood, taking their seats around the Ducal table.

Andrea Dandolo, still the youngest man in the room despite six years as Doge, stated that normal business of the Council would be deferred, in the interest of more pressing matters.

What followed was news of the discovery of a serious plot to overthrow the Councils, the Senate, and by inference, the entire constitution.

In November, an anonymous note had been placed in one of the *"Per Denontie Segrete"*, the Lions' Mouths built into the Palace walls. What set it apart from the usual "secret denunciations" arising from petty jealousies or resentments was the claim that men were holding secret meetings across the city. Discussing the overthrow of the authorities. Most chilling of all was the claim that the plot was being coordinated by powers from outside the Republic.

The Ten had applied for and received additional funds from the Magistracy, and spent the winter trying to learn if the assertion was true. Streets and waterways were trawled for intelligence. Additional men, and a few well-placed women were added to the payroll, supplementing the hundreds of paid operatives already embedded in the city's warp and weft. At the end of January, The Ten pulled in their senior assayers and placed the mountain of notes gathered in front of them.

The conclusion was shocking. For reasons unknown, a small number of English spies were actively recruiting support to bring them all down.

"The *Capi dei Dieci* sat there and told us they were following the movements of a small number of foreigners in the city, and that one man in particular might hold the key to what was really happening."

Malin's blood ran cold. "Bourchier?"

Soranzo's look was answer enough.

"They said they had issued a bill of attainder and acted immediately. He was apprehended in a San Polo brothel. They're questioning him now."

Neither man spoke.

Bourchier had been at the centre of the plot for as long as it had existed. Since introducing himself to Malin at his home, passing him the letter that demanded his appearance at the Upper Exchequer back in England.

Soranzo leaned across, his face only a foot away from Malin's. Fear was etched across his features. "So what I want to know. What I *demand* to know, is what you intend to do to protect me."

Malin needed time to think. He needed to know more.

"Do you have any further knowledge of how they knew to target Bourchier? Have they been following him for long?"

"What does it bloody matter? They have him!"

"It matters, because we need to understand which meetings have been witnessed. How many of us have been seen in his company?"

"Who knows. My guess is that they've been following him for at least a month or two, so it probably means everyone. Even you."

Malin thought this through. "And yet here we sit. Perhaps they know less than we think. If they knew, they wouldn't hesitate, would they? With so much at stake?"

Soranzo's voice was ice cold. "If Bourchier snaps, he will name us all. What should we do?"

Malin stood, and moved to the side of the room. He ran his hands through his hair, trying to retain control of his thoughts.

"We do nothing. Or to be more accurate, we do nothing to change our current behaviour. To do so will show them that we know about them. Our treason is already done. We have nothing to gain by cancelling our plans." Malin walked back to the centre of the room. "That said, I suggest we take extra care. Be vigilant." He fell silent for a few more moments. "And let's see if we can spot any signs of their activity."

Soranzo slowly nodded. "I agree we should do nothing rash. But we should tell our friends of Bourchier's arrest. They deserve to know."

Malin sat back down. "No. No. We should do nothing to alert them. It will only take one or two of them to panic, and we will all fall. Our best hope lies in helping everyone concentrate on the things they still need to do to be ready."

"So we mislead our friends?"

Malin spoke with increased force. "Do you really believe that none of the dozens of men we have worked with, *none* of them, would share what they know with The Ten to save their own skin?" He paused. "Should I worry about your own part in this?"

"How dare you!" Soranzo leapt to his feet, narrowly missing Malin's face as he rose. "You challenge *my* loyalty, when I sit at the Council table every week, inches from the men we seek to depose?"

Malin could feel his own anger building. "Please. Do I need remind us both that you have done this for your own reasons from the beginning? You are after power for yourself. Two or three more weeks, and that power falls into your hands. The dangers have not changed. They are simply more visible. It was always going to come to this." He felt his colour rising, and fought to steady himself. "I need your assurance that you will do nothing."

Soranzo's head dropped. His next words were uttered through tightened lips, almost a whisper. "You bear all responsibility for this. If we fail, it will be because you refused to listen. If we succeed, and I am rewarded as promised? Well. Then, we will talk again."

Before Malin could reply, Soranzo walked to the door, and knocked twice. His companion opened the door inward. The two men exchanged glances, and stood back from the opening to let Malin pass.

"Be very careful, Le Cordier. The Ten are not the only ones who see what is happening in our city."

Back on the street, Malin headed back to the bustle of the market, his eyes darting nervously about him.

★

Lucia was pulling her veil back from her face when Malin opened the door.

It was unusual for her to visit unannounced. Or to travel alone to Calle San Domenico, even in daylight.

Entering the house, she unbuttoned her thick outer coat. "I hope we can have a few moments to talk."

Malin called down the corridor. "Symon. Look who has arrived."

His friend greeted Lucia warmly. "On your own again? It must get tiring to constantly explain why you need no chaperone."

Lucia laughed. "I lost the desire to fight for my independence long ago. But fortunately, others demanding that I follow convention realised the error of their ways, and gave up well before that." She glanced around the office. "In any case,

130

I wanted to see for myself what was going on here. It's been a while since my last visit, and I find it refreshing to occasionally stray from San Polo."

The three of them spoke for a while about the ongoing recovery efforts, then Symon suggested that he be allowed to get back to work. Malin took Lucia into the reception room, and lit a fire.

She removed her coat and joined Malin in front of the hearth. "I have no intention of spending the afternoon in idle talk, Malin. I therefore ask you to brace yourself for a frank discussion between us. Can you do that?" She watched as he blushed.

"Oh dear. When others state such a thing, it normally leads to minor controversy about someone's dress, or the behaviour of one of the doormen at a friend's house. When it's you? I know I am in for something of a treat."

"Of course, you're free to make light of my preference for honest exchange. Yet I mean it, Malin. It is my desire to understand what it is that concerns you so."

Malin's smile disappeared. "What can you mean? My concerns?"

Lucia maintained her focus on Malin's face, sighing as if expecting his response.

"Malin. I understand that you have been out of sorts since your return from England. That in your disquiet, you have been taxing Symon with a number of questions or requests. He is worried about you. And when such concern about you is expressed by one so close to you over the years, I have to say I begin to worry also."

Malin's eyes searched Lucia's face for any sign that this might be one of her attempts to engage in witty or stimulating debate. No such sign could be found, and his eyes fell slightly, needing more time to consider her words.

She continued. "I must add, in fact, that I too have found you somehow different. And your behaviour on Saturday has been troubling me ever since we put you onto the gondola to get you home."

A look of mild recognition passed across Malin's face. The drinking. The bloody drinking.

"I can explain, Lucia. Perhaps I have been out of sorts a little."

"Out of sorts? I would hardly describe it like that. Quiet, perhaps. Sullen. Or the complete opposite. Jesting loudly with people who know you to be a reserved, thoughtful man. Not serious all the time, of course, but not prone to such *forced* jollity."

"I'm afraid you're not making any sense, Lucia. What do you mean, forced?"

"Unnatural. As if you are playing a part to mask other thoughts. I don't know. It just feels as though something is wrong. Symon feels the same way."

"What has he said to you?"

"Not too much, other than what I have just described. Please don't seek to deny what I am saying."

She sighed a second time.

"If you must know, he came to see me on Sunday evening. Malin, he's worried about you. We both feel that you are struggling with something, and that whatever it is, it is taking a toll on you."

Malin turned away. This conversation had become just as important as the one earlier in that half-derelict building in San Marco. Here was Lucia, staring straight into his heart.

And what was Symon thinking?

He turned to face her. To feel the gentle pleading in her eyes. He yearned to confess.

He tore his eyes away again.

Lucia sensed his retreat, and reached out her hand.

132

"Malin. My dear Malin. I can see just how much this thing troubles you. Please let me share it with you. We owe each other the right to honesty."

He had never been so close. How could he possibly survive the interrogations of The Ten, if he could not even navigate through an afternoon by the fire with Lucia?

"Please, Lucia. I need you to allow me time to order my thoughts. You are right to believe I struggle with important matters. But you must respect my need to reach my conclusions myself. I deeply value your concern, and apologise if my behaviour has worried you. But please. Do not push me on this matter until I am ready."

He clasped her hand. For a moment or two they sat motionless, each seeking to understand what had just passed between them.

"I wish you could open your heart to me, Malin. We have known each other for so long. It upsets me that you cannot express your true thoughts to me."

Malin smiled. "My dear Lucia. You of all people should know that when I have learned the substance of my own thoughts, you will be the first person with whom I share them."

With one more glance, Lucia sighed a final time.

She chose to leave without disturbing Symon.

Malin walked with her to the quayside, waiting until she was safely aboard her gondola.

He watched her slowly disappear into the fading light of the Canal, wondering how he had resisted his own desire to share.

And how he would admonish Symon.

Chapter 12

Wednesday 6th February 1348

Day 11 of the Quarant

Soranzo and Lucia.

Their words of the previous day reached out to him throughout the night. Moments after waking, they competed again for his full attention.

Two very different people.

Two very different sets of problems to solve.

He was due to meet Grisani, the Master Joiner, at his home in Santa Croce at noon, but needed time to think. He dressed, hurriedly broke his fast, and returned to sit on his bed. Two large mouthfuls of gentian tea would help.

Malin closed his eyes, waiting for his breath to slow.

If Bourchier was gone, he had only two options.

Continue, or run.

If he stood everyone down, he would not be able to stay in Venice. His reputation would be destroyed, and he would have dozens of new enemies. Some of them might even decide to go ahead and attempt the coup without his support. Another reason to leave?

If he did run, where would he go? Venice's reach spanned the maritime world. Failure back in Westminster would make his life both difficult and short.

He reached for his satchel, and pulled out his journal. He straightened up the sheets holding the sum total of his life's reflections. Looking through them had sometimes offered him, over the years, a new way to think about something troubling him.

He allowed himself the luxury of moving slowly through each page, recalling the circumstances in which some of the text was written.

No single observation or thought helped this time, but he felt himself relaxing. He drew comfort from the scattered thoughts of his younger self, written across almost thirty years.

He reached his last note, laughing quietly to himself at how easy he'd found it in The Tinsmith to ignore his own thoughts on drinking.

That thought brought him in turn back to Bourchier, and his calm was over.

Picking up his quill, he added a new line.

Listen to your own advice.

He had told Soranzo what to do. To continue as before, and show no sign that anything had changed.

He would do that too.

At least for now.

And what of Lucia?

He had believed his thoughts were his alone. That he had been successful in hiding his anxieties about the path he followed.

But Lucia's words the previous evening showed just how mistaken he was. Symon had sensed something was wrong, and helped Lucia to see that her concerns were not hers alone.

His replies to her had been vague. His promise of future clarity hardly helped.

And he knew he was tempted to tell all.

One thing was clear. Another month of this would end him. Possibly at the mercy of the interrogator's tools. Wielded by The Ten, or perhaps worse, by Lucia.

It was endurance that he lacked. So he had to help bring this to a close as soon as possible. Find a way to cope. Embrace the fear of discovery, or push it away for as long as he could.

Putting on his tunic and overcoat, he left the house without pausing to see if Symon was in the office or attending to matters in the city.

Walking to the quay, he accepted in his heart what he already knew in his head.

He was not cut out for this kind of work.

★

The *sestiere* of Santa Croce sat at the far west extent of the main Venetian island.

It took three separate boats to complete Malin's journey from his Castello home to the *Traghetto Vecchio*. Despite spending so much time considering ways to limit his exposure in the city, he found himself repeatedly standing on uncovered jetties. At least his route was sufficiently complicated to make it difficult for anyone following him.

Disembarking for the final time, he looked across to the Veneto mainland and the margins of the Margheran salt marshes. The closest any Venetian could get to real land.

The day had brought fresh winter skies, filled with the call of a far greater range of birds than those present in the east of the city.

The Canal had just one more turn before broadening out

into the wide basin of the western Lagoon. River traffic was light, but the vessels themselves were much larger than those nearer the centre of the city, carrying cargoes of food, cloth and salt between the city and the onshore Veneto.

He made his way south to the Campo de la Lana, along the wide, dirt-covered passageways that led to the guild leader's house. As the streets grew quieter, Malin became increasingly aware of Grisani's odd choice of neighbourhood.

As the senior representative of the joiners' and builders' guild at the Arsenale, he was needed regularly at the far eastern edge of the city. His willingness to commit to such a journey every day, even when not directly dictated by the long Arsenale working shift, was a real curiosity.

Then he turned onto the side street on which Grisani's house stood, and understood perfectly.

The houses either side were undistinguished timber dwellings, of the kind found throughout the less opulent areas of the city. In other sestieres, the conversion of houses from timber to stone was rapidly changing the entire character of the city. If the trend continued, the only wood used for building would be for rafters, and the *tolpi* piles keeping homes from sinking into the foetid Lagoon mud.

The proposal of such a renovation at the home of the Master Joiner, however, would be a crime.

Every aspect of the house was exquisite. Timber brackets carved in the shape of straining, burdened men. Portico facings depicting well-known city vistas. Window shutters, each portraying either the figure of St Mark or that of a winged lion. Every image drawn from the smoothest of woods.

Malin entered through the front gate and crossed a small recessed patio. As he approached the front door, carved frescos to either side revealed additional layers of detail.

A servant guided Malin into an upstairs reception room.

The inside of the house matched the promise of its external finery. An absence of wall tapestry was made up for by the craftsmanship and finish of every surface.

After a brief delay Romaso Grisani walked into the room, his voice loud and cheerful.

"Ah, Le Cordier. I am so glad you were able to grant me a chance to speak with you further. The room at Stornello's, while full of our friends, was uniquely distracting. I welcome the chance for more considered exchange."

Malin could not help liking the man. His questions were sensible, and put forward in a genuine desire to help. On the occasions when an answer was not possible, Grisani accepted Malin's promise to resolve it over the following days.

Their conversation extended into the afternoon, and wine was called for. Back for nearly two weeks, Malin began to feel a growing confidence in his own grasp of matters.

When it came time to leave, Grisani's invitation to stay for the evening was easy to accept.

Conversation over dinner was even more relaxed. Grisani had had no children before his wife died of a fever some twenty years earlier. Instead of starting a new family, he had thrown himself into his trade, building his reputation within the guilds as an honest and trustworthy business partner. Nobles increasingly approached him for his insights on how best to deploy joiners, boat builders and craftsmen.

After dinner, they retired to sit by the fire.

Malin remained curious about the reasons for Grisani's involvement.

"The nobles have been good to me, yet they seem always to lack the ability to learn. To take my advice, apply it, and understand what it might mean, success or not. Perhaps they have become accustomed to others doing their thinking for them. And then I began to wonder. If they can't be trusted to protect and use their own money wisely, then why should they be trusted to manage the wealth of the Republic? Especially when assigning themselves to positions for which they have little skill.

"Anyway, I'm not an ambitious man. I've no family to bestow my possessions on from my deathbed. But I do want to see the city cared for. In good hands. If the changes we bring end up putting more talented men into positions of influence, then I'm all for it."

Malin eventually made to leave, thanking his host for his hospitality.

The packed earth walkways were almost empty as he began his walk back to the Canal. The air was still, and Malin felt the moisture of a light mist settle on his face and neck.

A noise behind and to his left caused him to freeze in his tracks.

He heard the sound once more, this time closer. As he turned, a man appeared from a nearby junction, and approached him at speed.

A memory of the events of two nights earlier sprang into the front of his mind. He looked down to the man's hands, half expecting to see another roll of paper.

He saw instead the unmistakable glint of a knife.

*

Symon came to the door, responding to the muffled but insistent banging.

Malin stood to the right of the entrance, bent slightly over. His left arm was raised into his chest.

Symon leapt out and guided him inside.

"By God's soul! What has happened?"

Unresponsive, Malin collapsed onto the ground. His body convulsed in a series of deep, wracking sobs.

Symon returned to the street, glancing hurriedly first one way then the other. The dense mist prevented him seeing more than a few yards, but the street appeared empty. He re-entered the house and closed the door behind him.

"Malin. Can you stand?"

He slowly brought his friend to his feet, and guided him a little further into the safety of the hallway.

Malin, refusing to meet his eyes, continued to bend forward, his face hidden by his dishevelled wet hair. His clothes were filthy, and half his collar hung torn from the top of his tunic.

The man had obviously been involved in some kind of brawl.

As Symon put his arm around him, guiding him into the downstairs reception room, the smell of drink rose on Malin's breath.

Malin slumped down onto the covered bench opposite the fireplace, his left hand still hidden inside his cloak. "Symon. Please. I…"

He continued to look down at the floor.

Symon spoke firmly. "Just wait there. I'll bring something to clean you up."

He returned with a bowl of water and a clean cloth. Malin had barely moved. He would still not meet Symon's peering face.

"It's happened again."

Symon lowered himself onto the bench next to his friend. "What has, Malin?"

"My… mania. I just let…"

"Malin. You're not making sense. Let me take a look at what you've done."

Malin slowly shook his head.

Unwilling to tolerate his friend's continued resistance, Symon reached across and sought to lift his friend's face to meet his own.

As Malin's hair fell from his face, Symon froze at his friend's expression. He appeared lost, as though his mind dwelt in a place far from where they sat.

When Malin spoke, his voice was strangely flat.

"It's all happening so quickly. I've barely been back."

His hand dropped from inside his cloak. It was covered in a thick layer of dried blood. A dark, angry cut glistened in the low candlelight, running from his knuckles to the point where his arm disappeared into his sleeve.

"My God, Malin. What has happened?" For a second time, Malin answered him with a vacant stare.

Without seeking consent, he pulled Malin to his feet, removed his satchel, and pulled off the man's cloak. He then unbuttoned his jacket, and rolled the left sleeve of his shirt up to the elbow.

The deep cut terminated just above his wrist. Symon winced. "I'll be back in a moment. I need to get more cloth."

While he cleaned then bandaged him, Malin continued to sit in silence, content to be manoeuvred like a lifeless puppet.

Confirming the absence of further wounds, Symon stepped back.

"I think that's the best I can do. Now, for the love of Christ, will you tell me what happened to you? Were you drunk again?"

A tear fell from Malin's face. Then another.

"Malin. Please tell me what is going on."

His words, when they came, were chillingly steady. "I killed him. Before he could kill me. And I enjoyed it."

Over the next hour, pressed by Symon on why he had been attacked, Malin told him everything.

Everything about the attack, but then, after a few more questions, everything about the conspiracy.

Malin's reluctance to share the rest crumbled almost immediately. He only paused when asked to slow down, while

Symon sought to reconcile his own recollections of the past two years with Malin's confessions.

Malin's bitterness was evident when he returned again to the attack.

"I don't know if the man deserved to die. Maybe I don't care. But Symon, when he came for me. When I felt that first slash of the knife across my hand. It was just like Dupplin. But here, in Venice, not on some godforsaken highland bog. That's all it took. Just one movement, just one wave of a stranger's arm, and I became an animal again. I had no weapon. But I went for him, Symon. He was down on the ground, and I just kept kicking him. He kept screaming, and I kept kicking him. I didn't care who saw me. Who heard. I just wanted to… to tear him apart."

Tears began to roll down Malin's face.

"I've spent my whole life trying to become a different man. To be something other than Brenner. Other than the monster I was on that moor."

Malin's assailant had been completely unprepared for the savagery of his victim's reaction. His unconscious, bloodied body was either floating in the waters south of the Canal, or sunk in their thick silt bed.

Symon's sense of exclusion was profound.

"But how… why… did you keep this to yourself? Keep it from me?"

"It was easy at first. The summons to Westminster was a complete surprise. There was no indication of why they wanted me there. I half wondered if they had learned of the work I did for Antwerp, and wanted some of that for themselves. Or perhaps we owed them taxes. You were really busy with the *mudae* that spring, so I decided to go without worrying you about it."

Malin told him about how his two weeks at Westminster led

to him being initiated in the king's plans, and assigned to liaise with their man Ricaud Bourchier. And the fact that this man was now missing, believed under arrest.

When he spoke of Uberto's involvement, Symon fell silent.

On two points, Malin was emphatic.

Firstly, he could no longer handle this without Symon's help. Secret or not, he could see now that Symon was inevitably in danger from what he had been doing, however unaware or uninvolved. The Ten would take little convincing that he had been complicit from the start. He was sorry for misleading him. But unrepentant for trying to keep him out of trouble. If Symon would consider forgiving him for his deception, he would dearly like his help to complete his mission.

Secondly, Symon was to tell no one of any of this. Not of the plot. Not of the discovery by The Ten. And most importantly, nothing of this evening's events could ever be shared with anyone. Malin had no idea if his fight that night had been witnessed, but there was no possible advantage to be gained by ever discussing it again.

With anyone.

Chapter 13

Thursday 7th February 1348

Day 12 of the Quarant

No sooner had his head hit the pillow than it was mid-morning, and Symon was knocking on his door, checking that he had taken no further harm.

He sat up and took an inventory of his injuries.

His wounded hand had swollen beneath its bandages overnight. The muscles in his arms and back were sore. Bruises on his right leg and hip were consistent with one of his heavier falls while wrestling his assailant repeatedly to the ground. The toes of his right foot were tender. How many times had he kicked his attacker, feeling the crunch of flesh and bone on each impact?

He shook the thought away.

It would do him no good to dwell on these things. And if he had done nothing? It might be him, lifeless and gone on the canal bottom.

He was in no hurry to rise. He felt a calmness that had eluded him for months. Guilt too, yes, but also a quiet satisfaction that he had survived. He lay back down, pulling the blanket back over him.

His breath became steady and deep, exhaling slowly before taking the next lungful.

He allowed his mind to wander. To a time that made him feel part of something very special. Maybe even worth killing for.

As his pulse slowed further, he recalled a damp November day nine years ago. One of his most memorable and enjoyable with Uberto and his family.

The day had started inauspiciously enough, waiting under the shallow porticos of the Doge's Palace, a chill seeping into his bones.

Rain-laden gusts from the direction of San Giorgio found him, no matter how much he tried to use the columns for protection.

Many others had taken similar cover. The weather had been poor for days. The old Doge's burial ceremony would be a sorry affair if this continued.

Uberto, attending the Great Council meeting inside the Palace, had been insistent that Malin should spend the rest of the day with him. It was an easy invitation to accept. Time spent with his partner had evolved over the years into a unique pleasure. Each visit seemed to embed him deeper into his new life in the city, and into the heart of Uberto's family.

He heard them before he saw them.

Two of the outer doors swung in, releasing the sound of a thousand voices, liberated after hours in the main Palace chamber. The men themselves flowed like water through a breached dam along the narrow passageways. The earliest to escape had little choice but to continue their passage out beyond the porticos and into the driving rain, their violet caps doing little to shield them from the elements. After sitting for so many hours, it was a wonder that no stiff-legged noble fell underfoot. Most of the men wore black, in deference to the loss of their head of government.

Time passed, the flow of men from the Council chamber abated, yet there was still no sign of Uberto.

Malin moved toward and then through the nearest door, and into the gloomy, high-ceilinged entrance hall.

To his left, the huge chamber doors remained wide open. A warm glow of massed candlelight spilled through from within. He moved forward once more, registering the faint then increasingly powerful musk of recent male assembly.

Ten benches, each running the length of the hall, filled the floor of the enormous room. Two additional rows of chairs surrounded the permanent seating, lining three of the four walls. To his right, a raised dais boasted a large canopied throne, itself flanked by a further number of benches. Looking up, he saw the frieze running above head height around the room. Each scene within it appeared unique, its figures animated by the flickering candles not yet extinguished by the stewards.

He moved fully inside the huge space and, looking around the room, saw Uberto standing in one of several small groups of men.

Malin stepped back to stand just inside the main door, content to soak up the atmosphere. He watched his friend, noting how, when listening to others, he leaned slightly forward, his head tilted to one side. The way he moved his hands to emphasise his argument.

The group eventually dispersed, but Uberto sat down at the nearest bench, clearly unready to leave. Malin hesitated, then approached him, unsure if his interruption would be welcome. Uberto looked up, and a broad smile appeared on his face.

His embrace was intense.

146

"Ah, Malin. Of course. I am so sorry our business here has taken so long. Here. Sit." Malin looked around, checking on the location of the Ducal stewards. Uberto's smile widened further. "Oh, don't worry about them. I have every right to talk to my friends."

The energy coming from Uberto was new. His eyes shone, and his whole body seemed to emanate vibrancy and power.

The transformation in his friend, standing in this place, was undeniable.

"So this is where you disappear to every week."

Uberto laughed. "More like every day at the moment, my friend."

He gestured around the room. "Built for four hundred at most. There must have been at least three times that number here today. The seats become more crowded each day, and yet the amount of air available in here remains the same. No. I take that back. The amount of unused air dwindles each day. More speeches, more baying of agreement or objection. It's a wonder more haven't fainted in the crush." He pointed to the doorway at the far end of the room, to the right of the dais. "They took two away in the last hour today." He laughed gently. "I suspect that's just the beginning. More will arrive from the provinces tomorrow, once they've got wind of events."

Knowledge of the death of Doge Francesco Dandolo continued to spread across the Adriatic. The process to confirm his replacement had been invoked, pressing down on the pulse of government to the point where no other business was possible. For the last four days, at the instruction of the Doge's Court, all resident members of the Council had attended the designated emergency sessions. Each day, more nobles arrived from outposts of the Republic, replacing their increasingly bewildered deputies.

"You'd think that we would know what we're doing by now.

But every minor rule is being followed to the letter. Even when the rule itself is so vague that ten men could interpret it ten different ways."

Uberto no longer questioned his place here. Since his nomination four years earlier, he had moved from grateful recruit to confident, well-spoken and, by all accounts, influential member of the *Consiglio Maggior*.

"And the chaos this afternoon? You should have seen the look on Grimani's face when the nine called my name as one of the forty-five. He was not happy. Even though his turn will come when it matters."

Lucia had explained the process to him when he was last at the De Segna home. The electoral system, once triggered by the *signoria* of the Minor Council, was designed, over a long series of votes and drawing of lots, to reduce the possibility of collusion or favouritism.

"Thirty nobles are selected by lot, and their number is further reduced to nine by a second draw of names. These nine then have the honour of voting for forty colleagues. Twelve of these that survive the next draw of lots are then asked to select a new twenty-five names. Of these, nine nominate forty-five other nobles. After one more draw of lots, the eleven that remain are asked to choose the final forty-one men who will then finally cast their vote for the new Doge." Lucia had paused, looking up through her dark locks with the smirk that always drove him crazy. "Simple, really. Do you want me to repeat it?"

Clearing his throat, Malin had chosen to ignore the light-hearted challenge. "And this is supposed to *reduce* the chances of a tainted election?"

Back in the chamber, Malin could not hide his excitement. "So, Uberto, are you telling me you've been nominated to cast a vote for Dandolo's successor?"

"Ah, no, I'm afraid not. My name failed to come out in

the final drawing of lots. My colleagues will have the honour tomorrow of putting forward the final forty-one."

Malin blushed at his error. He should have listened to Lucia more closely.

Uberto put his hand on Malin's shoulder. "My dear friend. Do not look so distraught. Do you see me looking unhappy with the turn of events today? Look. Four years ago, I had given up any hope of being part of this great organisation. The door to entry was not just closed, it was bolted and sealed to all but the most exceptional cases. They saw fit to allow me to become part of their number, and I have striven to prove myself worthy of their trust. This week has been an extraordinary one. The Da Segna name has just been woven into the history of this great city."

There were tears in Uberto's eyes. "My boy, all is good. I have been recognised, and can now look forward to the coming division of roles when the new Doge takes his seat."

Two hours later, Malin sat with Uberto's family, having enjoyed their evening meal together.

All three Da Segna women were formally dressed. Malin had urged them several times in the past to relax their compliance with the sumptuary laws when he was the only visitor present, but recognised that after years waiting to enter the ranks of the privileged, the new protocols meant a great deal to them.

Across from him, Donata, ever the patient mother, continued to offer advice to her youngest daughter.

"So you see, Collette, it really is important that we all respect the seniority of the Soranzos. We must show deference to their long history of wealth and influence, even if it means agreeing with some of their more, shall we say, *questionable* views."

"But Mother." The young woman's voice hit the pitch most designed to set Malin's nerves a-jangle. "You tell us repeatedly that truth and honesty are virtues we must always seek to display, yet here you are encouraging me to dissemble. I'm sure I wasn't as rude as you suggest."

Donata paused, sighing quietly. He had no idea how the woman managed to keep her calm.

Lucia, meanwhile, continued to probe her father on the day's events.

"So how did the chamber react when your name was called?" Her hazel-green eyes flashed with their customary energy, leaning forward in her chair, eager to understand everything. "Did you learn anything about how you are seen?"

"Hah. If you mean, was their applause as sincere and genuine as that offered to all other nominees? Then I suppose they shared in my good fortune just as they shared in that of the others." His smile was understated, but Malin could tell that Uberto's elation remained undiluted.

"I understand. But to have been raised enough to be included in the final forty-five. That must have surprised a few of the more established houses."

"Well, yes. I suppose none of the other newcomers were much more than onlookers. I've done my best to build friendships. In the way you and Mother have urged."

"It is of course to your credit, Father. I only hope that when the new Doge is announced, no one in the chamber feels passed over. Or slighted."

"Well, if there was any slighting, it wasn't done by me."

"Hmm." Lucia's face tightened a little. "You know that's not the point. Some will assume that you have either been lobbying on your own behalf, or have been active in dissuading them from voting in line with time-honoured loyalties. Some people are greatly skilled in feeling slights where they do not exist."

Malin was captivated by this woman's mind. Her ability to find the essence of a situation. And how she simultaneously offered counsel to her father *and* a piercing critique of her sister's behaviour mere feet away.

Malin cleared his throat. "So, Uberto. Who will be proposed for Doge tomorrow?"

Lucia was unwilling to let the subject pass unresolved.

"No, wait. Father. Please. At least acknowledge that you may have given offence by playing your part. If there are those who love you less because of today, it would be wise to know who they are."

"Really Lucia. I have been mixing with these men for years. The ebb and flow of loyalties are not aberrations to be wary of on rare or important occasions. The effectiveness of the chamber would disappear overnight if everyone behaved in the honourable, virtuous manner you would have us all observe."

He looked across the table to Malin. "Every day in that place is like negotiating the most complex trade, with any number of affiliates or partners, each as likely as the next to be acting on behalf of some other undeclared party. I've learned to keep my wits about me, but continue to trust that the worst excesses of human nature will not visit me, openly or otherwise." He turned back to his daughter. "Please relax, my dear."

Lucia paused to consider his words. "I only worry that your success, which indeed it is, gives no cause for others to think ill of you."

"Well, I'm sure there will be some who would rather their name was called above my own. But this is simply, I hope, a sign that I am becoming accepted as a newcomer. I am sure all will rally behind the new Doge."

"As they should." Lucia's exclamation suggested he had hit a nerve. Donata and Collette stared at her, and the unexpected pitch of her voice. "It is the duty of the powerful to lead by example, and of those subordinate to respond with loyalty and honour." She showed no sign of allowing the conversation to move on, and her blush betrayed a level of passion that Malin had rarely seen.

The silence extended slightly beyond comfort.

Lucia brought her hands together in front of her on the table. "So, Father, regarding Malin's question. Who do you believe will win the vote tomorrow?"

Sensing the argument had moved on at last, Uberto regained his previous energy, shrugged and reached for his goblet. "Well, Dandolo's family and their friends seem keen to keep the position within their family. Andrea is a stunning, if young, candidate. No disrespect, Malin, but I'm not sure if the jump up from Saint Mark's Basilica to the head of the Republic is one that can be made by many thirty-three-year-olds." He glimpsed across at Lucia, and quickly continued. "Although great things have been achieved by young, energetic men, of course. He has a remarkable wit, and an even more remarkable grasp of the intricacies of law, by all accounts. The modernisation of Saint Mark's is little short of magnificent."

Lucia leaned forward once more. "So who else might prevail?"

"Well, believe it or not, our old friend Bartolemeo, the *podesta* of Ragusa, is being discussed. Your uncles and cousins back in Ragusa have very little good to say about him. As I understand it, he built a reputation for frivolous and lavish expense. But he has served us well as the prosecutor, putting the kind of theoretical knowledge that Dandolo possesses into practice in the courts for many years. That said, it's hard to imagine that nominating a man to any role, when he is already over ten years older than his dead predecessor, is a good way to build any stability."

He winked at Malin, and looked down the table to Donata, a glint of mischief in his eye as he raised his voice to address the whole table. "It's quite something for Bartolemeo to survive three wives, though. I'm still not sure if I'll outlive my first. Or if she'll allow it."

★

Malin's thoughts were pulled back into his room by the sound of Symon knocking on his door again.

"Malin, open up. I have a man here who needs to see you."

"I wish to see no one today, Symon. Please leave me alone." He would be happy simply to lie back in his bed, and idle the day away.

The door opened. "I'm serious, Malin. I have arranged for a physic to attend you. Allow him in."

Before he had a chance to argue further, Symon stepped aside and waved in the priest.

"This is Benasuto Penzini. He routinely attends the Patriarch, and has a fine reputation for matters of medical regimen. He will take a look at your injury."

Too shocked to object, Malin watched as the priest approached. His manner was a curious mixture of humility and self-confidence.

"Signor. I wish only to help. Your friend here offered to make a generous contribution to the coffers of San Lorenzo, if I were to offer my help in the matter of your wounds."

Malin lacked the will to resist, and submitted himself to the indignity and occasional discomfort of the priest's ministrations. First, the man removed the bandage applied by Symon the previous night. Malin almost swooned at the release of pressure and the immediate throbbing in his injured hand.

The cut appeared far worse in daylight.

The priest cleaned the wound, drying it gently with clean cloths he carried in a large canvas bag. At his request, Symon returned downstairs to bring more clean bandages. Penzini

153

went into his bag once more, and pulled out a large tied clout. Inside was a thick mass of foul-smelling paste.

He spoke to Malin in a calm, quiet voice, glancing up at Symon to include him in his explanation. "This might seem a little unusual, but I have had some success in healing wounds with this. While we are forbidden to read Vilanova's religious writings, his *Breviarium Practicae* is most clear on its effectiveness."

He applied the paste directly into the cut on Malin's hand. The pain was immediate, and Malin flinched instinctively, banishing his earlier malaise.

When the priest had finished, he turned to Symon and took the bandages from him.

"Ah, yes, these will be very good." He wound them around Malin's hand and lower arm. "I will leave you the rest of the paste. Please keep it cool and damp. You should remove the old poultice every two days, and replace it with the same amount of salve until it is gone. This should ensure that the flesh heals well, and that you will avoid fever."

Without any further conversation the priest rose, walked back out to the landing, and down the stairs. The two remaining men exchanged glances, and then Symon turned to catch up with the departing priest.

Malin sat back on the edge of the bed.

He would get dressed, and join Symon downstairs. They still had much to discuss.

Not least, the question of how that damned priest apothecary had magically appeared.

*

Symon had cleared his day to be with his friend.

Fresh from his confessions of the previous night, Malin held nothing back regarding his plans. "I should postpone some meetings today, just to get my thoughts straight. Could you arrange for five messengers to be here before the middle of the afternoon?"

In response to Symon's questions about the likelihood of further attacks, Malin was less forthcoming.

"It's hard to say. If they wished it, The Ten would already have me in custody. Last night felt more like a test. Why send one person to kill me when they have hundreds at their disposal? Perhaps they wanted to keep it discreet. Kill me quietly, with little fuss, and allow others under their eye to continue to implicate themselves. Either way, unless we hear of further assaults or arrests, I think it wise to simply continue. I just need to calm my thoughts."

Symon noted how Malin referred to "we", but said nothing. From the way Malin took the weight of his left hand in his right, he wondered if the assertion that nothing had changed was to be trusted.

An increasingly large pile of letters built throughout the day on the corner of Malin's desk. In each, Malin again advocated caution, but with further encouragement to hasten readiness.

His most challenging letter was for Libusch.

What should he instruct the man to do? Any orders could only be interpreted in conjunction with their situation on the ground, and Bourchier's last update on the mercenary's progress had been vague. He wasn't even sure where to send it. Knowing his forces were "travelling as expected" offered little insight into his current location.

He explained his dilemma to Symon, whose response was typically blunt. "Do you know what you want to happen? Enough to inform others of their part? This man Libusch may already have detailed instructions that match your requirements exactly. Or, equally possibly, hold the seeds of your failure."

Malin looked across at his friend. "That's just it. I could end up interfering in something that is already playing out perfectly, and bring the whole thing crashing down."

"So why not just wait for him to contact you, and then meet him to make the final arrangements? You don't have to react this way."

Malin's quill dropped to the desk.

Symon averted his eyes. He had said too much.

"You're right, Symon. And I'm sorry for putting you in this position. You asked for none of this. But you have no idea how good it feels to be able to talk about this with you. I know I have burdened you greatly with this knowledge. Put you in the same danger as myself. And yet. And yet I am so happy." He wiped his eyes. "I'm not making sense, I know."

He cleared his throat. "It is this that I have missed. For two years, I have missed the chance to examine each problem with you. Turn it this way and that. Thank you, my friend. Yes, I am sorry. But I am glad too. Do you understand?"

Symon nodded. He made to speak, but stopped himself, taking two deep breaths instead. "I understand. I hope we can find our way through this together. I know we will. But promise me one thing, if you can. Do not carry any more of this on your own. It was never our way."

After the last messenger had left, Symon disappeared into the kitchen. On his return, he carried two plates of the finest-looking grilled tench Malin believed he had ever seen.

★

His stomach full, and every muscle in his body aching, Malin took refuge by the well-set fireplace with Jerold's manuscript. He placed it on a low side table, vowing to suspend all thought of what awaited him the following day for a few hours. Taking

156

care not to knock his injured hand, he turned over the hard board protecting the pages beneath.

He knew nothing of Duns Scotus himself, but had previously obtained and read the four books of Lombard's *Sentences* before passing it on to Jerold. The old priest had probably spent many hours poring over it, seeking any apparent gap or contradiction in the man's arguments. The monks at Whitby, in keeping with their agreement to send only topical or controversial texts, had sent this work expanding on, and in some cases arguing against the *Sentences*. The manuscript took the form of several lectures, delivered by Duns Scotus in Oxford and Paris.

He read of the Trinity, and of how God's purpose could be observed or understood through worldly experience, becoming absorbed in the arguments and logic presented. The mysteries of how to read signs of God's plan.

As the room grew warmer, he found himself pondering how he had come to be sitting in his Venetian home, thousands of miles from England, nursing a bruised and bandaged body, while trying to think of a path for himself and his friends that would allow them to safely achieve their goals.

He closed the manuscript and sat back in the chair.

As he rested his eyes, he thought back to a day, still considering himself barely out of his teens, when Elyas invited him to meet two men in a side room of the Antwerp Kontor.

Six years had passed since Elyas had sailed out of Lynn with a confused and frightened fifteen-year-old boy. In those same six years, under the merchant's firm but caring protection, Malin had become one of the most promising young traders in the Low Countries.

At the age of twenty-two, he had moved out from Elyas' house on Wolstraat to a modest house of his own, just a few minutes' walk along the Jordaenskaai from the imposing Hanse building. He had completed trades along the entire western seaboard, from the Baltic in the far north, down to the ports of Catalonia in the south.

He was standing with Konrad, his own young apprentice, just beyond the entrance to the main boardroom, when Elyas found him.

"Malin, I need you to come with me. There are some people I would like you to meet."

Elyas opened the door and gestured him to enter. When the door closed, Elyas had remained in the corridor outside.

Two men stood to greet him.

The tallest of the two, a dark-haired, brightly dressed man, was the first to speak. His accent was thick and full, each word pronounced carefully.

"Herr Le Cordier, thank you for seeing us. My name is Accardi, and this is my colleague De Smet. We would like to talk to you about a matter of some importance."

The second man ran his hands over his smooth scalp. Malin recognised him for a local as soon as he opened his mouth. "Le Cordier, I have been working with members of the Antwerp ruling council for some time now. We wish to find ways to strengthen our diplomatic ties in the Mediterranean, and more widely into the Adriatic."

He looked a little nervously at Accardi, as if confirming his right to speak. "We are delighted with the way the city is developing, but feel that we must take additional steps to, shall we say, compete with our friends in Bruges. We feel there are a number of different and frankly, more *directed* actions we can and should take now. As a consequence, we are building a small but talented group of likeminded men who can use and if needed extend their trading practices to everyone's mutual benefit."

Accardi stepped in.

"We have noted your progress over the last two years in particular, in the quality of your deal-making. We believe that it is precisely men such as yourself, Herr Le Cordier, that can be of great help in our cause. Your sponsor, Scepene, has given us a clear sense of your talents and potential."

Malin felt the heat rising up his face. What had Elyas told them?

"I think I understand your aims, gentlemen. And I acknowledge any kind words from Elyas, but I'm not sure what to say. What services do you require of me?"

De Smet continued. "We know pretty much everything of your business from your declarations to the Hanse. No, please, there is nothing to concern yourself in this. We see how comfortable you are with entering new markets. And how you rapidly become a significant and trusted party in each of them. What is most impressive, in our view, is your record in non-Hanse ports or cities. In places where you are less able to operate under their protective blanket. It is rare for one so young to so quickly wean themselves off their domestic heritage, and embrace the wider opportunities that trading from the mainland represents."

Malin swallowed hard. He felt like a fly under a glass.

"What we are proposing, sire, is that we would like to work with you to move into a number of the key markets east of Genoa, and in doing so, increase our influence and standing with the governments of the region. We would of course ensure that such actions bring with them a guarantee of personal success that might otherwise take many more years to achieve. We would like to work with you to our mutual advantage. If God wills it, Antwerp can gain greatly, and your business dealings will see a considerable and permanent expansion. Advances that will also, incidentally, reflect much credit back on your sponsor, and this Kontor."

A log must have fallen in the grate, rousing him from his slumber.

Inspecting his bandages to ensure they would remain in place overnight, he picked up the manuscript, thoughts of God's unknown purpose still circling in his mind.

As he climbed the stairs to bed, his many bruises reminded him of their presence.

Chapter 14

Friday 8th February 1348

Day 13 of the Quarant

Malin stood out of the breeze in the doorway of The Stone Steps, a tavern on the eastern side of the Campo San Polo. He was a little early for his meeting with Uberto, but was happy to steal a few moments for himself.

His morning had been one long parade of discussions with minor officials and guild members. Time seemed to pass slower than usual, with each movement offering a sharp reminder of his bruised body and limbs.

He had taken Bourchier's earlier advice, and decided to meet as regularly with each of them as possible. The facade of summer trading, and the fate of his quarantined cargo on the Lido provided an effective mask for their real business.

Although none of the men had said it, all seemed to gain in confidence when being told of their importance to the scheme, and that each of their needs were taken seriously.

They only shared names of fellow conspirators when it was

unavoidable. He, Uberto and Bourchier had constantly striven to achieve the right balance between communicating the latest decisions or requirements, and the potential damage that might come if any one of them were compromised.

In a city of a hundred thousand souls, the number of plotters was tiny. Yet together, they represented all aspects of Venetian life.

All, that was, except for the clergy. The generally agreed view was that the priesthood and their masters would acquiesce in any outcome that left their power and position intact.

Citizens of the Republic had good reason to doubt their integrity, or place little value on their arguments. Forty years ago, the Church had turned on them, angry at the state's decision to oppose Papal forces at Ferrara. Their measures were shocking. City-wide excommunication. Withdrawal of the sacrament. Sanctions on Venetians abroad, including impounding of wealth, imprisonment, and in some cases, execution. When Pope Clement's corpse was reputedly struck by lightning five years after his death, many citizens of Venice expressed a tangible sense of satisfaction.

Still, Malin made a note to re-open this decision with Uberto over lunch. They could not afford to misjudge such a large constituency.

Leaning against the tavern entrance, Malin inspected his bandaged hand. Applying a new layer of paste under fresh bandages had been painful, but the wound had shown no sign of deterioration. Each occasional throb in his arm was a reminder of the need for care, but he was relieved that his right hand had escaped serious injury.

No one had come to the house to question him about the events of that night. He had evaded discovery. Another stroke of luck.

He reflected on the resolution made overnight. That he'd written in his journal on waking.

To approach each day with the attitude that every moment that passed without capture was a moment closer to the end of his mission.

He had also decided to reduce the number of journeys he made across the city each day, and in doing so, reduce his exposure to any eyes marking him out from the crowd. And he needed to rebuild his strength after his attack. Constantly moving had made him feel busy. Effective. But it could easily become a substitute for meaningful progress. He would seek to achieve more by doing a little less.

His mind set, he proposed meetings with a number of conspirators in a single location, but with a short time between each one.

He would learn if it was the right decision soon enough.

As yet, disaster had kept away. No cloaked agents of The Ten rushed through the Rialto stalls to converge on him and any one of his several visitors. No one dragged him away for interrogation or worse.

Yet he still felt watched, wandering and talking in hushed tones amongst the stalls and customers of the busy market.

By the completion of his fourth discussion, with a middle-ranking member of the *Signori di Notti* from Cannaregio, his growing sense of vulnerability was palpable and impossible to ignore.

Moments after wishing the man farewell, his gorge rising and his legs failing, he collapsed onto a bench at the edge of the market. Between each of several gulps of gentian, he cast his eyes around him, convinced the whole of Venice knew his thoughts. His journey across the bridge to San Polo had been an uncomfortable one.

Stepping aside from the doorway to allow two new customers to enter the tavern, he wondered how Symon was faring at the offices of the *Extraordinarri*.

Bourchier's absence had been a double blow. In addition to collecting and sharing information on the activities of their own number and their opponents, he was also the distributor of money needed to fund preparations. His earlier warnings about unusual financial dealings still rang in Malin's ears, yet they needed a way to address the shortfall.

Symon suggested seeking a partial short-term repayment of loans made to the government. In Malin's absence, he had already begun negotiations with the owner of a *panzone*, a medium-sized vessel that could sail soon after the return of the spring *mudae*. The ship would carry a number of cargoes through the Bosphorus to the Black Sea port of Sinope, and return with a hold full of cane sugar from Candia. His request for funds could be explained by their need to cover the costs of their next trading venture.

The idea was a good one. Symon, never one to delay, had left the house that morning to put his idea into motion.

Malin looked up from the doorway just in time to see Uberto crossing the remaining steps of the square.

"Here he stands! The man with the world in the palm of his hand." Uberto embraced him as though they had not seen each other for years. "Come, let us spend one or two of Dandolo's new ducats on the enviable charms of this fine establishment."

Malin was helpless in front of the man's good humour. They moved into the deep-set room of the tavern, seeking a table away from the windows. A powerful aroma of boiled vegetables, laced with a heavier, underpinning odour of damp rot hung in the air.

"Not the best place in the city, but close to home, and busy enough for us to talk." Uberto leaned over to his friend. "I doubt that anyone comes here for the quality of the food, but I've been on my feet since dawn, and am ready to eat almost anything put before me. I'll order for two."

Malin sat down behind at the table. He looked across at his friend, doing his best to ignore the stains covering much of the surface in front of him. Uberto's conversation with the landlord possessed a confidence that he, a mere ten years resident in the city, was still far from mastering.

Uberto returned with the wine. "I don't know if it's the exercise or the possibilities ahead, but my appetite has grown by the week. Here, let's do what we can to pass the time as affably as friends can. Business is business, but we can still enjoy ourselves. What have you done to your hand?"

A while later, having cleared what they could from two plates of barely edible pork, their conversation turned more serious.

Uberto had spent part of the morning with Sclavo at the Arsenale. "It's fair to conclude that tensions are mounting. Sclavo works hard to appear tough and assertive, but I can sense his fear. I hope no one else sees through him as easily. He has one genuine concern, however, and I need you to help provide the answer."

Most construction materials were supplied to the shipyard through well-established merchants. Disruption from the earthquake was already a daily challenge for the clerks in Sclavo's office. The Arsenale warehouses held just three months' stocks of building materials, and levels of replacement supplies arriving through the Arsenale gates had dropped by a third in the last two weeks. Any further disruption arising from changing faces on the Council, and other important positions within the state could further jeopardise the steady flow of timber and iron.

"So, my friend, in order to keep my son on just the right side of sanity, we need to show him how we will keep his workforce busy after the coup."

Malin saw it clearly. Sclavo was right to worry. The possibility of thousands of unemployed men wandering the streets of Venice with nothing better to do than hunt down those responsible for their newly inflicted poverty would be disastrous. "We cannot simply tell him to trust us. The shift from old to new must be rapid and smooth. Those of our friends who will be elevated to new positions must be aware of their obligation to maintain the integrity of existing supply arrangements, and to offer short-term help to those merchants who have been hit hardest in the quake. Could you visit these men, and make them understand? Gain their commitment? Without it, you cannot offer Sclavo any meaningful assurance. We need that assurance ourselves."

Uberto paused to consider the implications. "I'm not sure how some will take to the idea of gaining high office but still doing what they are told. But I can speak with them."

"And once it's done, you can advise Sclavo that work schedules and orders will remain unchanged. He should assure his *protomaestri* that this is the case, and that the *Arsenaleotti* will receive special consideration once the dust has settled. It is unlikely that they will be answering to the existing *patroni* for much longer. That should please them."

Their mood had become more serious, but a third flagon would do no harm.

Malin toasted his friend, drinking deeply.

"Uberto, now that we can put Sclavo's mind at ease, I wonder if you could do the same for me. I remain a little unsure of how the clergy will react to our changes. And there are significantly more of them than there are of us."

The Venetian priesthood was one of Uberto's favourite subjects. For every caring and sensitive cleric he could name, he would cite three others that exhibited at least three of the deadly sins.

He grunted instinctively. "As always, they react well to any suggestion that their power and influence will be maintained or

166

increased. If they perceive neither of these will happen, expect a letter to be sent from the Patriarch to the chaste and sinless halls of Avignon. I'm sure Clement will side with anyone who proffers the right amount of wealth, or confirms that they have no new argument with the French."

"But are we right to spend so little time on them? We have none of them in our number."

"I don't think they will cause any trouble. Although it would be worth suggesting a further *obligation* to our friends. That they are ready to assure the Church that they will still enjoy generous donations, even if they have new patrons to thank."

Neither of them appeared to have anything else pressing to discuss, but neither of them made any move to leave. The diluted wine played a part, no doubt, yet Malin had no desire to bring his time with his friend to an early end.

Many of the faces changed around them throughout the afternoon, but the tavern remained full. A few of the stallholders from the *campo* had finished for the day, and enjoyed a loud but light-hearted argument about one of their missing number, each man present expressing a view on the absent man's personal hygiene and skills in the art of love.

"So tell me, Uberto. Really. What do you see yourself doing when all this is over? When we can all go back to our own lives."

Uberto swirled the thin liquid around the rim of his goblet. "Ah, my friend. Is that even possible?" His eyes flicked around the room, keen to confirm their continued freedom from eavesdroppers.

Malin was quick to reassure him. "Do not fear. No one can hear us. And all they see is an old man and his handsome apprentice telling each other the way the world should be."

Uberto laughed. "Very funny. No, I just wanted to make sure Donata hasn't crept into the place, to witness my usual foolishness."

Malin could hardly imagine a less likely scenario.

"Anyway, my friend. I have been asking myself the same question for months now. When we started out on this *campaign*, I thought I knew. I really thought I did. I just wanted to regain the recognition of my peers, and show them it is as right now as it was then to trust me in matters that define and promote this great city." He sat up a little straighter in his chair. "To be able to hold my head up high once more, and feel that what I want to offer will be graciously accepted.

"I have no desire to progress further than the Great Council. I have no mind to wrap around the niceties of the law, however much I seek to stay on its good side. And in matters pecuniary..." He slurred the word, the wine weaving its influence. "In matters *pecuniary*, I have no interest in ducats and pounds, and the gaining of vast sums. What interests me most, has *always* interested me most, is what I can do with it. How I can help my family, my friends, *and my business partners*," he pointed at Malin, "feel safer in the world. Malin, ignore all the petty politics. All the small-minded aggressions and resentments. What you'll see, if you do, is a city perfectly set up to enable this feeling to spread to every one of its citizens. Not just to those whose grandfathers happened to be in a position of power fifty years ago.

"I can do things for this place, Malin. Things that will make our achievements today feel miserly and small. Once, I wanted to be the sole *Savii ai Ordini*. To be the one to specify which convoys go where. But not now. Now? I want to tear that all down. Kill the Council's stranglehold. Allow men, men who create new trade from nothing, to move us fully into the East. Let *them* find new ways to stimulate commerce with the Orient. Let *them* carve out a place for us in the *Oltremare*. Stand up against the jealous Genoese, the greed and avarice of Florence. The backward, clinging grip of the Church."

He sat back, staring off into the middle distance. When he spoke again, his calm had returned.

"And I want to work beside you to do all this, my friend. You and I. I know we can do this."

For the second time in as many days, Malin was speechless.

"Thank you, Uberto. Thank you. We will return here, the two of us, in a few weeks' time, and we will speak again of this moment."

One more flagon, and he would need to ask Tusco to arrange for his journey back to Castello.

Chapter 15

Saturday 9th February 1348

Day 14 of the Quarant

Saturday again.

Two weeks since completing his journey up the Adriatic coast and setting eyes on the damaged city.

Malin considered events since his return. Many things were in the sort of shape he could have only dreamed of when he left Southampton.

But it was Bourchier that dominated his thoughts.

He had held every small detail. He was the one that would best judge the precise moment when they would act.

And he was gone.

The Ten had him, and were unlikely to let him go.

Malin had heard nothing of his friend's fate since Soranzo broke the news four days ago.

He feared the worst. Making an enemy of The Ten made you an enemy of the state. And such enemies rarely lasted long.

At some level, Malin was unsure if the man's release,

posthumous or otherwise, would augur well or badly for their cause. Would Bourchier's death imply that The Ten knew everything? Or simply that his colleague for the last two years had taken all his secrets to the grave.

He had made two decisions overnight.

He would no longer squander his energies trying to second-guess what Bourchier's fate might be, or what it might mean. Despite how hard that would be. And within the constraints of his current knowledge, he would step in and execute those tasks he thought the agent would have done.

If he did not take his place, no one would. Only Soranzo, Malin and Symon knew the Englishman was missing.

Before leaving the house, he spoke at length with Symon. They agreed the previous evening that they would seek to share the latest information on their actions with each other every morning, and talk over any future steps they might need to take. There was no longer any question about Symon's involvement.

First, they discussed Malin's meetings the previous day, although Malin made little reference to his afternoon drinking with Uberto.

Symon wanted to know how Malin's wound was healing.

"I won't be rowing any lighters out into the Lagoon quite yet, but I might soon be able to button my tunic."

"And how many years has it been since you did any rowing of any kind *anyway*. I've never seen you do anything more than pass a coin or a grateful glance at any oarsman."

Malin laughed. "True. Yet in any case, the pain is manageable. I look forward to the moment when it becomes the source of the devil's itch."

Symon changed the subject. "Do you mind if I write the key points of our conversations down, Malin? I have no desire to create evidence against us, but I'm finding it hard to keep

171

all this new detail straight in my head. I don't want to forget something, or remember it wrongly."

Malin was unsure if the idea was a good one. "Perhaps, if you need to, just record the things you have to do, and then destroy the paper when you have done them. In a month's time, none of this will matter, and the less of it you remember then, the better."

Quill and paper in hand, Symon confirmed that they could expect to receive most of their loan money before the end of the following week. Malin greeted the news with a slow nod, and patted his friend on the shoulder. "Very good, Symon. Very good. At least we'll be able to offer funds without Bourchier being around."

Symon raised his quill, as if a thought had just struck him.

"Malin, I know you want to keep Bourchier's disappearance secret for now. But what I don't understand is exactly who amongst your number knows what. You tell me this alliance has grown over nearly two years, and I imagine you've had to be careful about how much you share with each of them. But I confess, I feel completely ignorant of how each man has been involved, and what it is safe to speak with them about. Can you help me understand? I think I could be so much more useful knowing the details."

Malin sat with Symon for the next hour, listing the name of each man known to have a role in the conspiracy, and, as far as he could, indicating what they knew, what they had been tasked with, and any outstanding difficulties or doubts concerning them. He did his best to mask any lack of current knowledge regarding each participant's readiness or challenges. The last thing Symon needed was any suggestion that the man stepping in to fill the gap left by Bourchier was uncertain, or just plain ignorant of how things stood.

By the time Malin went to look for his coat, Symon's earlier smile had been replaced by the concerned look of a man with too much on his mind.

They exchanged farewells from opposite ends of the hallway. Malin stepped out into the bright mid-morning with an overwhelming sense of relief that his friend was now entirely with him. And with the usual flutters in his stomach he always had, knowing that Lucia awaited him on the other side of the city.

★

Malin had barely set foot on the internal patio at Calle Donzella before Lucia descended from the terrace and whisked him back out onto the street.

Short of breath from his walk from the Canal, he could barely voice his greeting to the veiled woman.

"Good day, Lucia. I hope I find you well. Judging by your pace, I can only believe that you slept most soundly last night."

"Stop that at once." Her chiding lacked any sign of rancour. "We have much to do, and I didn't want you to waste my time listening to you talking to Mother. Come, this way."

They walked briskly, Lucia's arm laced though his own. The scent of fresh bread reached them briefly from a number of the bakeries lining the street, their doors open to entice customers.

Malin could no longer contain his curiosity. "Forgive me, Lucia, but I've reached that moment when to not ask of our destination or purpose could be construed as foolish trust. Or perhaps, in the eyes of some, gross indifference. Could you at least give me some sense of where we are headed?"

Her eyes, despite the veil, flashed a dazzle of green and brown.

She turned to him without breaking stride, her arm still

driving him on. "It will do you good to simply do as I say. You may learn something, and in the learning, do some good."

They emerged into a wider part of the street, the pale winter sun finally able to reach them after the cold, narrow streets. Lucia steered him to the right, into the small but busy square.

Lucia slowed. "We're here."

They stood next to a heavy cylindrical *vera da pozzo*. Its sides lacked the ornate decoration of other wells in the city, but its white stone, mounted on a further stepped structure, lent the square a modest, understated elegance.

Lucia stepped forward and ran the palm of her hand along the smooth stone face. She gestured to Malin to do the same.

"I wonder if you've ever had reason to consider the genius on which our city rests." Malin had the sense not to offer an answer, amused to see where Lucia was headed. "The marvel of a steady and generous supply of fresh water that slakes the city's thirst, while we sit on these unnatural islands, surrounded by the salty marsh Lagoon."

Malin was not to be easily outdone. "I believe you are about to offer a revelation regarding their use? Please, allow me to brace myself before you continue."

"Stop it. This is serious. It's the earthquake."

"What about it?"

"Father mentioned it last evening. Although I have to say he was fairly cup-shotten when he said it. He'd heard that one of the wells on the other side of the Canal had been closed. Its contents had turned to salt water after the quake. One of his merchant friends has offered to fund the work of pulling up the pavement and opening the cistern to see what damage has been caused.

"That led me to wonder. If anything similar might have happened in San Polo. There must be over three dozen wells in the *sestiere*, and it wouldn't take many of them to fail for it to cause real hardship. I thought I'd make my way through the district and investigate, if only to put my mind at rest."

She looked into Malin's eyes. "I would do this on my own, but I fear that some of the priests will look at me as though I have no right to even speak of my concerns. Let alone ask them to conduct an examination. Could you help me?"

Responsibility for ensuring that no one abused the right to free, clean water across the city was assigned to members of the clergy. Their tasks included the locking, unlocking and storage of the well lid, and ensuring the fabric of that part of the well above the surface was respected. For their service, they could request donations from wealthy families, who could see the well decorated in their coat of arms. Any remaining funds were welcomed as a donation for use within the church itself.

Lucia's intellect and compassion were well known to him. Yet even Malin was taken aback by her willingness to consider such a venture. Particularly given how her family had been so openly disrespected in the past.

"Of course I will."

He might have imagined it, but he thought he saw her eyes softening. Just for a moment.

"Then let's start right now."

She turned and walked across the square, to the raised entrance of the church of Sant'Aponal. "If anyone has had any problems with the water here, the priests should know."

Malin caught up with her, and together they climbed the steps and entered the high-ceilinged vestibule.

Over the following three hours, they visited the custodians of four more wells in the area. Their welcomes were not always warm, and in two cases, Lucia's fears that no woman would be taken seriously had caused Malin to step in on her behalf.

In one case, an early assessment of quake damage had

already been conducted, but for the remaining three, they proposed that an inspection should be completed.

Lucia offered her father's name as benefactor, but on the final occasion, Malin himself volunteered the necessary funds.

When the shadows of late afternoon began to creep across the southernmost boundaries of the *sestiere*, they began their walk home, just finding time to confirm the location of the three wells to the west of the Campo San Pantalon.

Their steps were more sedate than those of their outward journey. Their walk back north, Lucia's arm still through his own, resembled one of the more leisurely ambles they occasionally enjoyed together.

As they reached the site of their first visit, Lucia suggested that they re-enter the church for a while. "I need to talk to you, Malin, and I cannot do that at home."

Inside, incense still lingered from the Nones service. The church itself felt empty, yet a run of lit candles illuminated each side of the nave and its recessed altars.

They walked to the left, towards a small number of chairs positioned near the back wall.

Lucia seemed hesitant to begin.

"Tell me what is on your mind, Lucia."

She continued to look down at her grasped hands, a thumb running over the knuckles of her left hand. When she turned to face him, her face was transformed with fear.

"Malin. I vowed to myself that I would do this today. I will not treat myself well if I return without doing so. Please don't be angry."

Her words were quiet and faltering. "When I spoke to you last, you talked of your struggle to, what was it again? 'Learn the substance of your own thoughts', I think you said. And I was prepared to accept that. At least, I was then." She breathed in slowly, giving herself time to prepare her next words. "But I will accept that no longer. We have known each other for nearly twenty years. And you have been a constant for me during that time." She paused once more.

Malin sought to speak, but she raised her hand to his chest.

"No, Malin. Please. I need to say this without interruption. Allow me that.

"I have valued your company above all others. Initially, because you appeared to have earned Father's confidence. As little more than a girl then, well, I had no thought to question his choices. Of course, it didn't hurt that you were a figure from an alien land, full of unspoken histories that would turn many a girl's head. When Father told me a little of your background, I found it all too easy to warm to you. Not as a friend of my father's but as a friend of my own.

"And of course, that was before I found you to be such a tolerant and thoughtful companion. I know I have abused our friendship many times with my unguarded opinions. My candid thoughts about your own statements and behaviour. Mother chides me regularly in your absence because of what she sees as my disrespect for you. Sclavo teases me at every opportunity. But in your heart, you must know of my deep affection for you. Of my belief that you might care for me in the same way.

"So now, when you tell me there are things you cannot share, and I see the torment that I believe you to be in? The way you hide your injured hand from me? I cannot bear it. I will not.

"You must tell me, Malin. What is happening?"

★

They arrived back at the Da Segna home an hour later, and allowed family life to roll over them. The salve of laughter, of

177

Collette's regular outbursts of petty complaint and childish demand, the companionable, easy-going nature of Uberto's tales of his day.

Soon after dinner, Malin made his apologies and left.

By the time he arrived home, his energy was all but spent.

Symon was immediately worried. "You look terrible, Malin. Are you hurt again?"

Having no idea that his appearance could provoke such a reaction, Malin worked to put his friend's mind at ease.

"There is nothing to worry about. At least not in the sense you mean it. I am unharmed. Bring wine, and I will tell you of my day. I cannot hold it to myself."

His confession flowed unhindered, too tired to do anything other than share his honest feelings with his friend.

"I collapsed, Symon. Panicked. I was so close to telling her of the plot. Of how I recruited her father. Put him in harm's way, while all the while claiming to be his best friend. Her disgust would have been real, and justified. Her whole family have treated me like one of their own. And what I was close to telling her would have shown that their affection counted for nothing. That I was prepared to throw all that away to appease some faceless nobles in Westminster. And after how her father has been treated by the nobles *here*!

"I couldn't allow that to happen. I could not confess my betrayal, and live with their disappointment. Yes, Uberto is in this at least as deeply as I am. As you now are. But his wife and daughters?

"So I panicked, and dealt with my distress in the only way I knew how."

Symon's face was heavy with dread. "So what did you do? Is Lucia all right?"

Malin said nothing.

"Malin, have you harmed her?"

"Christ, man, is that what you think of me?" His rage was immediate, blood pounding in his head.

"I don't know what to think, Malin. You're not making sense. What have you done?"

Malin's breath was laboured and shallow. He almost screamed the words. "*I told her I loved her.*"

The two men looked at each other, each startled by the power of Malin's outburst.

Symon was next to speak. "I'm sorry. I really don't understand what this is about. Of course you love her. We've all known it for years."

"And none of you have been wrong. But I've never told her. And now I have, purely to cover up what we have been doing. And for what? Everything will be out in the open in weeks. And here I am, reducing our feelings for each other to a mere mask. A deceit.

"I've exploited something so important to me just to get out of trouble. And not even for long. The whole world could fracture any day, and my part in its collapse become common knowledge."

He fell silent, his hands to his face.

"Coming back from England, I spent the entire voyage worrying about the task ahead. About how we were going to get through this unscathed. I barely slept. My guts were like burning pitch.

"But when I heard what had happened in the city. What might have happened to Lucia. And to you. When I saw the carnage. Heard stories of death and the missing.

"Everything I'd been immersed in for weeks left me in a moment. In a blink. And all I could think about was how I'd wasted all these years never telling the people I cared most about, how I really felt about them. How much they meant to me. And now? Now, I've told the only woman I've ever loved that I can't live without her, and done it because I'm too frightened, too *ashamed* to show her the real nature of the man she cares for."

Symon sat quietly by the fire long after Malin had retired upstairs, the wine long finished.

By the time he snuffed out the last candle, it was almost morning.

Chapter 16

Sunday 10th February 1348

Day 15 of the Quarant

Attendance at Mass was unaffected by the early morning rain falling on the city.

The warnings issued from dozens of pulpits, however, left many with a deep sense of unease. The clergy stated as one that there was no room for doubt. The damage visited upon the city two weeks earlier was a strong and unequivocal sign of God's displeasure. Ways must change. God must return to the heart of the Republic, or greater harm would follow.

Malin travelled across the city to meet Uberto on his own return home from San Giovanni's. The rain had begun to clear, skies rising from the east, but the merchant's mood remained stubbornly flat.

"Cheer up, my friend. We are set fine for success."

Uberto grunted. "Perhaps that is what the priests are warning us about. Perhaps we are nothing more or less than the next blight to hit the city."

"What do you mean? We will cause no harm to those undeserving of it, and the city will benefit from new blood. And some old blood, of course." Uberto's eyes were fixed on a point between his feet. Malin gently nudged him, hoping to break through the man's mood. "If the people of Venice knew what awaits them, understood the wisdom of our actions, they would not be walking around with the melancholy face you wear today."

Uberto looked up. "If only that were true. But the priests have worried many of my friends. They do not merely stop at the rising of the waters, or the shaking of the earth as evidence of God's disappointment. They now claim that far from being a success, the casualties we suffered at Zara were also borne out of divine resentment at our pride. Several families at church this morning have men missing from their homes from that time. I wonder how long it will be before resentment at those who profited from our expansion rises."

How quickly, how easily, the atmosphere in the city could change. At Candlemas, it had felt as though a weight had been lifted from the entire population.

He continued his efforts to cheer his friend.

"Rather than anticipate God's view of our action, let us ensure instead that, once this is over, we give Him no further cause for concern."

Uberto met his eyes with his own. "How do you do it, Malin? I come to you with worry, and within moments, you find the words that pull me back up. Come, let's take a walk before we go to the *scuole*."

They had some time before their scheduled meetings at the confraternity house. Uberto led them west over the Ponte delle Tette, and then along the wide waterway of the Rio de le Do Torre. Signs of damage remained on every street, particularly on the facades of those houses standing on the narrow street corners. A few of the stones lining the Calle del Scaleter bridge were missing.

When they turned into Campo Sant'Agostin, Uberto's mood darkened a second time.

"Malin, I need you to see this. It is important that we have this conversation before we go any further."

They walked further into the square, and stood before an empty plot of land between two elegant villas.

Malin was confused. "What is it you wish me to see? There is nothing here."

"That's my point. A fine house used to stand here. It shared many of the features that now adorn my own home. But come. Walk with me a little further."

They turned into a quiet street to the west of the church square. At the rear of the church, Uberto slowed and pointed at a plain stone column, set in a small courtyard. The pillar had clearly been broken in two and then repaired. "Read the inscription, my friend."

Malin leaned forward, and scanned the engraved text.

"This land belonged to Bajamonte and now for his iniquitous betrayal, this has been placed to frighten others, and to show these words to everyone forever."

"It's harder to find now, since Tiepolo sent men to destroy it. But his revenge was hollow. By then, his family was smeared with the shame of treachery. He sat banished in Istria, but his entire family was condemned to *damnatio memoriae*. With the exception of this column, we are forbidden to remember that he or his family ever existed. That they ever drew breath here, let alone possessed a legacy of high office."

He took a step closer to Malin.

"Bajamonte Tiepolo came closer than anyone to

overthrowing the Doge and the Council. He'd planned his own coup for over a year, enlisting the support of the Querinis and Badoers. They hadn't allowed for a major storm hitting the city on the day they moved, but they failed for more fundamental reasons. They overestimated their ability to defeat forces loyal to the Doge.

"They thought the citizenry would support them. But they were wrong. Rather than turning out to help them, they either remained indoors, wishing to avoid the storm, or actively took the side of the government. They were also betrayed by men from within their own ranks, so the advantage of surprise was lost.

"I expect they believed they would celebrate their victory at the Feast of Saint Vitus but instead, all they achieved was the death and capture of a few good men, and the destruction of the Rialto Bridge as they retreated.

"Malin, there is only one thing I fear more than defeat. I fear for my family name. For my family's reputation, and the idea that my whole life may be condemned. Derided. I don't have generations of Da Segnas to dishonour. At least not here. But I bear an even greater responsibility. Ensuring we have a future here."

Malin moved to protest.

"No Malin. No. This also has to be said. The Ten did not even exist then. But in the thirty years since, they have eyes and ears everywhere."

He reached up, gripping Malin by each arm, and looking directly into his eyes. "I have never been one to fear a gamble. To back away from a potentially lucrative and beneficial trade. But we have reached this point now, my friend, where both lives and reputations can be lost. I need you to tell me that we have done enough. That when we sit down on the night of our action, we will be pleased with what we have achieved."

Malin's thoughts flew in all directions, but he had made promises to himself to see this through.

"Uberto. You have trusted me for so long now. And my love for you and your family is the reason why I remain here. I owe you so much. I will not deceive you regarding the chances we take. You are completely justified in your fears. I share them myself, although God knows, I have no reputation to protect, other than being known as a friend of the most honourable man in the city.

"If this man, this Tiepolo failed, he did so because he planned poorly, and placed his trust in the wrong men. He no doubt believed that he possessed enough force to overcome any resistance he might face, but he failed to mobilise his own forces in the right places where they were needed.

"We are well set. We will not make the same mistakes. The men of the Arsenale are fully behind us, and you know just how imposing they can be when they organise. They live in numbers all over the city, and are at the heart of civic defence. We have friends within the Council, and amongst all those families that feel, quite rightly, that they should be members themselves.

"And do not overlook the forces that will arrive. We will not be wanting for military support. In only a few days, we will have met the company's commander. Come with me, and be part of the final preparations."

Although Uberto's intensity remained, his grip on Malin's arms loosened a little.

Hesitating, Malin decided to address the final element of Uberto's concern.

"And as for The Ten, I'm not aware that they have any reason to suspect us. Have you had any new indication that they might have learned of our existence?"

"No. Nothing. And unless Soranzo has been party to any discussions in the Small Council, I imagine we remain unknown to them. Their reach is immense, Malin, and I pray they have other things on their mind."

Malin nodded. Uberto knew nothing of his conversation with Soranzo, or of Bourchier's disappearance. But this also suggested that Uberto's connections were not perhaps as extensive as he had always thought. As extensive as they needed to be.

They walked towards the *scuole*.

Their route took them past the magistrates' court. Several men stood by the entrance, waiting to appear as part of normal Sunday business, or perhaps discussing the outcome of an earlier case. They were barely feet past the building when the *Praedo* began his proclamation, publicly extolling the subject and merits of a case in the absence of its defendants.

They exchanged looks, and walked the remaining distance to the Calle de ca' Donà in silence.

Seated in the same small upstairs room he'd been in with Sclavo ten days earlier, they talked at length with a small delegation from the fraternity of oarsmen that provided most of the *caule*, the ferry boats that plied their trade along the Canal and across to the islands further from the mainland.

Boats would be needed to move their forces around the city on the day of the coup, and Uberto had nurtured an increasingly close relationship with the grey-haired, weather-beaten head of their *fraglia*, the fraternity that had represented the boatmen's interests for centuries.

Giacomo Favero had earned the right to speak on behalf of his brotherhood after a life spent working out of *cavanes*, the small wooden boathouses spread across the islands. His forthright speech was refreshingly different to the kind of language that Malin had spent his life listening to in council offices or merchants' chambers.

An unbidden, nostalgic smile often found its way onto

Malin's face, reminded of the coarse, uncomplicated men of his younger days, who spent their entire lives on or near the water. At the age of six or seven, Malin worked alongside men just like him. And had often wanted to *be* one of them.

A generous donation to the men of the *traghetti* was agreed in return for their future service. Malin would use some of the funds liberated by Symon. Uberto would continue to liaise with the old man until they were able to confirm their exact needs.

Hands were shaken, and Favero and his associates took their leave.

Uberto and Malin remained in the room. Malin continued to sense Uberto's subdued, almost distracted air.

He decided to change the subject.

"So, Uberto, have you had any time to work on next year's summer trades?" Uberto had always spent the first month of each year looking not one season ahead, but two. He attributed much of his success to this.

His mood picked up immediately. "Oh yes. I could not allow the winter to go by without considering where to make my next fortune!"

"So what's the Da Segna priority next year? And, if I might be so bold, which deals are you considering involving me in?"

"Hah. Though I might hear in your question a certain mischief, I assure you that I am almost landed on my best options."

"Is it the Eastern markets again? The taste for cinnamon and cassis grows unabated. Although I personally find cinnamon akin to placing my tongue in the fire."

"I'm less interested in whether the demand continues, than in the amount of competition. Too many cargoes sailing into harbour and the price will sink without trace. I'll get a better idea of which way to turn once the *mudae* are announced. Either way, fear not. We may be quite distracted at present, but you and I have much more business to do together, my friend. We should meet with Symon and Giradino in a few weeks' time to compare our intentions. Incidentally, I had a really interesting visit from the man you introduced me to at Candlemas. Del Chiaro, the Florentine?"

Malin vaguely recalled the man, but their conversation was dulled by the large amounts of wine that had followed that evening.

"Really. What was the nature of his visit? I remember him saying that he had money to invest?"

"We spent a most enlightening hour or two together. He has only just begun here, has already made quite a number of deals with men we respect. He seems to be a natural, and believes my own history makes me a potential partner."

The details of Malin's conversation that night were lost, but he vaguely recalled the man's tone. It suggested a familiarity with the nature of power. And of the places where it might exist.

"He seemed an interesting character, Uberto. If you are thinking of bringing him into your plans, I'm sure there will be good reason to do so. I look forward to hearing more."

*

Malin called in briefly when they arrived back at the Da Segna house.

Lucia came downstairs to greet her father, hesitating only briefly when she saw Malin was with him.

"So, no wells today, Lucia?"

Her eyes bristled at the challenge.

"No, Malin. All the priests appear to be too busy frightening us all today. My next visits can wait until tomorrow. Today offers me the chance of quiet contemplation, and the absence of unexpected interruption. At least for a while."

A blush rose from the base of Lucia's neck, painting her face in an involuntary beauty.

He felt his own scalp burst into flames. He wanted to turn, to see if Uberto could sense their shared loss of composure, but he dared not expose his own lack of poise. He had insisted that she tell no one of his declaration, until they had had more time to fully understand its meaning themselves.

His friend, perhaps seeking to divert any questions of their own activities that afternoon, began to talk about his daughter's plans for the following day.

There was no opportunity for the two of them to revisit the words of love that passed between them.

For the first time that he could recall, Malin made every effort possible to cut his visit short, and escape the confines of the drawing room.

He felt the heat of Lucia's gaze on his back long after he reached the Canal.

Chapter 17

Monday 11th February 1348

Day 16 of the Quarant

Dense, chilling fog hung over the broad waters at the mouth of the Canal. Buildings in Castello and Dorsoduro fell from Malin's view mid-channel. Sounds muffled in the still air, until all that remained were oars on water and the laboured, rhythmic breath of the gondolier.

The route was reserved for only the most experienced oarsmen, able to read and master island crosscurrents and the threat of collision with primary Canal traffic. Malin disliked this crossing. He had always thought the boats just a little too small, just a little too unstable for comfort.

The letter that had sent him scurrying nervously from the house that morning had arrived under the official seal of the *Extraordinarri*. It summoned him to appear at the Custom House at noon, "to present yourself in a matter requiring your attendance."

By convention, Symon was the one that dealt with shipping

and taxation. If the matter related to his partnership with Uberto, Da Viscia might attend, and in doing so attract the lower residential tax rate.

Yet that morning, Malin had argued with Symon that he, rather than his friend, should go.

"Symon, the note was addressed to me. If I'm not back by sundown, or have not sent you word, would you kindly let Uberto know of my whereabouts?"

The look they exchanged required no further explanation or instruction.

Malin's only visit to Dorsoduro since his return had been to meet Uberto. He wondered if his next steps on the island would be his last as a free man.

As the quayside solidified from the mist, he withdrew one of only three remaining phials of gentian. He had calmed his mind, but his body continued to defy him. Nothing would change.

At least not until this was over.

And what did *that* mean?

Malin had thought little of how the world might exist after the coup, beyond the need to keep their promises. To deal with any early provocations or protests and prevent the new reality unravelling. His part in such matters, if he had one, had never been discussed. Good. All he cared about was what he had to do to assure Uberto's safety.

And what of Lucia? What of himself? He reflected on his confession to her two days earlier. The central truth of it held no controversy. What chafed at him most, two days later, was why he had said it, and said it *then*. The mystery of it had held him hostage for the two nights since.

Moments from alighting from the ferry boat, he took a final draft from the green phial, closed his eyes briefly, and pushed himself up and onto the quay.

Resigned to whatever might lie ahead, he made for the main doors of the Custom House.

He was expected, and immediately accompanied to a private room. Inside, a man sat facing him behind a desk, and another sat between them, his back to Malin.

The clerk left and the man facing him acknowledged his arrival with a warm smile. "Signor Le Cordier. Thank you for coming at such short notice. My name is Stefano Morosini. I have the privilege of overseeing the more *unusual* matters that pass through this office. We appreciate your cooperation. It is important to ensure that visitors to our city are who they claim to be."

The man between them pushed the chair out and rose to his feet. He spoke before Malin had a chance to reply.

"Ah, sir, it is so good to see you again. I apologise for your need to travel here on my account, but I fear I had no say in the matter."

Malin took the man's outstretched hand and shook it. He was lost for words.

The man continued. "I do hope you remain well, sir, and that I am not too late to provide my services. I must say, the journey along the coast these last weeks has been most intriguing, despite spending the first week suffering from my lack of familiarity with the less attractive movements of a vessel. Nothing more than I deserve, no doubt, for sitting in the same Antwerp office these last twenty years."

He looked directly into Malin's eyes. Unsure of himself, Malin looked over the man's shoulder to Morosini.

The official was happy to pick up the conversation. "We simply need you to affirm that you summoned this man to help with your bookkeeping."

Malin glanced once more at the face of the new arrival. "Of course. Yes. I feared my summons had failed to reach him. The work I need done is most pressing."

"All is well, then." The official reached down to the desk, and turned over a sheet of parchment. "If you could sign to vouch for the presence and future lawful conduct of Signor Glyn, then we can all look forward to a most productive day."

They walked out of the building, saying nothing, and into a thick wall of mist.

Malin turned to the short, wiry man at his side.

"So, sire. I think it time that you told me just what the hell you're doing here."

★

Mainard Glyn.

The man behind the five barons of the Exchequer, controlling Edward's finances. Channelling the king's will, and funding the entire coup.

The man who stood beside him now, a mischievous smile sitting below amicable and twinkling eyes.

"Just to be clear, my friend. My sorry tale of the first week of the voyage was all too true. There were moments when I thought I would lose more than the bile of my stomach. I was right to never want to leave our shores. Not for fear of straying from matters of state. No. I hate boats. I hate water. And now look at me. On a floating island after a month at sea."

Malin returned his smile. "And yet here you are. Pretending to be my counter of coins."

"Well, in many ways it felt like a suitable falsehood. It seemed to work."

"Yes. Although it brings me no closer to the reason for your appearance here. Other than the fact that you wished to enter the city without anyone having knowledge of your real identity."

The smile finally faded. "Can we find somewhere safe to talk? Preferably as far away from this damned water as possible."

Several taverns stood less than an hour's walk from the Custom House, on the Calle Della Toletta. Each had been subject to the recent clean-up by the local authorities. The *sestiere* had doubled the night guard, following a series of unruly debates in the Great Council on the subject of increasing licentiousness, prostitution and assaults. Their expectations of local landlords were made clear, and over the last year, the frequency of assaults and thefts had plunged. No one, unfortunately, had shown any interest in the number of young women who could no longer feed themselves after losing their livelihoods. The magistrate, a man notorious for his love of wine and night-time sport, had been lauded as a role model for the remaining five districts of the mainland. Each of which were following his lead. Respectable citizens had slowly returned to the taverns and inns in large numbers, encouraged by a return to more sophisticated times.

A Monday afternoon, however, still unable to shake off the piercingly raw fog, evidenced few clientele. Malin and his visitor had a corner of The Bathing House to themselves, each of them glad to be out of the cold.

Mainard began by recounting the events of the last meeting called in Westminster by Humphrey de Bohun, the High Constable of England.

"It was the second Tuesday of the year. You had only set sail from Southampton a few days earlier. De Bohun had briefed me the day before. We agreed that we should gather to discuss the intelligence from Bourchier."

"Information that The Ten were aware of us? Ricaud told me of it when I arrived." Malin frowned. "They took him a week ago. I have no idea if he is alive or dead."

Mainard's shoulders dropped at the news. Malin told him what little he knew of his disappearance.

"So he told you? I'm sorry, Malin. If we had known just a few days earlier, things may have been different."

"Different how?

"Well, in the sense that we would have had more time to consider options. Anyway, when Grosmont finally walked in, late as usual, demanding to know why he had been told to attend."

Henry of Grosmont. The Lord High Steward. As Second Knight of the Garter, he was the natural intermediary between Edward, the three great offices of Chancellor, Treasurer and Keeper of the Seal, and their small group. Malin had never met him. Given Mainard's previous descriptions of the man, he had been more than happy about that. Hugely experienced as both soldier and diplomat, his reputation also extended to tales of anger and vicious tirades against any actual or perceived enemy. As Earl of Leicester and Lancaster, his seniority offered him broad licence. Some said Edward himself was often cowed in his presence.

Mainard continued. "De Bohun explained about the letter from Bourchier. It took him little time to realise the seriousness of the situation. If our plan failed and became public knowledge, our credibility would plummet. Our allies might reconsider the wisdom of aligning with us against France.

"Grosmont was clearly frustrated at our inability to be clear about what The Ten were doing. I did my best to assure him that our own work had been meticulous. That secrecy had always been our main concern. But that any breach in confidence could be calamitous.

"He demanded to know why you had mentioned nothing of this before your own departure. I told him it was because you did not know. That the news was received after you left. Then he asked how much longer it would be before we were ready to act. De Bohun confirmed it would be within forty days of your arrival back here. Earlier, if Bourchier and Libusch felt ready."

"So how did he react?"

"Well, I think he was a little unsure what to do. I don't think I've ever seen him like that."

Mainard hesitated.

"Malin, you need to know. I advised him that it was not too late to call things off. To recall you. The Ten might well have stumbled on the truth, but it would be far from easy for them to prove our involvement, if neither you nor Bourchier were present. We could withdraw, consider in good time what needed to be done, and reshape our plans to suit.

"He said nothing. So I reminded him just how valuable you were to us, with all your knowledge and contacts in the region. The years you'd spent here. He seemed unwilling to make a decision. So he turned to your father."

"My father? Jefferey was there?"

"Of course. You know he's been involved from the very beginning."

Malin was shocked. "I saw him that one time we sat together. Just after you'd explained what I was required to do. But that was two years ago. I had no idea he was part of this."

"He's been intimately involved in this from the beginning, Malin. His proposal to bring you in was merely a small part of his contribution."

Malin looked carefully at Mainard. The man looked uncomfortable. "What is it? What are you not telling me?"

"There *is* something else. But I need to explain all this in a way that makes sense. For now, just know that Grosmont sought your father's opinion."

"And what was it?" He could guess, but wanted to hear it from Glyn.

Mainard's eyes narrowed, recalling his exact words. "'To

turn back now achieves nothing, and chances all'. Malin, you need to know I argued for your safe return. Reminded everyone that we had no means to rescue you if we failed to act immediately. Reminded your father that it was his son in danger."

"And?"

Mainard brought his hand to his forehead, and massaged his brow. "And? And your father said nothing. He just looked at Grosmont. Who in turn sat there for a few moments, before rising to his feet. His last words before he left were to continue. To do everything we could to make things happen as soon as possible."

"So Jefferey did nothing."

Mainard snorted, unable to contain himself. "Oh, I think he did so much more than nothing."

"What do you mean? Did he send you here?" Maybe his father had reconsidered. Decided to help him after all.

"Hardly, my friend. Please. I need you to listen carefully to what I tell you next. It is vital you understand the entire nature of what is happening."

Mainard glanced around the room. No one showed the slightest interest. "This whole plan was borne from our need to defeat the French. But what you don't know, what we've not shared with you, is the truly poor state of our finances."

Malin recalled something that Bourchier had said.

About how every king wanted to spend more than he had.

"Edward, and his father before him, borrowed money from the Florentines, year after year. From the Peruzzi and the Bardi. It began as a means to keep his nobles happy, particularly after his father had permitted the Scots to retake lands north of the border. They both felt that they needed to buy loyalty and stability. When it came to it, Edward only really agreed to support Balliol in the raids on Scotland to keep the

Dispossessed from open rebellion. The extra borrowing flooded in after that. I had two men in the Upper Exchequer purely overseeing disbursements. Every so often, we would gift back small amounts, to maintain lender confidence, or negotiate *chevisance* terms on new loans."

"But how long did this last?"

"That's the key question, Malin. By 'forty, we owed between one and two million florins to Florence. But Edward was determined to pursue his claim to the French throne. I borrowed more money from English merchants, but their contributions were as nothing to what we owed Florence.

"So we did the only thing we could do. We told the bankers that we were cancelling our debt to them. They would get nothing. No capital, no *chevisance*. Nothing. We even cancelled their privileges in the wool trade. Our ability to borrow money since has been limited. In fact, almost impossible. If the Papacy had still resided in Rome, I think it would have been war.

"But Edward didn't really want to hear what the Exchequer or the Treasury had to say. Until, that is, his adventures in France drained us once more. By then, even if we wanted to go back to Florence, our chance had gone. Both families had collapsed. The Peruzzi in 'forty-three, and the Bardi two years ago.

"I never really understood until then just how one man, or perhaps one family, could affect the wellbeing of an entire country. More through his spending than anything won or lost on the battlefield. Through the power of money, or the lack of it.

"The campaign in 'forty-six broke the Treasury. We couldn't tax any more. Nobles would only contribute men-at-arms. Clerical tenths could not be raised again without losing the priesthood. That was when the Genoans approached us."

"The Genoans? But what have they got do with England, or conflict with France?"

"Well, that's the whole point. They had no interest of any kind in Edward's claims. No. They saw a chance to secure help for themselves, in return for the one thing he needed most. Money."

The Genoans were consummate maritime merchants, securing lucrative trade routes to the Black Sea, Adriatic and Aegean. Their rivalry with Venice was common knowledge. Their slaughter of innocent civilians in the Venetian quarter of Constantinople some fifty years ago still generated curses against them across the entire Venetian Republic. Even after taking their own bloodthirsty revenge on the Genoan population at Galata.

Mainard continued. "Genoa sees Venice as the one power able to rival them in wealth, reach and ambition. Their envoys approached the Royal Household. Described a world where Edward could, in addition to receiving new funds, expand English trade in the Adriatic and Black Seas. And in return, all he would need to do—"

Malin interrupted, his voice raised. "All he would need to do, is find a way to strike at the heart of Venetian power. To bring down the Doge and his Council?"

Mainard nodded.

"I'm sorry, Malin, but this plot, this entire endeavour is about Genoa. We are only doing this to provide money for Edward to win in France. To complete a task in return for bulging coffers, and the promise of new leverage here."

"But the Genoans… I've promised Uberto… He's staked his reputation and hopes on returning to the Council. To help shape the future of his city."

As he spoke, colour rose up his throat, and into his face. His hands flew up to grip the back of his neck. "You're telling me that once our work is done, we will be delivering Venice *to Genoa*?"

★

Mainard returned to the table with wine.

"You need to drink some of this, my friend. But you also need to calm yourself. I have more to relate, and it will fare poorly for us both if you are unable to control your feelings."

"But Mainard. You've allowed me to put my friend, his family, in extreme danger. And for what? For a false promise that he will have an opportunity to regain his position, and his self-respect with it?"

"It is the way things are done, Malin. It's unsavoury. I see that. But you would not have done all this had we been more forthcoming."

"What is this *we*, Mainard? I believed you to be an honest man. Why are you even here, if there were no friendship between us?"

Mainard took a full draught.

"You're right. I don't have to be here. In fact, no one is aware that I'm not on the ship sailing back to London. I left Westminster three days after the meeting with Grosmont. Sailed to Genoa, and collected the final large sum promised to the Treasury. I was supposed to accompany the money back. Instead, I have retained a small part of it, in case it is needed here, and instructed my deputy to return with the rest."

Malin tried his best to make sense of the man's actions.

"So. You're here to confess your guilty secret. How do you feel now that it is in the open?"

"Malin. Please. You have me wrong. I am here for all the right reasons."

"Really. And what in God's name might *they* be?" His frustration bled through every word. Mainard looked around them once more, still concerned for their privacy. When he spoke next, his tone was sombre and quiet.

200

"I confess that I'm not fully aware of them myself. It wasn't until I reached Genoa that I made up my mind to come here. But I have to tell you one more thing. One more thing you must hear. It concerns your father."

"I'm not sure I want to hear any more about Jefferey."

"And yet you must. It is of no little concern to your fate here."

"But you've already told me that it was my father who roped me into this."

"But listen. There is more. Much more. Your father is in prison."

Malin recoiled from the table. His eyes danced from side to side.

"It is vital that you understand what danger you are in. Jefferey was followed after our meeting with Grosmont. In fact, we had been watching his movements for some time."

"Followed? Why?"

Mainard took another large swig. "I have already explained to you about the Florentine money. The money loaned to the Treasury over many years, and administered on behalf of the Royal Household. Well, during the latter period of that arrangement, we now know that your father was receiving loans of his own, without any declaration to the authorities."

"How do you know?"

"We have been certain only since his full confession the day before I sailed from London. But I had been overseeing an investigation into his activities for over a year. We went back through the pipe rolls. All the annual proffers made by the High Sheriff of Norfolk and Suffolk. The Michaelmas returns show generous contributions from Wormegay each year. But in one of our routine checks, the Upper Exchequer discovered that far from generating your family's wealth, Wormegay Estate provided almost no money at all."

"We summoned the local sheriff, William de Middleton, who in turn reviewed his own records from the previous decade. He found that, far from thriving, your father's estate had run up many debts of its own. Crop yields had dwindled to almost nothing and, contrary to submitted records, they had sold no livestock for years.

"Your father had been living almost permanently in Westminster. Latterly, as Master of the Privy Wardrobe in the Tower of London. He allowed his estate to fail, Malin. He borrowed money directly from the Peruzzi to maintain his reputation in Westminster and London. To mask his own penury, for fear that he would lose his position as head of the King's Armoury."

Malin could hardly believe his ears. "But Wormegay? I know the place was falling into disrepair at one time, but we, Symon and myself, we put the estate on a really solid footing. When Symon joined me here, he told me that it was working so well, there were no challenges left for him. What did he call it? Yes, "profitable but boring". That's why he joined me. He wanted to learn new things. So how could this be?"

"We are not sure, but our interrogation after his arrest suggests that your father had become obsessed with succeeding in London. In achieving senior rank. In earning the king's favour by strengthening his armies."

"But that's a good thing, surely?"

"Normally, I would agree. Yet his obsession, and his means of funding it, led him into difficult territory."

"Difficult? How?"

"When the Peruzzi collapsed in 'forty-three, your father owed them a great deal of money. The family held Edward mostly responsible for their decline, and they had an opportunity to seek revenge. A pathway into the heart of Edward's government."

"You are not saying that my father…"

"I am saying that in return for further payments, and for withholding the fact of your father's financial misdoings from us, they recruited him to spy on our work with Genoa. With the ultimate aim to thwart Edward's attempts to avoid his own financial collapse."

Malin's mouth hung open. He had no sense of the next question to ask.

"Once our suspicions were raised, we observed your father closely. We had already established that he had a contact in London, an Italian claiming to be a small independent exporter of wool. A claim that was found to be false. The day after meeting Grosmont, we apprehended them both. Both were imprisoned in the Tower. The spy to the dungeon, and your father confined to his rooms there. We questioned them the following day.

"Malin, we no longer have any doubt that your father has passed details of your activities in Venice, and of the impending arrival of Libusch's forces, to enemies of the Crown."

"So it is true. The Ten have full knowledge of our plans."

"We believe so, but we're not certain. One thing is clear, though. One or more members of the Peruzzi know everything. And they hate Edward."

The questions that followed were eventually exhausted.

"There is one more thing I have to tell you."

Malin looked up, as if to plead for respite from any more revelations.

"I know that you have enough to think about. But this concerns you deeply. When we talked to Jefferey, he was clear on one more thing. Extremely clear."

"What is it?"

"There is no easy way to say it. It's part of the deal he made with the Peruzzi. He has secured the promise of your death."

Chapter 18

Tuesday 12th February 1348

Day 17 of the Quarant

When Malin emerged downstairs the next morning, his wound newly cleaned and dressed, he found Mainard talking with Symon. Their conversation appeared to have resumed where it ended the night before. Harmless talk of earthquakes and seasickness cures.

It had been a short evening. Mainard had enjoyed just one decent night's sleep in Genoa since leaving England four weeks earlier, and Malin was more than happy to retire early, his mind still raking through the whole distressing, knotted mess of Mainard's revelations.

"Good morning, gentlemen. How are you, Mainard? Given Symon's usual morning energies, I'm surprised you have not yet made your excuses and jumped in the Canal."

Their breakfast passed in the same light-hearted manner, but their mood slowly grew more sombre.

Malin made the first move. "So. Yesterday was quite a

day. We should think on what we now know, and decide what changes we must make. Perhaps we should start by explaining what is really going on to Symon?"

Mainard looked across to Malin. "Are you sure that is entirely wise?"

"Without question. I taxed myself beyond reason keeping our plans from him. I want no more of it. I no longer have any secrets from him, and I intend to keep it that way."

Mainard nodded, and took Symon through the facts as he knew them.

When it came to explaining Jefferey's role in the affair, he deferred to Malin.

Malin described his father's actions, and his confession in the Tower. "I am sorry Jefferey has put you in harm's way. I wish it were otherwise."

They gave Symon a few moments to make sense of it all.

When Mainard spoke next, it was with a firmness that hinted at the authority he wielded back in England.

"I have done nothing as yet to persuade you of any particular course of action. With all that I had to impart yesterday, I felt it unwise to press. But that time is over. Further delay brings additional danger to us all. In that sense, I fear that Jefferey was right. We must talk seriously about extracting you both from the city."

The two friends exchanged looks.

Malin spoke for both of them. "We've known of the threat of discovery for a while, Mainard. And we decided to continue. Telling us what you have does not make the threat greater. It merely offers us the chance to understand how we might be found."

"I cannot agree. I did not come here merely to tell you what you face. I sailed the length of the Adriatic to make sure you leave this place. I regret not acting on our intelligence about your father earlier, and how this delay may have affected Bourchier, but I cannot allow you both to suffer his fate."

Malin's response was swift. "But what of our progress since November? Of the many men committed to this, at our urging. If we leave, their destinies will be sealed. We will be handing them to The Ten."

Mainard's calm was wearing thin. "But it's clear you are already discovered. You told me of Soranzo. That he confirms The Ten are preparing to act. They have Bourchier. And you yourself have been attacked on the open street. The three of us must leave, to ensure our part in all this cannot be proven."

Malin rose from the table, took a few steps across the floor, and stood by the window, composing his thoughts.

He turned, and fixed Mainard with a steady, determined look.

"You are right. Each day could be our last. That has been the case ever since my return. But your conclusion is false. We are well prepared. More so than ever. I share your fears, but we must turn our thoughts to protection, not retreat. If we leave now, or if word of Genoa's involvement in this reaches our friends, all will fall into disarray. We might ourselves become the target of proud but cheated men. None of them would welcome the thought that they work for their bitter rival.

"You also fail to understand the difference your own presence here could make. I have found it hard to step into Bourchier's shoes. I just don't know enough. But you? You, de Bohun and Grosmont directed his every move. Who better to take his place? We can do this, and honour promises already made. We might even convince Genoa to look kindly on those who have assisted them."

Mainard looked at each of them.

"Look, Malin. Your commitment is admirable. We've both devoted much of the last two years to this. But loyalty to the king is best demonstrated by doing as I propose. I do not suggest withdrawal lightly. Our return will not be popular. But to stay, and still fail? The only good thing about losing our lives would be not surviving to hear our names vilified back home. As for keeping our part in all this secret? I would not withstand The Ten for an hour before confessing everything.

"And what of the Peruzzi threat? They have been working on our demise from the day of Jefferey's first involvement. They've known of our intentions much longer than The Ten have."

Malin returned to the table, but remained standing. He looked again at Symon before speaking.

"We will not go. I refuse. And in staying, I will do everything within my power, everything necessary, to make this happen. And you, my friend?" His voice lowered, his eyes seemed darker. "You will stay here with us to make this work. No one is leaving. I will not allow it."

Symon looked down at the table, unwilling to raise his head. No one moved.

"I believed us friends, Malin. I came here at my own peril to warn you. To help."

Malin stepped forward. His voice was raised. "You came here to ease your guilt, old man. You will share our fate, good or ill. And you will spend the next few days doing everything within *your* power to bring this whole, sorry affair to an end. We will meet any and all attempts to thwart us with cold fortitude or, if needed, a sharp edge."

He marched from the room, leaving Mainard and Symon staring at each other in disbelief.

★

One of Sclavo's clerks allowed Malin to wait in his office until his return.

Thoughts of his last visit to the Arsenale returned to him several times in the hour he was kept waiting.

He would choose his words more carefully this time.

He thought over his own behaviour with Symon and Mainard. It had been as much a surprise to him as it was to them.

Each day brought new and different problems. That was to be expected. But to admit defeat and leave with his tail between his legs, a broken cur? Even Uberto seemed to have lost some of his initial optimism. As for Mainard, he would need to step forward and demonstrate the necessary resolve.

Sclavo finally returned, his business in the yard complete.

One glance at the Englishman was enough for him to express concern. "Malin. Is everything all right? Something clearly troubles you."

He closed the door behind him, removing his damp coat as he walked round to his own side of the desk.

"Hello, Sclavo. I hope I have not caused you any inconvenience by coming here unannounced. I need to inform either you or your father of some developments, and you are considerably easier to reach. Perhaps I could ask you to visit Uberto later today, and pass on our discussion?"

Malin recounted his conversation with Soranzo. Of the special meeting between the Small Council and the leaders of The Ten. Of Bouchier's disappearance, and his own survival of the attack outside Grisani's house.

"I want you to talk to your father, and ask him to consider how we can find out what The Ten are thinking. See if he has any other contacts that might be useful. For all his tales, Bourchier has never spoken of being captured by anyone before. He may have taken our secrets to his grave, or told them everything. The Ten have had forty years to perfect their methods of questioning."

Sclavo nodded.

"Is Soranzo himself in any immediate danger? Do you think he has done anything to bring suspicion upon himself, and therefore us?"

"All I saw when I met him was a genuinely worried man. I do wonder how he hides his anxiety when in the Council chamber. But at this stage, we have to trust his fortitude. He has more to lose than any of us."

"Father will be most concerned by all this, Malin. As will all our companions when they hear. I suggest we are cautious about how we tell them."

Malin smiled to himself. *We have more in common than you think, you and I.*

"I agree. We should send out messages this afternoon, suggesting a brief meeting at the *scuole* tomorrow morning. Everyone should hear this the same way at the same time."

"I will see to it, Malin. But I must tell you, this is grave news. Bourchier was an impressive man. If they have him, what hope do any of us have?"

They agreed who should be summoned to the meeting.

"Let us strengthen our efforts, Sclavo. We are only a few days away from achieving everything we value most. Remind your father of that when you see him."

★

On arriving home, he liberated some wine and went straight to his room. He didn't care if Symon or Mainard knew he was back. If they thought he was avoiding them because of some sense of embarrassment or anger, that was their concern. For one night, let them think what they wanted. Apologies were needed, but could wait.

He needed time to think.

About the meeting tomorrow.

But more importantly, about his father.

He laid on the bed, his head resting against the back wall. Just enough height to avoid spilling the wine.

He closed his eyes, and heard Mainard's voice again. Felt again the pressure in his chest at his description of his father's confession.

He tried to imagine Jefferey's deformed version of sanity. How he carried his twisted desire for revenge so deep into the later years of his life. How he continued to live in a twisted form of the world in which a newborn child could deliberately take his wife from him.

Jerold had told Malin of his arrival in the world, eight years into the new century. The priest had learned much of it from Jefferey himself, in his tortured, angry confessionals. Erwan, Jefferey's Franklin, offered the rest of the story.

The story of a raw, silent, lightless day on the edge of the Fens. A day when the sun was drawn out so thinly that all colour seemed leeched from the world.

Jefferey had spent the day of his wife's fifth confinement alone in a downstairs drawing room in the manor house. Fear that he would be confronted once more by a child's small, lifeless body grew in him throughout the day.

Outside, mist topped the stones of the walled enclosure, masking the wide Norfolk skyline beyond.

Time in the drawing room hung heavy. Brenner had been sent to the rectory with one of the servants.

The boy hated being cooped up with the priest. Yet even Jerold would be better company than his own father today.

When Erwan entered the room, the candles had all but burned down to their metal bases.

Jefferey clung to his meditations for a few moments longer.

He had not moved since the Sext bells. The fire had

long since failed, and a winter chill had moved deep into the room.

He pushed his chair back over the floor. The sound of its scraping legs shattered the subdued hush. He was already convinced that another stillborn was about to enter the house. Two centuries of Le Cordier lineage would continue to hang by the thread of a single heir.

He looked into his Franklin's face. "Is it over? Tell me what I need to know."

Erwan hesitated.

"On second thoughts, say nothing. Remake the fire, and get these candles replaced. I will be back down soon."

He stood, and pulled back his shoulders. Gillian would search for signs of his disappointment, and he did not want this for her. The seventh Earl of Wormegay must display all the outward signs of nobility expected of him.

He moved to the door, past the cold fireplace embers and into the hall.

He wanted to curl up and howl at the dark. To tear at and destroy anything that spoke of hope.

Instead, he raised his head a little more, and climbed the staircase to Gillian's chamber.

Thank God again for Brenner. He could not believe just how precious, how essential the young boy had become to him.

He paused on the landing. Two deep breaths, one last nod of the head, and then he pushed the door in. His stride was deliberate and imposing.

It took him a few moments to take in the scene.

Earlier that morning, Gillian had released his hand and begged him to cast any concern from his mind. Concern based on memories of cold, bloody bundles of cloth. Of her last three desperate stillbirths.

She had promised him. They would soon have a second

child. Their prayers would be answered and Brenner would have a young brother at last.

The stillness was the first thing he noticed as he crossed the room. No one was moving. The bed was still. Above and beyond it, along the back wall of the chamber, a window was slightly open. No sound entered from the cold.

The room was weighed down with the smell of oils, a faint trace of sweat, and waste, and the unmistakable edge of blood.

The faces of the four women, standing to the right of the room, showed the ravages of a long day spent at his wife's side. They looked exhausted. And scared. Three of them looked straight at him.

The fourth did not.

She was looking down at the figure on the bed.

His eyes instinctively followed hers.

The covers of the bed were tidy. Gillian lay in its centre, not moving. Her hair brushed back from her forehead. Her hands resting by her side.

He drew closer. Her eyes were closed. Her face betrayed no sorrow, no grief. No disappointment at letting her lord down again. The reason for her stillness became clear.

"No. No."

His shoulders slowly dropped.

His vision clouded.

A small noise reached him from the direction of the women, its pitch too high to be drawn from their tears. It sounded again. He turned his head, and for the first time noticed a cloth bundle in the arms of the second woman. She tilted the bundle up, to reveal a small, crimson face. Puckered and folded skin.

"Sire. It is your son."

Time held still.

The woman repeated herself, unsure if he had heard.

A puzzled frown contorted his face.

"Take it away."

A few moments later, the room cleared, Jefferey sat on the side of the bed. He lowered his palm onto the back of Gillian's hand.

Behind the door, and in hushed tones, the women discussed what they should do with the boy.

Malin poured the last of the wine. His mind continued to wander.

His father had never remarried.

Erwan was left to manage the estate as best he could. He had found a wet-nurse and moved her, with the baby, into one of the rooms at the back of the house. It was left to the kitchen staff, with occasional visits from the Franklin, to see to the newborn's needs.

Many years later, Haylan, the earl's brother-in-law, had spoken to Malin of his visit to Jefferey three months after his sister's burial in the Le Cordier churchyard.

"I made that one effort to show him that I was willing to be his friend, after Gillian. I thought we might find some common ground in our shared loss. Your father is many things, Malin, but his love for my sister was powerful and real. He worshipped her. Gillian's troubles after Brenner's birth were a source of real pain for him, but he never let himself show it. She knew, of course, but she loved him all the more for his efforts to disguise his real feelings.

"So, was I wrong to try and reach him? He barely spoke to me. And when I asked after you, it was as if I'd tipped manure onto his hallway. What little conversation we had dried up. Something in his eyes sent a shiver down my back. I never visited from that day, and when you turned up at my door with Jerold, the only surprise was that it had taken six years to happen. Thank God Jerold had the balls to do what he did."

Malin finally blew out the candle and lay flat. His chest had begun to protest at the sharpness of the wine. He withdrew his last phial from beneath his pillow.

His final thought was of Symon. The look on his face when Malin had stormed out the room that morning.

He would try to begin tomorrow well, at least, before the next wave of challenges broke over them all.

Chapter 19

Wednesday 13th February 1348

Day 18 of the Quarant

The mood in the house remained sour. Conversation was limited to acknowledging each other's presence, or the passing of food around the breakfast table.

Malin, for his part, seemed deep in thought about something he had no intention of sharing. Symon mirrored his choice to say nothing, finding much to interest him in his cold cuts of beef. Mainard simply followed their lead, unsure if this was just another normal day in Calle San Domenico.

No one seemed prepared to take the chance of re-opening the previous day's arguments.

Malin finally broke the silence.

"The important thing about this morning is that everyone is placed on alert. But we must not scare them into doing anything stupid."

Mainard breathed a sigh of relief. "But we know even mentioning The Ten will change how people feel. It would help if we could tell them the steps we will take to remain in control."

"But we have always known that The Ten were there. These men should not be surprised that scrutiny is increasing. We have not chosen to work with fools."

Symon reacted to Malin's tone. "They are not fools, Malin. It is just that knowing something *could* happen is different to knowing that it *is*. Mainard is right. We must stay ahead of their fear. Offer assurances that they will be safe."

Malin shrugged his shoulders. "So perhaps now is the time to show our hand about Libusch."

Mainard looked at Symon, but his words were intended for Malin. "Let's just think through what that might mean. We have always agreed to keep that part of the plan hidden. Only Bourchier and Da Segna know about him. Most people react badly to the idea of foreign forces on their soil. Some of your friends might find that even less palatable than knowing constables are roaming the streets looking for traitors."

"I'm aware of the city's history, Mainard. Sclavo has been most enlightening on the subject of outside powers meddling in Republic affairs. The last time soldiers converged on the city, almost every man picked up arms and drove them out. But what other options do we have? Offering more money might have little effect. The offer of greater rewards after we have completed our task will only help if their more immediate fears are addressed."

"So why not ask Uberto to present the idea of armed help? At least it will look more like an internal action. They trust him. He's one of them, where we are not."

Until now, Uberto had been told to keep this information to himself. Uberto believed the money for the mercenaries came from the English Crown. Until a few days ago, Malin believed the same. Questions could become awkward very quickly.

"I would prefer not to involve Uberto."

"So how *do* you suggest we do it?" Symon sounded impatient.

Mainard was in no mood to concede. "Unless you have a better idea, Malin, I think Symon is right. Uberto is trusted, and given that he already knows of Libusch's part in this, he can speak with confidence that this is not some ruse conjured to ease their concern."

★

They arrived early at the *scuole*. Uberto was already there, keen to learn more from Malin about the message Sclavo had passed him the previous evening. Malin introduced Mainard, describing him as Bourchier's replacement.

Mainard was quick to raise the question of Libusch and his forces.

Uberto saw their reasoning. "I'm content to be the one to do it, but are you sure you want them to know? It's such a key part of the plan."

"There is no single right way to approach this. But if it's possible The Ten already know, why would we withhold it from our own?"

Men were beginning to arrive. As they discussed how they would run the meeting, Malin grew quiet.

Uberto was the first to notice. "Is everything all right, my friend?"

"All is good, Uberto. I am merely sorry to have had to ask this of you with so little warning."

"Please do not worry yourself. I am happy to do it. And thank you for your confidence in me."

Given the short notice, only four in every five of those invited were present. Despite that, the room at the back of the hospice ward was packed tight, even with all the seating removed.

The reaction of the room to news that Small Council business had been interrupted by the *Capi dei Dieci* was surprisingly muted. The announcement of Bourchier's week-long absence did little more than raise questions of which brothels had been searched.

After everyone had filed out of the cramped room, Malin pulled Uberto to one side, asking him to explain what had just happened.

"I think most of these men have already assumed the worst. You of all people should understand this, Malin. We're level-headed and positive in equal measure. Grisani's comments expressed how many of them felt. Their principal worry is that we are not moving quickly enough. They are impatient, and think we are trying too hard to perfect our plans. Things have never worked that way here. We see a chance, we weigh up the wisdom of pursuing it, and then we either take it or not. Hearing that Libusch will soon be waiting outside the city went down better than I expected, but you must tell them when we are going to act. Set the date, and tell them.

"I also think the shaking earth and the floods still weigh heavy on their minds. Is God's displeasure a signal that change is a good thing, or is his target the sin of their own intent? That question alone is enough to keep their feet on the ground. To them, that probably seems much more important than any concern over an English spy."

Relieved that their morning had gone well, the four men agreed that absentees should be informed of their discussions as soon as possible.

Malin, Uberto and Symon divided up the list of fellow conspirators, committing to visit each of them by nightfall. Mainard repeated his desire to meet Soranzo, to understand for himself the thinking within the Small Council. Malin was nervous about Mainard simply turning up at Soranzo's door without introduction. "I think Uberto should be the one to talk with him. There will be other opportunities for you to meet him."

Symon was first to leave, accompanying Mainard back to the house in Castello. A few moments later, Uberto left for Soranzo's offices at the heart of San Marco. They would meet back at Malin's home when they were done.

Malin closed the door behind them, and sat down on one of the reinstated benches. He reached into his inside pocket for the phial. It was empty, and it was too late to ask Symon to obtain a new supply. Just the thought of running out brought a small surge of discomfort to his chest. He pushed the flat of his hand against his ribs.

He would have to address this today. But not before his visits were complete.

★

He spent the afternoon moving slowly westwards into Cannaregio. His knowledge of the northwest corner of the city was fairly superficial, but he managed to navigate his way between each of the four addresses on his list.

His last visit, to the home of Stefano Bembo, a merchant living on the eastern side of the Calle dei Preti, was his most challenging. Bembo seemed unwilling to take his word for their improving state of readiness and the promise of armed assistance. Realising that his word alone would never be enough, he encouraged the man to talk to Uberto.

When he finally emerged back out into the overcast afternoon, the *campanile* had begun the Nones chime.

The day had left its mark on him.

Even before his last meeting, he had to reach out and lean against the nearest wall until the wave of pain in his chest eased. When the worst of it passed, he had continued on his way along the canalside.

He would not be able to eat or drink until his gentian was replenished.

Instead of heading back east, he turned from the merchant's house and headed north into the district of San Leonardo Fossamala, desperate to find an apothecary. He increased his pace, worried at the lateness of the hour. The buildings around him, some as grand as those in San Marco, were almost all made of timber, their roofs topped by the sturdy thatch from the local reed beds.

Stopping twice to ask directions, he eventually stumbled through the door of a dimly lit shop. As he stopped to catch his breath, scent from dozens of different plants and powders scraped at his throat. To Malin's relief the shopkeeper, a short man with long black hair pulled back from his face, looked up at the doorway and asked if he could be of help.

He explained what he needed. The man offered a seat, and ran his hands along shelves covering the wall. He pulled down a terracotta bowl containing small green leaves. "Here. Take a small handful of mint while I prepare the potion. It will only help a little, but it is better than nothing."

Malin put one of the leaves in his mouth and began to chew, and the man returned to his shelves. "I have a good supply of gentian root and bark, and can temper it with elderflower and verbena." He disappeared through a door at the back of the room.

By the time the man returned, the shop was in almost complete darkness.

"I apologise, sire. Allow me to find some candles. I have made what you require, but it would be best if we could finalise our business in the light."

Malin could barely restrain himself. "Perhaps you could first pass me a taste of your potion now? I am in sore need of it, and would be most grateful to wait no longer."

The man worked the flint and tinder while Malin took several long, deep draughts of liquid from the small phial offered him. The tension in his chest lifted. The poor light masked the moisture welling in his eyes. He counted out the right amount of coin for payment by touch as much as by sight.

The apothecary placed five small but heavy sealed urns in a cotton sack for his journey home. He promised to replenish his stocks first thing in the morning. Another five would be available for collection by the following nightfall.

Checking that the sack would bear the weight, Malin began the walk back to the Canal, noting the shop's location.

★

Uberto and Mainard were absent when Malin walked back into the kitchen at Calle San Domenico. Judging by the advanced condition of the meal under preparation, Symon had been back for some time.

"I thought Mainard came back with you?"

Symon nodded. "That was the plan. But he wanted to explore the city a little, so he jumped off the ferry at San Marco. I think he knows enough to stay out of trouble."

It was well past dark when Mainard finally appeared.

Symon handed him a goblet, glad to see that no harm had befallen him.

He joined them around the fire in the downstairs reception room, unable to stop talking of what he had seen. "This city is truly remarkable. I had some idea what to expect, having spent years looking over maps Bourchier sent back. Yet to see it in the flesh. The earthquake has done nothing to diminish its magnificence."

221

Symon agreed. "I felt the same when I came here to join Malin. And that was after years getting used to Norwich. And it's not just how it looks. You can buy anything, and I mean anything, in the world here. If you can't get it immediately, there is always someone who will obtain it for you within a sailing season. We've seen some sights, Malin and I, on our voyages, but nothing bears comparison with the relentless appetite of the people here. I don't think I'll ever get fully used to it."

Malin turned to Mainard. "Did you see all the scaffolding? Some of that has gone up in the last two weeks, to help with repairs. But at any one time, there must be dozens of houses being enhanced or rebuilt in stone. Did you see the rebuilding of the Doge's Palace, just on the edge of the square?"

"Only from a distance."

"Ten years ago, their plans to expand and improve the place didn't even exist. Now, instead of men standing on the scaffolding and seeing a plain stone facade, they can now get a close-up view of the most ornate porticos and arcades, and the most beautifully appointed brickwork. And Uberto believes there is at least a further ten years of work planned *inside*."

Mainard picked up on the mention of Uberto. "I was surprised this morning, when you introduced us. I was expecting the sort of man I have spent my life dealing with in Westminster. Given what I've been told of his ambition, mainly by you of course, I had imagined him as a determined, unapproachable man. Yet I found him to be most amiable. And humble. Not at all the scheming, suspicious type."

Malin laughed. "Don't be completely fooled, my friend. I have known him for fifteen years. His generosity of spirit is real enough. But his mind is sharp, and he is a practised judge of character. I am sure that as you spoke together this morning, he was already reckoning your worth. And not as a friend. He is a man who has only limited time to regain what he's lost. He is wonderful. A truly loyal friend. But he is also driven. And right now, he will be most interested in how well you can fill Bourchier's boots."

Symon looked on, saying nothing.

A look of displeasure appeared on Mainard's face. "Thank you for the lesson, Malin. You've made it abundantly clear where you believe I fit in. But let me remind you, before we go any further, that I am directly answerable to Grosmont, and through him to the king. You may know more about this city and its people than I ever will. But now that you've refused to leave, *my* job is to see that you fulfil *yours*. Given your decision, I will do my best to save the Crown's reputation, and my own. I considered you my friend, and still do, but I see now that you do not spare judgement on those close to you." He looked directly into Malin's eyes. "I did not see this side of you in Westminster, and it disappoints me to see it here."

Mainard leaned back. "There. It is said. And it will be said no more. I suggest we spend the rest of the evening discussing the outcome of our visits around the city. Symon, I believe we could all do with some more wine."

By the time Uberto arrived, the room was warmed through by the blazing fire.

"I'm sorry to be so late back. I felt it wise to return home for a while, to remind myself of my continued good fortune of having such a fine family. Donata sends her best, Malin, and wonders when you will next visit. She wishes me to tell you that all the women of the house will be pleased to see you."

Malin could feel his face burn.

"Thank you, Uberto. I will make a point of attending tomorrow. Now, please, let us share how our days have gone, and see where we stand."

Between them, they had met with almost all of those unable to travel across to San Polo that morning. With few exceptions, all seemed to share the views and feelings of the men at the meeting.

Uberto looked around the room. "Of course, no one as yet has any real sense of how our forces will be used, any more than when they will be here."

Malin was happy to admit his uncertainty. "I'm afraid I'm as unclear as they are. I got the impression from Bourchier that Libusch could arrive in the next ten days, but I've no real confidence in that. And I certainly don't know how his forces will be positioned. Do you know anything, Mainard?"

"Well, given where his forces were travelling from, your guess may be a good one. We needn't worry too much. If he hears nothing more from Bourchier, he knows to contact you instead, Malin. It just means that we have to live with the uncertainty a little longer. We can still save time later by thinking things through more now. Deciding those parts of the city where we would benefit from armed support."

Uberto then spoke of his visit to Soranzo.

"You're right, Malin. The man seems genuinely scared. I get the feeling that he has spent the last week or so looking constantly over his shoulder. He approved of our decision to tell everyone of The Ten. He said that he had heard nothing about Bourchier. 'But that makes me more worried, not less,' he said. 'They must be active in ways unknown to me. I'm finding it hard to sleep. Even with the additional protection I've arranged.' He's got at least one extra guard."

Malin was fairly sure who Uberto described. The surly, dark-clothed man accompanying Soranzo at their own meeting.

"Perhaps you should consider some protection yourselves? I don't think I could find a believable way to explain such a presence back in San Polo but then, you are not answerable to anyone here.

"Anyway, he confirmed he would continue his vigilance in

and around the Council, and let me know immediately if he learns anything new. I thought to put him at ease by mentioning the mercenaries, but that just had the opposite effect. He started to talk about the evils of civil war, and demanded that we tread extremely carefully. I assured him that we would use our forces sensitively, and maintain tight control over them once they entered the city. Like everyone this morning, he wanted to know when they were due to arrive."

"And what did you tell him?"

"Only that it would be soon. A matter of weeks."

Malin reached out and gave his friend a congratulatory slap on the arm. "That's really good, Uberto. It's good to know that we still have someone in the government that can keep watch on our behalf. No matter how scared he might be."

Symon rose from the fireside. "Good. So if we're done, I'm heading to bed." He bent down to pick up an unopened flagon of wine from the floor. "I wish you all a good night."

The three of them continued to sit around the fire.

Uberto entertained Mainard with tales of old Venice, and the many intrigues he had experienced or heard of during his public life. When he rose to return to San Polo, Malin accompanied him to the front door. Despite consuming a large amount of wine, Uberto looked first one way then the other along the street before stepping out onto the pavement.

Malin watched as he made his slow but steady way back to the Canal, and the private ferry awaiting him.

Chapter 20

Thursday 14th February 1348

Day 19 of the Quarant

Mainard left the house immediately after breakfast, eager to contact various officials courted by Bourchier at the Treasury, the Customs and the Magistracy. The gap caused by Bourchier's disappearance ten days ago had to be filled quickly. Men of power or influence were often the first to feel neglected or isolated if left untended.

Mainard was looking forward to meeting them. He might learn a few things that could be useful back in the Exchequer in England.

If he ever returned.

Malin had recognised only one of their names, Vincenzo Priuli, a senior clerk in the Magistracy. Five years earlier, the man had been part of a three-person panel handling a dispute in which Malin was involved. The man struck him as very ambitious, eager to dominate the panel's questions.

Most nobles worked for the state without pay, rewarded

instead with enhanced standing amongst their peers and for some, progression to higher appointments. Those written into the Golden Book at the *Serrata* dreamed of outshining their ancestors. But those occupying positions without the benefit of the right kind of ancestry often overcompensated with a more visible determination to succeed. Malin had nothing against such men. Their ambition was part of the reason why great cities became great. Yet he tired of the need to pander to them.

He thought again of Uberto. Of his long, gradual climb up the ranks of the hundreds of merchants plying their trade in the Republic. Arriving in Venice with nothing but a young, loving wife and a deep thirst for success. A desire to show his father, a fisherman making a living on the coast just north of Ragusa, what he could achieve in the world. His friend was different to these other men.

Symon was almost at the door, stepping out on his own business, when Malin asked him to collect the remaining medicine from Fossamala. The Scot muttered something about how he would seek to make his way across the city at some point, and then disappeared into the street.

Malin had the rest of the morning to get across to San Polo. Deciding to walk, he turned right from the house, and made his way at a deliberately slow pace. His thoughts wandered, prompted by Mainard's enthusiasm for the city, taking him back to his own first days there.

★

Their small merchant vessel had embarked from Ravenna six hours earlier, on a hot summer's day in 1329. Consignments of linen and fur were stored at the back of the ship, provided by the De Wiett brothers in Antwerp. Lunch was over, and the two

227

of them were back on the main deck, resuming their private conversation.

Accardi continued, with the customary thoroughness that Malin had lately found most endearing. "So you see, in this case, the tangled power structures will require you to step most carefully. Most, how should I put it, *delicately*. Political and commercial power are the same thing here. So a positive impact counts double, in Antwerp's eyes." He winked. "As does the opposite."

Malin's hopes for this first voyage were modest. Make some initial contacts, perhaps secure the promise of a trade or two accessible to outsiders.

His own curiosity about Venice had grown with every tale related in the Kontor, or in ports elsewhere around the Mediterranean. Tales of powerful regulation, huge state convoys, and low taxes for citizens.

Malin secretly enjoyed the Pisan and his obvious pleasure at sharing knowledge gained through his own respected place in the Flanders power structure. "When you disembark, make sure you make it clear to the *cattaveri* that we are here to do business with Da Viscia. That should get us quickly into the inspection queue. They hate the English, so give them no cause to exercise their enmity before we even get out of the docks."

"Of course. But are you going to do the introductions once we're clear of the warehouse?"

"We'll see how things look when we get there. As I understand it, word will soon get to Da Segna's man, and from there it should be relatively easy to get across to the Rialto. If anything, their efficiency will prevent you getting a better look around."

The view across the ship continued to reveal the slowly dropping coastline of the eastern Italian mainland. Huge flocks of seabirds threw mesmerising shadows onto the otherwise light blue coastal shallows. Malin walked to the stern, and sat on the wide bench immediately in front of the storage bays. He pulled out the notes he'd made before leaving Antwerp, refreshing his memory one last time of the different taxes he would need to discuss on landing. The *ripalico*, levied against their wharfage costs. Or the *ancoraggio*, imposed if they had to wait out in the Lagoon until a space was available to dock. The *teloneo* would have to be paid under any circumstance, safeguarding their cargo until reaching its new owners. Others would be determined later, once their goods were safely offloaded to their temporary warehousing.

The ship's bell rang, alerting the crew to prepare for their turn into the Lagoon. Malin raised his eyes from his study and took in the emerging view.

The frame to the west was dramatic. A continuous high white mantle of cloud ran the length of the mainland. Beneath it lay an equally solid band of dark mountain peaks, their line parallel to the thin band of the city beneath. In the foreground, the turquoise waters narrowed through two or three low-lying breaches in the stretch of land that acted as the eastern border of the Lagoon.

Accardi joined him. "Quite something, isn't it? One never gets bored with this approach. And trust me, you have no idea what lies in store for you this afternoon."

The ship emerged into the Lagoon from the narrow breach in the Lido. The offshore breeze abated, and rose instead from the shallower waters.

His business done at the docks, and Accardi's words of congratulation still ringing in his ears, Malin sat back in the gondola and watched the city flow past him, pressed in on the Canal as though ready to fall into the waters at any moment. As the distance between himself and the Pisan grew, Malin's confidence fell. While this first trade complied faultlessly with all Venetian regulation, his commission from the Hanse, a prohibited organisation in the city, might one day place him in conflict with the rulers of this place.

By the end of the following day, Malin had signed his first *colleganza*, covering a free voyage carrying pepper across the Adriatic to Ragusa. It would commence as soon as his initial cargo had met the forty-day Quarant conditions. The contract made no mention that Antwerp vouched for eight tenths of the cargo's initial purchase price.

His working relationship with Uberto had begun, although it would be five years before they met in person, in the Hanse warehouse back in Lynn. The house that Accardi leased, on the Calle San Domenico, was the scene of his first celebration later that night.

*

Entering San Marco, Malin walked beneath the imposing eastern facade of the Palace. His steps slowed, sounds coming to him in a jumbled echo of conversations from the shaded, covered arcade.

Standing at the epicentre of the Republic, he felt for the first time that he was being watched.

He cast his eyes slowly about him. To his left, just where the corner of the Palace pushed into the square, stood a group of men, all bearing the uniform of the city guard. They appeared to be engaged in light-hearted conversation. He shifted his gaze to the arches of the long porticoed walkway. There was no sign of movement. Then, as he watched, a couple emerged just to his right. Neither the man nor his well-dressed partner seemed to pay him any attention.

Finally, he looked back in the direction from which he had come. The pavement, up to the top of the steep wooden curve of the Ponte della Paglia, was empty.

Rather than continue on, he stepped back from the broad edifice, being careful not to retreat too far and attract the interest of the boatmen lined up at the quayside. Turning his back on them a few steps from the water's edge, he looked across to the beautifully patterned and smooth brickwork running above the colonnade's full length. Two separate scaffolding towers blighted the otherwise unblemished surface. His interest, however, lay inside the building. He gazed up, running his eyes along each of the seven large, evenly spaced windows.

Ten years ago, when Uberto was still an ascendant member of the Great Council, his friend had participated in the approval of the designs for the new Palace. The Council chamber was to be significantly enlarged, while the intentions for the Doge's reception rooms were little short of breathtaking. What occupied Malin's mind now, however, was the inclusion of a suite of rooms on the higher floors of the building. These housed the officers and staff of The Ten.

And then there were other rumours. The belief that a smaller suite of rooms, featuring low ceilings and no windows, had been inserted between the ornate and spacious areas of the ground floor, and the administrative and residential floors above. A dark and ominous space, for The Ten's exclusive use.

Malin shuddered. Was this where Bourchier had been taken? More disturbing still, was he captive there at that moment, beaten and bloodied, lying just behind these magnificent walls?

He lowered his head. And there, built into the wall at waist height, were the Lions' Mouths. Who had been feeding them with stories of plots and disloyalties?

The group of guards had dispersed from their earlier position. Not wishing to be seen loitering, Malin resumed his walk west, his bandaged hand pulled back up beneath the cuff of his jacket.

He wove his way through the streets of San Marco, and

into the Rialto. As he crossed the Campo San Salvador, heading towards the bridge, he passed two wagons, each topped by broken masonry and timber. A third stood next to them, its load of sand being shovelled onto the bare earth of the walkway.

The city was mending.

His welcome was a warm one. Donata insisted on inspecting Malin's wound, but seemed satisfied at how it was beginning to heal.

It was Collette who dominated the early conversation.

"Have you heard? Isn't it awful. I'm not sure it is a subject for polite company."

Her vexation and shock at the latest gossip was clearly feigned.

She couldn't resist. "But it *is* awful, isn't it? His excellency is such a pious, honourable man. He has brought so much beauty into the world. Look at the baptistery now – it is so gorgeous, I cannot but feel lightheaded just to think of it! All those little children, shown into God's blessings under such wonderful pictures of Saint John. How could such a man be guilty of such a crime! Even you, Mother, have said his orders to clamp down on lewdness in the streets and taverns has made Venice a much safer and more pleasant place to live in."

Donata spoke firmly. "Collette, I agree that his new laws have been beneficial. Yet even these are unsuitable topics for conversation, guests or no guests. And as for suggestions of questionable behaviour, well. That matter has no place in this house."

The city was, according to Collette at least, consumed by the story that Doge Andrea Dandolo was pursuing an affair with the young wife of the lord of Milan, Luchino Visconti. A state visit, widely acknowledged as good for the future prospects of both cities, had been cancelled at short notice.

Malin, far from being scandalised, simply found himself

instead in awe of this city's ability to move on from disaster at the slightest chance.

It was as though the earthquake had never happened.

Lucia was clear on the subject. "Whether we are aware of their actions or not, it is important that men in positions of power behave in a virtuous manner. We must be able to trust them, as they rightly have to make decisions that affect us all. And what better justifies our trust in them than that they honour God through their behaviour. I hope these rumours are untrue. I will do nothing to encourage their spread, and it saddens me that you do not feel the same."

Collette was undeterred. "Ah, Lucia. Ever one to take the higher ground. Not everyone can meet your standards, even those fortunate enough to be born into the right families."

There was little sign of surrender. "The right families are those that strive to set a good example to those around them. On this basis, our parents must feel that they have failed in at least one of our number."

The point seemed lost on her sister.

"Well, anyway, I can't wait to find out what happens next."

Donata seized her chance. "What happens next is that you and I will allow Lucia and Malin to continue to address the problem with the wells. Come, Collette. We will pick out your dress for this evening's dinner."

Lucia and Malin were left to bask in the welcome silence that followed.

Malin spoke first. "So, what is the dinner that demands Collette's preparations?"

"Father has been invited to attend the house of Pietro Selvo for the evening. I believed I would be busy all day with matters concerning the well surveys and repairs, so Father accepted the invitation on behalf of Mother and Collette only."

He knew the name from somewhere, but couldn't quite place it.

"I'm sorry. Selvo?"

"He works at the *Savii ai Ordini*. He and Father had business regarding the convoys."

"Ah yes. I remember him now. He struck me as a very modest, pleasant man. Perhaps he has good news about who has been nominated."

Lucia looked at him curiously.

"What is it?"

She shrugged. "Nothing, really. It just doesn't seem like you to have forgotten a man's name. I would have said it was one of your strengths."

He explained that it was Symon who had had the greater contact.

"Anyone would think you had other things on your mind."

Her mischievous tone had returned.

He chose to ignore her. "So how is it that you come to be here this afternoon, instead of continuing your good work around the *sestiere*?"

Lucia looked away briefly. "It is not a tale that I am pleased to tell. Particularly after chiding my sister."

Malin listened quietly as she described her morning.

"I have been forbidden to go any further."

"In truth? But did they give a reason for not wishing you to continue?"

"At first, no. Eventually, the clerk dealing with me left the office, and came back in with his superior, a man named Zorzi. I believe his grandfather was Marino, who was Doge for less than a year. Anyway, Signor Zorzi said that he had heard of my plans, and had concerns about their implications."

"Implications? You mean the cost of repairing those needing it? Surely they would need repair in any case."

"Well yes. But it's not the money they are concerned about. Well, not directly. Zorzi explained that a 'number of parties', I think he called them, had expressed their surprise that a woman was permitted to conduct such work. And that the funding of any repairs could be subject to any number of delicate discussions between many different departments. Some of the wells are positioned on public ground, so the *Officiali al Cattaver* would have an interest. If public funds were to be used, the *Camerlenghi di Commun* would need to be involved, particularly with all the damage to other parts of the city. Especially the waterways. And not forgetting, of course, the procurators of San Marco, who are busy pursuing additional loans from individual nobles for the restoration of the city."

She paused to check that Malin was following.

"Anyway, his point was that with so many *delicacies* involved, he felt it better if I stood aside, and allowed his office to ensure that things were addressed in a proper manner. A proper manner!"

Lucia almost choked on her last words.

Malin tried to think of the right supportive and caring things to say. But each time he looked at Lucia, his mind surrendered.

"I know, Malin. I know I should never have taken this on. But I feel so useless, sometimes. I can talk comfortably and sincerely about how it is our role as women to ensure that the men leading us are virtuous and informed. But sometimes. Sometimes, I just want to do something myself. Do something that makes a difference."

She choked a second time.

"Please don't think harshly of me, Malin. I want only what is best."

"That's enough. Please say nothing more. I understand completely." Malin got up from his chair and moved around beside her. "I cannot watch you getting upset. Or worse still, listen to you apologise for the way you feel."

He took her hand, and squeezed it gently. "Lucia. They do not appreciate you. Because they do not know you the way I do. And because they have no experience of a woman prepared to take action without first seeking permission."

He searched for a sign that his words had hit their mark.

"Malin. I want to be proud of what I can achieve. For myself. And now. For you."

They remained hand in hand.

"Lucia. I want you to know that I truly feel for you. The way you have been treated. How it must make you feel." He paused. "But I cannot sit here, with your mother or sister likely to return at any moment, without talking to you about what was said the other night. I have to know what you think."

She laughed quietly, and for the first time since his arrival, a single tear rolled down her face.

"Oh, Malin. Have I made your life so unbearable by listening to your words of love?"

Her wit was back. That was a good sign.

Lucia had kept her promise to say nothing to her father. But she had found it impossible to keep it from Donata. "She has promised to respect our privacy until you leave."

Malin was aghast. He had sat there all afternoon, unaware that Donata would be interpreting his every word and movement in the light of Lucia's confession.

"You need not worry. At worst, when her chance arises, she will chastise you for taking so long to express yourself. She believes you to be a brave and honest man in all respects but one. She loves you dearly, Malin, and is delighted that you have spoken your heart."

"But Uberto. I mean, your father. Will she—"

"Do not worry. I have asked her to say nothing for the time

being. But you will need to consider how long she is likely to keep her own counsel. She has made it her life's work to make my father happy, and she takes any secrecy between them to be a kind of betrayal."

"And what of you? What do you now think?"

"I hardly know what to think. A man I met when I was sixteen years old and already considered too strong-minded for marriage has just told me, a dozen years later, that he has been in love with me for much of that time. At this moment, I could die of happiness. Yet a few moments later, I could die of sadness that it has taken him so long to act on his feelings."

Malin withdrew his hand, but Lucia reached out to reclaim it.

"Do not worry, my love. I am simply stating the bitter-sweet nature of the moment. I bear as much responsibility for this as you."

The look she gave him caused his own eyes to fill.

It was dark by the time he left for home.

★

It was nearing midnight.

The three men had already agreed not to waste any more wood on the fire, and the room had noticeably cooled.

Loud pounding at the front door brought all of them to their feet. Had their time come?

Moments later, Symon walked back into the room, Uberto following immediately behind him. Although dressed in his best clothing, he appeared unusually dishevelled.

"I must speak with you at once." He bent over, as if catching his breath. "I think we have a serious problem. This can't wait until morning."

As Lucia had said, he had spent the evening at the home

of Pietro Selvo, but had sent Donata and Collette home with Tusco.

"A number of the other guests were there for the same reason as myself. He thought it a decent gesture to tell us, after we had eaten, that each of us had been successful in our bids to be part of this summer's *mudae*."

Symon could not contain his disappointment. "So are you telling us that our own bid has been dismissed?" He looked across at Malin. "I'm not sure how that can be. I spent nearly two days working on the details in his office, and the last time we discussed it, everything appeared very positive."

Before Malin could respond, Uberto interrupted.

"You miss the point. Allow me to finish."

Symon looked sheepish, but nodded.

"After the meal ended, a group of us were talking, and Selvo mentioned that the final decisions on the composition of the fleet were discussed and agreed by the Small Council two weeks ago. At their normal weekly meeting."

Malin didn't see why this was important. "That's how it usually works, is it not?"

"Yes, it is. But it is also normal for the discussion to take up the entire session. And it did."

"So, this would have been two Sundays ago. On the third?"

"Yes. They met straight after the Great Council meeting, and it was the only item on the agenda. Selvo himself attended, presenting the final recommendations on behalf of the five *Savii ai Ordini*. They finalised all the key aspects of the fleets. Two were to be despatched to the Black Sea, and a further two to Tunis and Sicily. Rates were set, and approval was granted to notify us, subject to acceptance at next week's Great Council, so we could commence setting up recruiting tables on the *Piazetta*. Capitanos for each fleet were agreed. They rejected the proposal that each convoy was armed by the shipowners, so Selvo was instructed to notify the Arsenale to prepare communal military escort."

Mainard could withhold his question no longer.

"But Uberto, please. What the hell has this got to do with us?"

Uberto turned to Malin, and looked pleadingly at him.

Malin looked around slowly at Symon and Mainard, and then fixed his gaze back onto Uberto's agitated face.

Malin spoke slowly, alert to any sign from his friend that he was mistaken.

"It's quite simple, Mainard. If Selvo is correct, then the Council had no dealings with The Ten that day. And if that is true, then Soranzo's account of events cannot be true. And if he is not telling the truth…"

He took a breath.

"And if he is not telling the truth, then why is he lying?"

Chapter 21

Friday 15th February 1348

Day 20 of the Quarant

They all looked up together as Sclavo's office door swung inward. Malin and Mainard had arrived just after Terce to inform him of Uberto's concerns about their man on the Small Council. It became increasingly clear that Uberto had been held up elsewhere.

For the second time in less than a day, they ran through all the possible implications of the news. All the ways it was possible to have misunderstood the meaning of Selvo's story. All the implications if Soranzo had in fact lied.

They quickly reached the same impasse as that of the previous night.

Malin had struggled to believe what Uberto was saying. "He seemed so genuine. His fear was real, and his accusations of our own laxity seemed heartfelt. We should have sought more evidence. Proof that The Ten had brought their suspicions to the Council."

Symon had tried to lift his friend's spirits. "But you had no reason to doubt him. And after you were attacked…"

Uberto was probably the angriest of them all. Angry at the implied treachery. At their own naivety. And at their growing inability to find simple, innocent explanations that would allay their suspicions. He had known Soranzo for years, working closely with him on the Great Council, and then as members of the *Pregadi*, shaping legislation prior to its submission for Council approval. Soranzo had been Uberto's steady and loyal collaborator. An honourable friend.

Uberto had left Calle San Domenico determined to seek further confirmation of their suspicions. When Malin warned him to tread carefully, Uberto's look was not an easy one to forget.

At breakfast, Malin had suggested that Symon should spend the day on progressing the *Seynte Marie* Quarant. "Its use as a cover for our activities might now be questionable, but we should still keep up appearances." Symon nodded, returning to his cold meats.

It was close to noon when Uberto finally arrived. He walked past the three of them seated around the table, and looked out over the sprawling mass of the shipyard. He seemed lost in thought. The tension in the room was palpable, no one wishing to disturb him.

When he finally turned to face them, Malin was struck by the look in his eyes. Not fear, exactly. Or sadness. Perhaps a slight hint of mania? Definitely tiredness. "What's wrong, Uberto? You look terrible!"

A weak smile appeared on the man's face, and his eyes softened a little. "Oh, nothing. Really, do not concern yourself, my friend. I have news for you that might help us understand our dilemma."

Sclavo could not contain himself. "Father? What have you done? You look as if you have just met the devil."

241

Uberto laughed. "Hah. Some might think so. But no, nothing so dramatic. And yet, for me perhaps, I have confronted one of his imps."

At first light, Uberto had travelled from his home in San Polo and into the heart of the Rialto. His destination was a large house on the Ruga Giuffa, on the boundary between San Marco and Castello. He had avoided the area for years.

He arrived unannounced at the door of Frederico Grimani, barely able to contain his feelings. "I can't say it was one of my proudest moments. But challenging times require challenging acts." He demanded to see the head of the household. The man singularly responsible for his removal from the Great Council four years earlier.

"I had not thought it would be so easy. Just turn up at his door and demand to see him. Perhaps he knew he would enjoy himself, seeing me suffer. Perhaps he was simply curious about the purpose of my visit. I don't know. In any case, I was shown in."

Sclavo was almost beside himself. The name Grimani was well known to the Da Segna house. "But what could you possibly gain from meeting that old bastard? His wealth is as objectionable as his name."

"That may be so, Sclavo. But hear me out. I would not have subjected myself to any of this were it not necessary."

Uberto moved to the empty chair opposite his son.

"He looked older than I remembered him, but he wore his satisfaction in plain sight. He has used his favour with Dandolo well. A full member of the Small Council. A fine example of what heritage and guile will gain a man.

"He seemed as surprised to see me there as I was myself. 'And how is it that we are sitting here together, Da Segna, after so many years? What threats have you come to deliver? Or perhaps you come here to ask for pardon for your past, how shall we say, iniquities.'

"I think he was enjoying himself. 'Or perhaps you have favours to ask. A loan, perhaps? It must be hard these days, to rely only on your own private acumen to provide for yourself, rather than sucking at the teat of Mother Venice.'

"I decided to back my instincts. 'I ask for no such thing, Signor. Although you are right. I do need something from you. I understand that you were most upset at my allocation of rights in the upcoming convoys.'

"Something akin to hatred flashed briefly across the man's eyes. 'How do you know of this?'

"'I simply asked myself how such an outcome could be possible when I know you have such influence. And such a rich opportunity to drive the knife in deeper.'

"'I will not dignify you with an answer.'

"'Why? Because you spent much of the Council meeting two weeks ago failing to stop my nomination? Expressing your opinion forcefully and clearly to your colleagues, but finding them unconvinced?'

"Grimani jumped up from his chair and began to point at me. 'How do you know what I did or did not say?'

"'Well, I just asked myself why you would happily support a venture that would benefit me. There is no way you would have done that. When they disagreed, did you feel you had lost their support? Their respect for your opinion?'

"That seemed to get under his skin. He almost hissed his next words. 'I never consider an afternoon wasted if I can spend it blocking your path back. Our city is better off without the likes of you. Dandolo was right to reverse the decisions of that old fool Gradenigo. He polluted our ranks by recognising you.'

"I'd have liked to have found out more about how long the meeting lasted, or who else was there, but I couldn't think how to do it without raising suspicion." Uberto closed his eyes. "And losing my temper with him? That could have ended badly, and perhaps led him to take a more active interest in us. Listening to him gloat like that, but walking away, was one of the hardest things I have ever done. But it's over."

Malin left him no time to dwell on his discomfort. "So you think Selvo is telling the truth? That the Council spent the entire session discussing trade?"

"I'm afraid so. I may have been fooled by Soranzo, but with Grimani?" He opened his eyes. "That hatred was real. He was there, and he failed to influence the rest of the Council. It must have happened the way Selvo suggested."

Mainard spoke next, his eyes fixed on the table in front of him.

"So we have some difficult choices to make once more. Do we continue? Or call everything off?"

He raised his head, and looked directly at Malin.

The two men stared at each other, saying nothing. Uberto and Sclavo simply looked on, unsure what was passing between them.

Malin turned back to Uberto. "So, what do we now believe we know about The Ten?"

Sclavo had listened enough. "Well, they might not have communicated their suspicions to the Small Council, at least not formally. But we cannot assume that they know nothing. If they have Bourchier, they have much of what they need to confront us all."

"True. But why is Soranzo playing games with us?"

Mainard leaned forward. "I don't know him the way you do. But I think he is up to something. I cannot think of a benign reason for his actions. We should be very wary of his intentions. And I agree completely with Sclavo. The Ten should never be underestimated. Their grip on the information that flows around the city will always be profound. What do you think, Uberto?"

Uberto cleared his throat. Again, Malin caught a sense of his friend's distress, there for a moment and then gone.

"I'm not sure. Of what is going on, I mean. But Soranzo knows more than he wants us to think. I wish I had not briefed him about our military plans. That was a mistake."

Malin stepped in. "You have made no mistake, my friend. If he is crossing us, the mistake is his. I hate to admit it, but he may have been playing us for fools for much longer than just the two weeks since I met him. Anything we have said or done over the last day or two may be as nothing to the real damage done over many months. And remember, Grimani hates Soranzo almost as much as he hates you. Even if he suspects your motives for visiting him this morning, it is unlikely that he and Soranzo are in league with each other."

Sclavo grunted. "Small comfort in that."

Mainard placed his hands down on the table. "So where is this all getting us, gentlemen? We cannot lose sight of the fact that we have been deliberately fed misleading information. And when that happens, in my experience, it means something is being covered up. So what is it?"

Malin's patience was at an end. "It's clear we don't know. We just don't bloody know what's happening behind our backs. But that is not good enough reason to throw everything away. I propose we hold our nerve, adjust our priorities, and take steps to find out what Soranzo intends."

Uberto jumped in before anyone else could comment. "And I suggest we follow him closely until he betrays those intentions. Or until we can piece them together ourselves. I was the one to recommend him as our key contact on the Council. Unless any of you object, I will happily take on this task." His spirit was back. "I will not allow him to continue in this deceit."

Sclavo rose to his feet. "Allow me to help, Father. I have men we can use. We have to know what he is doing."

Mainard's shoulders dropped.

No one was returning to England, and he knew it.

★

The two Englishmen left, allowing the Da Segnas to discuss how they would establish a watch over Soranzo's movements. Sclavo would pick the most trusted men from the Arsenale's own constabulary, a small but well-organised group that discouraged crime or violence amongst the fifteen thousand men working within the shipyard walls every day. Calm heads, and a willingness to follow orders had, in the past, prevented many minor disruptions escalating into full-scale riot. The head of security did not answer to Sclavo, but to one of the *protomaestri* Malin had met a few weeks ago.

Uberto would let them know how they would set things up on his way back home that evening.

Malin thought it would do them both good to take in the air before returning back to the city. They stood at the far end of the promontory behind St Elena, looking out across to the Lido.

The last place he had met Bourchier.

Mainard kept his hands in his pockets, protecting them against the chill east wind. "I think I have given up on any attempt to make you see sense, Malin. You are taking us all down a dangerous, possibly fatal road, but I see now that there is nothing I can do to stop you. There has never been any shame in taking yourself out of this situation. But you will not do it. I see that. So the only question now is how we can reduce our chances of failure from a certainty to something less. We need to buy ourselves a few more days in which we can all worry ourselves sick."

Malin laughed. "You certainly have a way of putting things, Mainard." He turned his back to the wind, looking back across the Arsenale to the scattered and numerous church towers across the city mainland. "Listen. I am truly sorry for my behaviour the last few days. I have not yet thanked you for taking such a leap to come here. It would have been so easy for you to take the ship back to London. I would never have known any different."

"Perhaps. But *I* would have."

They walked further north, a growing drizzle making the air feel even colder. "I do think, however, that you owe a similar apology to your friend Symon. He has done nothing to deserve your anger, and I sense he has done much to keep your head above water since your return."

★

It took Malin most of the evening to finally realise what it was about Uberto's expression that morning that so haunted him.

Symon sat over from him on the other side of the fireplace, legs stretched, his feet catching the rising warmth. Mainard had retired to his room, complaining that the chill of the day had gone onto his chest.

"Oh God." Malin's half-empty goblet clattered onto the table.

"What is it?"

"It was that look Uberto had when he was telling us about his visit to Grimani. He looked totally lost. As if he had been pushed into a corner, and had nowhere left to go. No choice but to follow through on what he knew, however much we wished he didn't have to. I don't think I've ever seen him so stunned by circumstances."

No one had shared this detail with Symon over their meal earlier.

"And just this moment, I remembered where I've seen it before. It was on Jerold's face."

"Jerold? Back in Wormegay?"

'Yes. And I need to share this with you. I don't think I ever have."

"This sounds good. Or maybe not. How intriguing! Wait there."

Symon jumped up and poured more wine. "This sounds like something best approached in a civilised manner."

Malin picked up the poker, and began prodding the logs in the hearth.

"I suppose it's of no consequence, in a way. But now I can place it, I have a better sense of how Uberto must have been feeling this morning. When it finally became obvious that he had been played by Soranzo. And that he would have to do things he would rather not. Things that he had never believed would be needed."

Symon just sat and listened as his friend related events from over forty years earlier.

Malin was six years old, standing in the entrance hall of the Carmelite monastery in Norwich.

But his story began a few months earlier, when Jerold had stumbled across him being bullied by his elder brother, Brenner.

"He saw me lying on the ground after one of Brenner's pretend sword-fights. I was sprawled in the courtyard dirt. I think I was crying when Jerold passed by on his way home from the manor house. He told me later that he thought I had finally had enough. Something about how I was sitting. Totally beaten. I must have been a sad sight.

"Anyway, he came over and picked me up. Brushed the dirt from my clothes, and talked about fixing the wound across my forehead." Malin ran his hand over the thin scar, still visible above his left eye. "He was on his way back to the rectory. He told me he'd just renegotiated his stipend, and was looking forward to a flagon or two of wine to celebrate. I can still remember how his shadow fell across my face when he bent to pick me up."

Malin put on his best Jerold voice. "'So, young master Malin. What scrape have you got into this time? Chasing the geese again? Or were they chasing you?'

"He pulled me up by my hand, and took out a cloth to wipe away the worst of the blood on my face. I told him Brenner and I were just practising, that he was showing me some new strokes. I told him Brenner didn't mean to hurt me, but I don't think he believed me for a moment. I didn't even believe it myself.

"The worst thing of all was my sword. My training sword. Brenner had stood on it after I dropped it, and the wood had completely split down the middle. Father would be really angry with me. Once I saw what he'd done to it, I gave up trying to lie any more.

"Anyway, Jerold told me to pick the bits of broken sword up, and then to walk with him back to the rectory. I don't think anyone saw us. Brenner had already run off around the back of the house, and all the soldiers seemed to be busy doing other things.

"Hah." He looked down at the fire, his arms outstretched. "This is exactly how I sat. When we got back to the rectory, Jerold lit the fire and went to get some water for my cut, and some wine for himself. I sat there by the fire with the poker until he got back. I used to do that all the while." Malin's eyes glazed a little as he remembered. "Maybe that's where I got it from.

"I always enjoyed being at the rectory. Jefferey never took any interest, and Jerold was always happy to add to the three instruction visits I had every week. He loved to tell me of the latest things he had read. Stories, or histories. Or strange new ideas about how God worked, and what good men should do. To be honest, Symon, he was the only friend I had then. Before Carsen and Radley. Father wouldn't let me mix with other boys on the estate, and Uncle Haylan stopped visiting with my cousins after my mother's death.

"I think it was after he cleaned and dressed the cut on my forehead that he decided to talk to Jefferey about sending me to the Benedictines. He had always said that they were by far the most interesting of the monks. That they respected learning more than any other order. I think he believed that if I stayed on the estate much longer, I would end up more permanently damaged. I remember him complimenting me on my new scar, telling me that it meant I had the beginning of my own collection of interesting stories that I could tell when I got older. He had a really good way of looking at things differently.

"Once I'd been attended to, he took another one of his books from his collection. I told you that most of them were stolen, from his time with the Greyfriars in Lynn? Even now, I picture him with one of his books open on his lap, chuckling at any occasional contentious claim or statement.

"Haylan told me later that Jerold had spoken with Jefferey, to ask if I could be sent away to become a novice with the Benedictines at Lincoln. He just wanted to get me away from danger, I think, and saw that as the best way to do it.

"But his plans went wrong. Father told him to keep out of things that didn't concern him, but then changed his mind. I think Jefferey saw it, even then, as a way to get rid of me. Instead of accepting Jerold's suggestion, he told him to enrol me with the Carmelites, at their House in Norwich. Jerold tried to argue with him, but it made no difference.

"So he drove me on a cart to Norwich, with Erwan on horseback and four armed guards. It took us two days, stopping at an abbey overnight. I can't really remember the journey very well.

"I do remember, though, just how impressive the view of the castle was as we neared the city. Even when we were right outside the city walls, you could still see the keep over the ramparts. The yellow-white stone just glowed in the sunshine. And the noise when we drove through the streets to get to the Carmelites. It was market day in Tombland. I'd never been in such a crowded busy place. 'Close your mouth, boy,' he said to me. 'You look like some unfortunate kicked in the head by a donkey.'

"I remember how we got off the wagon just outside the main door of the Priory. The walls either side were the height of three men, and stretched further than I could see. Erwan knocked on the door, and told them we were there. We went into a dark lobby. I can remember how cold it felt compared to the warm sun outside in the street. And how quiet the place was.

"A friar came to meet us. I remember him calling me 'uncommonly young', and how Jerold pulled a face when he said it. Erwan told them I would be seven at the turn of the year. Erwan called him 'My Grace'. He was the Dean of the monastery, but I don't think Erwan really knew how to address him.

"Anyway, the friar held my hand, and told me he would explain how he would 'meet the needs of my soul'. I remember thinking that I should do everything I was told, and be polite, otherwise they might not like me.

"Haylan told me later what happened when Erwan and Jerold were waiting for me to be brought back. They were told they could walk around to the inside courtyard, where there were a small number of places to sit.

"Erwan wanted to remain seated until it was time to leave, but Jerold wanted to look around. He'd heard rumours about the White Friars and their austerity. He decided to explore. It wasn't difficult. Nearly all the Houses in England are designed the same way, so his six years with the Dominicans and his visits to other Houses and their libraries over the years must have helped.

"He walked into the refectory, and saw a row of large oak doors along each wall. He pushed one of them open, and saw a rough, low wooden box positioned in the centre of the floor. It had a covering of straw that reached knee height. 'The rumour is true,' he told Haylan. 'Every monk sleeps each night in his own coffin. Isolated inside their own cell.'

"He then left the building and walked outside, into the wider monastery grounds. All the other rooms were laid out in the standard way. Granary. Garderobe. Infirmary. The misericord, a room normally offering the promise of minor respite from the rules. A glance inside suggested it had not been in use for some time.

"The gravestones were just at the back of those buildings. And next to them, three rows of open graves. Another rumour was true. Each morning, every monk was obliged to dig out a shovelful of dirt from his own future grave.

"The Dean eventually brought me back to the entrance, to say my final farewells.

"Symon, I have to tell you. *That* is when I saw that look on Jerold's face. The same one that I saw on Uberto's face this morning. He knelt down in front of me and tilted my chin up, and looked into my eyes. He then stood back up, and addressed the monk.

"'Thank you for hosting our visit, Dean. We have learnt much here, and are grateful for your hospitality. Yet time is against us.'

"He held out his hand, and I took it. 'Come Malin. We must not keep Erwan and our guard waiting.'

"A day later, when we were due to pass through Lynn, he had a second long argument with Erwan, and then told the party to head into the town and stop outside Haylan's house.

I remember waiting on the wagon while he spoke to Haylan. He finally stood at the door and beckoned to Erwan to bring me in."

"He still bore that look he had had in the monastery, but I could tell he was trying not to show how he really felt. To this day, he has never told me how he explained himself to Jefferey. But I know that his decision to stand up to him was one of the most frightening things he had ever done. And that, apart from these damned books we send him every year, I've never thanked him."

Symon looked down at his empty goblet.

"I'm sure he knows, Malin. Not everything has to be said to be understood."

Malin looked across at his friend.

"Maybe not. Maybe not."

"Do you think Uberto will be all right? It sounds like he has had a real shock."

"He should be here soon. We can draw our own conclusions then. But my guess is that with Sclavo behind him, he will have regained whatever balance he may have lost. Soranzo should look out, if the Da Segnas are on his tail!"

Chapter 22

Saturday 16th February 1348

Day 21 of the Quarant

Malin went to his bed unsettled, and breakfast the next morning was unusually subdued. Uberto had not appeared, or sent any message to describe how their plan to deal with Soranzo had developed. The plot had entered a new stage. The thought weighed heavy on them all.

Symon left to go to the Rialto, leaving Malin and Mainard to wait for any news from Uberto.

The man himself finally arrived mid-morning.

"I'm sorry for not coming last night. Rather than trust the men to get into position on their own, we both went with them across to San Marco. We needn't have worried, really. Although all eight of them work for the Arsenale, over half have worked privately for noble families across the city. It's a little shocking to realise just how often people wish to know the movements of others. Rivals in business. Or even love." He laughed. "Who knows which of the two offers the best rates!

"Anyway, we had three of the men position themselves around Soranzo's house, and one over the other side of the Canal, in the event that we need to follow him by boat."

Malin's relief was real, but he needed time to better understand what had been done. "Slow down, Uberto. I'm not following you. Where does Soranzo live?"

"Ah, sorry. Yes. His house is one of the large three-storey villas rebuilt a few years ago on the Campiello Santa Maria Zobenigo. It's in San Marco, as you'd expect, about half a mile west of the Piazza. A very nice area. The sort of place I would be living in myself had life not taken a different direction." He paused, lost in his thoughts for a moment. "Yes, it's directly opposite the Chiesa Santa Maria, with the Calle delle Ostreghe running along its southern side. It's a short walk from the *traghetto* station on the north side of the Canal. We've placed our fourth man at the Dorsoduro ferry station, so he can react quickly on both sides of the Canal if Soranzo decides to travel anywhere by water."

Mainard's eyes were clear and bright, having had a good night's sleep. "What have you told them to do?"

"That's fairly simple. Sclavo and I talked it over yesterday afternoon. We've agreed to share the duties of permanent overseer. I will take control during the day, while Sclavo will relieve me each day when he finishes at the Arsenale. The men will swap at the same time. I'm sorry if I'm a little unclear. We decided to share the duties last night, just to be sure that our orders were understood. We have both been up all night."

Malin was amazed. "I had no idea that the two of you would take such an active part in keeping watch."

"Well, yes, we did consider appointing a chargehand to run things. But this feels too important to leave to others. It goes to the heart of all our fates. And between Sclavo and myself, we have a fair chance of recognising many of those Soranzo might meet."

Mainard looked at Malin, and nodded slowly. "I'm impressed, Uberto. Bourchier would be proud of you both. Tell me, though, can these men be trusted?"

"As much as anyone can trust anyone else that skulks around the city for money, I suppose." Uberto smiled. "Don't worry. We can trust Sclavo. He is a good judge of men. They will want to keep their superiors at the Arsenale happy, and I'm sure their additional wages will serve to strengthen their loyalty. They just need to be nimble if and when Soranzo moves around the city. Who knows? If Soranzo is up to something, he may be doing it without even leaving his own house. We will record the name of every visitor to his villa over the next few days, and trace them back to their point of origin if needed." Uberto paused. "I suggest I come over here each day after I hand over to Sclavo, to let you know what we have learned. If needed, I can always pass any concerns or directions to him after our discussions."

Malin took a deep breath and leaned back in his chair. "That would work well, my friend. Congratulate Sclavo for organising this so quickly. We should run this for a few days at least, and then see what it can tell us."

"Excellent." Uberto stood. "Well, if you will forgive me, I'll return to San Marco. Our first full day must proceed in the manner we have agreed, otherwise the men will think themselves led by fools. Besides, if I sit here any longer, I'll fall asleep."

Mainard continued to speculate about Soranzo's actions. "I genuinely wonder what the man is up to. Maybe nothing? Maybe he just fears for his safety, and is exaggerating the threat from The Ten to ensure we take our secrecy seriously?"

"But how do you explain Bourchier's absence? He is hardly making that up."

"True. I'm afraid I don't know. I just want to hold on to the possibility that we are witnessing little more than the misguided behaviour of a worried man."

Malin chuckled. "How many men have you met in the last week that are *not* worried? Point them out to me now, and I'll consider them at least half lunatic."

The silence that followed offered few answers.

"So Malin. I'm not sure if this is the right time, but I don't think I've ever asked you. What will you do after all this is done? It's always seemed so far ahead of us, until these last few days."

"I have no idea, my friend. Like you, I don't think I've ever stopped to think that far ahead. In fact, I've tried not to. Before all this began, I was like Uberto. Always planning ahead. Never relying on the ships already at sea to protect my position. That's been part of the reason why I love the trade so much. Nothing is a given, and yet everything is there if you can find your own way through. Finding the best ways to make things happen, and then searching out others who can both help and benefit has always been my greatest joy. Since I hired my first ship to travel north from Lynn.

"But here? Now? I really don't know." He paused, drawing his lower lip between his teeth. "I would like to return to that life. Keep building up business with Symon. And Uberto. I just don't know if that chance will still be there in a few months."

"Would you consider coming back to England? The situation with your father could make things very different for you. I understand you are his only heir."

Malin did nothing to hide the bitterness of his laugh.

"His heir? I think I stopped being that the moment I drew my first breath. And Brenner's death made no real difference to that. As far as Jefferey was concerned, he only had one son worthy of the name, and he became childless the moment the news of Brenner's death arrived from Burton. If I hadn't been smuggled out of the country, just like some other cargo headed to Antwerp?" He fell silent. "I wonder if he would have even buried me in the Wormegay family plot."

Mainard let Malin's words hang over them, unsure how to respond.

"I understand. I haven't given much thought to the future myself, either. But I think the place I return to will be different to the one I left. Or perhaps it will be me that is different. I'm not sure what kind of welcome awaits me. Even if we succeed, I turned my back on orders to return home with the money from Genoa. And if Genoa meets its promises of further money after the deed is done, we'll still have the matter of funding an army in France to deal with. And as for how we will deal with Jefferey…"

He glanced up at Malin. "Sorry, I didn't mean to sound so… I meant no harm." He changed the subject. "I wonder if Ricaud will ever come back to us. If he doesn't, would you like to take his place?"

Malin laughed wryly. "A life spent spying on men at their worst, or becoming a regular in the worst brothels of any city? His current fate, however little we know of it, does nothing to attract me to his position."

Malin went on to describe his discomfort on his initial arrival in Venice, nurturing the appearance of being an ambitious but conscientious trader, abiding by all the regulations imposed on him. The city received its taxes, but concealing the true nature of his work exhausted him. Even as he fell in love with the city and its people, he was helping Antwerp and the Hanse undermine the Republic.

He shuddered a little. Perhaps he was more accomplished at deception than he was prepared to admit. It was a sobering thought.

Mainard asked again. "So what *will* you do here? After we're done."

He tried to picture it. The old guard of the Great Council replaced by members more pliable and sympathetic to Genoa's ambitions. The possibility that Uberto would find disfavour with his new masters, or they with him. And worse still, that Uberto would hold him, his greatest friend, responsible for leading him into a very real form of treachery.

He had no intention of considering what this would do to Lucia.

A knock at the door offered a welcome relief from such thoughts.

When Malin came back, he held a letter. He opened it, then handed it to Mainard. "Thank God. It's from Libusch, seeking to contact Bourchier. He will meet us at Murano, in one week's time."

The plot had felt a little more real when he had watched Uberto brief their colleagues at the *scuole*. Now, with words written just a few days ago by the mercenary leader, Malin found it hard to catch his breath.

He spoke next with a lightness he did not feel.

"So, Mainard. Let's get through the next two weeks before any of us start to think about what happens after that."

*

It was already dark when Symon returned to the house, visibly tired from his efforts in the Rialto.

"These merchants clearly refuse to make any allowance for our current predicaments, secret or otherwise. It's as if the earthquake never happened. I understand entirely if they seek to divert themselves from any thought of it. But do they really have to throw themselves with such passion into haggling over the most trivial of things? I need a drink."

Malin found it convenient to leave Symon to be the face

of the Le Cordier business in the city. It could not be easy. The deals being discussed were real enough, but the air of farce surrounding any plans beyond the next few weeks was hard to swallow.

Over a meal of dried pike and eggs, Malin explained the outcome of Uberto's visit earlier that day, and then moved to the subject of the following day's appointment at the dock. Although completely familiar with the regime, neither of them could believe how quickly the time had gone since Malin sailed back into the Lagoon.

The date of the mid-Quarant inspection had arrived. It was incumbent on him as principal trader to show all buyers that their cargoes were safe, and conformed to previously agreed definitions of quality. Although a Sunday, they would adhere to the long-established custom, if only to avoid any unwelcome questions.

Malin passed Symon the note from Libusch. "If we can show that the Quarant is fit to proceed, it could take us up to, and even beyond, the final steps of our plan."

Uberto returned, looking completely exhausted.

He had spent the entire day in San Marco. "As I told you this morning, Malin, the first day of a new arrangement should always be performed in the agreed way. I've just left Sclavo. In truth, he doesn't look much better than his father."

He described the main features of their first full day.

"Soranzo seems to have hosted his normal Saturday petitioners. There is never a shortage of men seeking to have issues raised at each Great Council meeting. Most of his visitors I recognised, mainly low-ranking nobles and family men. One of the local magistrates, and a deputation from one of the local confraternities, judging by their clothing. There were two men I didn't recognise, and we were able to follow them back to their lodgings. It seems they are clerks from the Treasury.

What business he had with them is unclear, but probably of no concern. It's quite usual for Ducal Councillors to discuss the funds for civic works. And God knows there are a lot of works commencing at the moment. Anyway, Sclavo will make enquiries at their place of work when they return on Monday, just to be sure that their roles are legitimate."

Symon offered him food and drink.

"Thank you, but I need to preserve my appetite, and my remaining strength, for a meal with my family this evening. I must find a convincing way to explain my absence last night. I might be head of the family, but that counts for little when it comes to the curiosity and logic of my wife and eldest daughter."

Malin knew he would have it no other way.

Chapter 23

Sunday 17th February 1348

Day 22 of the Quarant

M alin and Symon had been kept waiting at the Lido warehouse almost half the morning before their buyers arrived.

During that time, Polani entertained them with tales of shipping calamities and surprises. Handling mishaps. Miraculous transformations of spice into mutton at the point of a deceitful quill. Overly optimistic attempts to outwit men of the Customs.

Despite the delay, Malin was happy to be there. The house back on the main island had begun to close in on him. Every day men came and went, trailing with them the need for answers. Or demanding reaction to their latest discoveries. He needed to escape, if only for a few hours.

Returning to the Lido offered him one more irresistible boon. He counted the many days of his life spent on the berths, quays and docks of working harbours amongst his most enjoyable.

They had become his home soil. The places in which he felt most grounded.

He loved observing how each man knew what to do, and when and how to do it. How amongst an often-chaotic work site, goods magically appeared exactly where they needed to. And how vessel masters, apparently indifferent to the concerns around them, carried their air of quiet authority with them, confident their will would be done.

Here, outside the warehouse, one or two of the workers he saw seemed to carry with them a new sense of vulnerability. Perhaps friends or family had been lost in the quake. Perhaps they had just realised, for the first time, how fragile existence could be.

But the port was back in full swing.

The young man from the Grocer's Guild arrived just after noon, shortly followed by Stornello's representative. The validation of purchase agreements for the wheat and linen was largely symbolic, but Malin would breathe easier once it was done. The prospect of seeing Symon tied up for the weeks it might take to resolve any dispute could be particularly troublesome.

Stornello's man, a young half-cousin of the merchant himself, seemed keen to engage in discussions about the uses his linen might serve, and the possibilities of further imports from England. Malin, sensing that they were beyond the point where problems could arise, assured Symon that he would meet him back at the house, and walked back onto the quay.

Craving solitude, he turned and walked south. The wind had stiffened since their early morning arrival, and a thin but noticeable spume rose a few inches above the choppy Lagoon waters. He wandered the pathways between wharfs and warehouses, the surface underfoot alternating between damp, compressed soil and occasional slabbed stone. Half a mile along the strand he slowed, and looked for a place to sit. He spotted an upturned barrel, laying at the water's edge, just below a short wooden jetty. Checking that it would hold his weight he bent to sit, balancing on its damp, rounded side.

He studied the teeming movement on the surface of the Lagoon, and his mind drifted. Went back to a day with Radley in Lynn, just after his twelfth birthday.

He had loved their early morning rides to the Staithe together. Crossing Sunolf's bridge over the Millfleet, and gaining their first view of the river mouth. Stalling his horse on the crest of the bridge to read the signs of the day's weather. From there, he could see to the far shore of the Ouse, and any chop on the water. The massive skies to the east, that brought in most of any rain. The drift of smoke from Lynn's early morning chimneys.

On that day in June, he and Radley made their way through the southern part of the town. They rode along the priory's boundary walls. Seeing no sign of life in the courtyard beyond, Malin imagined the monks stuffing their faces in the Frater. Or straining to empty their bowels in the garderobe.

The Briggate Road rose gradually onto its banked sides, built to keep it above the spring floods. They reached the centre of the town, thriving under the dual towers of St Margaret's, and the Guild House at the mouth of the Purfleet. In the six years since his arrival, at least three dozen new merchants' houses had been built, extending to the north and south gates of the town. Uncle Haylan had left an already oversized town house for one of them, giving the boys a slightly longer journey to work each day.

The Tuesday market was already in full voice. The large new square, nestling between the Purfleet and Fisherfleet, already throbbed with the excitement of a hundred pitches. Customers already frequented the inns bordering the square's eastern and southern limits. First Radley, older by some three years and the more experienced rider, then Malin wove their way through the heaving grounds. Even on market days this was the best route to the Staithe, avoiding the boggy banks of the Purfleet.

They rode into one of the two lanes connecting the square with the riverfront. The hubbub fell away. Smells of cheap ale and stale piss were replaced by the equally pungent aroma of mudflats, exposed by the most recent ebb tide.

He recalled the stagnant ditches in the fields around Wormegay, but there was something more fundamental, more life-giving about the drenched mud here. In summers on the estate, the dry-baked fenland ditches lost their stink, their banks crumbling into scentless dust. Here, the river margin filled his lungs with a fecund rot all year around. Even the stench of untreated fleeces loaded in midsummer heat could only briefly smother the overpowering perfumes of the estuary.

Malin pulled alongside Radley to ride along the widening earthen concourse of the Common Staithe. "Is it your turn or mine?" The same question, every time the Searcher was due.

Radley had worked the Staithe for years, and knew almost everyone and their ways. "Oh, well now. If it's Fossard in charge, I'd better take the lead. He'll deliberately miscount if he thinks you're there to make fun of him again. And whatever figure he arrives at will not be in our favour."

His words were far sterner than the lighthearted expression his face conveyed.

Malin fought back. "Well, maybe he's brought someone a little more capable of adding up this time. Or he may just pass the cocket without bothering to check." Radley, unconvinced, but not really caring enough to think of a reply, offered his customary shrug. Nodded his head in the direction of the party ahead.

265

Several men and horses had gathered at the end of the quay. The only man he recognised at that distance was Fowler, one of the wealthiest and most colourful men in town. That amount of scarlet and turquoise could only be carried off by someone well-practised in its wearing.

Savouring the last few moments before their day's work began, the two boys rode on, to where a small vessel was moored up under the public crane. Malin noted the baskets of linen, three lined up on the dock, and another being readied for lifting. Not too busy today. Their own modest cargo of timber and iron would be dealt with soon.

The transaction at their own berth went smoothly. Malin had not seen this Searcher before. The man was efficient, balancing his accounting duties with just the right amount of respectful politeness when addressing Fowler, the owner of the goods.

The two boys remained attentive and compliant throughout the inspection. Fisher, the vessel master, seemed more interested in the breakfast brought from one of the market place inns than in the tallying of quantities.

When it was time, the men gathered above the walkway to sign off the cocket. Malin shook hands with all three of them, congratulating them on a successful voyage. He turned to follow the Searcher back to the Custom House to settle his uncle's dues and see the bond cancelled.

"Have you forgotten something, Malin?" Radley barred the way back to his horse, his arms crossed in front of him. His voice possessed the serious tone that Malin secretly envied. When no one else was around, he imitated it. "Gentleman Fowler is still here. You can catch him before you head off to the Custom."

Damn.

He had hoped Radley would overlook his boast of the previous evening.

Malin glanced briefly out at the wide mouth of the Ouse, composing himself before turning to face his best friend. "I've not forgotten." He passed the cocket to his older cousin. "Here, you take this, and I'll see you when you get back."

Running his hands down his jacket, making sure he was clean, he strode the thirty or so steps to the animated figure of Fowler, still engaged in final conversation with the ship's master. "Excuse me, sir, but could I have a moment of your time? I have a proposition I would like to discuss with you." He had caught Radley's tone exactly.

The man ignored him.

Completing his business with Fisher, the merchant began to walk back to the row of warehouses and offices.

Bastard. I'll show him.

Malin worked hard to keep up with him.

"Sire, I understand from reports in the Guild that you are seeking a carrier for your expanding wool trade at Whitby? And to transport goods back here and to Yarmouth?" He hesitated long enough to ensure that he still had the merchant's attention. "And that you would like to enter into business with a ship owner that is able to devote all their attention to your requirements."

Fowler, looking a little thrown, peered down at the small boy at his side. "It appears my wishes have kindly been made common knowledge by the Guild. On whose behalf do you enquire, young sir?"

So here it was.

Deep breath.

"On my own behalf, sire. I would take it as a great compliment if you would allow me to explain my plans further, and gain your confidence in my ability to serve you well."

Malin's legs trembled.

His first business offer. He couldn't wait to tell Radley.

The laughter, when it burst from the man's throat, struck him through the heart. It was accompanied by a look that no young man could easily withstand.

Malin took two steps backwards, and walked hurriedly in the direction of the Custom House. Fowler was calling his name, but he paid no attention.

He gathered his horse to retrace his route back to town. Lacking the strength to remount, Malin wandered slowly south, meandering past the few occupied moorings on the public staithe.

He looked around to see if anyone had witnessed his humiliation. The crane was still in use further along the quay. A stevedore gang carried sacks from the foreshore and straight into the relevant merchant's warehouse. One man fidgeted outside the public privy.

As he walked further, familiar faces occasionally shouted his name, preventing him slipping past unnoticed. By the time he reached the Purfleet, he had enough composure to at least return their greetings.

He had thought he could do it.

He'd grasped his apprenticeship under Haylan with both hands. Met every challenge set him, with help from Radley and his brother. After Carsen left to work in London, Haylan quickened Malin's development further.

He took a seat where the Purfleet's light grey waters joined the quay. Behind him, the stone warehouse of the Hanse looked out across the exposed promontory, its large doors tightly closed. He had worked with the Flemish and Dutch traders that came and went along the Common Staithe, but the Hanse remained a mystery. Even Haylan, a comprehensive source of all the latest happenings and talk at the Guild House, offered little on the Hanse's activities. The names of foreign ports, Lubeck, Hamburg, Novgorod, filled his mind with thoughts of adventure. Of waters presenting altogether different challenges to those of the sea around Lynn.

He had come a long way since Jerold removed him from Wormegay, and the fear of what each day might bring. He had mastered almost every task set him, and lived in a house built on kindness and good humour.

Feeling a little calmer, he rose to his feet. After a brief visit to the market for some lunch, he would ride back to re-join Radley, and share his comical new tale of the bumptious merchant and the stupid boy trader.

Back on the Lido, the strengthening breeze brought with it the first hints of rain. Malin pulled up his collars, and pulled the skirts of his coat over his legs. Caught in youthful memory, his thoughts returned to Lynn.

Later that same day, the two boys had sat in the main living area of the house. Radley, conscientious as ever, was preparing plans for what they needed to accomplish the next day. The allocation of duties almost complete, they were ready to head up to their chambers, when Haylan entered.

The man looked tired. He slumped down in the chair next to the empty hearth, closed his eyes and sighed with a mixture of fatigue, satisfaction, and most importantly, a need for their full attention.

"So lads, I understand you've had one hell of a day down at the Staithe."

Radley and Malin exchanged glances. Had they made any errors in the loading or offloading of cargoes? Harmed Haylan's profits?

"What do you mean, Father?"

Rather than answer, he told Radley to find the housekeeper and ask him to select the evening's wine.

Although addressing his son, Malin felt Haylan's gaze settle on him.

Radley left the room.

"Malin, there is something I need to discuss with you. Please pull up a seat."

There it was. The same tone Radley now used with such success.

The thought hit him. It's Fowler. It has to be.

Malin lifted one of the chairs from the back wall and brought it to within a few feet of Haylan's broad figure.

His uncle's expression remained unreadable.

"So, my lad. I had a very uncomfortable conversation at the Guild House this afternoon. A certain gentleman, important to this house, expressed some very strong views about a member of this household. More importantly, a representative of our company."

"I-I expect you are referring to gentleman Fowler? He was very happy with this morning's inspection and offloading." He decided to come clean. "I may have…"

"I don't think there is much of a 'may' about it, young man. You very much *did* act in a manner that caused him to bend my ear for well-nigh an hour this afternoon."

Malin looked down at his hands, as they wrung themselves tightly without any obvious instruction from himself. "I know what he probably said, sire." He searched the large, round face directly in front of him for any clue as to his fate. "I made him a business offer, and he chose to, well, to decline it."

His face flashed crimson.

"So what was it about the offer you made that caused him to decline it, young Le Cordier?"

The man only referred to him by his family name when poking fun at his legacy. Haylan held many of the nobility in low regard.

Before he could answer, his uncle continued. "Would it be perhaps, that you failed to hold his attention long enough for

270

him to understand even the barest details of what you were offering? That you left the conversation at a point that served neither of you well?"

Malin's eyes flicked left and right across Haylan's face. His thoughts ran in many directions. He held his breath, waiting for whatever came next.

"Relax, boy. It's true that Fowler was angry. But with himself. At his inability to take you seriously." Haylan leaned forward in his chair. "There are very few men in the Guild that have escaped my speeches about my three sons. My pride in each of you in mastering each stage of the merchant's way of life. You most of all, of recent months. He was annoyed that he had insulted the child of a dear friend. But what angered him more was that he didn't hear you out. Why did you not follow through on your initial approach?"

Malin remained silent. He wanted to answer, but wasn't sure what he would say that wouldn't make things worse.

Haylan snapped his fingers. "Tell me what it is that you think will make it worth Fowler's while. If I like what I hear, I will set up a meeting with him, and you can take him through it."

It felt as though he was looking straight into Malin's soul. All hints of light-heartedness had gone. "But remember, boy. Never, ever put someone on the hook like that and leave him hanging. Once you start something, have the guts to finish it."

Moments later, Radley had returned with his father's favourite Flemish wine. They moved on to their regular evening recap of the day's events, and the schedule for the next morning.

Hours later, fighting for sleep, Malin reflected on how Haylan had talked of him as a son.

*

Malin returned home on his own just before nightfall. The rain of the early afternoon had set in. By the time he stepped off the ferry boat at Calle San Domenico, he was soaked through and chilled to the bone.

He looked forward to a quiet evening by the fire, interrupted only by Uberto's evening visit. He might read more of the Duns Scotus before retiring.

The evening started well. Uberto arrived shortly after his own return, and shared a drink. Being a Sunday, Soranzo had walked to the Piazza and attended Mass in St Mark's. From there, he and two companions had walked the further short distance to the Palace to attend the weekly Council meetings.

Uberto made no attempt to hide his bitterness at his own exclusion from the main church of the city. He and his family had worshipped at St Mark's for almost nine years before his fall from favour consigned them to the lesser ministrations of San Giacomo.

"We picked him up as he left the church. He went straight to the Palace from there, in good time to attend the first of the afternoon sessions. Sclavo has always had a habit of catching up on his sleep on a Sunday, but he turned up at the Piazza in good time to relieve me and the other men. I expect he'll stay there with them until Soranzo returns home."

Malin told his friend about the successful completion of the Quarant inspection that morning. Uberto would pass on the outcome to Da Viscia.

Rain still fell as Uberto left.

Malin went back to sit by the fire, unable to get warm.

The evening seemed headed towards a peaceful conclusion. The words of Master Scotus occupied Malin's thoughts, while Mainard and Symon shared several flagons of wine.

The banging at the door late in the evening, and the agitated face of the messenger that appeared once it was open, took them all by surprise. His note, from Sclavo, demanded that Malin and Mainard meet him in San Polo.

The two men hastily put on their cloaks, and followed the man down to the quayside, where a ferry boat awaited his return.

Symon had sought to join them, but Malin was insistent. "You stay here. I'm sure there is good reason for just Mainard and myself being summoned. Tend the fire until we get back. It's still raining hard, and we will need to dry off when we return."

The messenger was one of the men assigned to observe Soranzo. He answered none of Malin's questions as they headed west. Mainard was silent, seemingly content to wait until their arrival.

They disembarked at the *traghetto* near to Uberto's home. Malin's anxiety grew, until it became clear that their destination lay beyond Calle Donzella.

Continuing further south, they finally halted just outside the Scuola di San Giovanni. At a signal from their guide, a figure stepped out from the dark entrance.

It was Sclavo.

"My friends. I am glad to see you. I have need of your counsel. It is not good news, I'm afraid."

Malin could barely contain himself. "What is it, Sclavo? Where is Uberto?"

"He is inside. Upstairs."

His grim face and tone did little to ease Malin's concern.

Sclavo sought to calm him. "No. Please. Uberto is unharmed. But you must come with me." He turned to their travelling companion. "Panelo. I need you to stand guard here until I come back."

Sclavo beckoned them to follow him up the broad steps and into the building. The large ground floor meeting room was unlit, save for the pale gloom entering through the windows in the front of the building.

"We need to go upstairs."

On Malin's previous visits, the steady, low murmur of voices had greeted him from the top of the stairs. As they climbed to the *ospizio*, he could hear nothing but their own steps.

They made their way across the small vestibule, and into the large dormitory.

Three men stood at the far end of the room. They turned at the sound of their arrival.

Malin immediately recognised the outline of his friend in their centre. "Uberto. What has happened?" He began to walk down the open corridor that cut through the lines of low beds. He was halfway across the room before sensing what was wrong.

He stopped, and looked down to the bed on his right.

There was no movement from the man lying prone under the bed's covers. No sound.

Malin looked across to his left, at the bed directly opposite the first. The same sight greeted him. Again, no sound. No movement.

He looked up, casting his gaze across the room. Thirty beds. All occupied. But all silent and still.

He looked back towards Uberto. Adjusting to the flickering candlelight, Malin saw his distraught look.

He turned back to look at Sclavo, still at the threshold of the room with Mainard. Sclavo's hand rested on Mainard's arm, restraining him from entering.

Malin turned once more and walked the few remaining steps to join his friend.

Neither of them spoke. Malin's eyes followed Uberto's eyes as he looked down.

To the bed just below them.

In the flickering light, and the unearthly silence, Malin saw a man's face. Part of a heavily bloodied corpse. The man's eyes were rolled back. His jaw hung loose.

Bourchier.

Uberto's voice was trembling. "Malin. I don't know what to say. It is so…"

Malin put up a hand. "How did he get here?"

"We don't know. A member of the *scuole* came to me at home, looking for Sclavo. As chief officer, Sclavo had to attend immediately. I told the man I would contact him and bring him here. I went to San Marco, to Soranzo's house, to get him."

Malin looked down at the body. "Please, Uberto. We knew he might not have survived his imprisonment. We have to be strong. And ask ourselves how he ended up *here*. In the place we meet."

"I agree, my friend. But it's just…" His voice failed him. He pulled himself up straighter, and made a gesture with his arm, sweeping across the whole room. "We have no one to ask. No one to tell us who brought him here."

Thirty old and infirm men and women of the San Polo *sestiere* lay in their beds.

"They're dead, Malin. All of them. Every last one of them. Strangled or stabbed. They will offer us little help."

As Malin looked back a second time at Sclavo and Mainard, Uberto took the three steps needed to reach the back of the room. Turning to lean against the wall, his legs gave way and he slid slowly to the floor.

Chapter 24

Monday 18th February 1348

Day 23 of the Quarant

"We need to talk." Symon paused, reconsidered. "No. That's not it. Not it at all. *You* need to *listen*."

It was early afternoon. Malin sat in the reception room at the front of the house, shrunk down into the chair by the window. The same chair into which he had collapsed when he and Mainard returned from the *scuole* just before dawn. Mainard was yet to come down from his room.

Receiving no response, Symon stepped forward and nudged the side of Malin's leg with his knee.

"Malin. This won't do. Listen to me."

Malin finally looked up at him through bloodshot, watery eyes. It was a look of defeat.

When they arrived home, the three men had sat together, trying to make sense of the scene back across the city. When Malin and Mainard finally went to their beds, Symon, considering his night over, ate breakfast and went to the office, determined not to lose a day's work.

When he heard Malin finally emerge from his room, he walked through to the front of the house to confront him.

Malin eventually acknowledged him. "What is it you wish to say?"

"Nothing you want to hear, I imagine. In fact, I don't really want to do this at all." Symon cleared his throat. "But I damn well will."

He had Malin's attention.

"I know you have had a shock. And that it's one of many over the last few weeks. But I cannot allow this to continue."

Malin reached up his hand, and gently circled Symon's wrist. "Really Symon. I am fine. I just need to think things through. To regather myself."

Symon pulled away.

"No. No. You don't bloody understand. Malin, this is not about you. Well, not in the way you think. This is about *me*."

"About you?"

Symon's anger grew. "Yes. You need to hear this. I need to bloody hear myself *say* this." His voice shook. "I'll try to be clear. I am your friend. I will always be your friend. But I will no longer stand by and take everything you throw at me. You presume too much. Making important decisions for me, or about me, without allowing me the chance to discuss them."

"I don't under—"

"I said I needed you to listen. For God's sake, grant me at least this one chance to speak my mind."

"You have never—"

Symon leaned forward, and grabbed his friend's arm. The force of the action surprised them both.

"Just shut up and *listen*. Thank you. I need to tell you that I cannot, no, I *will* not, put up with the way things are now. You arrived back here a month ago, lying to me. Pretending all was well. When you can't stand the guilt any more, or perhaps when

277

you thought I'd find out anyway, you tell me about this mad, ugly plot. And then you tell me I have to help hide it from view."

"It's not like that at all, Symon."

"Yes, it *is*. It's *exactly* like that. And then? You tell me that your contact has gone missing, and that I, not just you, may have been watched by the authorities here for anything up to two years. Without me even knowing!

"As if that wasn't enough, you come back here dripping with blood. Some yours. Some not. And you tell me you've killed a man. Before he could kill you. And all this without any mention of the additional danger this might have put *me* in. I've been wandering around the city, doing your business, without any idea if I'm going to be attacked in the same way.

"And last night, you pull me from my bed to tell me that the corpse of this man Bourchier has been dumped right at the door of your secret meeting place, and that three dozen innocent men have been murdered to cover his murderer's tracks?"

Malin looked down at his lap, his head bowed.

"The worst bloody thing, though, is how you've been since you got back from that damned visit to England. I hardly recognise you. Even Mainard thinks you've changed. For God's sake, Malin. You're settled here. You *live* here. *This* is where your friends are. And you've lied to your best friend here, the man who has done everything for you over the years to help you settle here and make a life. Even now, with death coming closer each day, you're still not telling him the whole truth.

"And what of me, Malin? I know the part I play here, and I have willingly accepted it. From the moment we came here. But I never thought that you would treat me like this. Like anyone you could fob off with half-truths and pretence. Keep me at arm's length doing all your chores, like some low-paid errand boy."

Symon paused. "I know how you feel about your father. About how he has punished you at every opportunity for being born. But at least you *had* a father. And an uncle that could step in to fill at least some of the void left by your mother. How can you treat Uberto the way you do? He has been every bit the father to you that Haylan was, yet you still let him walk around believing that his time will come."

Malin found his voice. "Symon, I wish it were otherwise. I truly do. I did not seek this. I did not get involved to give him false hope. You have to believe that."

"But don't you see, Malin. You did it anyway. I know you've only been aware of Genoa's part in this for a week. But did you really think that Uberto would come out of this unharmed, even if the whole thing was just England's idea? Everyone believes that this place works on family history and the willingness to use it to make money. But that's not true. It demands the one thing Uberto will never be able to enjoy again, no matter what position he is granted. Malin, he would never be *trusted* again. And for him? For him, that would be like sticking him with the most treacherous of knives."

"I... I didn't think it would—"

"No, I'm sure you didn't. That's the problem. You've stopped thinking about anyone but yourself. All that talk the other day about how Mainard must stay here. Must! He only came here because he cares about you, and you're ordering him to plunge as deep into this as you are.

"And as for me. Well. You know how I feel about you. We never speak of it, because we have never needed to. But you have shut me out. Treated me like just another one of the men with a part to play in this madness. I've done my best to do everything to help you through this, these last two weeks. But I've become little more than a runner of errands. Chasing around the city all day to complete menial and bloody pointless tasks to cover your tracks, or worse still, to keep me out of your way."

Malin snapped. "That's not true. I've never sought to avoid you. You have to know that. We are partners, you and I."

"Well it doesn't feel like it. Not since you came back. And I don't want to do this anymore."

"But I don't want any of this either!"

"Yet you continue to behave as though we're all just here to be moved around like puppets in some great scheme that only you control. One where anyone can be sacrificed."

Seeing that his words had hit finally hit their mark, he stepped back. He found it hard to get his breath. He turned as he walked to the door.

"Malin, you told me how Brenner used to pick on you. Treated you the way that a brother never should. The way you have used me over the last month is little different. Things have to change, or none of us will be able to protect each other. Or even want to."

He walked out.

An hour later, just after the Nones bells had rung across the city, Mainard came downstairs.

He found Malin and Symon in the office. Each seemed distracted by their own thoughts, but there was also a distinct air of tension in the room.

Assuming they remained preoccupied with the overnight discovery at the *scuole*, he withdrew to the reception room to wait for Uberto's arrival.

★

Finally released from Malin's embrace, Uberto looked into his friend's eyes. "What was that for? I've not even removed my coat, and you're greeting me as though you've not seen me for years!"

The four men sat at their usual places around the table. Their new routine, a mere three days old, had already become something of a comfort against what felt like an increasingly hostile world.

Uberto had been busy. He had left the *scuole* at dawn and resumed his position outside Soranzo's house. Sclavo had remained to address the matter of how to dispose of all the bodies.

"Where Sclavo's ability to cope comes from is a mystery to me. Neither myself nor Donata have ever had such a force of will. In better times, I had hoped that none of my children would ever need such skills. But the carnage of last night?" He shook his head. "Brutality of any kind must be confronted and dealt with. But facing it robs you of something, doesn't it? Leaves a stain that will never fade. Anyway, Sclavo will work with the *banca* to arrange for the preparation of the bodies for burial. They'll notify each family that their loved one has passed. No one will learn of so many deaths in one night."

He looked across at Mainard. "What would you like to do with Bourchier?"

"I think it wise to dispose of him as though he were one of your own, Uberto."

Malin was curious. "And what of the attendants? How will they be handled?"

"Ah. There lies a dilemma of a different sort. Their bodies were not found. Sclavo sent one of his men to me today to confirm that three of them have not reported for duty. Not that they would have any patients to attend to if they had. We think they may have been taken by the same men that had Bourchier. All three are ordinary citizens, known to Sclavo for many years. But they also possess information of use to our enemies. They will have seen us parade backwards and forwards through the hospice for our meetings many times over the last year. A list of our names will allow anyone to guess at the nature of our conspiracy."

Talk stalled for a moment or two while each man considered the implications.

Uberto was looking increasingly tired. "So they know who we are. Where we meet. They knew Bourchier was one of us. So why have they still not seized us? Every day they delay, we are more prepared. What benefit do they enjoy by holding off?"

Mainard tapped his lips with the side of his forefingers. "I'm not sure, Uberto. But equally, how sure are we that what happened last night was the work of The Ten? Is this really something they would do? Kill thirty harmless old men just to send a message with a corpse. Seize three more innocents, simply to confirm what they probably already know?"

Uberto looked around the room. "But if it's not The Ten, then who is it?"

Malin could feel Symon's gaze. "I don't know, my friend. Perhaps The Ten have changed their methods. Perhaps they are having their sport with us. They might wish to push us into premature action. Force our hand. Their behaviour seems strange to us, but only because it lacks precedent. Perhaps our view of them can no longer be trusted. Their leadership changes regularly, and Dandolo's requirement of them may have altered. Perhaps he has granted them additional freedoms. They may even be answerable to no one. In which case, anything is possible.

"Right now, we don't know for sure who our enemies are. Yes, The Ten are duty bound to oppose us. But to be safe, we should assume that anyone outside our immediate group might bear us ill. So let's discuss what our own actions should be, but ensure that they account for any possible adversary. First, then, can we all agree that our meeting with Libusch should proceed as planned?"

There were no objections. Malin would travel to Murano with Uberto and Mainard on Saturday. In addition to confirming Libusch's readiness, they would confirm the date and precise details of their joint action.

Mainard continued. "Our priority now, beyond handling last night's damage, is to confirm with each delegate that the men that they speak for are truly prepared. Uberto, I assume you and your son will continue to follow Soranzo?"

"Hah! In all the discussion of last night's events, I have failed to describe my many trips across San Marco today. He has been visiting his main supporters in the *sestiere*, no doubt informing them of the wonderful way he represented their interests in yesterday's Council meeting. It's hard to know what they have discussed for certain, but his day appeared similar to those Mondays I myself used to experience. And yes, Sclavo is at the *campo* with his men. I think we should continue as planned. At least until our trip to Murano."

Malin confirmed that the cover afforded by the Quarant remained solid.

They ended the meeting by running through their list of friends to ensure they had overlooked nothing of importance.

Symon offered more wine, but the lack of enthusiasm was obvious.

They said their farewells, and Malin walked Uberto to the dock. "One last lungful or two of Lagoon air will do me good."

The street was in darkness, with only one lamp lit between the house and the small jetty where Uberto's oarsman would be waiting.

Malin noticed that Uberto's step had lost a little of his customary liveliness. "And how have you coped with what we found last night?"

Uberto slowed. "Ah, well. I don't suppose I shall forget that sight for a long time. There's something very sobering about

283

looking upon death close up. I've been to my share of funerals over the years, but to see such a wanton act. Such a total lack of compunction..."

He moved out from the centre of the street, and leaned against the blank wall to their right.

"I'm coming to hate this, Malin. Any excitement I felt at the possibility of a return to our life before has almost gone. Look what it's costing. There were always going to be casualties. I'm not naive enough to believe otherwise. But it was Sclavo and myself that were pleased to offer the *scuole* as a regular meeting place. We congratulated ourselves on such a convenient and credible venue. Some of our number were already active in the confraternity before any of this even began."

He looked down at the flagstones. "But those men, Malin. Lying there. Robbed of their final dignity. Visited by an evil that only knew of their existence because of the choices *we* have made."

"The responsibility lies with all of us, Uberto. Don't take the weight of this only on yourself."

Uberto looked to the end of the street. The dark water at the quayside was just visible, a mass defined only by its lack of stone and substance.

"Last night, amongst those beds, I saw into the real nature of what we are doing. Perhaps for the first time. Many more people may get hurt, Malin. Many of them strangers to us, who deserve no such fate. And what of our families? Our friends? We may hurt them too."

"Uberto, you are tired. You must not allow these thoughts to trouble you. They are not unsound, but you need your full strength to deal with them."

"And what of you, Malin?" Malin looked a little startled. "What of you? Is this what *you* had envisaged when this began? I thought you looked particularly uneasy tonight. You more than any of us knew Bourchier well."

"I miss having him to rely on. And of course, share your worry that what was once in his head is now the property of our enemies."

Uberto looked at him curiously.

"Please take no offence, but I have to say it. You seem almost hardened to proof of his murder. And to the violence visited upon the patients of the *ospizio*. I have to ask you. Are you as unaffected as you claim? There is no shame in sharing your anxieties with your friends."

Malin shook his head. "We just need to stay on course. We will have time to mourn, to reflect, when this is all done." His tone softened. "But thank you for being honest with me. Please do not worry. My hand is healing, and I am grateful to have avoided Ricaud's fate."

At that moment, Malin's head began to spin. He reached forward to steady himself on Uberto's arm. "I fear the grippe is on its way, after my drenching at the Lido yesterday."

They walked the remaining distance to the quay, and Uberto stepped down onto the waiting boat. "Well, my friend, make sure you sleep well. I will see you again tomorrow."

Malin walked slowly back to the house, still a little lightheaded.

Unable to consider sleep, he sat by the fire in the front room. A light sweat beaded his brow.

Symon would give him hell in the morning for maintaining his silence about the Peruzzi. He would nod respectfully, and defend himself as best he could. Even if he knew he had failed his friend once more.

Waking up in the chair some time later, he made his way to the stairs. As he climbed, he began to consider all the things he had learned since the morning, and how he would find the right words for his journal.

Chapter 25

Tuesday 19th February 1348

Day 24 of the Quarant

He was right, of course. Symon wasted no time the next morning in berating him.

"But he deserves to know. Why hide it?"

Malin stumbled through his half-hearted justification.

"He has enough to worry him at the moment. It would undermine what little confidence he still has, and at the same time, offer little practical advantage to our efforts."

"That's not good enough. I'm new to all this. But even I can tell that no one believes that The Ten are the only ones active in the city now. Is it because you don't want to talk about your father's treachery?"

"Stop. I'm not discussing this any further."

"It is, isn't it. But don't you see? Uberto would never hold that against you. He knows everything about your father that matters. Everything about how he has treated you."

"But not this. No matter what Jefferey has done to me in

the past, it has had no impact at all on Uberto or his family. I do not want him to know that I have somehow dragged my own problems into this. Made them his."

Symon tried hard to remain calm.

"*You* might not have dragged anything in, but it still threatens Uberto. It's not right. How would you feel if he kept something like this from *you*?"

Malin had no intention of storming out. He didn't have the energy to stamp and rage. His head was sore, and he just wanted this conversation to end.

"Symon. I'll consider it, all right? But at the moment, please respect my judgement. I have not taken this course lightly."

The conversation ended. At least for now.

As he travelled to San Polo, he reflected on his temporary victory. Mainard and Symon would spend the day creating a detailed list of all issues to be addressed at the weekend meeting with Libusch. The Peruzzi name would inevitably come up.

At least if he wasn't there, he would not have to fight his corner again. His head had been thumping since waking that morning. The minor fever that had crept up on him during the night was still lurking. He was glad to leave the thinking to others today.

He walked to the apothecary on Calle Paglia on his way to Uberto's. His partial new stock of gentian had almost gone, and after their conversations of the last two days, he had no intention of asking Symon if he had collected the remaining supply.

Perhaps, while he was there, he could ask for something else to help with his headache.

On his last daytime journey across the city, Malin had stood beneath the Doge's Palace, wondering if Bourchier was somewhere within its walls.

Today, he did everything within his power to use the widest, busiest streets. He had no wish to find himself isolated on any narrow thoroughfare, vulnerable to ambush or capture away from any observing crowd. He wove his way through the city, frequently looking into the faces of passers-by, searching for any suggestion that their business was somehow feigned, a mask for more sinister motives.

The deeper he immersed himself in the bustle of the city the more nervous he became. His chest burned. By the time he crossed the Ponte Storto, the last bridge before the apothecary, he had stopped bothering to return the phial of gentian back into his jacket pocket.

A small throng of people stood at the apothecary door. Despite their proximity, no one was talking. More men and women still stood inside, equally silent.

The shopkeeper was nowhere to be seen.

He wandered across the room to the far door, from where the man had emerged on his previous visit. He was unsure what to do. He could not remember the apothecary's name, and was reluctant to invade the man's premises. Deciding to wait for him to appear, he stepped back and leaned against one of the walls.

He looked around him at the other customers. Several of them looked unwell. One man was slightly bent over, clutching his middle. A thin, tidily dressed woman stood in the centre of the room, her face flushed and red.

In the time it took for the apothecary to appear, a further three men entered the room, each clearly in need of help.

It took some time for Malin to work his way to the front of the queue.

"I'm sorry, sir, for keeping you waiting. I have asked my wife and brother to come and help me cope, so the delay should gradually get shorter."

Malin asked if he could collect the remaining part of his gentian order.

"But I gave the remaining urns to your friend at the end of last week, sir. He was most clear that he was collecting them on your instructions."

Symon. As reliable as ever.

"I'm sorry, then, for troubling you. I'm sure he has put them somewhere safe. But while I am here, I wonder if you might be able to offer me something that will ease my headache? I have a growing chill and fever, and would prefer to treat it now, rather than see it worsen."

The apothecary laughed wryly. "I do not mean to be rude, sir, but take a look around you. I have been working day and night since the weekend, and my stock of willow bark is long exhausted."

The man pushed back his long black hair from his forehead. He looked genuinely tired, and Malin wondered if he might not be on the verge of illness himself.

He walked back into the street, and looked more closely at the crowd of bystanders. Many of them appeared to have the same sheen of sweat on their faces. Perhaps their heads were sore too.

★

It was almost noon when he arrived at the house on Calle Donzella.

Donata's embrace when she joined him in the reception room was as warm as ever. "Ah, Malin. It's so good to see you. Uberto told me that you're both sinking under the weight of all the paperwork needed for the *mudae*. It seems to get worse every year. Perhaps Sclavo made the right choice to avoid following in his father's shoes."

Malin laughed. "I think Sclavo's skills are perfectly suited to the work he does at the Arsenale. The respect they have for him there is truly remarkable."

Donata's face beamed with pride.

"And I'm sure he was only trying to do his best for the family by following a different path to Uberto. I've seen how much he loves his father. How much he admires the way he always repays the trust his partners and friends have in him. And yes, this time of year? Insurances, submissions to Customs. The magistracy? It does seem as though we are working simply to keep the authorities busy."

Donata gestured to Malin to take a seat. She took care to rearrange her skirts on the crimson upholstery.

"My dear. Lucia and Collette are aware of your arrival, and await you upstairs. But I wanted to speak with you alone first. Just for a few moments."

Her tone was light, but her hands were clasped tightly together.

"What is it that concerns you, Signora Donata?"

"Concern? Oh no. Nothing of the kind. I do, however, need to tell you of my feelings. Regarding Lucia and yourself."

Malin's smile disappeared immediately.

"I believe you know that Lucia informed me of what has passed between you in the last few days?"

"Yes, I do. And that it is you, and only you, that is aware of our changed circumstances."

"Oh. Please. I promised her I would say nothing of these matters to her father. And I have honoured that. No. It is because of that promise that I must speak to you now."

Malin could not help but sound defensive. "Please, Signora. I had no desire to behave disrespectfully, to you or to Uberto. I simply wished to give Lucia some time to consider my words."

Donata raised her hand to stop him. "I have no argument with you, Malin. Please know that. But I want to tell you some things about Uberto and I. Things that might give you a better understanding of us, and how we feel about Lucia. About all our children."

Donata relaxed into the back of the chair.

"You must understand, Malin. When we arrived here, Uberto and myself, we had almost nothing. Outsiders from Ragusa. A small son, less than two years old. We shared a large single room in a *cavane*, with the families of three ferrymen on the Giudecca shore. It was Uberto's first job when we got here. Taking ships' crew to and from their berths. It was the only way he could get some kind of foothold. It took him over a year to find a way to begin as a merchant here. Our money had almost run out by then. But he was determined to make it work. When Lucia was born, two years later, we rented a place of our own, a little further inland.

"He worked so hard, Malin. You see him now, and perhaps think of him as a conscientious, hard worker. But then? He barely ever slept. Always planning his next venture. Working in any one of dozens of warehouses or yards across the city. I see some of that in Sclavo. And his sharpness of mind? I definitely see that in Lucia.

"By the time our daughter took her first steps, Uberto had chartered his first ship. I remember how he took us to see it. Dwarfed by the ships around it, but to us, it was majestic. I was so proud of him that day."

Uberto had shared little of his origins with Malin. He knew he came from humble beginnings on the other side of the Adriatic, but little else. For all his charm and openness, Uberto had been very protective of his past.

"Anyway, Uberto grew his business, just as he and I raised our family. You could say that these two things became the great purpose of our lives. They still are. There are many things about Uberto's business that even now I don't fully understand. The same holds for our children. Sclavo became his own man a long while ago. When Uberto had his 'fall from grace', as he calls it, our fear was that the Council would replace Sclavo at the Arsenale as a way to further humiliate us. But it is to Sclavo's credit that it didn't happen. They overlooked his paternity in the interests of the Republic, you see. The whole city knows how he keeps the heart of the shipyard beating."

She leant forward and patted Malin's leg.

"Listen to me talk like this. You must wonder what I am trying to say. What I want you to know is that our family has been our shared work. It took Uberto the full twenty-five years to be formally recognised as a citizen. Unheard of, as he was already voted onto the Council by then. Far, far longer than his success demanded. But he had persevered, because he wanted it for his children. Their lives here were stable and tolerable, but they were still outsiders. And then, to see our family name in the Golden Book? He could not have been happier.

"He is a proud man, Malin. Bitter, yes, about losing his nobility so soon after it was granted him. He feels for your own story, too, deprived of your own position as an Earl's son. Nothing of that is lost on him. He has never really understood why, with your obvious affection for Lucia over the years, you have not taken this step before. When he fell from favour, he thought that you had finally decided that we were not good enough for you. But he still loves you like a son.

"So tell me, Malin. Before I tell him. Why did you spend so many years keeping your feelings for Lucia secret?"

Malin had no idea where to start.

He had met her for the first time when she was just sixteen, on his second visit to Uberto's home. He immediately recognised her fierce intelligence and unflinching honesty. At that time, he still only had a basic grasp of the language. Several months later, Uberto had confessed to censoring some of her translated retorts for fear that he would take offence.

Then, as he was slowly taken into the heart of the family, he found himself increasingly looking forward to sharing with her his latest news of foreign trade and travel.

"I'm afraid I cannot answer that, Signora. I am often a mystery to myself."

He felt the guilt shift in his chest. Were it not for his growing alarm at the challenges facing him on his return to Venice, and his inability to hide it from her, he would never have made any move at all. It was the true answer, but one he could never give.

"I am gratified that you consider me a fitting suitor for your daughter. But I would ask you to continue to honour our wishes, and withhold this news for a little longer still."

Donata looked puzzled. "But why?"

"You have said yourself that Uberto is under a great deal of additional pressure. I would rather we wait until the news can be enjoyed in a more relaxed manner."

Her face softened. "I imagine a few more days will make little difference, even though both Lucia and myself dislike secrets. But in return, I have a favour to ask."

She told him of her growing worry about her husband. Of the dramatic recent increase in his time away from the house. "He's no longer a young man, Malin. He's not even the middle-aged man that took solace in his business when his political life ended. In the last month he has hardly been here. And when he is, his mind seems elsewhere. Would you speak to him for me? Help him to understand that he might not be as sturdy as he thinks himself?"

When Donata rose to take him to meet Collette and Lucia, Malin followed at a distance that allowed a swift mouthful of gentian, and a furtive run of his sleeve across his damp forehead.

★

293

The afternoon had gone well.

Lucia and Collette were inseparable. Which meant that the conversation, while at times unpredictable, rarely wandered onto dangerous ground. No talk of love. No talk of future plans.

Malin relaxed to the point where time simply passed.

He had just begun to think about getting back to Castello for their evening meeting with Uberto, when the man himself walked in.

One look was enough to see that something was very wrong.

"Ah, Malin. It's good to see you." He walked up to the younger man, slightly out of breath, and embraced him in his usual manner. "I see you've decided to enjoy the company of these lovely ladies. But could I have a moment or two with you to discuss something that involves us both?"

Waving off Collette's demands that he remained for dinner, Malin followed Uberto into his private reception room.

Uberto turned to face him as soon as the door closed behind them. "Malin, I have to talk this through with you. I have thought myself into a maze, and I need you to lead me out of it."

His day had begun as his last few had, travelling the short distance across the Canal to relieve Sclavo at the Campiello Santa Maria. Sclavo had little of note to report, beyond the movement of one or two servants. About mid-morning, just after the Terce bells, Soranzo left the house alone. This *was* quite unusual. His previous journeys had been in the company of his surly, dark-clothed bodyguard.

Uberto took two men with him, and followed at a safe distance. Soranzo headed north, up towards the border between San Marco and Cannaregio. When he turned into a shaded alley, lined on each side by semi-dilapidated houses, they returned to the earlier junction to wait for his reappearance.

"We stood there until noon. I sent one of the men to circle

around and position himself at the far end of the alley, in case Soranzo chose to continue his journey north.

"When he emerged, he was with two men. One of them I recognised immediately, even at that distance. It was his bodyguard. But I had no idea where he had come from. He had certainly not accompanied Soranzo at any point. We stepped back, seeing they were headed in our direction.

"When they passed, we had a clear view. The other man, Malin? I'm sure it was Del Chiaro. The businessman from Florence.

"Anyway, we tailed Soranzo and his man at a safe distance. It looked as though they were heading back home. Del Chiaro, if it was him, left them as they reached the bridge at Calle Fuseri. I don't know where he went after that, as the man I'd set at the top end of the street in Cannaregio had not yet re-joined us.

"When we got back to San Marco, my mind was chasing in a hundred directions at once. What the hell was Soranzo doing with Del Chiaro? Of course, it could just be Del Chiaro pursuing another business venture. But why meet in such a rundown part of the city, and why was Soranzo's bodyguard with him?

"I sent a messenger to Giradino. Told him to go to the Admiralty Office, and ask to see their records. To look at copies of any contract lodged with them over the last year that featured Del Chiaro as partner, buyer or seller. It cost me a pretty sum to see the request processed in haste. Anyway, the clerks confirmed that they had no record of a Del Chiaro ever having done business in the city. None. And he was not registered as a foreign merchant or trader."

Uberto paused, clasping the back of his neck with his hands. Malin had rarely seen him more uncomfortable.

"What do you think is going on, Malin? Why do these men know each other? I hope you don't mind, but I've sent a message to Sclavo at the Arsenale. I think he should join us at your house this evening, before he takes on the evening watch."

Thoughts of the Peruzzi roared through Malin's mind. And then, of Uberto's unquestioning openness.

"Yes. Yes, of course. That's a good idea."

There must have been something in the way he said it.

"Malin? What's wrong?"

A wave of fatigue swept over him, his headache returning with force. This must end. He no longer had any choice.

"My friend, I have to tell you some things of which I am ashamed. Things that you have had every right to know. I told myself that it was better to keep them from you. I see now that I was wrong."

He told Uberto everything. The Peruzzi's vow of revenge against the English. Their blackmail of Jefferey. His father's treachery and betrayal.

But nothing of Genoa.

That was too much to expect Uberto to bear. And too much for him to confess.

Outside the door, Donata and her daughters prepared for dinner.

The men gave their apologies as they left to travel back east together, to Malin's home in Castello.

*

Sclavo was already there when they arrived. "So this is where you share gossip every night. What have I done to be honoured with such a summons?"

Uberto was in no mood for jesting. "It is good that you could be here. The night watch at Soranzo's is still needed, but the men are well practiced now in what is required. Your time here is more important."

Uberto outlined the events of the day. Malin left him to explain how this might now suggest that Soranzo was in league with the Peruzzi. He made no missteps in describing the bankers' activities in England. Mainard and Symon sat quietly, glancing at Malin as each new revelation passed between father and son.

"So as you can see, Sclavo, we have not been in possession of the full truth in these matters. If you are angry, I fully understand. For myself I have decided, in the time spent travelling here, to bite down on my own anger. I take no pleasure in knowing that these men have deceived us. But there is nothing to gain from lashing out. We have much to discuss."

Sclavo's initial cheer was long gone.

Malin wondered if this would be the moment he would receive his second beating at the Venetian's hand.

Mainard was the first to break the brooding silence.

"So, forgive me, but we must keep our thoughts on what we now know. It seems safe to assume that Soranzo and Del Chiaro, if that is his real name, are working together. It is also possible that it is *they* and not The Ten who took and killed Bourchier. That *they* seized the attendants at the hospice. Yet we still cannot rule out the possibility that The Ten are also aware of our presence."

Symon groaned, his eyes rolling back in his head, and rose from the table. "Sweet Jesus. Anyone need a drink?"

No one objected.

Malin could still feel Sclavo's eyes burning into him. "So what do each of you think we should do?"

Symon argued that they should call off the whole plot. Sclavo called for immediate action against Soranzo and 'the bastard Florentine'. Mainard advocated continued adherence to their plans. Uberto agreed with Mainard, but expressed a wish that they hasten.

Malin just listened.

They decided to sleep on it overnight. Sclavo suggested that they meet in his office at the Arsenale the following morning, after he returned from his night watch.

When Sclavo moved to leave, Uberto rose to accompany him.

Malin stayed seated as they left. They would need more time together to absorb what they had just learned, and explore their feelings about how their closest friend had kept so much from them.

Chapter 26

Wednesday 20th February 1348

Day 25 of the Quarant

Malin's sleep was troubled by dreams of sneering fathers and despairing friends. On each waking, his sheets were drenched further with a cold sweat. Repeated attempts to quell thoughts of the previous day's events provoked a resurgence of burning in his chest. Seeking a position to ease it, the sheets tightened further around his body.

He surrendered at dawn, unrefreshed but determined to find some distraction. At least the intensity of the chest pain abated a little, helped by a generous dose of gentian.

He continued to revisit his conversation with Uberto at Calle Donzella. Saw again the look on Uberto's face as he listened to his confession.

At least the truth of Genoa remained hidden. It would have to stay that way.

Malin's head throbbed after descending the stairs, but with less severity than the previous day. Hopefully, it would clear with the walk to the Arsenale. He made a note to add something to his journal later, that only young men should sit for hours in the rain.

Symon and Mainard greeted him, and returned to their breakfast. Malin was about to sit down and join them, but abruptly stopped.

"Oh, Symon. With all that happened yesterday, I forgot to mention that I visited the apothecary. He told me that you had been there last week. I fear I have not thanked you for making your way across."

Symon's face betrayed his surprise. "I was pleased to do it. Although I'm not sure where we might source the next batch from, should it be needed. The man I spoke to sounded very unsure of whether any of his supplies would see out the illness in the city."

"Well in any case, I wanted to thank you now, for fear it leaves my mind again. I expect we'll have further things to think about today."

Mainard chuckled ruefully. "Well whatever they are, I hope we are able to make more sense of the way ahead than we did last night. Did either of you stumble across any inspiration in the realms of sleep?" The glances that followed were answer enough. "We cannot just leave things as they are. Our Venetian friends will expect us to have something to offer."

Symon shuffled in his chair. "It's not that easy though, is it? This whole scheme of yours. Sorry, of *ours*. The way I understand it, any Florentine threat has been there all along. If Soranzo has been involved with them from the start, could he have told them more than Bourchier? If not, then the only new problem is that Uberto and Sclavo know about it now."

Malin considered his friend's words. "And Uberto has suspected Soranzo for days already, else he and Sclavo would not be marching behind him all over Venice. Do you think there is a chance that Uberto will walk away from the conspiracy?"

Mainard shook his head. "That won't happen. He is as stubborn as you, Malin. But this could badly damage his confidence."

Malin finally had an idea. "So perhaps we encourage them to see that this is simply one more example of how the current regime cannot be trusted. That they are even more corruptible than Uberto already believed."

"And can you honestly say that Uberto and his colleagues see themselves as behaving honourably?" Symon seemed unwilling to meet the eyes of the other two men.

Mainard reacted first, anticipating opposition from Malin. "It's a fair question?"

Malin turned to Symon. "None of this is about honour. I'm not sure it ever has been. For Uberto and his friends, this has always been about being excluded from the ranks of those that decide on how the Republic advances. If pushed, all of them would admit to having a selfish reason for gaining influence.

"But that does not mean they lack merit above other men. It saddens me more each day to see them daring all to change things here. Even more so when I consider what fate might lie ahead of them, successful or not. But they have a right to their beliefs, and they have the right to pursue them."

Leaving the house, each of them wondered how the Da Segnas would greet them.

★

Father and son were already in the office when they arrived.

Uberto seemed to have aged ten years overnight. His shoulders were lower, his head held a little further down. When he looked up at Malin, it was clear that he was still shaken.

Sclavo told his clerk that they were not to be disturbed, and

301

then closed the door. "I trust you have some useful suggestions for how we proceed?" His abrupt tone suggested impatience.

Malin glanced at Mainard and Symon, checking to see if any of them wished to speak.

Sclavo stepped in before he had a chance to respond.

"No. I thought not. I think it is time to stop all this damn talk, anyway. It's all we've been doing since you got back, Malin. And what has it gained us? We are getting nowhere, and it's clear that you don't trust any of us locals. Judging by the last two weeks, it is only you and Glyn here that are entitled to know everything."

Malin leaned in. "Please Sclavo. You misunderstand. It is simply that some aspects of our endeavour have been so uncertain, or so potentially distracting, that they have not merited the telling."

Sclavo sprang to his feet, unable to control his anger.

"So *you* decide what is worth knowing and what is not. *You* decide if *we* are to be trusted. Are we children, unable to cope with matters above our heads?"

"It's not like that, Sclavo."

"Well it damn well feels like it. We've recruited and mobilised men across the city. And we've done it as part of an alliance *of equals*. But now, after all this time, we find that you have been withholding truths from us. It's not just about trust. It's about *respect*. And it's clear you offer us neither!" He turned his back on them, striding the small distance to the window looking out over the shipyard.

Uberto went to his son and put his arm around the taller man's shoulder. Sclavo shrugged it off, whirling round to face him.

"Don't try to soothe me. These things must be said, and be said now. I know you feel it too, yet you will not say so."

Symon slowly rose to his feet.

302

"Sclavo. Listen to me. Much of what you say is true. And I know the pain you feel when finding that important things have been kept from you. Until three weeks ago, and again more recently still, I have been in a similar position. In part due directly to the secrecy of yourself and your father."

Malin began to interrupt.

"No, Malin, let me finish. Sclavo, Malin only told me of your plot three weeks ago. I believe he kept it from me to protect me, not to diminish or disrespect me. It hurt like hell at the time, but I see now that he meant no harm. Perhaps he thought he was strong enough to manage matters on his own, and therefore had no need for me to ever know of them. It no longer matters. My point, and this is as true for you and Uberto and all of your friends as it was for me, is that his intentions have always been honourable, and borne from love. His father's betrayal hurts him at least as much as it does us. More. And it changes nothing. Nothing of importance. Unless you let it."

Symon sat down.

The room fell silent.

The colour in Sclavo's face slowly lessened, but his struggle to retain control of his emotions remained obvious.

"I understand what you say, Symon. And I can see why Malin has become so dependent on you for so many years. Yet you are wrong. His reluctance to tell us all has changed everything."

Malin could listen no longer. "In what way?"

Sclavo looked directly at his father as he answered.

"In every way. I have Soranzo."

★

Uberto was as shocked as the rest of them.

303

They sat, open-mouthed and grim, as Sclavo told of the night's events.

On his way back to San Marco, Sclavo had decided to act. On reaching the north side of the quay at the end of the Campiello Traghetto, he parted from his father and gathered his men from the Arsenale together. They confirmed that Soranzo had remained in his house since arriving back from his meeting with Del Chiaro that morning. He then sent one of them to take a message to Giacomo Favero, the head of the ferryman's guild, requesting that a boat and four of his most trusted men be brought to the moorings at the end of the street.

Returning to the Soranzo house, they waited for news of the arrival of Favero's boat, and then made their move. Breaking into the house through its secluded back entrance, they quickly found Soranzo's second floor chamber. They tied and gagged his wife, and escorted the Councillor back downstairs. The servants either slept through the entire event, or chose to keep out of trouble. Although expected, Soranzo's bodyguard was nowhere to be seen.

They left the house as quietly as they entered it, and made their way across the square to the waiting boatmen. Soranzo was passed onto the boat, Sclavo boarded, and the party made their way along the Canal, heading east towards the Arsenale.

"And Soranzo offered no resistance?" Uberto could not believe his ears.

"Stripped of his attendant, and the protection of his rank, he was timid. Affronted at the assault, and no doubt unfamiliar with the rough ways of the street. A dagger held to his throat, and a promise that any complaint from him would cause us to use it, seemed enough."

They disembarked at the main gates of the Arsenale and Sclavo vouched for their entry. They then escorted their prisoner along the deserted quaysides to one of the many supply warehouses at the far end of the yard.

"So, you have him here right now?"

Sclavo had walked back to gaze out of the window. "You can't quite see the roof of the warehouse from here. It's just a little further in and around."

Uberto could barely contain himself. "But this is outrageous, Sclavo! What were you thinking? He's a *Signori*. One of the members of the Small Council!"

"Do you think I did this lightly?"

"Of course not. But to take such a step now. And without us having a chance to discuss it?"

Sclavo's anger returned. "Discuss it? You've seen what our discussions have achieved. We drift along, seeing each day a new signal of the growing threat of discovery, and what do we do? We discuss. We talk. And we do nothing. Well, no more. We must take control. And to do that, we need to know much more about what we face. Who is against us, and what they are doing. What they are *going* to do."

It was Mainard's turn to express his exasperation. "But to strike at the heart of things before we are ready. Is this the kind of action that will help us win? You have started something that we may not be able to bridle. How will you handle Soranzo now you have him? He leads a very public life, so surely he will be missed?"

Sclavo was in no mood to back down. "At this moment, I don't care. The chances are that the only people that miss him will be those he has appointments with this week. We made it clear to his wife that if she wanted to see him alive, she must tell no one of what we have done. The next Council meeting is not for another four days, which gives us ample time to get the answers we need. We can decide how to deal with him once we have them."

Sclavo's plan was to keep the man hidden within the boundaries of the Arsenale, and spend the next few days learning the truth from him.

It was Malin who finally demanded to see him.

"Why do you want that? Do you trust me so little on this as well?"

"In truth, I'm not sure. But how secure is he? How safe is it to keep him here? Do you really believe you can hide him here for days? Thousands of men come in and out of here every shift."

Sclavo clenched his jaw. "If there are two things you *can* trust, Malin, it is that I will do nothing more to put my father in danger, and that I know how every inch of this yard works."

Uberto reached across and placed a hand on Malin's shoulder.

He looked at his son.

"If you can do so safely, I would like it very much if you could show us where he is being kept. Then we will talk once more."

★

The day had gradually brightened.

The bell tower at the entrance to the shipyard, casting a shadow across their stone pathway, seemed to Malin to be just one more place from which their movements could be watched. The hair on the back of Malin's neck bristled at the thought of prying eyes.

They headed further into the main construction yards.

Sclavo was accosted by one of the *protomaestri*. Malin could hear the two men talking, but nothing of what was said. When they finally parted, Sclavo returned to their party.

"Is everything in order?"

Sclavo brushed away Malin's concern. "It's nothing. Our workforce appears down by one in twenty today. It's actually good news for us in the office, as a few shipments of timber and sailcloth have also failed to arrive. Each shortfall will conceal the other."

They continued along the eastern quays.

The scale of the place was unrivalled, expanded thirty years earlier to increase its capacity for building and repair. The yard was capable of producing up to three new vessels every week, as long as materials flowed smoothly into their many warehouses. They had begun making their own rope, but Sclavo was responsible for ensuring all other materials arrived at the front gates well before being needed.

As they turned into the main basin of the Arsenale Nuovo, they were offered an almost uninterrupted view of the entire construction process. At the far end of the basin, hewn from the reclaimed island and reinforced with new dock walls, were the bare, incomplete ribs of several new ships, three of them still in dry dock.

The nature of the work done in each area of the yard dictated where each guild enjoyed their greatest influence. Where ships' frames were the main construction task, joiners, shipwrights, and those skilled in the creation and application of pitch were strongest. Grisani's guild members were well known for the number of victories won for the workers at the expense of the patrons.

They walked past ships that appeared complete, awaiting only their final outfitting before beginning sea trials out beyond the large defensive tower at the north-east entrance. In happier times, Malin could have spent days there, just admiring the yard's organisational prowess.

Sclavo finally turned from the quayside and towards one of four dark, wooden warehouses. The smell of fresh timber filled their nostrils as they left much of the hammering and shouting behind. Gesturing to a small side door, Sclavo entered the building. They left the bright sunshine and stood just inside the door, waiting for their eyes to adjust to the high-roofed gloom.

Footsteps approached, and Sclavo moved forward to greet three men. After a brief conversation, he indicated that they should join him. A few more yards, and they stood in front of another small door.

"You'll see a set of stairs off to your right. When I go through this door, I want you to ascend them, and then hold your counsel while I speak to Soranzo. He will not know you are there if you remain silent."

He opened the final door and entered. Two of the three men followed him, and the third turned his back to the closed door, his arms crossed.

Malin led the way, moving up the stairs onto a narrow balcony positioned a dozen or so feet above the bare soil. He watched as Sclavo moved across the room to a seated figure. The man had his back to them.

Sclavo walked behind the man, and checked the ropes securing him to the chair. He looked up to the balcony, confirming that all four of them had taken up position. He drew back his hand, and brought it down hard onto the man's skull.

★

When they emerged back into daylight, Sclavo spoke to them with a firmness that invited little argument.

"I am assuming that none of you wish to share Bourchier's fate, so I am not about to apologise or seek permission for Soranzo's treatment. He will stay here until he tells us every aspect of his deceit.

"I also propose that we assign our *Arsenalotti* to track down

308

Soranzo's bodyguard and Del Chiaro. I hope to learn of their location from Soranzo, but we cannot wait until he decides to talk." The hint of wildness in his eyes was enough to discourage any disagreement. "Father, will you continue to take charge of their work? I will work in the office during the day, while spending my evenings here."

Mainard suggested that he joined Sclavo when the workers left each day. "I am keen to understand more about this Del Chiaro, and might be of assistance if we are offered any information concerning his origin."

Sclavo shrugged, indifferent to his proposal.

They made their way back to the supply office. Sclavo left them at the door, intent on spending the rest of the day there. Orders still required payment, and stock still demanded tallying.

The rest of them departed in silence, each trying to come to terms with what they had seen.

Chapter 27

Thursday 21st February 1348

Day 26 of the Quarant

E motions were raw on their return to Calle San Domenico. None of them felt capable of rational discussion. Symon spent the rest of the day in the office, working on accounts and contractual papers. Mainard said something about rereading the notes for the Libusch meeting, disappeared upstairs for a while, but then left the house. He returned with a strong smell of drink on his breath. For his part, Malin spent the afternoon with the Duns Scotus manuscript on his lap by the fire. By the time he went to sleep, he could recall little of what he had read.

At breakfast, their discussion was brief. Sclavo's reaction had been as unpredictable as it was violent, but at least one thing was clear. The Da Segnas were not withdrawing from the conspiracy.

When Mainard left to meet Sclavo at the Arsenale, they continued to sit at the table.

Malin took the lead, his tone deliberately light. "So how are you coping with all this, Symon? Are you glad I no longer have any secrets?"

Symon laughed ruefully. "It's curious that it takes imminent arrest, or removal at knifepoint of a high-ranking Venetian noble for you to suddenly take an interest in my feelings." His tone was harsh. "Sorry. That sounded worse than I meant it to. My feelings are probably the same as your own. We're caught in something that becomes harder to work through each day. And the way we're speaking to Uberto and Sclavo now? I thought we fitted in here. That we've earned our right to be here. But I'm less sure now. And I also see how this is affecting you. Perhaps I was too blunt with you the other day."

Malin smiled. "No. I deserved it, Symon. But that's not the point. It's you that I care about right now."

"Well, thank you. It doesn't need to be said, but thank you for saying it. I hope that if the day comes when it's no longer true, you would tell me. I just wish you'd found a way to keep us completely out of this mess."

Malin nodded slowly. "I've been thinking back to how this all happened. I never really tried to escape any of this, you know? There must have been a time, a moment when I could have just walked out. Left Westminster, and got the first sailing back here. But I didn't do it. And even now, I'm not sure why." He frowned. "I felt its grip tightening, Symon, but I just allowed it to trap me. I suppose I didn't want to jeopardise everything we'd built, or give anyone the chance to hold it over us. Threaten us with its destruction. But perhaps it's not too late to do something."

"What do you mean?"

Malin got up from the table and leaned against the wall.

"I'm not sure I care as much as I did. About what we've built, I mean. No one can deny our achievements, and I'm proud of them, but I'm beginning to think that other things are more important. Do you think you could find some quiet way to resume our efforts to pull our money together? A small enough amount to escape attention, but enough to offer a future away from here? I know I told you to stop looking into it. Don't repeat this to Uberto or Mainard, but that's beginning to feel like a mistake."

"So, what is it you would like me to do?"

"I'm not sure. But what of our unsettled contracts? Could we find other traders to buy them from us?"

Symon was quick to respond. "Even if it means taking a loss? Are you prepared to do that?"

"Honestly, Symon? At this moment, if the only thing keeping us here was the money we have in the banks, I could happily lose all of it. But for now, it would be just be good enough to know if we could put our hands on a modest part of it without it being noticed."

The sound of a visitor at the door brought the conversation to an end.

A messenger passed over a note addressed to Malin, in Lucia's familiar handwriting. He broke the seal, read it, and told Symon he would be out for the rest of the day.

★

He found her waiting on the corner of the Basilica, sheltering from the morning breeze crossing the Piazza.

It was rare for them to meet openly in the city. Their greeting, a brief touching of hands, was as awkward as it was fleeting. Lucia kept her veil in place, unwilling to dispense with formalities. Her voice, though, was full of warmth.

"Malin, I am so pleased you have come. I could not bear for our next conversation to be shared with Collette. Come, let's get out of the wind. The *Chiesa D'Oro* has never felt so attractive."

They walked briefly back onto the Piazza and past the high arches and colonnades of the church. Four huge bronze horses towered above them, their flanks glistening in the mid-morning sunlight. Pillaged from Constantinople, installed as a permanent reminder of the Republic's military and commercial power, their nostrils flared with the energy of unconstrained flight.

Malin looked around them as they moved under the high, ornate curves of the main door. The threat of being followed weighing on him still after his journey from home. He smiled to himself. It would be harder for anyone to follow them undetected inside.

He turned to Lucia. "It's not that much warmer in here than out there."

"True. Yet it is possible to gain great warmth from all this surrounding beauty. And it does us no harm to meet in a building that bestows an unassailable air of chastity and devoutness."

Her boldness was astonishing.

"Follow me."

She continued along the broad flagstones of the narthex, and entered the main body of the church. Malin had not been inside for many years. The view took his breath away.

Far ahead, the high altar stood ablaze with candles. Thousands of gemstones, embedded in the arch above, glittered with reflected light. A new addition since his last visit. A series of recessed domes stretched the length of the roof, each featuring elaborate gold mosaics. Ceiling recesses were further illuminated by windows around their circumference.

Lucia beckoned him forward. He lowered his eyes, and made a conscious effort to stop his jaw dropping. Catching up with her, they moved to the right, through a large doorway.

The Baptistry.

He had heard Lucia and Donata talk of its restored beauty.

Dandolo had made his name with all these ornate additions, despite being the youngest ever Procurator of the church to hold office.

Yet Malin was ill prepared for its effect. He felt as though he was swimming in a sea of gold.

They walked to the opposite side of the room, around the imposing baptismal font and its towering cover. "May we sit here for a while, Malin? I find that to remain still, and simply move my eyes from one scene to the next, is to allow any form of worry to be lost. To be forgotten amongst such artistry." As she spoke, she lifted the veil from her face, allowing it to fall back over her shoulders.

"Worry? What is it that has worried you?"

"Over the years? Oh, many things. Or perhaps, it is better to say that it has been a small number of things, yet ones that remain stubbornly persistent."

"But surely, apart from your father's recent misfortune, your family have enjoyed a long period of calm and relative peace?"

Lucia patted the space beside her, inviting Malin to join her on the long marble plinth. "I see I need to be clearer. I love my family, and I am entirely devoted to it. But I exist as an individual too, Malin. As a woman without the blessing of youth, or, until recently, the prospect of personal happiness."

Malin welcomed her glance. "And what was it that had previously caused your lack of happiness?"

She continued to look at him. "A number of things, perhaps. The plight of a woman blessed with curiosity, or some small talent for mature thought? My desire to find a rewarding way to serve the great men of this city? Besides entertaining them at dinner."

Malin laughed. "And how did your efforts fare?"

"This is not a matter for humour. I have devoted most

of my life to find some way to fulfil my duty. Yet each time I found a man through whom I could do it, he would fall short in some way. I am not speaking of marriage. I have long since dismissed that from my mind. No. I speak of my duty to assist men of character to improve the lot of our fellow citizens. To help *them* become more principled and virtuous. But such men are truly hard to find. And when they are found? Well. They struggle to appreciate a woman's honest attempts to help. It's like the incident with the water supply last week. A competent woman will always be discarded in favour of an uninterested, less motivated man. It is all these things that cause me to seek refuge here."

Malin had rarely heard her speak this way. He said nothing, sure that Lucia would say more.

She nodded in the direction of the brightly coloured mosaic above the door. "Perhaps I should look no further than that terrible image to understand the place I occupy."

The mosaic portrayed the figure of a beautiful woman, dancing in a brightly patterned red dress, a hand provocatively raised as her feathered sleeves fell to the floor. Her other hand held a golden plate above her, on which lay the severed head of John the Baptist.

"We are either whores or murderesses, or else creatures of such little importance that our help is deemed worthless. I have often wondered if Collette's view on life might not be the most useful one to cling to."

"That is terrible, Lucia! I've watched for years as you've shown your understanding of your father's business, and the ways of the city."

She lowered her eyes. "So what should I do now, Malin? Now that you have told me of your feelings for me?"

"Do?" Malin was wrong-footed. "I don't understand."

"I would think it a simple matter. You tell me you love me. I

315

have shared with you that I have loved you for over half my life. I am no stranger to love's cruelty."

Malin heard the bitterness amid the tenderness.

"I'm not sure what to say, Lucia. My declaration to you was sincere."

"I don't doubt it for a moment. But why did it take you my whole adult life to tell me? We have both seen our best years pass us by, have we not?"

He looked at the exquisite marble patterns beneath his feet. At Lucia's profile, as she looked down onto the beautiful marble floor.

"So here is what I want to do. I am going to spend the rest of our time in this room speaking bluntly and honestly. One of us must. May I speak my mind?"

Malin nodded.

"My mother brought me up to believe in family. Integrity. Duty. And although she rarely voiced it, I knew she also believed in love. In the love she and my father shared. I saw it in some of the smallest ways. In the way she listened to him tell of his latest trade. In the glimpses she would steal of him as he greeted someone at church. Even how she gently teased him at home over dinner. She spoke to me often about what I should aspire to, but her behaviour always affirmed something different. *That* spoke of the value of love. The bonds that build and strengthen, offer protection. And yes. Happiness.

"As I grew up, I saw the truth in this, and yearned to experience it for myself. With someone else, outside the family. I saw Sclavo's strength. His determination to follow in Father's footsteps and to make him proud. I felt that way too, but for me it was impossible. Mother would sometimes speak of some striking young man of commerce, usually the son or nephew of one of Father's partners. I knew she was ready to exert her influence over Father to make things happen. But no one attracted me enough to wish to follow that path. I think she sensed that. And if others came looking for me? Well, I always found it easy to show my own mind. Perhaps even compete with them. By the time you first turned up at the house, Mother had already begun to give up on me. Or at least, give up on finding me the kind of happiness she thought I would want.

"I hold no grudge against her, Malin. It is a wonder to me that she and Father had so much patience. When Collette became the centre of their efforts, I didn't mind. I welcomed it.

"And, for different reasons, their ambitions for her failed too. Father cared so much for our wellbeing, Malin. Not wishing us to marry badly. I know he yearns for grandchildren, though he will never admit it. He lacks the necessary cruelty, and now, it is too late. Every so often, though, I see it in his eyes. That look that had me walking across the Rialto and into this place today."

"But none of those men deserve you. They do not see what I see."

Lucia sighed. "Yet it has taken all these years to say so. What did I do that was so wrong, Malin? That prevented you speaking openly to me. My love for you was so ready to declare itself, in those first years you were here. Nothing you did or said dampened my attraction to you. But bit by bit, I felt your indifference. Your inability to see how I felt for you."

"But I did see it, Lucia." His thoughts ran back through the years. "I knew something of how you felt."

"So why did you do nothing. Say nothing?"

He hesitated, as if trying to understand his actions himself. "I don't know. I was new in the city, and your father was my only real ally. I suppose it was cowardly of me but—"

"Cowardly?"

"Well yes. I wasn't frightened of your father. That wasn't it. And I don't think I was frightened of you, although a rejection

317

would have made any future visits uncomfortable. I think I lacked the belief that I could make a success of myself here without your father. And that I should do nothing within my power to upset him. Including taking his daughter from him, and depriving him of any chance that the Da Segna name could be linked with one of the noble families here."

Lucia's face reddened. She turned away from him.

"Lucia, I'm sorry."

She did not move. He reached out and gently pulled her arm. Her initial resistance slowly weakened. When she turned back to face him, the tracks of silent tears stained her face. Still she said nothing.

"Please speak to me, Lucia. I am truly sorry."

He took her hand.

She looked down to where he held her, as if watching something of interest, yet of no direct relation to herself. She pulled away slowly, and moved her hand up to her face, wiping away her tears.

"You fool. You have thrown away the best part of both our lives. And sit there as if it's merely a matter of apology. Don't you feel it? Doesn't it tear at you?"

Tears came once more. This time, anger was laced with the sorrow. Her body tensed as she struggled to suppress it.

"Lucia. I feel it too. I can't explain why I found it so hard to talk to you. I've never found it easy to share my feelings. I may appear cold to you. Or that I am indifferent to what I have done. It's true that I gave you no sign of my real affection. After those first few years, I grew accustomed to the idea that we would never reach a point such as this." He swallowed hard. "But like you, I can no longer tolerate it."

A cry burst from her. He immediately brought his head up, believing her to have given up her fight for control. Instead, she was shaking her head, a wry smile quivering where he least expected.

"This is not the behaviour of mature, rational people. Yet here we are, you and I. Mourning over our lost life, unable to explain how we allowed it to happen. Perhaps we don't need to understand. Perhaps we can just be grateful for the chance to rescue something from it."

"I want that, Lucia. Really. Please allow me to make it happen."

Lucia laughed again. "So now it's the man's task to build our new life, is it?"

She brought her hand up to his cheek. "Perhaps, given our individual failures, we should think about making it work together. Come. Let's get away from all this terrible beauty, and talk of less exhausting things. Such as how you will tell Father about the years you have spent in fear of upsetting him."

They walked the narrow streets of the city all afternoon, Lucia's arm through his, no longer caring who saw them.

An unescorted single woman strolling brazenly with a foreign trader.

A man planning the downfall of the Council, uncaring of any spying eyes.

As they walked, they formed ever more incisive questions for each other. And shared answers that ground their reserve into dust.

★

The house on Calle San Domenico was empty when Malin returned alone.

He was glad to sit down. His anxiety levels had dropped with every hour spent with Lucia but now, lacking distraction, he could not help taking stock of his physical condition.

The pounding in his head. The mild but insistent sense of fever.

Uberto arrived from San Marco.

319

"Ah, so you're on your own this evening? A rare pleasure. I'll join you for a relaxing drink or two, if I may. For some things, the bottom of a cup is the only remedy."

They sat, each savouring the opportunity to do so without interruption or distraction.

"You can tell the other two when they return, that the watch over Soranzo's house has revealed nothing untoward today. A few tradesmen, a couple of suitors no doubt soliciting support for their plans in the *sestiere*. But no sign of the constabulary. Soranzo's wife has remained inside all day. I have no sense of what she is telling her husband's visitors, so we're following each man as they leave to establish if they might do anything concerning over the next day or so."

Malin nodded. "It's all we can do. I still can't believe Sclavo could have been so hasty. Does he really believe the man's disappearance can continue unnoticed?"

"I don't think he cares. He should, of course. But when he acts, he does so with little thought of the consequences. For him, once the decision is made, he simply acts on it. I just wish he had told us what he was planning. Perhaps I have lacked the sense of how this was likely to develop, but it was only in the last few days that I've realised there would be violence. It's taken my own son to show me how ignorant I have been."

"And what of Soranzo's bodyguard. Or Del Chiaro?"

"Well, they both remain a mystery. All we have to work with is the house near Cannaregio. I've got two men in position there. I wish we'd had the numbers to follow Del Chiaro after he left Soranzo. I've no idea where he is staying, or of his movements. So for now, we wait. And remain patient."

"And how patient do you feel?"

Uberto took another mouthful of wine. "That's not a helpful question, my friend. But we have no choice. Perhaps Sclavo and Mainard will have more luck with Soranzo."

Malin refilled their goblets.

"So Malin. I think we should talk about the things you shared yesterday. It does no good to pretend that nothing has been said."

He had been dreading it, but this was best dealt with now. For good or ill. "Yes. It's only fair that you tell me how you feel. Without Sclavo around to offer his own perceptions, I mean. But can I begin by saying that if I felt it would gain us any advantage, or reduce the danger facing us in any meaningful way, I would have told you before. I first heard the truth from Mainard when he arrived. I knew nothing of bankers stepping in to foil us."

"No, my friend. You misunderstand. It's true that I've been trying to fathom the reasons for your reluctance to share the possibility of a new adversary. Part of me remains disappointed that you could not trust me with that knowledge. Sclavo's reaction might well suggest you were justified. I don't know. No. What I am more concerned about is how you now see your father. And of the true nature of his feelings towards you."

Malin was stunned.

"It must be hard to learn that your father's hate has been so constant. I cannot imagine what unspeakable things must have caused him to behave in such a way. His own son! You say Mainard told you. You've known about this for ten days, but never felt you could talk to me about it?"

"I couldn't, Uberto. I really couldn't. It would have compromised our plans at a time—"

"Malin. Stop. This has nothing to do with any plot. And you know it."

Malin looked across at his friend. At the man who had supported him for twenty years. Protected him from the ambitions of those who might have wished *him* ill, while facing severe challenges of his own.

For the second time that day, Malin felt tears pushing their way forward.

Unlike that morning, where he was able to drive them away, he allowed them full rein.

Uberto moved over and sat beside him.

When he put his arm around him, Malin's collapse was complete. And the bliss of his release, when it came, was unbridled.

Chapter 28

Friday 22nd February 1348

Day 27 of the Quarant

S ymon returned late the previous evening, having spent the day approaching possible contract buyers.

He found Malin sitting in his usual position by the fire.

"I did nothing to suggest why we needed to move quickly, but these men know a desperate man when they see one. It's quite a skill. I'll continue tomorrow, and bring back the best offers I can, but they will be certain to strike a hard deal."

Malin listened without comment. He seemed uninterested, perhaps even displeased with Symon's efforts. Asked what was wrong, he confessed to an overwhelming sense of fatigue.

Symon looked closer. His friend's forehead was covered in a thin film of sweat, and his eyes had deep black rings under them. Responding to Symon's suggestion that he go to bed, Malin seemed unable to rise from his chair.

He woke the next day in soaking sheets for a second time. He tried to raise himself up in bed, but could barely lift his head from the pillow. His neck creaked and burned. All he gained for his efforts was blurred vision and a shooting pain running down his arms.

He lay back, trying to remember his plans for the day. His time with Lucia and then Uberto had been so intense he had barely spared a thought for what was needed. Unable to complete the task, he slowly allowed his grip on the day to weaken, and closed his eyes.

Symon finally roused him later that morning, concerned at his absence downstairs.

"You look no better than you did last night. Love sickness, no doubt. One day with a woman, even when it's spent almost entirely in a church, is clearly too much for you."

Undaunted by his friend's lethargy, Symon proceeded to list the contracts he would address that afternoon. When the promise of hot food finally came up, Malin swung his body onto the edge of his bed. The room whirled, but he was able to get dressed. His slow descent of the stairs was almost amusing.

He submitted to Symon's inspection. "You really don't look well. Shall I get you more gentian?"

"I don't think it would help. Perhaps I'll feel better after I've had something to eat."

He sat down. "Living here is becoming more demanding by the day."

"Things have certainly changed since your return. Perhaps it has something to do with the new world you are seeking to create."

Malin failed to suppress a soft laugh. "Uberto would argue that it's more the case that we are seeking to return to an older form."

"Maybe. But it's a shame that it can't be done without us. We've had some challenging times, you and I, but we've always found a way to pull ourselves out of the midden. I'm not entirely sure that we'll be able to wash the shit from our clothes on this one, though."

Malin could feel some of his strength returning, and gestured at the plate in Symon's hand. "Some decent meat for once! I'll see how much of this I can get through, and then perhaps you could pass me the list that you made with Mainard, so I can be fully ready for tomorrow's meeting. Is the boat to Murano organised?"

★

He took a seat near the fire, five scrolls of parchment resting on his knees. Symon left for the Rialto. "I should be back in time for Uberto's next visit. But I hope to see you a little stronger when I return."

In the quiet that followed, he worked through each sheet, and then more slowly a second time. Mainard's notes were exhaustive. Bourchier had always offered meaningful answers to his questions, but it was clear from these papers that he should have asked many more than he did. How they would have coped if Mainard had just followed orders and sailed back west from Genoa?

Malin's knowledge of state power and its ways bordered on useless. He dealt in ducats and crowns. Bushels and bales. Bourchier traded in things at once less substantial, yet much more dangerous. Operated under the noses of bishops and kings.

Mainard was different again. Although lacking Ricaud's vivacity, he brought a rational, level-headed mind to bear on problems. His gift was to break down any situation into its smaller parts, and address each in turn. He did nothing to get the blood pumping, but inspired instead a steady confidence in those around him.

Sitting by the fire, the man's thoughts laid out in Symon's clear hand, Malin familiarised himself with every aspect of the task ahead. He felt his spirits rise. If, perchance, they resolved these last questions. If, perchance, everything else in these sheets happened the way it should, then maybe. Maybe they could succeed.

Later, he woke from his light slumber to find the scrolls around him on the floor, mercifully spared from the diminished fire. He bent to gather them, and when he sat back upright, the room revolved again. Recovering, he walked to the kitchen and poured himself some beer from the pantry.

This weakness was beginning to worry him. He had succumbed to the occasional cold or fever over the years, much to Symon's amusement. His friend always enjoyed suggesting that his frailty stemmed from the vast difference in their years. A difference that neither of them could quantify, given Symon's admission that he had no idea of his own age.

He promised himself that he would be careful of his energies over the next few days. God knew he would need every last drop of strength to ensure they all came out of this safely.

He thought of Lucia. Their intimacy seemed to have crept up on them without warning. Their mutual trust had been there for years, but their new openness had taken them to a place at once unfamiliar and enticing.

He closed his eyes and turned to feel the fire's heat on his face. How would their lives have changed had they reached that point years ago? Had he overcome then his reluctance to speak as he did now.

Those first few years in Venice had been the most exciting, the most stimulating of his adult life. Beneath the invisible, protective embrace of Antwerp lay the intoxicating promise of success in the most exotic and bustling port in the world.

Was it fear of letting that promise slip through his hands that prevented him following his heart with Lucia?

His declarations of love to her now had been prompted by a different fear. By anxiety and self-recrimination. But now, his eyes still closed, he knew the truth of the matter.

He loved Lucia, and had always loved her.

He slipped into a further light slumber. Into a world where their love held them both tightly, and nothing else mattered.

★

Daylight and much of the fire's warmth had fled the room by the time Symon returned.

"I need some more of that wine, my friend. I don't think I've ever had two such days of hard bartering in a single week. We have reason to celebrate."

Symon recounted his discussions with three of the largest importers in the city. "That Pancrazio, the one with the tight red beard. Do you remember him? He fights his corner for his master as if his life depends on it. He always seems one breath away from panic or violence. At least the other two agents, the ones representing the Sagredo brothers, helped keep our conversation on just the right side of madness."

Symon had sold on all of Malin's future import contracts. He apologised for losing one tenth of their value, but Malin was delighted.

"Symon, you said so yourself. These men can detect a whiff of desperation from the other side of the Adriatic. Yet you sat with them mere feet away, and still did this." The wine was going down well now. "What else is to be done?"

"Well, that depends on how far you want to go in offloading your warehoused goods. Quick sales are always possible, but not without substantial loss. And there's the small matter of our newest imports, the wheat and linen awaiting the conclusion of the Quarant."

Malin considered how much his friend had already achieved. "Let's leave everything else for the moment. Secure the funds from today's deals. That will offer at least some security. Let's see what happens over the next week or two."

In the comfortable silence that followed, Malin's thoughts turned to Soranzo.

"I wonder what's happening at the Arsenale? Sclavo has been acting more and more unpredictably of late." He rubbed his chin, recalling the moment he found himself prostrate on Sclavo's office floor. "At least he has the concerns of the Arsenale to distract him during the day."

Symon grimaced, recalling the blow to Soranzo's head. "He seems determined to do whatever he can to protect us. But carrying off one of the most well-known men in the city, and hoping that no one notices enough to come looking for him? I have no idea of where this will lead."

Malin agreed. "At least Soranzo can do no more harm. And we only have to hold him until our task is done. I just hope Mainard can keep Sclavo from doing anything else without discussing it first."

Uberto arrived soon after dinner.

Symon filled another plate for him. "You look starving, Uberto. Another day of fresh air and walks across the city?"

"Indeed. Yes. And becoming a witness to something unwholesome. The streets are slowly emptying. It's Friday, yet many of the market squares are but half occupied. There is a growing fear of contagion. Everyone is talking about it."

Malin and Symon glanced at each other.

Symon spoke. "What sort of contagion?"

"It seems there is fever afoot. And it is spreading through each district. We crossed the canal three times today. Walked many of the streets of Dorsoduro, Giudecca and Santa Croce. The place feels unnaturally quiet. It was all we could do to find ways to remain out of sight of Del Chiaro."

"What? You found him? How?"

Uberto put down his empty plate. "We went back to where we last saw him with Soranzo. The run-down street? Anyway, we watched him arrive, and then followed him when he came out again. Since then, we've seen him enter and depart from three more properties. I've left men outside the last house we tracked him to, a small terrace on the Calle del Forno. Just west of the Campo Santa Margherita. I'll travel home that way, just to check with the men that he is still there. It's possible he may simply be visiting another contact. But it could be where he is living."

Malin could barely hide his delight. "And what do you think he's doing?"

"It's hard to say. He doesn't seem to be carrying anything of any weight or size, and he enters and leaves alone each time. We'll continue our watch overnight, and through tomorrow. If we discover anything important, we'll send a message to Sclavo. Is everything set for our journey to Murano tomorrow?"

With no new information to discuss, and no changes to the following day's plan, Uberto took his leave.

"He does look tired, Malin. Do you think he is able to cope?"

"If there were no end in sight, I would have to say he is not. But he is an amazing man. Even at his age. Finding Del Chiaro will be success enough to keep him going for another few days. Once we have met Libusch, we will get a better sense of how much longer we must keep this up."

It was long after Vespers before Mainard arrived back from the Arsenale.

"I'm sorry I missed Uberto. I felt it important to remain at the yard with Sclavo."

They told him of Uberto's news. Mainard's relief was obvious. "Thank God. Perhaps now we can use Del Chiaro himself to betray his secrets."

Mainard had spent almost all day in the dingy, poorly lit warehouse, with two *Arsenalotti* for company.

"The day has been a long one. I possess little of the local language, and Sclavo's men are unschooled in our own tongue."

The exchanges between Mainard and Soranzo had been short and intermittent. "His haughtiness is astonishing, given the circumstances. I don't know how he keeps his calm. If I were in a similar situation, I would be undone many hours ago. It is as though he feels no sense of threat. As though all will go well for him, and he will simply return to his accustomed position of power and prominence. He saw his own wife threatened, his home invaded, and has been confined for almost two days. Yet his mood seems no different from when we first saw him.

"When Sclavo arrived, he was eager to learn of any progress I might have made. When I told him that I had achieved nothing, he walked straight across to Soranzo, and gave him the most awful stare. Soranzo seemed to hold his nerve, initially, but he eventually looked away. Sclavo suggested I leave. That it was unnecessary to remain. But I wanted to see what would happen.

"Malin, I'm sorry, but I don't have the stomach for this. For what Sclavo began to do. I knew he was getting frustrated. He started to shout at the man, leaning over and pushing his face right into Soranzo's. When Soranzo said nothing, he started to hit him. On the top of the head, just as he did yesterday. And then in the face.

"The two men untied him from the chair. When they lifted him up, his legs failed. He'd been seated there for the whole day. They tied him back up against one of the beams that held up the staircase. The blows began again. This time to his body. Blood started to run down from his forehead."

Colour leeched from Mainard's face as he relived the scene.

"I asked Sclavo to stop, and he did. But I could see he wanted to continue. I walked up to the man, and asked him to tell us what he knew. He just stared at me. I think he knew what was coming. I asked Sclavo to repeat the questions. He shrugged his shoulders, but did as I asked.

"Soranzo answered this time. I'm not sure what he said, but it seemed that Sclavo was almost disappointed. They spoke some more. I couldn't discern their meaning, but it seemed as though Soranzo had finally started to speak of the things we wanted to hear.

"Sclavo told me to leave. That he would brief us when we returned from Murano, and would pass anything useful to the men looking for Del Chiaro as he learnt it.

"I did what he told me. Gladly. I don't want to see what he does to him next. It's strange. I'm meeting a mercenary leader tomorrow, to finalise plans that might lead to many deaths. And I am at ease with the idea. And yet, standing in that warehouse, hearing each blow land. Seeing the damage that one person, a civilised person and our ally, can inflict on another. It was more than I could stomach."

Malin nodded. "It is done for today. We must leave Sclavo to do what he believes is needed. He, more than any of us, understands how the men in this city think and act. More than Uberto, perhaps."

Mainard stayed downstairs with them for a while, then retired to bed.

Malin placed more wood on the fire and told Symon he would remain there for the night. Symon brought him a blanket, and left him staring into the flames.

Chapter 29

Saturday 23rd February 1348

Day 28 of the Quarant

The day began unfortunately. With an argument in full view of any passer-by at the Calle San Domenico dock.

Malin and Mainard awaited the arrival of Uberto's boat, the morning chill working its way into their layers of clothing. The sun was still low, bleeding into and through the thin layer of mist wreathing the Lagoon. The calm surface of the water suggested a smooth journey ahead to Murano.

Malin tightened the top button of his coat, determined to retain as much warmth as he could. His neck remained stiff and sore.

He already looked forward to returning to his position by the fire. But today was too important to miss.

The plan was to make their way as discreetly as possible to the meeting point agreed with Libusch, and be back in Venice well before dusk. Uberto would then visit the Arsenale, to seek the latest news from Sclavo.

A boat emerged from the broad mouth of the Canal. Uberto rose to his feet to greet them. A second man sat in the stern.

Mainard spurned Uberto's outstretched hand. "I am in need of an immediate explanation." He nodded to the second passenger. "What is Signor Caloprini doing here?"

"Ah, yes. A small change to our plans. I hope you approve. I thought it to our advantage to be able to move around the island under the protection and support of a resident. I have no reason to doubt his commitment."

"That's hardly the point." Mainard's tightened lips added venom to his words, despite his attempt to keep his voice down. "You know how important this is. And how long we have been planning it. And here you are, inviting a well-known member of the community to join us?"

Signor Gian Caloprini.

The near legendary head of the glassmakers' guild. Perhaps the most gifted *maestro* on the whole of Murano. His glassware was exquisite, commanding the highest prices. As his business grew, he had bought several other glass bead furnaces, securing his supply and gaining further influence over his peers.

His future seemed set, until the day of his arrest for leaving the Lagoon without consent. He was brought back to Venice from Trebizond in chains, having been caught establishing a new furnace and workshop that would exploit the emerging Far East trade routes.

Since their ejection to Murano at the end of the previous century, glassmakers had been granted many privileges, in return for one key condition. They would never be allowed to leave the Republic, for fear that their secrets could be learned and imitated by rival cities.

Justice was served. Caloprini was convicted, and the sentence was severe. A small platform was erected on the corner of the Piazza, just outside the Ducal Palace, and Caloprini was relieved of not just one but both his hands. In recognition of his excellence in business, he was permitted to continue ownership of the bead furnaces, but his time as a *maestro* was over.

To his surprise, and in an act of unprecedented solidarity, his peers on Murano proposed Caloprini as the next head of the guild. The Small Council, fearing the consequences of objecting, took the equally unprecedented path of restraint, and allowed the appointment.

The guildsman was one of several recruited into their cause. The man had not lost his sense of humour. "Like my brothers, I'm allowed to carry a sword, just don't expect me to swing it."

Uberto responded to Mainard's objections. "Please do not worry. Gian is probably the most trustworthy ally we have. He will ensure that others on the island keep a benign watch over us."

He looked across to Malin, anticipating more discussion. Malin held his gaze for a moment, and then stepped forward to the edge of the dock. "Let us be on our way. My feet are cold, and we have much to accomplish."

They stepped onto the broad vessel, and walked the remaining few steps to the rear of the boat to greet their new companion.

★

The boatman took them around the headland, the city passing by on their left.

Masts of new and partially constructed ships thrust up from the foreground, joined by the many campaniles and church towers behind them.

As the thin mist began to clear, Malin felt a growing sense of exposure. A month since his return, and he had only left the city mainland twice, each time to attend matters on the Lido. This felt different. A journey undeniably bent on treason.

Before arriving back in Venice, he had considered this day as the point when the end game would begin. Despite Bourchier's loss, and the recent discoveries about Soranzo, it was still happening.

They made their way along the north Castello shore, and then began to cross the bay separating Venice from the islands of Murano.

The earlier tensions of the dock had reduced, but conversation was anything but cheering.

Uberto was talking of the illness sweeping the city.

"The *banca* at the *scuole* lifted their restrictions on admissions two days ago. Of course, they started with many empty beds, but they are already considering extending the hospice facilities downstairs. There seems no pattern around who is falling ill. Men and women. Young and old. And the symptoms all seem the same. We have had to recruit more attendants from the Rialto to help cope."

Caloprini shared the concern of other guilds around the city. Workers were falling ill in increasing numbers, and supply lines for basic goods were coming under pressure. "My neighbour sells fish on the Ruga del Spezieri, and has had to cut down on what he buys, as prices are already rising due to scarcity. It seems that even those working in the fresh air every day are falling ill."

As if on cue, their boat passed to the east of the Isola San Michel, a well-known gathering place for fishermen plying the waters north of the city. Nets were spread out at regular intervals along the shore, with boats tethered at the numerous jetties thrusting out into the bay. Malin's eye was caught by several white-robed figures, perhaps working the gardens outside the imposing walls of the Camaldolese Monastery. If things were as bad as Caloprini suggested, would the monks not be back on the main island tending the sick?

They entered the waterway leading into the centre of Murano. The level of activity on the shores either side of them increased. Caloprini confirmed they would be met at the ferry station on the Riva Longa.

The boatman brought them alongside, and Malin and his companions allowed the guildsman to disembark first.

"I will get my men and return for you. Wait just a few moments, please." Malin could not help glancing at Uberto, wondering how they had all suddenly become subservient to a man who, until yesterday, was just one more member of their wider fraternity. Uberto smiled back with a characteristic shrug of his shoulders.

Three men arrived, each appearing well acquainted with the physical demands of the island's furnaces. Caloprini would remain at the ferry station, pledging to watch for any sign that they might have been followed.

It took them little time to walk to the western end of the island, skirting the Campo San Bernado and remaining close to the buildings running parallel to the southern shore.

They approached a small redbrick structure just beyond where the street became a rough track to the west dock.

A man stood on each side of the low entrance to the building.

They paused while one of their escort approached the men.

When he beckoned them forward, they entered the house.

Their eyes were still adjusting to the dim light as a voice reached them from the far side of the room.

"So which one of you is Le Cordier?"

★

Their meeting lasted deep into the afternoon.

Malin drifted in and out of the conversation, happy that Mainard had full grasp of the many details needing attention.

He studied the diminutive Silesian. Malin had known Viet Libusch's name for well over a year. During that time, he had conjured and slowly refined an image of the man's appearance. Tall, stocky, wearing his hair long and unkempt. Bearing many unpleasant scars.

But the real Libusch could not have been more different. Of average height, head and chin clean-shaven, with piercing blue eyes and a restless lean frame. His voice was remarkably smooth and even-pitched.

A man of intelligence. But with a distinct air of danger in his every move. The kind of man he was pleased to have as an ally.

Libusch untied a collection of worn maps, and described the steady movement of his troops over the six months of their travels from the Duchy of Strasburg.

His forces were currently waiting in fields and small villages across almost fifty miles of the Veneto, in numbers small enough to avoid attention. Ten here, fifteen there. A total force of four hundred men, many of whom had followed Libusch since his time in the *Compagnia della Colomba*, the Company of the Dove.

In those days the Silesian had been just one of many mercenaries flocking south over the Alps, seeking their fortune in an army organised by John of Bohemia, the King of Poland. Libusch had learned quickly that the most powerful men had bulging coffers, and were prepared to pay others, including himself, to protect or increase them.

Survival, rather than victory, was often the only skill required to find a new master. Over a series of engagements, Libusch built a formidable reputation. Other men followed him, and by the time he signed his name to the Company of

St George, he brought two hundred or more battle-hardened companions with him, and stood on his own merit as the only *condottierie* from beyond the Alps.

Ten years on, his reputation attracted the attention of Genoa. The city state's recommendation accompanied the initial delivery of gold to Edward's household. The deal was struck, and Westminster took the first steps to hire him.

Libusch traced a number of thin lines featured on the maps, connecting points marked with names and small flags. "We had just one mishap, losing four men in a dispute over food and the use of some local women. But we remain undiscovered. I am able to pass messages to each of these small companies from my own position just outside Treviso."

Mainard and Uberto then described their own circumstances in the city. As he listened, Malin recalled his conversation with Uberto at the Tiepolo marker stone. As they took Libusch step by step through their preparations, he could not help feeling proud. Even Grosmont and de Bohun would be rightly impressed.

Mainard passed over a heavy bag of coin.

Time to talk through their final arrangements.

Every member of the Great Council would see their action for what it was. A threat to their family's power, and their removal from lucrative or prestigious roles. But its fifteen hundred members were spread across all six districts. Some of the most influential families were not even resident in the city at all, having been offered or inherited roles elsewhere in the *Oltremare*.

The proposal was therefore to time their attack to coincide with a session of the Great Council itself. On a Sunday, after their summoning by the Trottiera bells, between the daily chimes of Sext and Nones.

Uberto strongly favoured the idea. "All the nobility in one place. A single cage holding almost every songbird."

Libusch was not prepared to agree until he had heard more of the plan.

Mainard removed a detailed map of the city from inside his jacket. The many hours he had spent wandering the city had been well spent. The detail was astonishing.

They discussed the locations that would be vital to their success.

The Ducal Palace was by far the most important. It not only held Andrea Dandolo and his family, but also the main pillars of the city's administration. The Armoury was critical. Cut off the supply of weapons, and it would be less easy for a counterattack to form. The prison cells were in a state of disruption, given continued rebuilding, but they would need them to detain their most prominent enemies. Finally, and perhaps most importantly, the Palace held the central offices of The Ten, with the three *Capi dei Dieci* permanently installed there. The Doge's personal bodyguard would have to be dealt with swiftly.

One fundamental problem remained. The Palace was situated in the central *sestiere* of San Marco. Any invading force would be vulnerable as it made its way in from the outlying districts. To overcome this, they would neutralise the constabulary in each of the six *sestieres*, stationed near each of the Ducal Councillor offices.

The militia, drawn largely from the *Arsenalotti*, would follow the instructions of the *protomaestri* recruited by Sclavo.

Mainard strongly advocated sending a party to secure the Zecca, home of the city Mint and holder of the city's reserves of domestic and foreign coin. Additional funds would help enable the planned transition of power.

Uberto listed where their support would come from. "We have several of the guilds prepared to stand aside and resist any call from the authorities for assistance. Favero has placed almost two hundred members of the *fraglia* at our disposal, to allow us to move around the city quickly. No member of the *traghetti* will accept an order to transport anyone seeking to resist us along the Canal. The *Arsenalotti*, at the ringing of the Arsenale alarm bells, will disperse across the city and take all the main bridges. They should be more than a match for any *shirri* despatched by the magistrates, and will ignore any orders to join the Palace guard or defend the Zecca."

Libusch seemed impressed. "So how will you ensure that everyone does as they are expected?"

Uberto cleared his throat. "We will keep a close watch on how things develop. Myself and Mainard will position ourselves near the Palace, and enter the building once the initial move has been made. My son, Sclavo, will maintain oversight with the *Arsenalotti*, staying in touch with their senior foremen. Malin here will attend the Mint, and his colleague Symon will take up position at the main Custom Office on the Lido, from where he can monitor any ship movements."

Their thoughts turned to how Libusch would transport his forces to the island, and where they would disembark. It took them little time to select the most obvious landing points. Mainard took note of their location to pass them on to Sclavo and Favero.

The mercenary returned to the decision of when to commence the attack. "So, Uberto, with respect, with all these elements of the plan in place, we should not be constrained by the sitting of the Council. It seems that none of them have any forces of their own, save perhaps their own personal bodyguards, and once our other locations are secure, they will have no choice but to comply. In fact, once we have succeeded, I suggest that you find a way to suspend their meetings for a while. Men with time on their hands and something to lose should be kept apart, in my view."

Everything was set. Libusch would pass word to each of his brigades, and instruct them to march to a single launch point.

They would make their final move just before dawn on the first of March.

In exactly one week.

Mainard, Uberto and Malin were the first to leave. Libusch held back to ensure they would not be seen together.

They re-joined their escort, and began their walk back to the ferry station. The mist had begun to draw in once more, and Malin felt the cold biting into his bones almost immediately. By the time they re-joined Caloprini, his head was spinning, his nausea was back.

They instructed the boatman to take them back to the city mainland by the shortest route. Once landed, they would make their way home on foot.

They had just passed San Michel when Malin collapsed with no warning, narrowly avoiding a fall into the cold water of the Lagoon. Unable to rouse him, and taking care not to rock the boat, Uberto and Mainard eventually managed to lay him in the centre of the vessel.

When they landed on the north shore of Castello, Uberto left the Celestia dock to hire a small handcart. With help from the boatman, they lifted Malin in. They bade farewell to Caloprini, and with a shared anxiety neither wanted to show, steered the cart south, heading first around the perimeter of the Arsenale, and then back to Calle San Domenico.

During the half mile of their journey, they saw two other groups pulling similar carts. Each of them contained at least one prone and unmoving passenger.

Chapter 30

Sunday 24th February 1348

Day 29 of the Quarant

A tormented night.

Over in moments, yet lasting forever.

Flames in his mind. Ice through his veins.

Malin woke with a jolt.

Where was he?

His surroundings slowly resolved. The familiar door to his left. His bedchamber.

He recalled the slap of the Lagoon on the side of the boat as they crossed back from Murano. The flocks of birds beginning their evening swoop and swing in the skies above the city, preparing to roost. A surge of nausea. Tingling at the base of his neck, rising to his temples, and then? Nothing.

Symon sat beside him.

"Ah, there you are. I was wondering how much longer to give you." The lightness in his tone felt a little forced.

"What happened?"

"Everything and nothing, I suppose. Agreed to invade the city next week, then decided to save yourself the boredom of the trip back by closing your eyes and letting your friends carry you home. Anyway, now that you're awake, we need to talk. A letter has just arrived from Mainard. He wants to know if you can make your way to The Tinsmith. Something really urgent, he says." He peered forward. "I just need to decide if you're well enough to do as he asks."

Malin brought his hand up to his face. Pain shot through the side of his chest and up through his shoulder.

"When does he need us there? It seems an extreme way to avoid Mass."

"He's there already, according to the messenger. I told him that one of us would be there as soon as we could." He looked down at Malin, but avoided eye contact.

"Symon, what's wrong?"

His friend sighed. "Nothing. I just wish you could throw off this illness. More importantly, throw off this lunatic scheme of yours and sail away from this whole damned thing."

He continued to look anywhere but into Malin's eyes.

"You know that can't happen. It's gone far beyond that point." Malin paused, and brought his other hand up to probe the sides of his throat. "Bring me some water, let me get out of this foul-smelling bed, and I'll know if I can handle a brisk Sunday walk to the brothel."

In the end, they left the house together. Symon set a slow pace, for which Malin was grateful.

★

Descending the shallow arc of the Fondamenta Rimedio bridge, Symon reached out to prevent Malin's stumble taking him to the ground. As he caught his arm above the elbow, arresting his fall, Malin's cry of pain took Symon and several passers-by on their way to church by surprise.

Malin apologised. "I don't want to attract any more attention. Could we walk just a little slower? I will be more able to keep my feet."

When they arrived at The Tinsmith, Symon held the door open, resisting the temptation to put his hand out to help his friend in. Malin looked exhausted, but he did not want to damage his friend's pride in front of Mainard.

Malin had not missed the place. A rough tavern, and for all he knew an even rougher brothel.

He looked around the room, half expecting to see Bourchier propped up on his stool, looking as relaxed as any regular visitor to such a place. Malin missed him. His vulgarity, yes, but also the charm of the man that made his coarse edges so much easier to forgive. He shook his head, casting off the image of the man's torn and bloodied corpse in the hospice. He was gone, his body in a pauper's grave at the marshy fringes of the city.

He saw Mainard. The man next to him was bent forward, his dark dishevelled hair hiding his features.

As Symon and Malin approached their table, Mainard nudged the stooped man. He raised his head.

It was Sclavo.

"Hello, Malin. Come to gloat?"

Mainard stepped in before Malin had a chance to ask the obvious question. "Thank you for coming. I'm glad you were well enough. Sclavo wanted you to hear what he had to say. How are you feeling?"

Mainard himself looked ashen. His eyes were sunk deep.

For the first time, Malin thought he looked vulnerable.

Something had shifted. The day had barely begun, yet something dark and ominous sought to envelop them.

Sclavo had been drinking. Not yet noon, on the Lord's

Day. As if to confirm Malin's suspicions, Sclavo reached down beside him, and raised a pewter tankard from a pool of spilled ale.

Having received no answer to his earlier question, Sclavo offered another.

"So, Malin, are we happy now?"

"What the hell is going on, Mainard?"

Sclavo slammed his cup down on the coarse wooden surface. "That's right, Mainard. Tell him."

Sclavo had spent the previous day attending to an increasing level of disruption across the docks. One in five of his men were absent, and there had been work stoppages out on the wharves. He had not stepped out of the facility for four days. Each day he worked to stabilise the office, and each night he sought to break Soranzo. The Councillor had finally begun to talk. But instead of rewarding him, Sclavo had pressed him with increasing violence.

"The man had been using us all for months. Years. He must have thought us stupid. Easy prey. When he started to confess, I could hear it in his voice. That *superiority*. That arrogant, smirking look that says everything about his own sense of nobility, and everything about how he sees our lack of it.

"I couldn't help it, Malin. With each new admission, I hit him. And him? He seemed to enjoy seeing me lose control. Revelled in how he exploited Father's trust. Said how easy it had been to make a fool of him."

Sclavo's companions had stood by while he beat his prisoner, first with his fists and then, when the man slumped to his side and onto the dirt floor, with his feet. The bound man eventually stopped grunting, but Sclavo paid no heed. He finally fell to the ground himself, spent and unthinking.

The bloodied corpse had sneered at Sclavo's family for the last time.

By the time Sclavo's confession was over, tears and snot ran down his face. Malin could sense his self-disgust.

Mainard summarised what they had learned.

The Councillor had been approached by Del Chiaro within weeks of his recruitment by Uberto. His proposition was a simple one. If the plot was foiled, Soranzo could take credit for its defeat. His place on the Small Council, along with his position as Ducal representative for San Marco, would be secured for life. If, on the other hand it succeeded, his duplicity would never be known, but he would receive similar reward, this time from Uberto and his collaborators. If he refused to work with Del Chiaro, the Florentine would expose him immediately as a traitor.

"He fed information to Del Chiaro for months. At the end of last year, they spread the idea that The Ten suspected the existence of a plot. Del Chiaro believed that this would cause us to panic and make mistakes. He hired men to follow our movements. They were already operating in the city well before you came back to Westminster for final instructions."

Symon did his best to keep up. "So the man that attacked Malin. He was working with Del Chiaro, not The Ten?"

"Yes. But the attack in Santa Croce was Soranzo's idea. Del Chiaro told him of his agreement to kill Malin for his father, and Soranzo wanted him dead immediately. He was unsettled by Malin's behaviour at their meeting, and the possibility that he might learn that Bourchier was being held in the very next room."

Malin could barely believe his ears.

That room. The atmosphere of rot and damp. Soranzo's anxiety had been genuine.

Malin's head reeled. "So why did they not try to kill me a second time?"

"I don't know. Perhaps they felt that they could wait. Or

perhaps they were genuinely surprised by your ability to defend yourself, and decided to wait for you to be arrested with the rest of us."

Symon asked his next question. "So, dumping Bourchier's body at the hospice?"

Sclavo lifted his head. "The bastards wanted to give us another fright. And to cover their tracks. But mainly to show us their power. By killing defenceless old men." His venom was plain. "They took the attendants to confirm what they already knew, and to fill any gaps. Nearly every one of us has attended one or more of our meetings there. Those men knew us all."

Malin took a deep breath. "So, Sclavo. Is this all my fault? Your anger. Why you sound as though you hate me?"

Sclavo eyed Malin across the table. "You mean how you dragged us into this, put us in peril from The Ten, and then found a different way, through your bastard of a father, to place our family in the way of ruin?"

Symon reacted first. "Now wait, Sclavo. Stop. This will get us nowhere. You're bloody drunk." He drew back, aware of his raised voice. "I understand why you're feeling the way you are, but lashing out will achieve nothing. I won't stand by and allow you to blame Malin for your desire to return your family to its former position. Or for your own savagery."

The three men held their breath, waiting for an eruption that never came.

Instead, Sclavo seemed to shrink in on himself. "I have to tell Father of Soranzo's death. The Small Council meets this afternoon, and his absence will be noticed." He looked down at his hands. "I am sorry."

Mainard folded his arms.

"Let's think this through. Sclavo, did Soranzo have anything to say about how he would inform The Ten of our intentions?"

"No. Only that when he did, he would be rewarded for his service."

"So if it was Soranzo that was going to tell them, do The Ten remain unaware of us?"

"I think so, yes. We have had Soranzo since Tuesday. So Del Chiaro is the only one left who could have informed on us since then."

Malin thought it through. "Four days, and Uberto has been following Del Chiaro since Friday. And he hasn't been anywhere near the Palace since then."

Mainard turned to him. "So it's possible that our work remains secret. We have six more days to stay hidden."

Sclavo was unconvinced. "But if Del Chiaro is as good as we fear, he'll know you've met Libusch. And that you would only have done that as close as possible to the day we act." He lurched to his feet. "If you're determined to talk about this now, you'll have to do it without me. I've had no sleep for three days, drunk more of this than I should have, and need to get to Father before The Ten or Del Chiaro's men do. I won't have him learn the truth of what I've done from anyone else."

He left to find his family at Chiesa San Giovanni. Malin wondered how his wild and unkempt appearance would be received at the Mass.

Mainard placed his hands palm down on the table. "So, let's go back to Castello and give this some thought."

★

Malin decided to remain downstairs when they finally arrived home, despite his exhaustion. He took up his usual position by the fire, and was joined by the other two men.

One key question dominated their afternoon.

"If we leave any reaction to Soranzo's absence to take its

course, who knows where investigations will lead. If they learn of his connection to Del Chiaro and question him, we might be in trouble very quickly."

Malin decided to remain hopeful.

"But they've had two years to uncover what we've been doing, and it seems they suspect nothing. Do you really think that they can catch us in less than a week?"

Symon laughed incredulously. "But they've never lost one of their own before. Someone from the very top of the tree. They won't hesitate to react. Would you expect any different back in England, Mainard?"

"Sadly, you are right. If a duke or earl went missing, the court would be in uproar. De Bohun would have every man out searching for them."

Malin considered his words carefully. "We know they'll act, and do so with urgency. Perhaps we should consider how we make them look in all the wrong places. We wouldn't have to delay them for long. Just long enough."

They needed Uberto's intimate knowledge of how minds in the centre of government worked.

Malin finally admitted defeat, and told them that he needed to sleep. Symon brought down a fresh blanket, and then left with Mainard to compose messages to each of the main conspirators, confirming that Saturday, the first day of March, would be when they made their move.

★

Malin's dreams were haunted by memories of his last visit to Elyas, his old friend and mentor in Antwerp. He had always found time to visit him on each return to the Low Countries.

Disembarking at the Hanse dock on the Scheldt, he had wandered into the Kontor, fully expecting to see the old man immersed in some matter of trade, or offering guidance to his latest apprentices. Instead, he learned that it had been a year or more since Elyas had begun to work entirely from his home on Wolstraat, just past the church of St Carolus.

When he arrived there, he was told to take a seat in Elyas' office at the front of the house. Eventually, a servant that Malin had never seen before carried his old friend into the room and placed him into his chair.

Time had treated him cruelly. His wife had died from the sweating sickness three years earlier. His sons were based in ports along the Baltic, and had not visited since her death.

They talked of business.

Malin spent most of his energy masking his sadness at the old man's cracked voice and shallow breathing.

He finally moved his chair closer to the frail man, leant forward and took his hand.

"Old friend. I will be gone tomorrow, and may not return for years. Have you all you need?"

A weak smile appeared on Elyas' drawn and sallow face. "Please Malin, fear not for my ease. It was lost so long ago that I barely miss it now. Visits to my door will continue. The physic will continue to provoke me with promises of cures, even as the Scepene coffers continue to swell without any real effort from me."

Malin grasped his hand tighter. "You have to know. I need to tell you just how much—"

The old man shook his head and interrupted. "Please Malin, you need say nothing. You must know that the pleasure has been all mine. I know you will continue to thrive. You have made a solid friend in Da Segna, and you will have each other to watch your backs. I hope only that you continue to allow your instincts to guide you, and that you place your trust only in trustworthy men."

A short time later, Malin walked slowly along the Jordaenskaai, accompanied by the baleful cries of gulls swooping above the waters of the Scheldt.

On waking, his face wet with tears, Malin wondered how many of his friends in Venice would live to see their old age, or have the same grace to accept their fate.

He fell asleep once more.

*

Symon greeted Uberto at the door an hour after nightfall.

He removed his cloak, and gestured with his eyes at the door to the reception room.

He walked into a room filled with the sour, biting tang of illness.

The silence continued, as Uberto took a seat and looked across at his friend.

"Symon wanted to open a window, but I was too cold. I hope you don't mind."

Uberto looked subdued. "Malin, it's important that you look after yourself. There are many across the city feeling equally unwell now. Not all of them are as lucky as you to have such a caring friend as Symon."

Malin nodded. "The strangest thing about feeling this awful, is the burning in my chest. It's been my constant companion since Dupplin. And it's gone. Once this illness is ended, perhaps I will no longer have to travel the world with any more of those damn phials."

Their quiet laughter served as a signal for Mainard and Symon to join them.

"Gentlemen, Sclavo has told me everything. Soranzo's removal was necessary. But his death now leaves us in peril. It would be normal for the Council, missing one of its members, to invoke the help of The Ten.

351

"We must protect ourselves, and those that have come to depend on us. I have told Sclavo to return to the house, and get some rest. He has never been a brutal man. But I confess my shock at his actions. And I am sorry that our names might one day be connected with…"

His voice cracked.

"I believe his actions were wrong, and his sin will stay with him until God decides to relieve him of it. I will leave it to Him to reflect on when that might be. We do not have that luxury. None of us are served well by this. But he has gained us the knowledge we needed. And we must use it wisely."

Malin thought he knew his friend. Thought that he had the measure of this intelligent, caring man.

He had barely skimmed the surface.

Uberto told of his journey there that evening. How it had given him time to make sense of events, and imagine the steps that would make this right. Or at least less wrong. He had been distracted only once. He had just passed the Palazzo Malipiero built, as coincidence would have it, by the Soranzo family some two hundred years earlier, when a low, wide pontoon passed him, travelling west. Its entire deck was filled with bodies, swathed in black cloth.

He returned to the question of how to proceed.

"We can still put the hounds off the scent. Send them in the wrong direction, until it is too late for them to stop us."

He and Malin had each stumbled on a similar approach to the problem. Turn the efforts of their enemies against them. And allow themselves time to deal with Del Chiaro. They discussed what they could do, and then Symon and Mainard returned to the office. They put their earlier letters to the conspirators to one side, and Mainard began to compose the words that would give them the time they desperately needed. Symon began to scour the office for a range of inks and parchments.

Back in the reception room, Malin changed the subject.

"Did anyone notice Sclavo's appearance at San Giovanni?"

Uberto laughed. "He had the sense to wait outside. He approached us in the *campo* as soon as we left. Collette has not yet stopped talking about it."

They both stared into the fireplace, neither sure where the conversation would lead.

"Malin, my friend. I must ask you something. Sclavo's actions have shown me how a plan such as ours can cause decent, law-abiding men to do the most atrocious things. It doesn't help to know that Soranzo's fate could easily be visited on us, dealt out by other seemingly decent men. Did you ever wonder what this would do to us? To how we will make our way through life when this is over?"

"If anyone had asked me if I would commission, or at least exploit the murder of a man in cold blood, just to obtain some justice for my own cause, I would have laughed in their face. No. Not that. I would have scorned them, for even suggesting me capable of such a thing.

"Yet here we are, you and I. A lifetime of working together. Building a certain level of respect for ourselves. The love of our family."

Malin flinched at his last words.

"No, I don't mean your father. Symon has been family to you for as long as I've known you. Longer. And I have always thought of you as my second son. As a brother for Sclavo. Donata loves you so much, Malin. And, of course, Lucia."

Malin searched his friend's face.

He knew.

"Yes. It was far too much for the woman to keep to herself. Lucia has no idea that I know. At least she has not yet said anything to me directly. But we both, Donata and I, rejoice in your love for each other. Even now."

Malin could not speak. For the second time in a week, after decades of friendship, his tears began to fall in the man's presence.

"That's why I have to tell you of my decision, my friend. I can no longer keep this whole business from Donata. Or from the girls. I wish it were otherwise, but they deserve to know what danger they are in. And to know that you and I will do all in our power to keep them safe."

Malin lacked the strength to argue. They would ask Symon and Giradino to work on a plan to secure passage for the women out of the city. Even if it meant they had to return a week later to share in their success.

Uberto saw himself out, leaving Malin to imagine the scene at Calle Donzella when his friend reached home.

Chapter 31

Monday 25th February 1348

Day 30 of the Quarant

S ymon returned before Malin woke.

Five messages, all using different paper, different quills, and different words. But all conveying the same meaning.

Each featured the name Soranzo, mention of a plot, and the suggestion that at least one other Ducal Counsellor was involved. None of them offered a date.

These, and Soranzo's continuing absence, should be enough to provoke a reaction. Although dangerously close to the truth of the real conspiracy, the suggestion of a broader internal coup should keep The Ten busy for the final days they needed. Any eventual connections back to them would be too late to make any difference.

The Lions' Mouths along the Palace perimeter would be emptied before noon.

Malin could still sense Symon's excitement when he joined him in the office.

When Malin finally appeared, Mainard was still learning more of Symon's adventure. "Are you sure no one saw you, or followed you back here?"

"As sure as I can be. The columns of the new porticos offered good cover from the palace guards. The *cesendeli* along the passage were still lit, but I used the shadows to move between each Mouth. I checked regularly on my way back that there was no one following me."

His eyes sparkled.

"So it's done."

The morning had already been busy. Moments after Symon's departure, the first of half a dozen messengers arrived. Each letter leaving the house contained a single line. The date of the first of March. By noon, every leader in the conspiracy would know it.

Like Caesar crossing the Rubicon, they had taken their final, decisive step. Their plans would be hard, if not impossible, to reverse.

Even Malin, his body a single knot of aching muscle, felt a small tremor of excitement run through him. This was going to happen.

In just five days.

He declined Symon's offer of food. "At least take some drink. You must have sweated through your clothes overnight."

Malin took the hint, climbed the stairs as best he could, and reappeared in clean clothes.

"Where has Mainard gone?"

Symon placed a jug of weak ale on the table by Malin's tankard. "The messengers brought stories of many deaths across the city. And of many more fallen ill. He wanted to see for himself." He paused. "And what of you, Malin. How do you feel today?"

Symon's look rested and remained on his friend.

"Not as well as I would wish, that's the truth of it. It seems my ailment is not one to visit briefly then leave." He smiled. "I fear I too have the illness. I will make it my business to speak with Mainard on his return."

Symon looked across at Malin's tankard, and grabbed one for himself. "Not yet Terce, I know, but I think I'll join you."

Malin poured, and they each toasted the day.

"Symon. I know I have been sending you on one task after another these last few weeks. And I have been so glad of your help. But I need yet one more thing from you. Something I think you will find the most difficult. But I have no one else to ask, and you are the only one I can trust."

Symon slowly lowered his tankard.

"I spoke with Uberto last night. About the dangers of this final week. And how he no longer wants to see his family in harm's way."

Malin shared Uberto's intentions.

"He wants them out immediately. Before Saturday. At the very latest. I told him you would help him. Symon, will you do this for me?"

They discussed the details. Uberto wanted them to leave by sea. To give them the freedom to travel short or long distance. Yes, they would be prepared to stay away as long as needed, but with the possibility of an early return.

"Could you meet with Da Viscia today? Uberto is having this same conversation with him this morning. Between you, you probably have the best contacts in Venice. I know you've just got back from the Palace, but could you go and meet with him in the Rialto?"

When Symon had gone, he returned to the reception room, and remade the fire. His body yearned for rest, but his thoughts offered little peace.

By now, Donata would know of their entire scheme. And if Donata knew, it would not be long before Lucia knew too.

Knew everything. And of his part in it.

A sharp spasm ran down the right side of his torso, jolting him straight in his chair. The pain was excruciating, then gone. He explored the area under his arm. The side of his body felt tender, but there was no second surge.

Wiping the moisture from his eyes, his thoughts turned once more to Lucia. He pictured Uberto and his wife talking in hushed tones late into the previous evening, but agreeing to say nothing to their daughters until the morning. Donata would learn of Sclavo's involvement. Perhaps Uberto would tell her of Soranzo's death, or at least his capture, to convince her to leave the city.

Or instead, simply describe what he and his friends had planned for Saturday.

Stop.

Stop these thoughts.

The detail no longer mattered. Even one small part of the truth would be enough to tip his world, and the world of his friend's family, into chaos.

His turmoil continued through the morning. Three more times the pain beneath his right arm returned. On the fourth attack, the nausea returned with it. He found a bowl just in time.

The Sext bells had long since rung when the front door opened. Mainard was back.

"Malin. I'm pleased to see you upright still. But you look pale."

Malin passed off his inquiry with a shrug. "I am fine, my friend. Relieved, if anything. All our friends have certainty on when we move. And all is set. It seems an age since we discussed making this happen, that first time in Westminster."

Mainard took a seat at the other side of the fire, pausing to put two more logs into the hearth. "In truth, sitting here with you now, two thousand miles from home, I barely recognise either of us as the same men."

He crossed his arms, and stretched his legs out straight.

"Before I left Genoa to come here, the Exchequer was all I had ever really known. An entire life. Learning how it worked, finding ways to fight any challenge to our accuracy or fairness. I could click my fingers and command the immediate obedience of some of the most gifted men in the kingdom. Not all of the rank that you enjoy, of course, but their talent and dedication made up for any lack of noble birth. Many of them could have made more money, enjoyed a more than comfortable living, doing other things. Yet all of them chose to help me oversee the foundations and integrity of our country's wealth. Burning candle after candle to ensure that all records were above suspicion.

"I tell you now, Malin, even sitting here in this most foreign of cities, that being part of that has been a privilege. To witness and sometimes shape the plunging and soaring wealth of kings. To see and understand the real story of how our kingdom works. To witness the making of fortunes, and those less fortunate lose even the roofs over their heads. To plant coin in ventures that yield wonderful harvests.

"Yet here, my friend. Here, I have met my match. The intricacies of this place. Every aspect of this city's existence is balanced and organised. Nothing left to chance. Even the manner in which it heals itself after disaster.

"I have spent most days here, in part at least, wishing I had returned to England as instructed. Back to my own realm, where I am master.

"But being here? Seeing with my own eyes how this huge, crammed *miracle* of a city responds to adversity? To events that would overwhelm anywhere else? It has been worth every troubling, upsetting, brutal moment."

Malin had never heard him speak in such a way. He thought back to the day, barely two weeks ago, when he forbade his departure. How much he had done since then to help rescue their plans.

As Mainard recounted his journey through the streets and waterways that morning, his admiration for the man's ability to adapt sank slowly under a mounting sense of dread.

Members of every confraternity in the city had been mustered, urged in part by the words of the priests at Mass the previous day.

"A Council edict is on display in every square, Malin. The authorities have decided to adopt 'extraordinary and decisive measures' to account for the growing number of corpses."

Bodies were to be presented at two city monasteries for immediate burial. Requirements for the dead to be buried within their local parish had been suspended. Instead, the edict continued, the graveyards of San Marco in Boccolama, and San Leonardo in Fossamala would be used. Where relatives could be identified, their names would be taken, and costs reclaimed at a later date. All citizens of the *arengo* were charged with ensuring that they remained respectful of the constabulary, allowing them full access to their homes and family members. The *Pregadi* had drawn up emergency laws, which would be approved by the Great Council when it next met.

"The entire citizenry has been enlisted to help. Can you imagine such a thing happening at home?"

Malin tried to imagine groups of men, dressed in the coloured robes of their brotherhoods, working slowly and deliberately along the streets of London, or Norwich, or Lynn. "Would it really be any different? I'm not sure. But tell me. What of the illness itself? Is it really killing people in such numbers?"

Mainard hesitated, not quite hiding a momentary flash of panic. "I have made it my business today, despite covering what feels like every mile of the city, to keep my distance from any corpses. But word has it that bodies appear covered in lesions, as though deeply bruised from many blows. I heard one man tell of how his brother had large swellings in his groin and on his neck. How they burst and flowed with putrid liquids."

"And how does it start, Mainard?"

Mainard froze. "I... I don't know for certain."

"Mainard?"

The man looked away. His next words were soft, barely audible.

"It's said it starts with a fever. Aching limbs, and vomiting."

They both fell silent. Malin sank into his own thoughts, while Mainard considered ways to leave the room before being asked more.

★

Malin had been sleeping for some time when Symon returned.

"I wish *I* could sit there next to the fire, and just let the day drift by." He reached over and patted his friend amiably on the shoulder. "I'm almost as tired as you look. I'll get us some food, and then we can talk over what each of us has been doing. You can go first, as I doubt that will take long."

He left the room, a whirl of cloak and legs, imagining Malin's smile on his back.

"I see Mainard has been back for a while. There are piles of parchment all over the table. Where is he?"

Malin shrugged. "I don't know. He was here earlier this afternoon, but may well have gone back out again. He's worried that some of our friends may be affected by what's happening in the city. With this illness that's spreading."

"Well, I've put all the paper away, in case of any unexpected visitors. If he does return, there's some nice tench in the larder.

Here, let's get the fire going again, and sit and enjoy the remaining evening."

Symon settled in the chair vacated by Mainard.

"So, to put your mind at ease, Uberto won't be here tonight. I saw him just before I left San Polo. He asked me to tell you that he was needed at home. He has been out with his spies today. Del Chiaro returned to the old house up in Cannaregio. The one where Uberto first saw him with Soranzo. He arrived on his own, left on his own, and took a ferry back across the Canal to his place in Dorsoduro. Uberto will discuss it with Sclavo tonight. Sclavo's not been to the Arsenale today, but plans to return in the morning. I got the feeling that they're going to take a look inside the derelict house, and find out what it is that keeps Del Chiaro so interested."

"And how did you fare with Da Viscia?"

"Well, that's a tale that would be almost as tiring to hear as it was to live through. I've never sat through so many short, fruitless meetings with ship owners and charterers in one day. I think half of them had their minds on their colleagues out walking the streets in their robes and pointed hats. It's just as well Giradino has such extensive connections. We covered most of the Rialto and San Marco, barely retracing our steps, visiting perhaps ten or fifteen different offices. He didn't even have a list. It was all from memory."

"But did you find someone that would provide us a ship?"

"That's just it. Even those not pulling the dead and dying from houses seemed unwilling to see past their noses. They are so accustomed to following convention. And so worried that if they struggle to get labour and crew organised, they could be accused of breaking contracts. Giradino did everything he could to reassure them, and I offered to waive many of the usual contract conditions, but they seemed more rather than less cautious as a result. I'm sorry, Malin, but we could find no one prepared to help us."

Malin's face fell. "No one? Really? We can offer whatever is asked for. And more."

"I know that. But Malin, the better news is that we may not have to."

"No? Why? What do you mean?"

A smile returned to Symon's face. "So you have to picture us there. Myself and Giradino, relating the same tale of our day to Uberto. Donata and Collette sat nearby. Like you, Uberto was unwilling to accept it, but couldn't come up with any new ideas.

"Then Collette walks over from her mother. Says, in that way she always says anything, that she would take a different approach. We had no idea she was even listening. I could see Uberto thinking about how to dismiss her without hurting her feelings. But Giradino asked her what she meant.

"'You already have the ship in Quarant. The *Seynte Marie*. On the Lido. Malin's been back for at least a month now. She should be free to go on her way soon. And her crew will no doubt want to leave with her.'

"I tell you, Malin. All four of us, Donata included, just sat there. We could hardly believe it. It seems that all this while, far from being the daughter that thinks only of what her friends are wearing or doing, or the latest gossip, she has been taking a full interest in Uberto's business! Visiting his offices. Asking his staff about the latest, fluttering her eyes and then seeking their discretion. Half the time she's supposedly been visiting friends, she's been doing no such thing!

"So the three of us thought about her idea. How that might work. What it would take to make it happen. You sailed in on the twenty-sixth. So the Quarant runs until next Thursday."

"But that's too late, Symon. We move on Saturday. And that assumes that nothing happens between now and then. They need to get to safety much sooner."

"Yes, I know. Uberto will accept nothing that keeps them in danger that long. Collette had an answer for that, as well."

Malin laughed out loud. If it wasn't so serious, this might just be turning into the most fantastic conversation he'd ever had.

"People are starting to leave Venice. To run away from this illness. Each day, they take ferry boats to the mainland. The richer they are, the easier it is for them to organise their departure. Many of them, like Uberto, possess their own private boat. Collette knows of three families who have already left. Their houses stand empty. She believes they could stay hidden in one of these for days. They could wait for the Quarant to end, and then take a short trip across the Lagoon. All we would need to do, while telling only those that need to know, is to ensure the ship is ready to leave by then." He paused. "Uberto has instructed us, myself and Giradino, to look into the crewing of the *Seynte Marie* first thing tomorrow. And Collette has agreed to check, amongst her acquaintances, exactly who remains, who has left or is leaving. What do you think, Malin? Could this work?"

Symon disappeared into the office, returning with the documents relating to their last cargo. The crew had been hired in the Low Countries with the ship, then sailed to Southampton to load their cargo and bring Malin on board. The deal was that they would man any return journey, assuming a worthwhile cargo could be arranged.

Malin finally asked the question that interested him the most. "And what does Lucia think of this idea?"

Symon hesitated. "I'm not sure, Malin. I only saw her briefly, just before I left. I think she had spent most of the day in her room, away from the rest of her family. It looked as though she'd been in tears most of that time. I've never seen her look so, well, so *broken*. You know how strong she is."

Malin thought back to the last time they met, wandering the streets after leaving the Basilica. And of her tears when relating her exclusion from working on the city's water supply.

Symon reached into his jacket, and brought out a small folded piece of paper.

"But she did ask me to give you this. I promise I have not read it. I'll be in the office if you need me, my friend."

Malin took a deep breath, raised the letter to the hearth, to the point where the words were illuminated by the flames, and began to read.

I write this because I do not trust myself to speak these words to you. My father told us everything this morning.

Of what will happen in just a few days' time. And of the danger that all of us, innocent or otherwise, are now in.

I thought you our friend, Malin. I thought you a loyal, caring partner to my father, and a beloved, long-standing part of this family. I find now that I am mistaken. That you are none of these things. That you are prepared instead to involve us in something shameful and wicked. Something that honours no one, and exploits the people it claims to help. This city, for all its clumsiness and pursuit of wealth remains, at its heart, a place where law and justice play their part. Where, for the most part, citizens are free to admire beauty, and act with a mutual trust that we must not gain at other's expense.

You have deceived me, in your work with my father, and in your declarations of love to me. I see now that, since your return to Venice, but possibly for longer, you have played my affections in order to mask your real intentions. To misrepresent your feelings for me such that, in my belief that our love is mutual, I will see nothing of your true intent.

Please know this. Whatever feelings I have had, or might still have now, disgust me. Our last time together has turned from the most precious jewel to the foulest dust.

I will never forgive you for how you have used my family, *or used me. Consider our friendship, built on such deceit and* *dishonesty, at an end.*

Malin let the letter fall to his lap.

He closed his eyes, and yearned for the abyss.

Chapter 32

Tuesday 26th February 1348

Day 31 of the Quarant

"I'm sorry, Uberto, but I need you to slow down."

Malin bent over his knees, a few steps short of a complete collapse. They had to get to the Arsenale as quickly as possible, but at this pace, he would not get there at all.

Uberto returned along the cobbled pavement to reach his friend, and placed his hand gently on Malin's back. "I'm sorry. I expect this is becoming too much."

It was fast turning into a day for apologies. Malin laughed to himself, before straightening up. "Let's just get there with enough breath left to speak to your son."

After reading the letter from Lucia, Malin had left the fireside and gone up to his room. Losing the comfort of the fire was easier than having to face Symon.

The night that followed brought no oblivion, but it did offer periods of exhausted void. In periods of wakefulness, his neck and shoulders felt like hot lead. When dawn finally came, he walked back downstairs, hoping that Symon would not hear him. But his friend was waiting, with a pitcher of cold water and the remnants of the previous day's pork laid out for him by his chair.

Symon handed him Lucia's note. "You left this here last night."

Malin took it. "I suppose you've read it?"

"Yes I have. I probably shouldn't have, but it is done. Malin, I'm so sorry. She's right about many things. But wrong about your feelings for her." Malin folded the letter slowly, placing it inside his jacket. "What will you do now?"

Malin considered the question. "With Lucia? I'm not sure there's anything I can do. She is not known to change her mind easily. Particularly when it comes to judging a man's character. But for our wider plans? It felt like yesterday went well for us."

Symon made a quick but thorough study of his friend's condition.

"Yes. Mainard feels the same way. If the Council and The Ten have seen our notes, they may have already visited Soranzo's wife. Which could well give them much more to think about, and more choices to make, none of them straightforward. Equally, they may have dismissed the contents of the warnings, and continue to do nothing. Either way, I think we have done the right thing."

Part of Malin no longer cared.

More than ever, he resented how matters of state in England, Genoa and Venice had destroyed the path his life had been on. How an accident of birth and a motherless childhood had pulled him into this potentially fatal circus. And led to his rejection by Lucia.

"So, Symon. Do you still think Collette's idea might work?"

"I'll find out for certain today. With Giradino's help, we can contact the original crew. If we need more men, we'll go to the Rialto and hire them."

Malin had been resting for most of the morning when Uberto burst into the house.

"What the hell is it? You look like you've been chased here by the devil himself!"

Wild-eyed, Uberto moved from foot to foot, unsure where to put himself. "The boat from Dorsoduro felt as though it would never get here."

"Take a breath, Uberto. Please." His neck was coloured a deep red, but his face was a deathly, wan grey.

Uberto dropped his head, and took three loud, deep breaths. Malin had never seen him like this, even in the days of rage and disbelief that followed eviction from the Council.

"I need you to come with me to the Arsenale. I have to know if Sclavo has him. Or if he's been taken by our enemies."

Malin was back to full wakefulness.

He motioned Uberto to take a seat, who finally calmed down enough to tell of his morning following Del Chiaro.

"He left the house on Calle del Forno soon after dawn, and headed over the Canal. We caught up with him as he approached the Ruga Giuffa. At Grimani's house. And then he went inside." Uberto took another deep breath. "The Small Council, Malin. I think he has another connection with them.

"He was there for at least an hour. By the time he came out, the streets were busy, and he had quite a wait when he got back to the ferry station. We stood there so long, I thought he would be sure to recognise me. Anyway, he made his way back to his house. He had just turned the corner to walk the last fifty yards, when men ran towards him from north and south. They must have arrived after we had all left to follow him.

"They took him, Malin. Snatched him from right under our noses. By the time we realised what was happening, and managed to gather as a group, they were out of sight, turning into San Croce. We lost them."

369

It was Malin's turn to find breathing difficult. "But what... who?"

"That's it. We don't know. At least not for sure." Uberto looked down at the cold hearth. "I didn't recognise anyone. It was so quick, and I was looking around for my own people. But last night, when I talked to Sclavo, I got the feeling that he was determined to do something further to protect us. Mother and the girls. I think it was him, Malin. I think he has taken Del Chiaro, the way he took Soranzo."

Malin had had no choice but to accompany his friend to the Arsenale. They needed to know if Sclavo had him. More importantly, to learn if Del Chiaro was held by someone else. Malin's blood ran cold at the thought.

By the time they reached Sclavo's building inside the compound walls, Malin could hardly stand upright. Uberto took his arm for the last few yards, and helped him up the steps to the office door.

The door swung open before they reached it. Sclavo walked out, and gestured for them to return to the bottom of the steps.

He spoke abruptly. "I know why you're here. I was expecting you." He took a closer look at them. "Father, please do not be concerned. Malin? Are you sure you should be here?"

Sclavo's behaviour was enough. They no longer needed to ask who had the Florentine.

As they walked along the dock, retracing the route to where Soranzo was held, Sclavo seemed content to talk about the continuing problems at the yard. "We've moved those men that are still showing up onto working the ships closest to completion, but I don't know how long that can last. Some trades are hit more than others, and we'll run down our stocks of timber within two or three weeks. Nothing's coming through."

It was a different guard at the warehouse door, but inside, the positioning of Del Chiaro sent shivers down Malin's spine.

Same part of the building. Same chair. Maybe even the same ropes. He avoided looking beneath where the man sat, fearful of seeing any older stains seeped into the dark soil.

Del Chiaro turned his head as they approached. He appeared unhurt. Sclavo nodded to one of the nearby men, who stepped forward and removed the strip of cloth gagging the man's mouth. No one attempted to conceal their identities in front of their captive.

They moved to stand directly in front of him. It was the man from the Candlemas ball at Stornello's house.

"Good day, Le Cordier. I trust you had a pleasant journey through the shipyard. I would greet you more warmly, but, as you can see, your friend here has made that quite difficult."

He seemed quite unperturbed.

Had they made a grave error?

The man continued. "It seems that you have an urgent need to speak with me. I would have been perfectly willing to do so from the comfort of my friend's home. I'm a little disappointed that you chose to remove me in such a rough and undignified manner."

Sclavo took two steps towards the man, and squatted down until their faces were level, less than a foot apart. His voice was calm, his words slow. "I need you to understand something that Soranzo did not. If he had, his suffering would have been much less. I will learn everything I need to learn from you. I loathe the violence and hurt that men can visit upon each other, but that hatred will have no bearing on what I will do to you."

He reached forward and gripped Del Chiaro's ear. The man jerked his head back in an attempt to pull free, then tensed as the pain grew worse. He pushed his feet down into the soil, two of the chair legs leaving the ground. His groan was deep-throated and long.

Sclavo relaxed his grip, and continued to speak as though

nothing had happened. "You see, Soranzo relied in part on my reputation as an honest servant of the Republic. As a man no doubt seen as disciplined and direct, yet incapable of truly uncivil behaviour." Sclavo crouched down a second time. "But what he did not know then, and what *I* know *now*, is that when it comes to the safety of my family I am capable of great *incivility*."

Malin had seen enough. He turned and walked out of the room.

Uberto joined him, back into the irregular sounds of hammering from the construction wharves.

"I hate this as much as you do, Malin. What Sclavo did to Soranzo sickens me. But if that man stands in the way of our success, and the safety of Donata and the girls…"

He took a moment to compose himself.

"The last two days have been among the worst of my life. Our plans descend into brutality. My family could be arrested at any moment. My son has lost much of his humanity. And my best friend, unfairly rejected by my eldest daughter, grows more ill by the day."

Malin made to answer, but Uberto raised his hand.

"I bear none of the resentment that Lucia does. You and I are grown men, and have shown each other nothing but the utmost respect since our first meeting. We make our choices as well we can, and once made, honour their implications. We can adjust our stance in matters of detail, but will not bleat like lambs when things turn against us. The outcome of the next few days remains uncertain, my friend. But I want you to know, my love for you remains unsullied, and I will continue to believe that you feel the same."

Without waiting for a reply, he turned and began walking into the late winter sun, beginning its descent above the distant bell tower of St Mark's. He paused after a few steps.

"Come, Malin, we must return to the city, and see what

Fate has in store for us. Let us leave Sclavo to his butchery. I must return home and spend what little time I can with Donata and my two beautiful daughters. We will walk at a pace you can match."

★

Mainard was back at the house when he returned.

"Our luck seems to be holding, Malin. Grisani wouldn't see me, so he may have fallen ill. But Favero, ever the blunt one, said that although he believes one in ten of his boatmen missed their shift yesterday, he would happily 'row a damn boat myself, with a third shaft up my arse for additional power if need be' on Saturday. We still have three days to go, so the disease could still hurt us. But the same applies to those that oppose us."

Malin told him of the events concerning Del Chiaro.

"I'll get something to eat, and then head out there. I might be of greater assistance with Del Chiaro than I was with Soranzo. Sclavo knows little or nothing of the Peruzzi, whereas I have dealt with them for years."

Symon was the last to return.

Like Mainard, he looked tired, but had good news to recount.

He and Giradino had found the crew of the *Seynte Marie*. All but three of them had agreed to return across the Lagoon to prepare the ship for departure in exactly one week's time.

When the matter of their likely cargo arose, they had told them that it was still to be settled, but to assume that they should present themselves for boarding at Nones on the fourth of March. That would give ample time for any loading required.

Giradino would recruit the remaining men, and Symon would deposit the necessary securities for the cargo with the *Consoli dei Mercanti*.

Early the next morning, Symon would return to San Polo and learn more of Collette's efforts to confirm a suitable place to hide.

Malin barely had the strength to pull himself up the stairs a few hours later.

As he lowered himself into bed, the dark outline of Jerold's gift caught his eye.

He must remember to give the manuscript to Symon in the morning.

Chapter 33

Wednesday 27th February 1348

Day 32 of the Quarant

Malin's skin had taken on a mottled, shiny hue. The swellings in his neck had distended overnight, and were painful even without the pressure of bedsheets. The black lumps under his arms were the size of small goose eggs.

Despite his lethargy, he rose from bed, determined to remain as connected as he could with his friends' continuing labours. When he found the house empty, he allowed himself the chance to steady himself on the furniture. No need to keep up appearances.

He had no appetite, and retched up each of the three cups of water he poured himself. Sitting by the empty fireplace, his fever returned and his mind wandered.

It was as he slipped in and out of a fevered doze that the thought came to him. The moment it became fully shaped, blood surged through his body, and his chest lurched.

Genoa.

In all the effort demanded of him yesterday, he had completely overlooked the Florentine's knowledge of Genoa's role in funding their conspiracy. And Sclavo was intent on learning everything the man knew.

He had to get back there.

Campiello Tana seemed endless. As if to mock him, the day had become one of those early spring days that suggested warmer days still to come. Crisp, clean air. A high sky.

Every step took its toll. Every footfall jolted his neck and shoulders.

When he reached the gates, he could barely straighten to speak Sclavo's name to the guard. He dropped to the bench outside the tower, not caring for his appearance. He leant back on the warming brickwork while a messenger was despatched to the supply office.

He closed his eyes, and concentrated on bringing his rising panic under control. Perhaps Sclavo had not yet broken his prisoner. Perhaps there was still a chance. Ridiculous. Sclavo's success was vital to their survival, but he almost wished for his failure.

This was the point to which he had come.

Unsure which he desired more.

He finally received clearance to enter, and made his way along the familiar paving to Sclavo's office.

Sclavo sat behind his desk.

Malin hesitated, waiting for him to speak, but the silence continued. He could feel his legs begin to fail at Sclavo's hostile glare. Not wishing to show any more weakness than he could help, he walked forward and took a seat opposite the glowering man.

Closer now, Sclavo's appearance was truly wretched. His hair was ratted and wild around his face. He had clearly not shaved for days. His skin had a clamminess that caused Malin to wonder if he too had fallen prey to the sickness.

The silence continued. Perhaps he should be the one to speak first.

"Good morning, Sclavo. Thank you for seeing me."

Sclavo grunted, but remained motionless.

"I felt I must come to offer my support, and learn of your dealings with Del Chiaro."

"Del Chiaro, you say?" His aggression remained undiluted. "I know of no one by that name." He brought a hand up to his forehead, and moved his fingertips across his temple. "Tell me, Malin. What do we mean to you? Father and myself."

Where was this going?

"I'm not sure what you mean, Sclavo."

"No more and no less than what I ask. How do you see us?"

Malin tried to swallow, but his mouth was dry. Sclavo's tone scared him. He had rarely seen the man so calm, yet so prepossessed.

"As my dearest friends, of course."

"Really. And how do you think we regard you?"

Despite his fear, Malin's patience was running out.

"I'm sorry, Sclavo, but why do you ask me these things?"

Sclavo's tone lifted slightly, gesturing behind his guest. "You've seen, no doubt, how thin our numbers have become? The empty desks? The lack of noise?"

He nodded, still unsure where the conversation was going. "Yes. The illness seems to have affected many across the city. Mainard and Symon have brought many stories of suffering back to the house."

"And to what do you ascribe such suffering, Malin? So soon, a few weeks at most, since our last calamity. Since the earth shook the stones and timbers of the city. Since the waters tore down bridges and swept away peace of mind. How does a city such as Venice suffer such adversity when honourable men like my father wander its streets? Men like yourself?"

377

"I have no idea, Sclavo."

"No. I am sure you don't. The last few weeks have been hard on all of us. Tell me. Have all our actions been those of honourable men?"

Malin was silent.

"It's many years since I first began to contribute to the workings of this city. More yet since I began to help Father in his more ambitious dealings in the *Oltremare*. During that time, particularly when his colleagues treated him with anything but honour, I have striven to keep my feelings for his enemies separate from my feelings for the Republic. From our duty to do what we can to enable the city to thrive, and be safe for all who live in it.

"I agreed to help you out of duty to my father. I did not choose to promote your cause, Malin. I chose merely to protect my family from its possible failure. Largely, until your return, I met my obligations. Without threatening my sense of who I am. Of the man my father brought me up to be.

"I work hard here, because I believe that the hard work of honest, well-meaning men can make a difference. Can be the simple difference between having a place to live, and living in a place to be proud of."

Malin interrupted. "And you still can be proud of it. More so, once the right men are able to steer it on its path."

"But who are those men, Malin? Is it Father? He will soon lose the integrity of which he has been rightly proud. And what of me? I have done things this last week…"

Sclavo sprung to his feet and took the four or five steps to the window overlooking the shipyard. "Come here, Malin. Come and stand next to me."

Malin did as he was told, unwilling to provoke the man further.

"Look at this place. The power here. Its ability to flood the oceans with commerce or war. It must be led by men of honour, else not just the city but the world itself could face a poisonous future."

He turned to face Malin. "A few weeks ago, you had to kill a man. In self-defence. I know how much it shook you. What it cost you. This last week, I have killed two men with my bare hands. They were both unarmed, tied up. With Soranzo, I almost drifted into my final attack on him. The blows I dealt were simply a consequence of his reluctance to speak. But even at the end, my anger took over.

"But this latest? I began with *him* where I left off with Soranzo. And took pleasure in it. Do you understand that, Malin? With every blow, every slash of the knife, I was less interested in what he had to say, and more interested in vengeance."

He brought up his hands. Held them in front of his face. "These hands have forced words into my ears that I cannot unhear. Words that confirm our treason. You have ensnared us both, Malin. And for what?"

He lowered his hands, and turned back to face the window. "If we fail, we are dead men. If we win, we hand victory to Genoa. Gift ourselves to our greatest enemy, and make traitors of us all. Father would sooner fail and hang in the Piazza than die of shame."

Sclavo had tears in his eyes. "In any case, Malin. This man. This Florentine. He has undone us from the grave."

They sat back down.

And Sclavo told him everything he had learned from the doomed Italian.

★

Del Chiaro's real name was Filippo Peruzzi. He had spent much of his life working in his family's banking business, with the most recent eight years as head of the Paris branch.

He had stood by and watched as the effects of Edward's refusal to honour his debt to the family had slowly wreaked its damage.

His own dealings with the French court and its nobles were initially unaffected, but when first one then another of the Peruzzi's business dealings collapsed through lack of funds, or loss of confidence in their ability to remain solvent, his own business came under greater and greater strain. By 'forty-three, his family were declared bankrupt throughout Europe and he returned to Florence.

The Bardi, their fellow Florentines, had sunk into bankruptcy three years later. Despite having lost even more with the English king, each family were seeking ways to re-establish themselves.

Filippo bitterly resented how his life had been torn apart. His family were more than capable of amassing a second fortune, but he wanted something else.

Revenge.

Philip VI was openly antagonistic to Edward, each of them disputing the other's right to the French throne. So it wasn't hard to use his connections with the House of Valois to help him infiltrate the English establishment. Several members of their nobility had secured secret Peruzzi loans over the years. Their level of debt, even after the collapse of their lender, offered the leverage he sought.

Filippo learnt of the emerging arrangement between Genoa and England. No one in France wished to see an increase in England's influence in the Adriatic, or of the gold in its coffers. The French agreed to help him pursue his covert activities amongst their enemy.

Through a contact in London, Filippo cultivated a relationship with the seventh earl of Wormegay. Jefferey, with his position in the Household and participation in the inner circle of Westminster, became a rich source of intelligence. When English plans were confirmed, Filippo began to develop his own body of Venetian spies, finding men more than happy to take the offer of coin in return for information of the growing plot. Six months after Bourchier was sent to Venice to live, the Florentine found a local merchant prepared to rent him his home in the Dorsoduro *sestiere*.

"So he has had men following us, just as we have been following him and Soranzo?"

"Yes. And I think he developed quite a taste for spying. Wanted to have a personal hand in the thwarting of his enemy." Sclavo hesitated. "We have the same feeling here. Revenge is a deeply personal thing, if it is done properly.

"It took him little time to determine Soranzo's involvement. And even less time to turn him. Soranzo offered Peruzzi the same advantages that he offered us. Knowledge of the preoccupations of the Small Council. A connection to The Ten. And the ability to operate unchallenged in his own streets as Ducal Councillor."

Malin frowned, recalling Bourchier's fate. "And he learnt more of our plans from Bourchier?"

"Yes. Although he already knew much of them by then. Bourchier simply confirmed his thinking, and offered more detail on our weaknesses. On where we were ready, and what else remained to be done."

"Does he know about Libusch?"

"Yes. He observed your trip to Murano on Saturday. He already had men on the island before you left home. By then, it didn't matter that Soranzo was gone. I think he already felt confident that he had all he needed."

"What was he doing during the week you and Uberto followed him?"

"Just ensuring that the names he had gained from the

attendants at the *scuole* were correct. He held them in the same house where Bourchier was held, by the way. They were killed there as well. Two days ago."

The day after Sclavo killed Soranzo. The day both he and Sclavo had stayed in their homes, reflecting on their own descent into violence and murder.

"We were too late, Malin. By mere hours. The Council and The Ten knew nothing of our plans. It was all Soranzo and Peruzzi. They had us running from our own shadows. We tipped their hands with yesterday's notes in the Lions' Mouths, but they had no real knowledge of anything we've been doing. That all changed this morning. That bastard gave them everything. Gave Grimani a full account. Names. Dates. And his guess that Libusch's forces will arrive within a week of our meeting in Murano.

"So this is what you have brought us to. You. Mainard. Your cur of a father. The Ten will convene today or tomorrow at the latest. And then our fates are sealed."

Malin was not prepared to give up. "But we can still contact Libusch. See if we can bring his arrival forward by a day or two. Everyone else is ready. Mainard is sure of it."

"For what, Malin?" Sclavo's calm was at an end. "To march on the Palace, and see your bloody English king hand over the Dogeship to anyone prepared to sit in Genoa's pocket? Either the people will not stand for it, and spill more blood on the streets than you or I can imagine, or Genoa will be gifted the *Oltremare*. Peruzzi is dead, sinking into the mud of the Lagoon. But you have sunk us all, Malin. I wish you had never come here."

"So what do you intend to do now? If things are so beyond rescue?"

"I don't know. That's part of my rage at you. You have left us so little choice."

"But we must continue. Anything else is certain death. And the reasons for doing this remain solid. Venice needs people like your father to fashion its future."

"I don't doubt that you believe that. But do you think Father will feel the same, once he knows the truth?"

"So don't tell him. Keep his dreams intact. Let him believe only that we must act quickly, and nothing more. Let him get your family out of the city. We will face the next few days as we have faced all those before. Together."

★

Malin sat in the office with Symon, and told him everything that had happened at the Arsenale. And of his uncertainty about whether Sclavo would withhold the full truth from his father.

A large flagon of wine sat untouched between them.

In return, Symon related how Uberto had approved of the hiding place suggested by Collette, a spacious and recently renovated stone villa near the Chiesa Dell'Angelo Raffaele, in the southern part of Dorsoduro. Far enough away from the more affluent areas of San Marco and San Polo, and offering quick access to the waterway between the main island and Giudecca, from which they intended to cross to the Lido.

But things had become difficult.

Lucia and Collette had gone upstairs to begin packing essentials for their departure in the morning, but Donata had refused to leave.

"Uberto was walking from room to room, slamming doors and swearing at nothing and everything."

Malin could imagine the scene. Uberto's frustration would be immense, but Donata's refusal to leave her husband, no matter what danger lurked outside their door, was entirely in character. "I hope she sees sense. Perhaps I could talk to her."

"That's one thing you should *not* do, Malin. Donata has made that very clear. Go nowhere near that house. You would not be received."

"And what of Lucia? How is she?"

"I'm not sure what to tell you, Malin. She remains beaten down. She responds to every suggestion with a meekness I had thought foreign to her. She seems happy to be pushed around by whatever wind is blowing."

Malin's heart sank.

He had no stomach to remain downstairs. Asking Symon to share the latest with Mainard upon his return, and consider sending a message to Libusch to hasten his arrival, he returned to his room.

Upon removing his shirt, he found it stained with a yellow fluid. The angry and leaking lesions under his arms were surrounded by pale red rings. Smaller blotches ran the length of his arms. He could feel their heat on the palms of his hands.

Shaken, he pulled on his nightshirt and climbed into bed. For the first time, since his arrival five weeks ago, he felt the meaning of true fear.

Chapter 34

Thursday 28th February 1348

Day 33 of the Quarant

His clothes clung to his chilled yet sometimes burning body. Encased him as he endured waves of heat then cold.

Fever was a constant presence.

Yet his mind enjoyed long spells of clarity.

In two days' time, he was expected to join some of the *Arsenalotti*, and thirty of Libusch's men in their assault and occupation of the *Zecca*.

It was time to face the truth.

He doubted if he would even be able to stand by then.

Every part of his body was rebelling. Commanding it to do even the simplest things – move slowly around the house, sit, rise, keep down the small amount of food he could still eat – exhausted him in ways he would have thought impossible a week ago.

He considered how he could still contribute. Perhaps help Mainard send information around the city. Relieve Symon of his writing duties.

And what of Symon himself? Lucia and her sister would be taken out of harm's way. But what of his oldest friend? His eyes would be vital at the city docks, yet that duty could be his death sentence.

Everything came down to this final handful of days. It had all once seemed so far away.

Would he have questioned things this way if he were in full health?

Possibly.

Would he still have felt the tightening circles of Fate?

Or that Peruzzi's claims regarding Grimani were genuine? What if he was lying?

Perhaps their unnecessary anxiety was the only remaining legacy of the man's revenge. The Florentine might be gone, but he could count their late loss of confidence as part of his victory.

I'm still alive, though.

Jefferey's side of the bargain had not yet been met.

Sclavo had told him that after the failed attempt on his life in Santa Croce, Soranzo had argued that no further move should be made on him, for fear that Uberto might begin to suspect him. Even though the Florentine knew nothing of Jefferey's arrest, Peruzzi had already begun to feel that an early end to the English merchant was a worthless indulgence.

So here he sat, by the fire once more, reflecting that that failed assault had merely allowed him the time to fall ill.

But also to finally share his feelings with Lucia.

Perhaps his illness was a price worth paying after all.

He rolled up his sleeve. The mottle and blotch of his arm was complete to the elbow. Several of the smaller marks had begun to blister. He felt the growing pressure from lumps on his forehead and beneath his beard.

Symon came back to the house just before noon.

Malin struggled to hide a sudden surge of affection for his friend, when he saw how Symon tried to mask his reactions to his appearance.

"Symon, I thought you were accompanying Da Viscia." The plan had been to escort Lucia and Collette to the vacant house in Dorsoduro. "Are they hidden safely?"

"That's what I need to talk to you about."

"What? They got out without…"

"No, Malin. No. Wait. Nothing has gone wrong. It's just that there has been a small change to the plan. Collette is there now with Giradino."

Nothing he had said was helping.

"Listen. There is nothing wrong. It is simply that Lucia chose to delay her departure."

Exasperated, Malin threw his blanket to the floor. "She needs to see sense. This is so like her. Her stubbornness…"

Symon decided to just say it.

"She's not there, Malin, because she's here. Uberto insisted that she see you. They're both outside. I just thought that, given your… condition, that you might appreciate a little warning."

★

"Malin? What are you doing?"

He sat with his back to her now, beyond the bed and facing the window.

After Symon had told Lucia she could enter the house, he had escorted her to the office and asked her to remain there until Malin could receive her upstairs. Confirming she would do as asked, Symon then checked that his friend was ready to see her.

As she reached the landing, Symon joined Uberto

downstairs in the reception room. Lucia pushed open the door and walked into the bed chamber.

"Please, Lucia. Take a seat." She looked down to see a chair between the wall nearest her and the bed. Malin continued. "I am glad you are here, but sorry that we have to meet in such a way. I cannot allow us to sit close to each other. I fear this illness may spread."

"Malin, please. This is so unnecessary. At least turn and look at me."

"I would like nothing more than to see you. But it is important to me that I spare you my appearance."

"Your appearance? But Malin…"

"Please. I could not bear it. The disease has worsened greatly since we were together on Sunday. It would be too much."

"Do you not think I can decide such a thing for myself, Malin? I am here, after all. Symon pleaded with me to see you before we leave."

Symon once more.

"And Father would no longer allow me to dwell on my 'sadness', as he called it. As if two days mourning the loss of something so dear is somehow beyond reason. I have no desire to disobey him, so here I am. And I find you unwilling to even look at me."

Malin was not ready to concede. "Let us just agree to remain like this for a while. It eases my mind to know you are here, although you should not be moving across the city in broad daylight. Neither should your father."

Her tone was sharp. "Do you not think it a little late for that, after what you have done?"

His head dropped visibly. "I have no words that will make amends."

"You assume that it is amends that I seek? I do not."

"Then why *are* you here? Apart from your need to obey your father."

He resisted turning his head to look at her in the silence that followed.

"Do you claim not to know? Do you not feel it? This whole, stupid thing that you have done. That you have inflicted on Father? Using him as you have. My better instincts scream at me, even now, to hold to the decency of having no more to do with you. To do what I can to put you from my mind. Yet I cannot do it. When we met in the Basilica, something changed. I could look to the future in a different way. With an excitement at what was ahead of us.

"How could you do this, Malin? I feel so let down. I don't think I will ever fully understand why you deprived us of a shared life."

Malin thought carefully before answering. "I'm still unsure of the reasons myself. And I see now, even more than when we sat in the Baptistry, just how foolish I was. Your father. I so value—"

Lucia jumped to her feet. "Will you stop putting Father at the centre of things. I'm talking about *us*, Malin. About *you* and *me!*"

Malin flinched.

"In truth it is yourself you have let down, Malin. I may not be the greatest catch in all of Venice, now if ever, yet we could have made a life. What angers me most, is that I believe we still can."

Malin wanted nothing more than to turn around. "But your note? I thought those feelings were over."

"When I wrote it, so did I. Firmly, and with an anger and resentment that I could barely contain. I have been useless to my family these last two days. Were it not for Collette…" She paused. "Your betrayal cannot be forgotten. Yet both Symon and Father believe you were not entirely free to choose the actions you have taken. Or responsible for their outcome."

Her voice softened. "It is so sad, Malin, that you still seek approval from your own father, who so little deserves it. You remain a prisoner of your past. Just as I have been imprisoned by your unwillingness to speak to me honestly. By leaving Venice without seeing you, I would be turning my back on the chance to free us both. And that is something I could not do."

She rose and stood at Malin's side, placing her hand gently on his shoulder.

Malin made no move to pull away.

"Symon has told me how your illness has worsened. It is your pride alone that prevents me seeing you as you are. But I don't care, Malin. I don't care."

Malin turned his head away from her. The swellings and blisters on his neck were now clearly visible.

"My poor, poor Malin."

He could resist no longer. He continued to avert his face, but brought his hand up to gently cover her own.

"I cannot tell you how your words have offered me consolation. If I could take things back. Have a chance to do them again, it is possible that I would do the same once more. But the one thing I would not repeat is my reluctance to tell you of my true feelings. My determination to keep secrets from you in the belief you required protection. You are strong, Lucia, in ways I am not. And I am sorry for not seeing that. Or believing that I could not lean on that strength for both of us."

Lucia sat down on the edge of the bed, keeping her hand under his.

They sat that way for a while.

Few if any words passed between them.

When she rose to leave, Malin rejected her plea that he join her sister and herself in hiding, and from there escape together.

He insisted he would offer her father the help he needed, and promised that they would meet again once it was safe. At their next meeting, they would sit close to each other once more, and consider how to make up for their lost years.

Uberto climbed the stairs and confirmed that he would take Lucia back across the city immediately. That she and her sister would remain hidden until either boarding the *Seynte Marie* or returning to the family home.

Malin thanked his friend for bringing his daughter, and wished him God's speed for his safe passage. If no disaster befell them, they would meet the following morning, here at the house on Calle San Domenico, to talk over any response from Libusch.

★

After their departure, Malin returned downstairs. Symon replenished the hearth, and spent the next few hours with him.

Their conversation was wide-ranging. Symon's indiscreet confidences with Uberto and Lucia. The *Seynte Marie*'s Quarant conditions. Final title deeds for ownership of the linen. Settling fees for use of the city warehousing.

Symon saw no major barriers to the ship's departure back into the Adriatic, but was less happy with how they would finally decide that the women should leave the city.

"We know they can't leave for another week. But how will you judge, between when Libusch arrives and the following Thursday, if they still need to leave? And for how long?"

Malin had no answer. At no point had he sensed the need to think more about exactly how this should all happen.

What else had he missed? And how much was due to his fall into illness?

They explored it further together. Arrest of Uberto and

other ringleaders in the next two days, or a complete routing of their forces on Saturday, while disastrous, at least offered an unarguable certainty. They should get out, and probably never return.

But would they be safe in the city when, following success, the conspirators sought to strengthen their new power?

Another thing troubled him.

How could he be sure that the women would reach the boat, ready for the first available tide after the Quarant conditions were finally met? They would have to reach one of the ferry stations, cross the Lagoon unhindered, and gain access to the *Seynte Marie* without being intercepted or challenged by those alert to their intentions.

"Uberto may well have considered all these points, and possess perfectly well-reasoned answers. If so, we could all relax a little. Would you speak of it with him tomorrow morning?"

He put his head back in the chair. Talking with Lucia and then Symon had exhausted him. He would just close his eyes for a few moments, and try to think of a way to persuade Symon of one last thing.

★

He regained consciousness just as light was beginning to fail.

Symon was kneeling beside him, speaking his name.

He allowed his friend to lift him from where he had fallen onto the floor, and back into his chair.

Symon brought him some water, and sat next to him.

"This must stop. You can no longer behave as if you will be capable of working with us over the next few days. If you do not rest, you will join the hundreds each day that lie on the pontoon decks, shipped for burial."

Malin took a few slow, careful sips.

He tried hard to remember what he had been thinking of before he fell asleep.

Symon was keen to tell him where he had been.

"Listen. I've caught up again with Uberto. We needn't have worried. All is in hand. He had already told Giradino to join the women in Dorsoduro on Friday night. He will observe events in the city from there, and act accordingly. If he believes they still need to leave, he will accompany them to the ship when it is time, and based on how he sees things, instruct the captain regarding the number of days' sail they should make."

Malin felt weaker than ever, but his spirits rose a little at the news.

"Thank you, Symon. It's good to know that at least Uberto remains sound of mind."

He finally remembered what it was he had been planning to say.

And now was the time to say it.

"I agree with you that it is time for difficult choices, Symon. Time for cool, deliberate talk. I have realised many important things today. One of them is to speak with total candour to those most dear to me. So please, listen to what I have to say, and do not challenge me. I will not have it. Not now."

"You sound serious, Malin. What is it?"

"I want you to leave. With Lucia and Collette. I want you away from here. And while it pains me to say it, I do not trust anyone else, not even Giradino, with Lucia's safe keeping. I will explain to Mainard, and we will find someone else, perhaps Da Viscia himself, to take your place at the docks on Saturday. Now that I think of it, that would make perfect sense. He knows his way around at least as well as you do, and he can also keep an eye on the *Seynte Marie* until she's ready to leave."

Malin raised his hand to suppress Symon's response.

"No. No, Symon. You need to hear this."

"Apart from those few years in Antwerp, you and I have shared every key moment in my life since we met. Even when you were back in Wormegay, I wanted you with me. It was only my desire to see you prove to yourself just how damned capable you were that prevented me calling you across earlier.

"We've been to places we never even knew existed. Had more than one or two close calls, but always looked out for each other. I never intended to deceive you, and I will not deceive you now. I love Lucia, and need to know she is safe. But I love you too, my friend. Dearly. And I need to know you are out of this place too. Away from The Ten. Away from the abomination consuming this city. And, now, because of it, away from me."

Symon readied himself for argument. But Malin's expression seemed to pull the air from his lungs. He slumped back in his chair. "Please don't ask me to do this. Your words mean a great deal to me, and I'm flattered that you trust me to look after the women. But please don't send me away. We should face these things together. As we have always done."

Malin would not be moved. "Spend a while gathering the most important documents from the office. And the money stored upstairs. When you are able, make your way back to Dorsoduro. Tonight. Continue to check that you are not followed. And then stay there. I will speak to Mainard this evening."

"And will you be sending him away too?"

"I don't know. I've had no chance to think that far. But that is of no concern to you today. If he turns up at your hiding place, it will either be to tell you that departure is no longer needed, or that he will join you."

"Malin, he wanted to leave here, and take you with him. Weeks ago. And you refused."

"I know. But he is his own man, and has his own opinion

394

about what he needs to do. He has a wife and children, but he is also a loyal servant of the Crown."

Symon could see it was pointless pressing further.

"Before you leave, could you bring me a quill and paper? I wish you to take a message to Lucia for me. And one to Jerold."

When Symon was ready to leave, Malin carefully rose to his feet. He tried hard to conceal the difficulty of even such a small movement.

"Please do everything in your power to be safe, Symon. I will be thinking of you dearly as you leave this maddening place. And know this. You will always be my brother."

The door to the street closed, and for the third time that day, Malin found himself alone.

Chapter 35

Friday 29th February–
Wednesday 5th March 1348

Days 34–39 of the Quarant

This house could have belonged to anyone. Or at least anyone with a good deal of money and taste.

In the courtyard, the bronze *bochali* and cups displayed in the beautifully carved cistern cupboard seemed to mock any possibility of theft.

Inside, large draperies hung in the public rooms. A pair of heavy, high-backed oak chairs were placed around a hearth.

Everything spoke of entitled affluence.

But here, deep in the San Leonardo Fossamala, all he needed to know was that the house owners were no longer present.

Dead? Or absent, fearful of contagion arriving at their door? Well, he thought wryly, *both could now be true.* He should care, but the lives of people unmet and unknown no longer held his interest.

Sanctuary, on the other hand, and the ability to put distance between himself and those he loved, was of vital importance. Important enough to overpower a lifelong respect for others and their property.

His willingness to violate the sanctity of a stranger's home was sharpened by his four earlier failures. And a public flogging, the punishment for trespass, had become laughably irrelevant.

It took only one voice from within each house to drive him away.

The servant's reaction to his appearance at the second house, his instinctive and violent revulsion, did nothing to ease his anxiety.

When he stumbled back from the door, pain shot through his torso. He half-ran, half-fell from the confrontation.

But this unsecured courtyard offered a promising stillness. Entered directly from the junction of Calle Emo and Rio Tera San Leonardo, its high brick wall and gate sheltered it from the street.

Sequestration of the area for the dead and dying increased the chance of him occupying the house without disturbance.

Obtaining no response to his repeated knocks on the front door of the house, he had withdrawn his dagger and used it to prise open the latch. The pummel binding offered some protection to the sore and blistered skin on his hands, but the effort involved, and his rising fears of being seen, robbed him of much of his remaining strength.

The cold brazier ashes in each of the downstairs rooms were encouraging. The villa might have been empty for days.

He dragged one of the heavy chairs out to the entrance. With the lock broken, any unwanted visitor would have to work hard now to join him inside. The harsh truth remained. He would be incapable of offering any meaningful defence of his new, deserted realm. It was enough for now to know that he had the place to himself. No point thinking about what might happen next, or never happen at all.

A polished alder staircase rose from the hall in the centre of the house. Clinging to each baluster on his right, he pulled himself up each of its impossible steps. It was slow work, but his determination to find somewhere to lie down was enough to urge him on.

He entered a bedchamber overlooking the courtyard.

Crossing the room, he fell onto the crimson-draped bed. The pain in his temples and the next full rage of his fever arrived with a savagery that took all awareness of his surroundings away.

★

His journey there had begun two hours before dawn. After just ten steps along the Calle San Domenico, he felt sure he would collapse within sight of his own front door.

The cold, clean air, after two days indoors, conspired with his weakness.

He glanced up and down the street.

The streetlighters had been assigned to more morbid duties, so the *cesendeli* remained unlit beneath heavily overcast skies.

If night constables or agents of The Ten were waiting for him in the dark, he would be helpless. Yet if his plan was to succeed, every step was needed, unobserved or not.

Do this.

And don't look back.

He continued towards the quayside and the chance of a ferry boat.

No. Keep off the Canal.

He retraced his initial steps and headed north to the church at the top of the street. He stayed in close to the houses on his left, grateful for the additional gloom offered by their overhanging balconies, and for the chance to steady himself against their brick and timber exteriors.

He had decided to leave after his last conversation with Symon. Concealment in Dorsoduro would keep him and Lucia safe, but now he needed to protect Uberto and Mainard from falling prey to his illness.

They would feel abandoned. So be it. His absence would change little. Their plans were robust, and they knew it.

Better to make his move while he still could, even if they thought it an unforgivable act of cowardice.

What he needed now was bravery of a different kind.

Before bed, he had pulled together the few items he would take with him.

His satchel. A cloth purse with enough coin for any future bribes or payments needed for survival or escape. The loose pages of his journal. His dagger, withdrawn from a low cupboard for the first time in a decade or more.

He sat with the Duns Scotus in his hands. He'd forgotten to give it to Symon. He hated the idea that Jerold would never receive it. Or worse, the thought that Symon would disobey him and return to recover it.

It would just fit in his bag. And he had just enough strength to carry it.

He had almost finished packing when he heard Mainard return.

The nagging voice in his head since their confrontation almost three weeks earlier had never let up. Malin had blocked Mainard's withdrawal, first by refusing to leave the city himself, and then insisting that the man stayed to see the work through.

They had great need of his skill, without doubt, but he would always be ill prepared for the danger.

So ill prepared that, by his own admission, he would be

unable to withstand any forceful questions put to him if captured. And it stood to reason that the location of any of the conspirators or their immediate families would be of early interest to them.

He could not jeopardise Lucia or Symon's safety. Mainard could not be given the location of the safe house. Which meant in turn that Malin could not offer him the same opportunity as Symon.

He told himself, for the hundredth time, that of course they would succeed, and hiding would be unnecessary.

Malin lowered his head into his hands on the side of the bed, remained in his room.

By the time either Mainard or Uberto came looking for him, he would be gone.

He set his mind on departure.

*

Progress through the streets was slow. Anyone following him would find it easy to keep up.

He avoided as many of the wider streets and *fondamentos* as possible, retracing his steps twice in the continuing darkness of unfamiliar walkways. In a third case, a street remained closed due to uncleared debris from the earthquake.

Most of the streets were deserted. Those citizens he did see seemed eager, like himself, to avoid contact. Perhaps a curfew had been declared. Or perhaps, like him, each of them feared the consequences of contact with strangers.

His satchel became increasingly cumbersome. The trembling in his legs, already weak from days of inactivity and an inability to keep food down, caused him to stop frequently, leaning into the walls of houses or courtyards. He felt particularly exposed on the bridges that lay in his path.

There was activity in a number of the small *campos*, usually outside the porches of local churches. He twice glimpsed men in red robes, their identity hidden further in the pre-dawn light by the tall, hooded masks that made them look so unworldly. And intimidating.

In one square, another group of red-robed men stood over an immobile mass of bodies, no doubt awaiting the arrival of the blankets used in the absence of coffins. In another, just by the side of San Felice, four constables stood guard over a number of men and women seated on the damp soil. As he watched, one woman crawled slowly away from them, towards the base of the well in the centre of the square. One of the constables pulled away to reach the lowest step at the well's base while the woman remained a yard or two from her apparent objective. The constable stood directly in front of her, stooped as if to say something, straightened, and then with no warning, drew back his foot and delivered a crunching blow to her head. The woman fell still immediately.

Malin walked on, wishing to see no more and to not be seen. The weight of his satchel was becoming too much. The decision to jettison the manuscript could be avoided no longer.

I'm so sorry, Jerold.

He pulled up the collars of his jacket before continuing, determined not to look back.

By the time he crossed into San Marco, the first signs of daylight had begun to penetrate the streets. They would soon echo with the sounds of men and women going about their early business. His fear spurred him on further into the city, to the district where he believed he would have the greatest chance of finding sanctuary.

★

He woke with a start. Vomit stained the pillow beneath his head. The faltering tremors of the spasm that had put it there still gripped him.

He closed his eyes, seeking any point of calm to which he could cling. His breathing slowed, and the fluttering in his chest receded.

At least for now.

He looked around him. It was still daylight, but he had no idea how long he had lain there.

I did it. I got here.

To his left, a large window offered an uninterrupted view of houses on the other side of the street. Of San Leonardo's broad, tiled roof. The sun was high enough to suggest there was still some of the day remaining.

He tried to lift his head from the bed, to get a better view of the street below, beyond the few visible tiles of the room's sheltered terrace.

Pain shot up from both sides of his neck into his forehead.

Tears filled his eyes. If he wanted to see more, he would have to drag up his whole body.

And find a way to cope with his worsening condition.

He pulled back the finely woven bedspread. He swung his legs over the side of the bed, using their motion to rise from the damp linen sheets beneath him.

The room revolved and then settled. Shivering, he moved his weight forward. He twisted at the waist to gather the thin blanket around him.

He removed his jacket. A sour, rotten smell rose on the sudden release of warmed air.

His shirt was covered in blood.

When he probed under his armpits, both hands came away stained. He did not need to raise his fingers to his nose to know that the swellings were burst and putrid.

Instead, he wiped his hands on the exposed bedsheet, and raised them once more, testing the swellings on each side of his neck.

Pulling the blanket up over his shoulders, he leant forward and rose to his feet. When his head steadied, he approached the balcony window.

Beyond the lip of the tiled balcony floor, he could see the hard-packed soil of the street. Its dark, glistening tone suggested there had been rain since his arrival that morning.

He moved forward and opened one of the windows. Despite the street below him looking deserted, and the closed shutters of all the houses opposite, the faint underlying hum of the city reached in to greet him. With it came the unmistakable scent of the sea, and the marsh from which the city rose.

Times were far from normal, but he thought he should still be able to detect the signs of men and women doing their best to cope. Instead, as a gentle breeze ran across the blistered skin on the back of his hands, the whole area had a sense of holding its own breath. Of a mournful stillness that whispered quietly of siege and abandonment. Or fear.

He lost track of how long he had stood there. The tolling of Nones bells reached him, drifting over from St Mark's and then answered by every other campanile in the city. Some practices would persevere until the end of days.

A sharp pain shot through his groin. He stepped back from the window, unfastened the top of his leggings, and pushed them down to just above his knees. A large black swelling sat at the top of his right leg. Further down, each leg was covered in smaller, raised blisters.

He shrugged the blanket from his shoulders, and rolled up his sleeves. He saw the same pervasive pattern of blemishes, more numerous than had been the case the previous day. Not as fiery as those on his hands, but sensitive when touched.

A chill settled into his bones, and his shivering returned. He pulled his clothes back on, and pulled the blanket back around him.

How many of the corpses laid out in the squares possessed similar marks?

He wondered if Mainard and Uberto had met yet. They should be talking about the final hours before they mobilised to join Libusch's men.

They would be aware of his disappearance. He knew his absence would distract them. After two years of work with Mainard in Westminster, and many more since that extraordinary first meeting with Uberto, it was inevitable. He hoped they would keep their minds clear, and think only of those things needed to make the next day a success.

His thoughts strayed to Symon. Had he followed his instructions? Done what he begged of him, and reached Lucia?

He wondered again at how he had crossed the city without any obvious sign of being followed. Perhaps this meant that Symon was able to do the same the previous evening. That the letters of denunciation, or any accusations passed to Grimani had caused just enough ambiguity to confuse The Ten.

Perhaps Peruzzi had been lying all along, never committing any of his knowledge of their plan to writing, and never handing the details to Grimani.

Perhaps Grimani *did* receive the documents from Peruzzi, but choosing not to believe him, had decided not to pass his allegations on. Perhaps he wanted to avoid being implicated himself.

Everything mattered, but nothing mattered. Malin could barely hold it all straight in his head.

He hoped that when his friend reached Dorsoduro, he would pass Malin's letter to Lucia unopened. Inside it, Malin had placed an additional final letter to Symon. He had wanted to say so much to each of them when he sat with them the day before, but the words wouldn't come. Habits that grew from an initial reluctance to show his feelings as a child had stealthily hardened into a firm and unbending refusal to speak of anything that dug deep into things that really mattered. Jerold, the old priest, had been the only man with whom he could be truly open. And they had not spoken for years.

Now, apart from a few scrawls of ink on two small pieces of paper, he might be silent forever.

Slumped with his back against one side of the closed window, he craned his neck to look down at the street again. If he looked long enough, would he spot Symon's familiar gait, the slight favouring of his right leg since his brutal time on the battlefield, a young man thrown into a bloody chaos that would cause even the most experienced fighters to quake. Despite their lighthearted chiding, Malin knew that the bond he felt with Symon was shared.

He had just wanted to have one more chance to make everything clear. Make it true and clear for both of them.

He felt the next surge of heat engulfing him.

This would be hard.

Where was Symon?

★

He was still on the floor by the window when he woke, awash with sweat, his body a furnace beneath the blanket wrapped tightly around him.

The waning moon cast a ghostly light through the window, drawing long shadows along the wall behind him.

His eyes adjusted in the gloom, and traced the outline of a large cabinet placed against the wall. The *ancona*'s ornate

405

carvings stood in stark relief from the sharp corners of its walnut doors.

He blinked.

Had he seen one of the carved figures, a man shown offering a cup to a group of other men, move his arm first up, then down? Was he taunting them?

Many of the more established families regularly gathered around their own personalised shrine. Those that Uberto considered overly sanctimonious enjoyed private visits from clergy, keen to offer a private communion in return for an expression of generosity they could easily afford. The top surface of this shrine was bare, suggesting the removal of silverware. A chalice, perhaps a bowl, might have sat there. Perhaps the absent family, despite worries about their health were, after all, still capable of sparing a thought or two for their more valuable possessions.

A sudden need for water hit him. The image of a cool draught, once conjured, would not be dispelled.

You need to go back downstairs.

Hard now, but perhaps impossible later.

He'd witnessed the plight of men short of drinking water at sea. Felt for himself, once or twice, the creeping insanity of a slowly parched mind.

You have to do this now. Or sit here and burn up.

His attempt to find and bring water back to the room began well. Holding onto the railings at the side of the stairs, he used them to keep his balance, lowering himself to sit each time his legs faltered. He shuffled down, one tread at a time, gripping then releasing each baluster. Taking a rest on each of the split landings, he managed to reach the ground floor without falling.

Little light penetrated into the lower part of the house as he made his way to the front door. The sound of scraping chair legs was harsh and loud in his ears as he cleared a way out to the courtyard.

He picked up one of the heavy water jugs from its shelf, walked to the low wall of the cistern, and stooped a second time, lowering it into the still, clear water. His movement dispersed the image of the moon from its smooth, untroubled surface.

As the jug reached his lips, his thirst overcoming his wish for warmth, he barely noticed his blanket dropping at his feet.

The first mouthful of water offered a sensation close to bliss. He greedily took down four more large mouthfuls before forcing himself to take more care. His mind sharpened, but with it came the early, unmistakable signs of nausea.

He refilled the jug. Putting it down on the floor, he removed another from the store and filled it in the same way. He picked up his blanket, placed it over his shoulders, and took first one jug then the other back into the house. He stopped for a moment to reposition the heavy chair at the back of the door.

After the pale night sky of the courtyard, the house seemed in complete darkness. He walked slowly back to the stairs, holding the first of the jugs in one hand and his blanket around him with the other. He shuffled his feet along the floor, careful not to spill any of the water.

He looked up to the first landing. This would be harder than he had first thought.

It took five trips up and down the stairs, the last to recover the blanket he had left at the base of the staircase, to complete his quest. Finally, back in the strengthening dawn light, he could look across from his bed to the two large jugs of water, positioned almost ritually on the top surface of the family shrine.

He drifted back into an exhausted sleep, wondering if the carved figure across from him, of the man holding a cup in his outstretched hand, would appreciate the treasures that stood just inches above his head.

Any sense of achievement he might have felt slipped effortlessly away from him when sleep came.

★

He is seated on the damp grass on the banks of the Great Ouse. Above him, gulls wheel and bicker in the early spring drizzle. Their plaintive cries give voice to his own anguish.

Accardi is sitting beside him, his arm around his shoulder. The surge of emotion that first dropped him to the ground grips him even tighter.

His sobs are easing.

How long have they been there?

His head is just a foot or two above the reed-fringed bank. The wind paints small ripples on the surface of the river, moving against the strengthening tide.

Accardi is visiting from Antwerp. Back for more than two weeks. They've spent each of these days together, walking this stretch of the river several times. Time spent away from Haylan lowers the tension in his uncle's house. If only for a while.

Accardi had been speaking of his latest voyages. Cyprus. Acre. As far east as Famagusta. Of the women.

"Tripoli, Malin. That's where the best times are to be found. A feast for the eyes, and more besides."

Without warning, enjoying tales of the life he had shared before being ripped from it into England and war, his first wrenching sob had stopped him in his tracks. The second took him off his feet, his lungs suddenly emptying.

He finally spoke. "I thought I could see this through. Help Symon. Bring the estate back. But I hate it. I hate it here. I shouldn't be here. Haylan doesn't understand. I didn't choose any of this, Accardi."

The Pisan pulls away, believing the worst over. He rests his wrists on his bent knees, and weighs his words carefully.

"Malin, I've seen this before. Men can heal from wounds that usually kill without mercy. Pull themselves back from God's grasp and refuse to give in. But many carry scars that cannot be seen. That they themselves cannot see.

"You need to put what has happened behind you. Push whatever you are feeling back onto your father. He should carry this, not you.

"It's tearing you apart, but Haylan has had enough of your anger and selfishness. Let it go, and get your real family back. They love you. But they'll not put up with you behaving like a man who hates the world and everyone in it. Not any longer."

Accardi shrugs off Malin's eventual apology.

"It's your father that should feel remorse for your wounds, not you. And it's him you should be burying, not any remaining love that your family and friends might still feel for you."

"It's not my wounds, Luchas. It's the way that bastard put me into that situation. Knowing I would die. Hoping for it. That monstrous rage I felt, hacking and gouging. That I still feel. I can't face him. And it's pathetic."

Accardi's face hardens. "So decide, Malin. Confront him, or get as far from the people who love you as you can. Before they have had enough of you."

Malin looks out across the bleak landscape stretching beyond the far bank of the river. A flash of red to his far right draws his eye. Three figures resolve and then vanish.

It is time for him to resume his life in Antwerp.

★

Morning.
How long have I slept?

409

A shaft of light fell onto the floor to his left. The drifting dust motes within it demanded his attention.

He tried to roll to his left, wanting to sit back at the base of the wall by the window. A good place from which to gain a view of the street.

His right arm refused to move. He carefully separated the cloth of the bedsheet and his sleeve. Dirty ochre stains were mirrored on both sets of cloth. Pulling the sleeve up beyond his elbow, he saw that his entire arm was covered in suppurating sores. He raised his hand as he gagged. The back of his hand featured the same angry welts, interspersed with a number of soot-dark blemishes. His left hand looked no better. The scar from the assassin's knife, still a deep crimson, was almost hidden by the spreading affliction.

He finally sat up, and felt the shirt across his back tug against his skin.

Grimacing, Malin rose from the bed.

He'd been sitting at the window for a while before the thought came to him.

It's Saturday.

The first of March.

He slowly got to his feet, leaning against the window shutter to keep his balance. He fought to ignore the new level of pain in his upper arm where it contacted the cool, smoothly planed wood.

He searched for any sign that the attack had started. The sound of fighting. The sight of men hurrying through the streets, seeking to attack or defend territory. He raised his eyes for any signs of smoke.

Is Uberto already standing in the Council chamber?

A shudder ran the length of Malin's body.

Or did Sclavo tell him of Genoa, and cause him to withdraw?

He saw and heard nothing.

He tried to determine the hour. Dawn seemed long behind

him, suggesting that at least part of the attack should have concluded. Where did the *Zecca* lie from here? He could see the campanile of St Mark, proudly extending to more than twice the height of any other tower across the city. Had Libusch reached the Piazza? Overcome any resistance to enter the Palace with Uberto?

Straining to see past the shutter, the world began to spin rapidly.

He was vomiting before his head hit the floor.

★

He is twelve years old, and the wind blowing across the deck is making its way past him the lazy way. Through rather than around him. He is salt-drenched, and each gust pushes the cold, damp material against his body. He adjusts his footing to account for the ship's irregular pitch and yaw.

Haylan has told him that if he wants to understand trade at sea, he must experience it himself. Not simply watch as cargoes load and unload at the Staithe.

"Get out of the Guild Hall, get your hands dirty, and see how money is really made."

He looks to port, across to the low coastline north of the Humber. He thinks he recognises it from his two previous voyages along the German Sea.

What was Radley doing right now? Still friends, their relationship was now an adult one. On both sides.

He presses his elbow into his side, confirming for perhaps the fiftieth time that day that his papers remain safe in his satchel. His lack of ship's duties, his right as ship charterer, makes the job of keeping out from under the feet of Master Langland and his crew that much harder.

He moves to the other side of the ship.

411

Turns into the full force of the growing wind.

Poor skies mask the horizon, but he can still make out where sea and sky come closest.

The sound of the wind quietens in his ears.

He is in that calm place again.

That place where he is at his greatest ease.

Relaxed into the meaning of himself.

This is his element.

He cannot wait to learn where it might lead.

He looks down at his bag, and the papers held within it. They offer a sense of the next one or two steps on his path, but nothing more. His deeper journey, his dreams of how it will feel when he moves further east to lands beyond even this distant horizon, bring an unaffected, innocent smile to his face. He will never tire of wondering what is sitting just beyond view.

The next day, he climbs a steepening path that leads up the East Cliff.

Below him, Langland's crew move the first of seventy sacks of corn, their return cargo, onto the ship.

St Mary's disappears for a few steps, then returns, as the path meanders round to the left. The square towers of the church soon dwarf the houses at the cliff's base.

He's onto the open hill. At the edge of the high, empty moor.

His stride lengthens, his blood quickens. Thoughts of the return voyage recede.

The full facade of the Abbey explodes into view.

Its central tower sits like a squat castle keep. The ornamental towers either side take his breath away. They stretch up and away from their foundations, thin needles seeking to escape the earth beneath them.

He continues on, until he sees the next tower, the true high point of the Abbey.

How many are there?

He enters the gate, breaches the low outer wall that surrounds the whole building.

Two monks break their conversation as he approaches the entrance.

"What do you want, boy?"

He swallows his fear.

"Where do you make the manuscripts?"

★

Later.

Still daylight.

The water had gone, so Malin slowly repeated his efforts of the previous day.

His bowels had emptied of their meagre content while he slept.

He paused at the cistern, undecided whether to introduce the cold water to his filthy but burning skin.

He thought of Lucia while he washed. Of her love for him.

He finally regained the bedchamber, the replenished water jugs again sitting on top of the shrine. Shivering uncontrollably from the drenching downstairs, he dried himself as best he could on the blanket, then climbed back into bed.

His sleep, as troubled as before, offered partial respite from the growing pain in his lower back.

Have I awakened again?

It hardly mattered. His thoughts were wild and random. Nothing made sense.

Ships and books and bodies under blankets bleed together into echoes of conversations held and not held.

Men clad in armour. Horses screaming their battle distress. Horseless riders screaming on a highland moor, their horses stationed at the bottom of the hill, unable to retain a safe distance from enemy footsoldiers.

The gross insult to men's cold flesh, crawling with maggots and the torment of their stolen lives.

A woman holding a severed head, blood dripping onto freshly written letters.

And beneath it all, the agony in his back.

★

"Why are you here?"

The disembowelled corpse seems to be addressing its question to him.

"Is it important I tell you?"

"Not to me. But perhaps you would like to know for yourself."

Every face in the pile of bodies on which the corpse lies turns to look at him. They appear interested in the answer, even if his questioner is not.

Malin breaks into laughter.

"What is it that amuses you?"

"Well. Your lack of curiosity. Asking a question, but not concerned with the response. And really, given the nature of your death, I would have imagined you would have more important questions requiring answers."

The corpse considers his words.

"No. I think all such matters are already resolved. Purgatory has a special place for me. One that will take me from these carrion crows."

Flocks of black birds are scattered across the moor. They pick and hop their way around the fallen.

"I am safe from all illness now. It is you and your friends that should be asking yourself why you are here."

The scenery shimmers, fades.

Becomes the view of the Lagoon from the ferry station at the end of Calle San Domenico.

The corpse remains directly in front of him, floating on the surface of the water.

"Saint Mark's. Dupplin. The Lido. Does it matter where we depart from?"

Malin wants to argue.

His anger comes at last.

"We are none of us dead yet! You may wish us to join you. But we are not ready!"

"Hah. Ready or not, I will not be alone much longer. She may be in hiding, but I know where she can be found. The crows will soon feast on more than just the flesh of deserving men. Innocent women have no promise of escape."

Malin shapes his reply, but the corpse is gone, pulled beneath the surface.

He runs to the edge of the dock, and dives into the unwelcoming waters. His eyes pierce deep into the murk, but no sign of the cadaver remains.

When he surfaces, he sees a wall of water heading towards him across the Lagoon.

The giant wave lifts him up.

Up high above the city.

Releasing him for the plunge to come.

He looks around, and sees that he is not alone.

*

The sounds of grating wheels and snorting horses reached him from the street.

A two-wheeled cart swung into view above the upper line of the courtyard wall. He couldn't make out what it carried.

Another followed. They each headed towards the southern corner of San Leonardo's.

Malin tightened his eyes further to see what was being moved.

The first cart was already beyond sight, but he could see the second was fully laden.

From his position in the upstairs chamber, its contents were easy to see.

Malin's breath caught in his throat. A memory of his earlier hallucination rushed back to him. Of the men he had killed, high on the Perthshire battlefield.

On the flat bed of the cart, bodies laid one on top of another. Many of them shared the tell-tale marks of the illness blighting the city.

And besieging him.

As he watched, one of the bodies reached up its arm, as if pleading for help. It was not only the dead being brought here for disposal.

The cart moved out of sight, heading for the burial ground the other side of the church.

The image of the raised hand and its empty grasp stayed with him long after the sound of the last cart faded.

*

He was awake, though rarely in full possession of his senses, for every moment of the following night.

The almost exquisite tenderness of his skin, and throbbing of the ruptured swellings in his neck, armpits and groin were dwarfed by the overwhelming, all-consuming agony seated around his middle. With each pulsing onslaught, he fought against a desire to succumb to its demands. Release was becoming increasingly desirable.

But to surrender would be the end of him. And he still could not allow that to happen.

Not until he knew Lucia was safe.

★

Hours came and went. He no longer had any sense of what day it was, or of how long he had been in hiding.

He wondered how pages of his journal had come to be spread across much of the floor between the shrine and the window. They moved with each breath of breeze entering from the street. He must have tried to read them, but he had no recollection of doing so.

His thirst, strangely, had diminished. The remaining water went untouched.

His fever was now a fierce, dry, brittle thing.

He experienced moments of remarkable clarity.

On each occasion, whether laid flat on the bed, or on the floor propped up against the wall, he thought of one thing only.

Of the possibility that, regaining enough strength to stand at the window and beckoning to the street below, he would see Symon and Lucia. That they had spent the days since his retreat, helped by constables under instruction from Uberto, searching every part of the city for him. Seeking to bring him back into their care.

The idea grew, until it was the one overriding wish of his life.

If he saw them, would he have the energy to signal to them? Would he, still aware of contagion, pull back from the window? Hold to his initial resolve to spare them his own awful fate?

These brief moments, more than any of the pain that now consumed him, shook him in their teeth like a raging bear.

He imagined Lucia, the look on her face as she recognised him from the street. Her relief at realising their quest had ended, and that she could nurse him back to health.

Such thoughts were both sweet nectar and deadly poison.

But they proved he was still alive.

His head hurts where Brenner has hit him.

He can taste the dirt of the yard.

The dry, chalky grit coating his tongue is horrid.

He opens his eyes. There's something sticky in one of them.

Brenner stands over him. The toe of his shoe fills his view.

He wants to get up, but his head feels bad.

As though it belongs to someone else.

"What's the matter, Malin? Don't you have the guts to get up and show me what you've learnt?"

He knows what will happen if he gets up. How the next blow will put him down again.

He should say something.

He tries to speak, but his mouth won't work properly. It's little more than a grunt.

Brenner copies him.

"You're useless, aren't you?"

He tries again. Another grunt.

Brenner laughs.

"You see? Father is right. Some people cannot be taught. And some people don't deserve to be."

He knows it's unfair. Brenner is almost twice his size.

But he won't complain. Brenner would love it if he did.

And it would just make things worse. He would hurt him more.

He already hurts me. Father lets him.

Malin hears some footsteps heading his way, scuffing on the dirt of the castle courtyard.

Brenner's foot disappears. He hears him run off in the opposite direction.

He's gone.

His head is a little less heavy, even though he still can't see out of his left eye.

He uses one arm to lift himself up a little. His head is out of the dirt.

He feels the tears come. Brenner isn't there to see them now.

The sun is not as bright as it was. Someone is standing over him again.

Brenner? Please, no.

The light dims more.

"So, young master Malin. What scrape have you got into this time? Chasing the geese again?"

It's Jerold.

"Or were they chasing you?"

His wooden sword is broken. Father will be furious.

"Let's take this back with us. We can mend it together."

He feels the heat of the summer breeze on his face as he walks with the priest on the dried out road to the rectory.

Feels the comforting pressure of his hand being held.

The cool water of the cloth that dabs his forehead, washing the blood from his face.

★

On waking, Malin traced his finger along the old scar above his eye.

His finger, black and swollen, is dead to the touch.

But he can feel its pressure on his forehead.

And the memory of cool water returns.

★

Malin is not certain, but it feels as though it is the last light of the day entering the room.

He wants to sit once more by the open window.

But he cannot move.

419

The world outside has fallen quiet since the mid-afternoon bells.

He takes a long breath.

Again.

He is beyond pain now. Beyond struggle.

He might not know it, but a shallow smile appears on his face.

"Lucia. My love."

"I'm here. We can leave now, you and I."

He feels her caress on his cheek.

Her face, inches from his own, has the serene ease of the day they sat in the Basilica, having shared their deepest fears and desires.

His eyes remaining closed, he reaches out to return her caress with his own.

Chapter 36

Thursday 6th March 1348

The Quarant

The three women sat at the back of the small wooden shack behind him, amongst the strong smells of tar and damp rope. The night had been cold, and they missed the large fire in the house in Dorsoduro.

Symon could see Collette's arm around her mother, but couldn't tell if they were asleep or awake.

Lucia sat a little to one side.

He had known of this place, and places like it, for years. There were dozens of them along the Lido wharfeside, offering dock workers shelter in summer and winter, and a place to store their belongings and tools.

Undoubtedly not intended for gentlewomen. But this made it the last place where anyone searching for the wife and daughters of a wealthy merchant would think to look. Better still, this particular hut stood no more than two hundred yards from the *Seynte Marie*.

It had taken Symon much longer than he imagined to persuade Donata to leave the house the previous night.

She was clearly terrified of being recaptured. "But it's too soon! If we go now, we'll be there for so long before the tide, we're bound to be discovered. You cannot put the girls in that much danger. We should wait until the morning. Please!"

They came here anyway. There was no real choice. They could not chance crossing the Lagoon in daylight, and to wait longer in the city would simply increase the threat of capture. He knew from Donata that it wasn't the women the authorities were seeking.

It was him.

He peered out from the shack door again. Still no movement on the quayside.

The ship's crew were already on board. Glad to escape the contagion, they had taken up position the previous morning. It had been an easy day for them, with no cargo to load. They had brought provisions as directed, so there would be enough food and water to last crew and passengers alike until they reached a safe port further down the coast.

The tide would be ready for them shortly after dawn. He and the women would board when the ship was almost ready to depart. The night guard might still move to impound the vessel, and it wouldn't do for them to be on board if that happened.

The possibility of being called back into the city by a joyous Uberto, their departure no longer necessary, had vanished with Donata's arrival at the house three days earlier.

Symon felt certain that she had led their enemies to their door, but as the hours and then days passed, it appeared they had lost all interest in her.

They had just released her. Told her she was free to return home.

The appearance of San Polo constables at her door at noon

on the previous Friday had shaken her badly. Five men, armed and uncaring of the damage they might cause, combed the house in search of her husband. He wasn't there, having left for Calle San Domenico earlier that morning. She had never felt so alone, but clung to the thought that Lucia and Collette had made their escape the day before.

Three of the men remained in the house, in case her husband decided to return home. The two remaining constables marched her along the Calle Donzella, the shame of her arrest visible to all who cared to see. The waiting ferry took them to San Marco, where she was escorted off the boat and into the Palace.

Guided through a maze of corridors, she was met by two men.

One of them stepped forward. "Signora Da Segna. My name is Frederico Grimani. I am sorry for any roughness in your treatment, but we need to take every step necessary to achieve the capture of your husband. Where is he?"

Receiving no answer, he instructed one of his colleagues to take her into a nearby room.

"It was the longest afternoon of my life, Symon. Men were searching the city for Uberto and Sclavo, and I had to sit there on my own, for hours, wondering if they had been caught or not. Fearing what they could be doing to them."

The light was failing by the time Grimani walked through the door.

"Ah. Signora Da Segna. I have to tell you that we have your husband and son. They are currently answering our questions downstairs."

Downstairs. The prison quarters.

"We will need to keep you here for the time being. Until we learn all we need to. We hope you understand this."

"Uberto spoke of him many times. And never favourably. But to hear him speak on behalf of the whole city…"

423

She was held there for two days. Never disrespected. Never threatened. But deprived of both liberty and news of her family.

On Saturday, she sensed a heightened level of activity around the Palace.

Grimani returned on Sunday afternoon.

"You will be free to go shortly, Signora. But I'm afraid the news is bad for you. We have concluded beyond any question that your husband and son were plotting to overthrow the Council, and no doubt the Doge. A force of several hundred men, mercenary scum from the north, were apprehended yesterday, as they attempted to land in various parts of the city. An Englishman, caught with your husband at the home of his countryman Le Cordier, has confessed to organising the plot."

Donata's voice trembled as she continued her story. Symon did nothing to interrupt her. "Then he told me, Symon. That Uberto and Sclavo, along with almost forty other men, had been executed. They had been questioned, charged and killed within a day. It would have happened sooner, had the Small Council met earlier. How can they be so brutal?"

Symon had no answer.

"I'm so sorry, Signora. I have no words that might help."

"I know. I know. But they didn't even let me see him, talk to him before…"

The one question he so desperately wanted to ask would have to wait.

Was Malin amongst those captured?

The rooms in the house on Calle Donzella felt empty and desolate. Giradino was nowhere to be seen. Donata feared the worst for him. Any man close to Uberto had probably suffered the same fate as her husband. How else to explain his absence?

After one day back in her home, she decided to join Lucia and Collette.

Packing a small bag of belongings, she left money on the

reception table for the two servants, and left the house she had lived in for almost twenty-five years.

Unsure if she was truly moving unnoticed through the streets, she made her way south, and finally knocked on the door of the villa in Dorsoduro.

Her daughters were overjoyed to see her. She told them nothing of the fate suffered by their father and brother, saying that she had simply changed her mind to join them, and that Uberto and Sclavo were fully occupied with matters of the city. She demanded that Symon honour her wishes to spare them any additional anguish.

There were three more days before the expiration of the Quarant. Then they would make their move.

*

A pale, crimson dawn sharpened the edges of the warehouses opposite, and the intermittent stone-paved sections of the quay began to take form.

Symon heard the three women whispering to each other behind him, but did not turn to see them. His concerns lay outside the hut, his senses attuned to any sign of human activity.

After sunrise, time slowed down further.

Small groups of gulls took to the air, landing to inspect and fight over any unclaimed detritus. A stiff morning breeze began to build.

Symon's patience was all but spent. They were isolated and vulnerable here.

Collette moved forward a few steps, and crouched down beside him.

"Symon, is it time to move?"

He turned to look at her. Over the last week, he had seen a completely different side to the woman. Just as Lucia had sunk

425

back into herself, so Collette seemed to grow in confidence. He had been glad of her support in keeping up the spirits of the other two women as the day of their departure drew nearer.

"Not long now. The place seems to be pretty deserted. Midweek, an hour after dawn, and still no sign of any wharf teams."

The ship's captain, a swarthy, ill-kempt man from just outside Bruges, offered a possible explanation when they met briefly the previous evening.

"I hear they're no longer able to keep up with the burials. Over in San Marco alone, they claim there are two hundred new corpses every day. God knows how many across the whole city. They'll have to start burning them soon."

Seaman's tales. Always prone to falsehoods that made them more interesting. Yet even if his numbers were twice what they should be, the death toll was still enormous. Under such conditions, the authorities would struggle to assign many men to chase down the remaining plotters.

He turned to Collette, still close to his side. "Tell your mother to be ready to move soon."

They had got this far. Kept out of sight for almost a week. Secured passage across the Lagoon from one of the depleted number of ferries at the San Basilio station. Remained undetected inside the damp, pungent shack.

When he finally led them onto the quay, it was clear that things were still far from normal. Where he expected groups of men, pulling carts or carrying crates between them, Symon saw instead empty dockside. No *consoli*, or other representatives of the *Levant* preparing to confirm that crew sizes were acceptable for departure, or that they had been paid the correct wages for their place on the voyage.

They walked as briskly as their cold, stiff legs would allow.

They passed two other ships to reach their own, but they each seemed to be empty.

Symon gestured to the women to wait on the quayside by the *Seynte Marie* gangway. When he reached the ship's bulwark, a man appeared.

"About time. The tide is on the turn. And this place is cursed."

Symon beckoned to the women, who needed no second request to join him on deck. He passed each of their bags to the lookout, who begrudgingly began to move them below deck.

A few moments passed, and the captain appeared. Symon wondered how much ale had been consumed after he had left the vessel the previous evening.

"So. You're here. Good. Let's get you out of sight. We're ready to sail."

They passed several men as they went down the steps to the lower deck. As they looked for somewhere to sit, the sound of ropes chafing on wood came down to them, broken now and then by the grunting and cursing of men raising sails for departure.

After some further shouted commands, and corresponding actions from the men on deck, Symon felt a shift in the ship's hull.

They had left their berth.

He resisted the temptation to go back out on deck. The ship's movement was of great comfort, but he should stay with the women for a while longer. Donata had not been on board a ship this size since she and Uberto first sailed into Venice from Ragusa. Her two daughters had never once left the city. His place was with them, at least until they reached a point of relative safety.

When he finally climbed the steps to the main deck, the sails were full and, judging by the rate at which the land passed on their port beam, they were making good speed.

Sailing barely two hundred yards from shore, they were

already approaching the end of the Lido. They would soon leave the Lagoon and make their way south to Chioggia.

He walked to the starboard side of the ship, and looked back across at the city, a broken line on the horizon representing each of the main islands.

He heard footsteps behind him, and turned to see Lucia walking towards him.

She put her arm through his, as if to stabilise herself. Neither of them spoke, as they each looked back across the calm stretch of water.

Lucia broke the silence. "The mountains still hold a little snow."

Symon tried to pick out some of their detail. The long upland range, dark and indistinct despite the brightness of the day, was fringed by a long, intact line of white, softened only by the shadows cast from a handful of high clouds.

Lucia spoke without turning from the view.

"Do you still wonder? What has happened to him, I mean."

Symon nodded, then lowered his head.

"If anyone managed to avoid The Ten, it would be him, wouldn't it?"

Lucia's eyes were filled with tears that seemed determined not to fall.

"Yes. Of course. He just needs to shake off his aches, regain his strength, and re-join your father. The two of them…" He found it hard to continue. "The two of them have achieved so much together. Once everything returns to normal, your father and Malin will build new businesses that will be the envy of the whole city."

He couldn't look her in the eye.

She spoke again. "I never knew how small the city looks when viewed from here. The mountains seem to completely overwhelm it."

"Yes, but they offer Venice much of its power. It's those hills that make the sea here such an enticing place on which to move goods. To keep the world supplied with what it needs."

"And much of what it doesn't."

Symon laughed. "True, and with it, enough wealth to keep the whole damn place afloat."

She leaned into him.

He felt her shiver.

"Do you think he is all right, Symon? Really?"

He hesitated, unsure how to answer.

Lucia could detect a falsehood better than most.

"He has done what he believed was needed. For our survival, as well as his own. If we honour the chance he has given us, I am sure he will do everything he can to do the same."

Lucia pulled her arm from his. Pulled his sleeve to force him to face her.

"What did he tell you in his note?"

Colour rose up his neck.

"I could ask you the same question."

"Yes, but I have shown the courage to ask first. What did he say?"

Symon put his hand inside his jacket, and removed a small piece of paper.

"Here. Read it for yourself. I cannot bring myself to speak it."

She took it from him, her eyes still fixed on his downturned face.

She unfolded it, and fell silent as she read.

When she looked at him again, her tears had given up their fight, and flowed freely. Yet she smiled through them.

She moved her own hand into her cloak. Withdrew a similar piece of paper.

"Here. You may read mine. It's almost exactly the same."

Moments later, they both stood at the side of the ship, content to maintain their silence.

The *Seynte Marie* turned into the narrow gap in the Lido.

First the city, then the mountains finally disappeared from view.

DRAMATIS PERSONNAE

ENGLAND
Wormegay Estate, Norfolk
Jefferey Le Cordier: The seventh Earl of Wormegay.
Gillian Le Cordier: Jefferey's wife. The sister of Haylan Rowbern.
Brenner Le Cordier: Eldest son of Jefferey and Gillian.
Malin Le Cordier: Youngest son of Jefferey and Gillian.
Jerold: Priest on Wormegay Estate.
Erwan: Franklin of Wormegay Estate.

Bishop's Lynn, Norfolk
Haylan Rowbern: Merchant in Lynn. Uncle to Malin.
Carsen Rowbern: Eldest son of Haylan.
Radley Rowbern: Youngest son of Haylan.

Westminster
Edward III: King of England and Lord of Ireland.
Henry of Grosmont: Earl of Leicester and Lancaster. Lord High Steward, and Second Knight of the Order of the Garter. Soldier and Diplomat.
Humphrey de Bohun: Earl of Hereford and Essex. Lord High Constable.

Mainard Glyn: Senior civil servant. Leads the King's Upper Exchequer.

Ricaud Bourchier: Agent of the Royal Household.

ANTWERP

Elyas Scepene: A Burgher of Bruges, and member of the Hanse.

Luchas Accardi: A Pisan working as an independent trade advisor.

Lennet De Smet: Politician.

SCOTLAND

Symon: Peasant boy from Glen Lyon, in the Central Scottish Highlands.

VENICE

Uberto Da Segna: Trader and Merchant. Ex-member of the Great Council and the *Pregadi*.

Donata Da Segna: Wife of Uberto.

Sclavo Da Segna: Only son and eldest child of Uberto and Donata. Head of Supplies at the Arsenale.

Lucia Da Segna: Eldest daughter of Uberto and Donata.

Collette Da Segna: Youngest daughter of Uberto and Donata.

Giradino Da Viscia: Senior Administrator for the Da Segna family.

Tusco: Domestic servant.

Penina: Domestic servant.

Political and Noble Class

Andrea Dandolo: The 54th Doge of Venice.

Nicolo Soranzo: Member of the Small Council, and *consigliere ducale* for the San Marco *sestieri*.

Frederico Grimani: Member of the Small Council.

Pietro Selvo: Senior clerk of the Admiralty.

Vincenzo Priuli: Senior clerk of the Magistracy.

Stefano Morosini: Senior clerk in the Customs Office.

Gabriel Polani: Port official overseeing all imported goods.

Merchants and Citizens

Antonio Stornello: A leading cloth merchant.

Romaso Grisani: Master Joiner, and head of the Carpenters' and Builders' Guild at the Arsenale.

Giacomo Favero: Head of the ferryman's fraternity, or *fraglia*.

Stefano Bembo: A merchant living in Cannaregio.

Franco Stolado: Owner/operator of warehouses on the Lido.

Others

Pietro Del Chiaro: A businessman from Florence.

Veit Libusch: A senior commander of a company of the *Condottieri*.

Benasuto Penzini: A priest, permitted by the Church to practise medicine.

Gian Caloprini: Head of the Glassmakers' Guild.

GLOSSARY

Acqua Alta "High water". Exceptional tide peaks that occur in the northern Adriatic.

Arengo The Venetian citizenry. Citizenship was based on the duration of a family's residency within the city (normally a minimum of twenty-five years), and formal acceptance of an application for membership.

Arsenale, The A complex of shipyards and armouries, extended extensively in 1320, in which the state's naval and merchant ships were constructed and maintained.

Arsenalotti Workers in the Arsenale who act as part-time reservists for the city, in times of need.

Banca The committee elected to lead a confraternity.

Basilikon Currency in use in medieval Byzantium.

Bills of Lading Legal documents between a merchant and shipowner that describe the type, quantity and destination of goods being carried as cargo. The documents are also used as goods receipts on delivery at their destination.

Camerlenghi di Commun Financial magistrates, involved in the allocation and audit of public funds.

Campanile Bell tower.

Campo A city square.

Capi dei Dieci The three elected leaders of The Ten.

Capo Sestiere The senior representative of any one of the six districts of Venice. Responsible for public order in their district. Each *capo* has a seat on the Minor Council.

Caule A type of ferry boat, wider than a gondola.

Cavane A small wooden boathouse, used by ferrymen (see Traghetti).

Cesendeli Street lanterns lit at the public expense.

Chancery (England) The main writing office, producing all official documents on behalf of the King's Household, and Westminster offices.

Chevisance A form of official lending and borrowing of money that avoided the appearance or practice of usury.

Chiesa Church.

Chiesa D'Oro The "Church of Gold", the popular nickname for St Mark's Basilica.

Citizen The right to be known as a *"cittadini originarii"* is earned thorough twenty-five years' continuous residence in the city, although the payment of "public burdens", or *"faziono"* could reduce the wait to as low as two years. The children of citizens could claim citizenship *"de intus"*. Certain offices were reserved for these men. A *"citizen de extra"* sails under the protection of San Marco, and can trade in Venetian markets.

Colleganza A limited liability contract used extensively in Venice.

Commenda A limited liability contract used extensively in north-western Europe.

Compagnia della Colomba A company of fortune, available for hire as mercenaries. Founded by John I of Bohemia.

Condottierie Captains in command of mercenary companies. The *Condotta* is the contract by which such a force agrees service to a city or a lord.

Confraternity An association of often wealthy lay people who on a voluntary basis promote and perform charitable works.

Consigliere Ducale An advisor to the Doge, sitting on the Ducal Council. Each of the six *sestieres* had one councillor.

Consiglio Maggior See Great Council.

Consiglio Minor See Small Council.

Consoli dei Mercanti One of the state departments regulating private ships. Has particular responsibility for ship rating.

Doge The senior elected official in Venice, and the chief magistrate and leader of the Republic.

Exchequer, Lower (England) Westminster office that oversees the receipt and issue of all non-clerical tax revenues and gifts on behalf of the king.

Exchequer, Higher (England) Westminster office where accounts are rendered and calculations of tax made.

Extraordinarri An administrative board of customs officials charged to oversee maritime affairs, including the collection of freight taxes.

Fraglia Venetian guild of ferrymen.

Great Council The "Consiglio Maggior". Consists of approximately 1500 to 2000 members. Its sessions largely involve electoral duties. Meets on Sundays and High Days. Members are summoned by the tolling of the *Trottiera* bell of St Mark's.

Gentian tea A liquid or potion made from the roots of gentian, a herb that grows a long slender stem and produces blue-green leaves and yellow flowers. Widely used as a digestive tonic.

German Sea The North Sea.

Golden Book, The A formal list of the all the recognised nobility of Venice. Following the "closing of the Council" (see "Serrata"), entry of new names to the list was highly unusual.

Hanse, The An organisation of affiliated commercial guilds, originating in cities around the Baltic, that dominated trade along the coasts of Northern Europe.

King's Council Predecessor of the Star Chamber, the Council was a key body of executive government, taking decisions with the king. Membership included Chancellor, Treasurer and Keeper of the Privy Seal, a number of bishops and senior officials.

Kontor A trading post of the Hanse.

Maestro Master.

Massari The Venetian Mint.

Mudae A state-sponsored fleet, sailing together for mutual protection, on a seasonal basis. Composition and size are determined by the Savii ai Ordini.

Narthex The porch that acts as the main entrance into a church.

Nones The ninth hour of the day (mid-afternoon).

Officiali al Cattaver Venetian inspector of goods.

Oltremare The cities, ports and lands of Venice's maritime empire.

Ospizio Hospice.

Patroni The three officials appointed to oversee the Arsenale on behalf of the Small Council.

Podesta The chief magistrate of a city state within the Venetian Republic, or Oltremare. The position was filled by a Venetian noble, nominated by the Minor Council.

Ponte Bridge.

Populari The ordinary men and women of Venice who are neither nobles nor citizens.

Praedo An employee of the courts, required to pronounce publicly the order of cases to be heard, and proceeding outcomes.

Pregardi The permanent Senate of Venice, responsible for preparing and recommending legislation for approval by the Councils.

Protomaestri Foremen of the Arsenale workforce.

437

Quarant, The A forty-day period, during which all imported goods were required to be warehoused, pending checks of all commercial documents and calculation of duties. It was common practice for ship owners to keep their vessels in port during that period, in the event of any problems.

Ragusa Modern-day Dubrovnik.

Ripalico A tax levied on all ships using Venetian wharves.

Royal Household, The (England) In addition to servicing the king's accommodation, it includes roles such as Deputy to the Chief Steward, Deputy to the Chamberlain, Keeper, Controller and Cofferer of the Wardrobe. The military household features fifty to a hundred bannerets and knights, and about thirty serjeants-at-arms who protect the king.

Salammoniac A mineral, often used as an astringent in the cleaning of stained glass.

Savii ai Ordini Five senior officials responsible for deciding the military and commercial provision made for the following year's fleets, or mudae. This assists merchants in their own planning, and offers stability.

Scuole The buildings in which the confraternities of Venice are based.

Searcher Customs official employed at bonded quays tasked with checking onboard goods against entries in merchant's cockets.

Serrata "The Locking", or closing of the Council. An action taken in 1297 that restricted membership of the Great Council to those families already represented on it.

Sestiere A Venetian district. San Marco, Castello, Canareggio are on one side of the Grand Canal, Santa Croce, San Polo, and Dorsoduro are on the other.

Sext The sixth hour of the day (probably noon).

Shirri Guards of the magistracy.

Signoria: Members of the Small Council (see 'Consiglio Minor')

Signori di Notte "Lords of the Night". The night police.

Silesia A region of Central Europe, bordered by the Holy Roman Empire, Hungary and Poland.

Small Council The "Consiglio Minor." A body of forty members, with the collective authority to supervise the actions of the Doge, and a power of veto.

Ten, The The Council of Ten, established to provide internal state security following the failed insurrection of 1310.

Terce The third hour of the day.

Teloneo A form of underwriting tax.

Tolpi A form of pile, usually made of oak or pine, used to create the foundations for heavy structures.

Traghetti The boatmen who operate Venetian passenger ferries.

Vera da Pozzo A large stone wellhead, often featuring ornate carvings.

Vespers The twelfth hour of the day.

HISTORICAL SIDE NOTES

1. An earthquake, its epicentre eighty miles north-east of Venice, occurred on 26th January 1348. Damage reports and archaeological findings are consistent with a force of 8.0–9.0 on the modern Richter Scale. Eyewitness reports describe the draining of the Venice canals and Lagoon, and the subsequent tidal wave that followed, which caused additional damage and loss of life. The trauma was such that it was rumoured that every pregnant woman in the city miscarried.

2. The Black Death, although now no longer believed to have been transmitted by flea-infested rats, arrived by ship in Venice in March 1348. Its impact was so rapid that a state of emergency was declared the following month. By August, the government issued an edict dissolving itself, on the grounds that too many of its members had died to allow them to function. By early 1349, Venice's population, at that time the greatest city in Europe, had reduced from 100,000 to an estimated 40,000.

3. In 1297, the Great Council of Venice passed a series of laws known as the *Serrata*, formalising a trend towards freezing out non-member families. There was no such thing as nobility in the Western European sense, only those

voted onto the Council. This effectively set a glass ceiling for anyone seeking upward mobility or political influence in the future. Very few exceptions after 1297 were granted, with all families written into what became known as the Golden Book. This system lasted for about four centuries.

4. In the years between 1297 and 1340, there were five failed coups in Venice. The most well known, in 1310, led to the (at the time) temporary creation of the Council of Ten, whose goal was exclusively to prevent future treason. Its role grew from that point, becoming a permanent body, with increasing power and independence. It became the precursor of all modern state intelligence and counter-intelligence organisations.

   There is no record of a failed coup in 1348, although this may easily be explained by the city's descent into chaos.

5. Quarantine was adopted by the Venetians as an innovative way to limit the spread of plague on its frequent returns to the city *after* 1348–9. The practice has its origins in the earlier administrative practice of holding imported cargo in warehouses for a forty-day period, during which all import processes could be completed. The period of forty days itself had religious significance, derived from the story of Christ's fast in the desert, and the subsequent duration of Lent.

6. The English Crown, under first Edward II and then his successor, borrowed large sums of money from the Bardi and Peruzzi families of Florence, recompensed in part by a number of import and export concessions. The commencement of the Thirty Years War with France depleted Edward III's coffers further, and part of his response was to renege on his debts. By 1346, both family businesses were gone, although they each sought ways to return over the decades that followed.

7. The Battle of Dupplin Moor was fought on 10–11th August, 1332, on a highland plateau above the Earn valley in Perthshire. It was the opening battle in the Second War of Scottish Independence. Edward III secretly supported the English forces, led by Henry de Beaumont, a survivor of the Battle of Bannockburn. It is known to be the first use of dismounted men-at-arms fighting alongside archers in an English army, a formation that was then used extensively by the English against the French in the Hundred Years War. The Scottish forces were heavily routed, with many of their nobles killed.

8. The earthwork remains of a motte and bailey castle, probably built after the Norman Conquest, can be found in the parish of Wormegay, some seven miles south of modern-day King's Lynn.

BIBLIOGRAPHY

VENICE

Ackroyd, Peter, *Venice: Pure City.* Chatto & Windus, London, 2009.

Crowley, Roger, *City of Fortune: How Venice Won and Lost a Naval Empire.* Faber and Faber, 2011.

Hodgson, F.C., *Venice In the Thirteenth and Fourteenth Century: A Sketch of Venetian History From the Conquest of Constantinople to the Accession of Michele Steno, A.D. 1204–1400.* George Allen and Sons, 1910.

Horodowich, Elizabeth, *A Brief History of Venice: A New History of the City and its People.* Constable and Robinson, London, 2009.

Jansen, Katherine L., Drell, Joanna and Andres, Frances (Eds), *Medieval Italy: Texts In Translation.* University of Pennsylvania Press, 2010.

Madden, Thomas F., *Venice: A New History.* Viking Penguin, London, 2012.

Martin, John & Romano, Dennis (Eds), *Venice Reconsidered: The History and Civilization of an Italian City-State, 1297–1797.* John Hopkins University, Baltimore, 2003

Molmenti, Pompeo, *Venice: Its Individual Growth From The Earliest*

Beginnings To The Fall Of The Republic. Part One: The Middle Ages. John Murray, London, 1906.

Norwich, John Julius, 'Andrea Dandolo and Marin Falier (1342–1355)' in *Venice: The Rise To Empire.* Allen Lane, 1977.

Norwich, John Julius, *A History of Venice.* Penguin, 2012.

Winchell, Sean P., 'The CDX: The Council of Ten and Intelligence in the Lion Republic' in *International Journal of Intelligence and CounterIntelligence,* Volume 19, pages 335–355. Taylor and Francis Group, 2006.

ENGLAND

Brown, A.L., *The Governance of Late Medieval England, 1272–1461.* Hodder Arnold, 1989

Cushway, Graham, *Edward III and the War at Sea: The English Navy, 1327–1377.* Boydell Press, 2011.

Maddicott, John, 'The Origins of the Hundred Years War' in *History Today,* Volume 36, 5 May 1986.

Mortimer, Ian, *The Time Traveller's Guide to Medieval England: A Handbook for Visitors to the Fourteenth Century.* Vintage, 2009.

Ormrod, W. Mark, *Edward III.* Yale University Press, 2013.

Page, William (Ed), 'Hospitals: Hospitals In Lynn' in *A History of the County of Norfolk, Volume 2.* London, 1906.

Stober, Karen, *Late Medieval Monasteries and Their Patrons: England and Wales, c. 1300–1540* (Studies in the History of Medieval Religion, Volume XXIX). The Boydell Press, 2007.

Whittle, Jane, 'The Food Economy of Lords, Tenants, and Workers in a Medieval Village: Hunstanton, Norfolk, 1328–48' in Maryanne Kowaleski, John Langdon and Phillipp R. Schofield (Eds), *Peasants and Lords in the Medieval English Economy: Essays in Honour of Bruce M.S. Campbell.* Brepols Publishers, 2015.

Willard, James F. and Morris, William A. (Eds), *The English Government At Work, 1327–1336. Volume 1: Central and*

Prerogative Administration. Medieval Academy of America, Cambridge Mass., 1940–1950.

SCOTLAND
Haldane, A.R.B., *The Drove Roads of Scotland.* Birlinn, 2015.

MARITIME TRADE
Blockmans, Wim, Krom, Mikhail and Wubs-Mrozewicz, Justyna (Eds), *The Routledge Handbook of Maritime Trade Around Europe, 1300–1600.* Routledge, 2017.

De Lara, Yadira Gonzalez, *The Secret of Venetian Success: A Public-Order, Reputation-Based Institution.* Universidad de Alicante, 2008.

Dotson, John E., *Merchant Culture in Fourteenth Century Venice: The Zibaldone da Canal.* Binghamton, New York, 1994.

Fusaro, Mari, *Political Economies of Empire in the Early Modern Mediterranean.* Cambridge University Press, 2017.

Lane, Frederic C., 'Diet and Wages of Seamen in the Early Fourteenth Century' in *Venice and History: Collected Papers.* John Hopkins Press, Baltimore, 1963.

Lane, Frederic C., 'Maritime Law and Administration, 1250–1350' in *Venice and History: the Collected Papers of Frederic C. Lane.* John Hopkins Press, Baltimore, 1966.

Lane, Frederic C., 'Venetian Merchant Galleys, 1300–1334. Private and Communal Operation' in *Speculum, A Journal Of Mediaeval Studies,* Volume XXXVIII, April 1963.

Lopez, Robert S. and Raymond, Irving W., *Medieval Trade In The Mediterranean World.* Columbia University Press, New York, 1955.

Mackay, Angus and Ditchburn, David (Eds), *Atlas of Medieval Europe.* Routledge, London, 1997.

Postan, M.M., *Medieval Trade and Finance.* Cambridge University Press, 1973.

Puga, Diego and Trefler, Daniel, 'International Trade and Institutional Change: Medieval Venice's Response to Globalization' in NBER Working Paper Series No. 18288. National Bureau of Economic Research, August 2012.

Salzman, L.F., *English Trade In The Middle Ages.* The Clarendon Press, Oxford, 1931.

Turner, Jack, 'The Spice That Built Venice' in *Smithsonian Journeys Quarterly,* November 2015.

Williams, N.J., *The Maritime Trade Of The East Anglian Ports, 1550–1590.* Clarendon Press, Oxford, 1988.

Wubs-Mrozewicz, Justyna, 'The Late Medieval and Early Modern Hanse As An Institution of Conflict Management in Continuity and Change', Volume 32, Special Issue (Merchants and Commercial Conflicts in Europe, 1250–1600). Cambridge University Press, 2017.

FINANCE

Bell, Adrian R., Brooks, Chris and Moore, Tony K., *Accounts of the English Crown with Italian Merchant Societies, 1272–1345.* Volume 331. List and Index Society, 2009.

Farrell, Joseph P., *Financial Vipers of Venice: Alchemical Money, Magical Physics, and Banking in the Middle Ages and Renaissance.* Feral House, 2010.

Hunt, Edwin S., *The Medieval Super-Companies: A Study of the Peruzzi Company of Florence.* Cambridge University Press, 2010.

Kunal, T., 'The Crash of the European Financial System in 1345'. *The Financial Engineer* (thefinancialengineer.org), March 2013.

WARFARE

Historic Scotland (Alba Aosmhor), *The Inventory of Historic Battlefields: Battle of Dupplin Moor (A Designation Record and Summary Report).*

Lepage, Jean-Denis G.G., *Medieval Armies and Weapons in Western Europe. An Illustrated History.* MacFarland & Company Publishers, Jefferson, North Carolina, 2005.

THE PLAGUE

Aberth, John, *The Black Death: The Great Mortality of 1348–1350. A Brief History With Documents.* Palgrave, Macmillan, New York, 2005.

Singer, Maximilian, 'What Did Venice Do To Combat The Plague?' Quora.com

ACKNOWLEDGEMENTS

This book would not have reached this point without the assistance and support of a significant number of people, to whom I will always be grateful.

Firstly, I could not have moved through the early drafts of the novel without the unswerving support of Dennis Tardan, interviewer and comms coach guru. Our transatlantic 'Skypes' have had a profound impact on the emotional journey within the book. Thank you for introducing me to the writings of Christine de Pizan, many of whose thoughts find expression through Lucia.

I'd also like to thank my editor, Imogen Palmer, for her empathetic oversight and challenge, at the time I needed it most. Her insightful readings of the work offered me every opportunity to improve the coherence and rigour of the story.

Matt Wood, John Smith and Mike Dyer, friends on this side of the pond, have also had the courage and kindness to offer their impressions of the work as it has matured. Matt, and Nicky Thomson, thanks for access to the thoughts of your reading groups.

I've also benefitted from the *esprit de cour* of my fellow alumni of the Moniack Mhor writing course in May 2017. Detailed comments from Pam Macintyre, Annie MacDonald and Julie

Williamson have been key to a number of improvements in the writing and plotting, and Ian Hall, well, what can I say – your challenge at the right time made all the difference.

I'd also like to acknowledge the assistance I've received when researching the period in which the novel is set. Thank you to Erla Zwingle, freelance journalist based in Venice and author of a fascinating set of articles on the city, and Sandra Cardarelli, for her early advice to embrace the historical record wherever possible.

I also want to thank Sarah Ralph, Robert Reid, and Helen Allen of the Scottish Highland Library Service for their help in researching and obtaining the large number of secondary sources that helped inform the book.

Finally, and most importantly, thank you Joanne, for having faith in me, and allowing me to stay home.

Graham Bullen
June 2020
Invernessshire

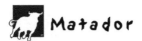

For exclusive discounts on Matador titles,
sign up to our occasional newsletter at
troubador.co.uk/bookshop